FLAME IN THE NIGHT

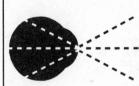

This Large Print Book carries the
Seal of Approval of N.A.V.H.

Flame in the Night

A NOVEL OF WORLD WAR II FRANCE

Heather Munn

THORNDIKE PRESS
A part of Gale, a Cengage Company

GALE
A Cengage Company

Farmington Hills, Mich • San Francisco • New York • Waterville, Maine
Meriden, Conn • Mason, Ohio • Chicago

LIBRARY OF CONGRESS CIP DATA ON FILE.
CATALOGUING IN PUBLICATION FOR THIS BOOK
IS AVAILABLE FROM THE LIBRARY OF CONGRESS

ISBN-13: 978-1-4328-6159-9 (hardcover)

Published in 2019 by arrangement with Kregel Publications

Printed in the United States of America
1 2 3 4 5 6 7 23 22 21 20 19

For Rich Foss,
my friend

Prologue:
Where Do We Go?

Elisa Schulmann took the last pin out of her mouth, slipped it gently into the silk of the skirt she was altering, and picked up her needle. She glanced up; Madame Mercier was watching her, standing in the open doorway that led to the front of the shop. Elisa kept her hands steady under her employer's frown, taking a tiny, careful stitch.

"Wash your hands."

Elisa laid down her work. "I washed them when I came in, madame."

"Wash them again. You're sweating. Do you know how much silk costs these days? If we have to replace that I'll dock every *centime* from your pay. Anyway, put that aside for now, I've just gotten a rush order from Madame Boutet. I'll need you to stay till it's finished."

Elisa sat up very straight, glancing at the doorway of the windowless workroom and the narrowing stripe of afternoon light. She ducked her head, keeping her hands still on the linty black fabric of her skirt. "I'm truly sorry, madame, but you know that on Fridays —"

"You will make an exception tonight."

Elisa lifted her head and looked Madame Mercier in the eye. "I'm truly sorry, madame," she enunciated.

The woman's cold frown sharpened. "You people shouldn't work in Christian shops. I ought never to have hired you. Always rubbing your differences in people's faces — too good to drink a cup of coffee with us. I wouldn't be so proud if *my* religion was based on doing cruel things to baby boys —"

Elisa was on her feet before she knew it, blood pounding in her ears. She froze. "Excuse me, madame," she said through lips stiff as clay. "I have a personal need." She turned her back and walked carefully to the shop's tiny bathroom, then locked herself in and sat on the toilet lid, shaking.

"God, help me," she said in a harsh whisper. "Help me, please." She closed her eyes, thought of the lines in Papa's face last week when he'd told her the rent had gone up again. *Their* rent, not the neighbors'. *All Jews have gold under their mattresses, didn't you know?* She remembered the day last year when Papa had asked her to take this job. The day David Schulmann, who once was able to provide what was finest for his family, admitted he needed his daughter's help. A tiny, burning coal had lit somewhere behind her breastbone at that moment. It was burning still. *I will not fail them.*

She took a deep, silent breath. *Help me.* She loosened her bun and re-pinned it carefully, then rose and opened the door. Madame Mercier was measuring a hem. Elisa stood silently till the woman finished, then spoke quietly, eyes down. "I apologize, madame. I will try to wash my hands more often. I apologize for my attitude and I will do as much as I can for you tonight."

"Till it's finished?"

"Till nine, madame."

Madame Mercier blew sharply through her nostrils and rolled up her measuring tape.

By nine Elisa had the new sleeves of Madame Boutet's dress pieced, pinned, and the first seam stitched, and she was exhausted. She showed Madame Mercier her work, ignoring the breathy sounds of her displeasure; they were good signs, signs that breath would be the only consequence tonight. She kept her face respectful as she

9

said *bonsoir.* She walked out of the shop and heard the door close behind her, and filled her lungs with the open air.

The narrow streets of Lyon were deep in shadow beneath the three-story houses, clouds already brightening to pale sunset gold in the sky above. Elisa walked quickly, threading her way to the dingier quarters. Going down her familiar alley, she hugged the gray wall, away from the stench of the sewer drain where something seemed to have died. She let herself in the back door and climbed the stairwell, shutting her ears against the sound of angry voices through thin walls. At her own door her fingers rose instinctively, her eyes on the two ragged nail holes where the mezuzah used to be. They always tightened her stomach a little, those holes. She passed them by and let herself in the door, into peace.

It smelled like brisket. It smelled like Shabbos. The deep, sweet peace of Saturdays in the house in Heidelberg came back to her with the scent, and her eyes stung. Her right hand lifted to the small, bright mezuzah nailed in its new place on the inner doorframe, and for a moment she thought of nothing but the holy words inside. Then she heard her sister's voice: "Just *stop* it!"

10

She set her jaw and walked down the little hallway to their bedroom. Her brother, Karl, sat on the bed, arms crossed and face defiant, as their sister, Tova, fingers tangled in her half-made braid, wailed, "I'm going to have to redo it all!"

"Karl," said Elisa.

"I *didn't,*" said Karl hotly. "I just asked if I could share the washbasin a minute —"

"You hit my elbow!"

"I didn't mean to!"

"But you did," said Elisa. "Apologize. Tova, I'll fix it."

"Sorry," muttered Karl to Tova's shoes.

"Thank you," whispered Tova, tears appearing in her eyes. She gave Karl a wavering smile. She was the only one of them who used her Hebrew name for everyday; it had stuck, Mama said, because it meant "good." And wasn't that just like a parent, thinking pliable was good — even now, at thirteen years old? Elisa worried for her.

"Shh now," Elisa soothed as she braided her sister's thick, wet hair. "It's all right."

She gave Karl his turn at the basin and then shooed them out so she could change. She heard clinking from the kitchen as she peeled swiftly out of the sweat-stained black working dress. As she combed her hair something rustled behind her. A slip of

11

paper appeared under the door — then flicked back out of sight. She turned her back. *Do you know what I do for this family? I'd like a minute's peace sometime.* Rustle. Flick. She glanced behind. There it was, then — *flick* — a grin seemed to hang in the air. The corners of her mouth softened helplessly. Whispers from behind the door, a giggle. She twisted her hair into a bun, shoving hairpins in ruthlessly, and dove for the paper as it slid forward again. "Ha!" She threw open the door and displayed her trophy. "I win."

"Come to the table," Mama called.

As she followed her siblings down the hallway she glanced aside into her parents' cluttered bedroom. Her smile fell away as she took in what lay on the bed.

Mama's jewelry box. Open.

Her heart tightened, then began to pound. The open lid, which ought to be locked and hidden in its place under the floorboards, spoke to her as if aloud. *It's not all right.* Tova and Karl were almost too young to remember the days back in Heidelberg when the automobile had gone, and the carved walnut furniture, and the piano. Her first piano. She'd cried and cried. The next day Papa had taken her to watch a rally from a friend's third-floor window, her dark curly hair carefully hidden under a hood. She'd heard words she still couldn't burn out of her mind. "We must leave this country," Papa had told her quietly, as she shivered in the dark shuttered room afterward, hearing the last fierce, joyous voices in the square below. "I am so sorry, Lies. I would not have sold your piano for any lesser reason than this. You see, they will not let us leave with our money. That is the price."

"It's not fair," she had whispered.

"It's not fair," he'd said gravely, as if they were reciting a lesson together. Then, "We will pay them and go."

She leaned on the doorframe, staring at the box. *Who are we paying now? Where do we go?* The handful of bright things in there was all their savings. *Not enough.* Papa said so. He said over and over that the rumors from Paris must be exaggerated; it was impossible to know what had really happened at the Vel d'Hiv stadium, with the reports contradicting each other so completely. Even if the Nazis had done such a thing in the Occupied Zone, he said, it was another matter here. This was still France.

He had written to a friend in Paris to try to learn the truth. He hadn't had an answer yet.

The gold in the box spoke its silent question. "I don't know," she whispered, and turned away. She walked down the hall to the dining room, to where the table with its pure-white cloth stood against the scarred wall, laid with blue-and-white plates, clean napkins by each one. To Mama, behind her two tall candles, and Papa by her side smiling. To Shabbos dinner, and peace for tonight.

CHAPTER 1
WHEN THEY COME

Julien smiled reassuringly at young Chanah — *Anne, you've got to call her Anne* — and gave a tug on the rope harness that held her to the high oak limb. The girl watched him with eyes bright and brave and a little too white around the edges.

"Did I tie it right, Julien?"

"Exactly right. You do it exactly like that when they come."

Anne nodded vigorously. Julien gave her another smile. His father's words beat in his mind: *They say they are planning a census. That is a lie.*

Around him the treetops glowed green and golden with afternoon sunlight, sweet as if no darkness had ever touched the world. Around him hidden by those summer leaves, Jewish children were strapping themselves into rope harnesses high in the trees, and from round the massive oak trunk came his sister's voice, telling the little ones in the concealed treehouse to lie down. "You'll have to be quieter than this when the police are here."

A week. That was what the *préfet* had said three frantic days ago: *A census, in a week.* Julien's Scout troop had been assigned to the Les Chênes home, where more than half the sponsored refugee children were Jewish, an hour later. An hour after that, they'd been out in these woods tying ropes, hoisting boards, their wiry troop leader, Marcel, pacing the forest floor beneath them shouting, "I can see you! Move that board! Don't nail *anything* down till you're sure!"

Julien's father had barely been home these three days. When he was, he'd stand moving his lips, folding a sheet of blue-lined paper over and over in his fingers as he stared at nothing you could see. Then striding into his study, locking himself in there with Marcel, with Madame Thiers, with Pastor Alexandre. No words for his son except, "Don't be late for Scouts."

They'd been entrusted with more than Scouts usually were. But Julien was eighteen now, and Marcel was twenty. They couldn't be soldiers. But they could do this.

Julien steadied himself on the oak limb, high in the green, and quizzed Anne on the alert signals. She recited them breathlessly,

16

word-perfect, head high; Julien could see her at a blackboard, bright eyes on the teacher, and his throat twinged. *This isn't a test. You kids could get everything right —* *Or maybe it is a test. But not of you.*

Marcel had chosen this oak. He'd played in it with his brothers, he'd told Julien with a reminiscent grin: pretending to be Huguenot pastors hiding from the soldiers, if they could resist dropping acorns on them. *My family's been here six hundred years, you know,* he'd said. *One of our ancestors was a martyr.* The people here remembered. They had done this before.

A young rough voice rose from the other side of the oak, somewhere above the treehouse: "I'm nine years *old,* I can —"

"Don't be an idiot, Jean-Marc!" Another young voice, shrill with indignation. "Why don't you *ever* —"

"Wait here," Julien murmured to Anne. "Don't untie by yourself yet, all right?" He began to climb upward.

His sister Magali's voice snapped up from the ground like a whip: "Marek, *no!*"

Marek? As in *Guess what Marek did today?* Magali asked that almost every night at the dinner table, after her workday with "her kids" at Les Chênes. Usually rolling her eyes. *Guess what Marek did today,* Julien's

17

mind babbled as he climbed feverishly, *he fell from the top of an oak tree and* —

The scream struck through him to the roots, like lightning. He braced for the sound of a body hitting the earth — then scrambled desperately upward as the boy shrieked again from up high. And there he was, a small form dangling by one armpit from a loose harness, legs kicking, free hand flailing in the air.

A lanky boy shot into view from above, flung himself belly-down on Marek's branch and wrapped his legs around it, reached down and caught the loose end of the harness in both hands, screaming: "Stop kicking! *Stop!*"

"Wait — wait!" Julien crawled toward them along the limb, not daring to look down. The lanky boy was twelve at most, barely heavier than Marek — he'd be yanked off the branch. "Don't take his hand — just wait . . ."

He made it, braced himself, his face almost in the boy's determined face — *Étienne, his name's Étienne* — and they grasped the rope together. They hauled up: ten centimeters. Twenty. Marek's free hand found a branch jutting from their limb and locked around it. Julien reached down and took the boy under the armpits, fingers knotting in his sweaty shirt. Étienne took up the slack and secured it around the limb with a quick and fumbling hitch.

"That branch — down there." Julien barely had the breath to speak. His shoulders were trembling, and he didn't even have Marek's full weight. He'd never be able to lift him all the way onto their limb. "If we can get his feet on that one — he can stand."

Étienne scrambled down to the lower branch, not quite within reach of Marek's legs, and held out his hands, ready.

Marek was shaking his head.

"You have to — let go," Julien gasped. "I swing you — sideways — Étienne puts your feet — on the branch. Have to."

Marek's eyes were huge. Tendons stood out like bars in his thin wrists. He shook his head again.

Sharp terror stabbed through Julien's gut, and the strange, cold knife of memory: the *préfet*'s voice, the *préfet*'s cold eyes: *Nothing you can do, nothing you can do* — eyes on Papa — *nothing you can* —

"Let go!" he snarled, guttural, and his body was hot suddenly with inexplicable rage.

Voices rose from the ground.

"We're under you."

"We'll catch you."

19

The Scouts — Marcel, Pierre — the Les Chênes workers, his sister, and — was that *Benjamin*? Julien looked into Marek's wide eyes: the whites glaring, a mere rim of brown around the huge black pupil. Then he felt it, the boy drawing breath, the eyes going up to his hands — Julien's knuckles spasmed into their tightest grip.

And Marek let go.

Pain flared through Julien's back as he swung the boy sideways, Marek's hands digging into his shoulders, both of them gripping like death. The limb tore his shirt and scraped his chest as he pushed himself forward along it — and Marek's feet found the branch and Marek's hands found Étienne and the weight lightened and was gone, and Julien did not let go. He could not let go. Deep, rough breaths rasped in and out of him, and the world was green and tilting, and the voice of the *préfet* was in his ears, was everywhere.

Do not obstruct us. The eyes on Papa. *Or it may be* you *we are forced to deport.*

"Your turn."

Julien's eyes flew open.

"To let go," said Marek, looking at him with concern.

Julien's hands sprang open. "Sorry. Sorry. I . . ." He pulled himself up, drew a steadying breath. "That was amazing, Étienne, that was — well done."

Étienne's shoulders grew straighter, his over-bright eyes meeting Julien's. Then he turned and growled at Marek. "You'll stay in the treehouse when they come. Or I'll *drop* you next time."

"Okay," said Marek. "Sorry."

Julien lay back down on his branch and closed his eyes.

The *préfet* hadn't said it only to Papa. He had said it to Pastor Alexandre as well.

Because of the letter.

Three days ago, Julien had stood in the church courtyard among the other young people of his town, waiting for a visiting official from the collaborationist French government in Vichy to walk out through the dark church doors. Marcel stood at the head of the group with a protest letter about the Vel d'Hiv roundup in his hand. Julien still had the torn flap from the envelope, a tiny ball of paper in his pocket, soft now with handling.

We know what you people did in Paris. We know, and we do not condone.

They might have had no warning of the census if they hadn't provoked them with the letter. Papa said so. Papa said it was the

21

right thing.

The smile had faded off the official's face as he read the letter; he stammered something about Jews not being his business, thrust the letter at the *préfet* beside him, and fled to his automobile. The *préfet*'s hard eyes dismissed the young people with a glance, and came to rest on the pastor and his assistant, Julien's father.

A census, the *préfet* had said, dusting his hands. There was nothing in this talk of deportation. He didn't want to hear another word about arrests in Paris; here in the Unoccupied Zone, France made her own laws. Eventual resettlement was a possibility, the *préfet* had said, but what was it to them? Yes, in about a week.

A word to the wise, messieurs les pasteurs. *Do not obstruct us.*

Julien rolled and unrolled the ball of paper in his pocket between his finger and thumb as Marcel came to him under the tree.

"That was well done."

"I never," said Julien in a low voice, "*ever* want someone hanging over certain death from my hands again."

Pierre butted in between them, his farm-bred shoulders taking considerable space, and glanced up far too casually to gauge the distance. "That wasn't certain death.

Broken ankle. *Maybe* two. Or I'd have broken an arm catching him, I guess."

"Better if it was you," said Marcel quietly. "Four more days."

"Mmm." Pierre looked toward the children's home. "There'd be ways to hide him. Root cellar maybe. I figure, you tell 'em how sorry you are about the rats, but the traps'll take care of them soon. They ask what kind of traps, you tell them to step carefully. City man won't set foot underground after *that*, you watch."

"I'd rather not, thanks," Julien told his old friend coolly. "Not sure I'd enjoy the show."

Pierre grunted, looking grim.

Under the oak tree, the Les Chênes director was gathering the children, a commending hand on Étienne's shoulder, Anne on his other side. Brother and sister, Julien remembered suddenly. He looked past the children and met the eyes of his best friend, Benjamin, slight and pale among the suntanned Scouts, wiping his glasses on his shirt. Julien beckoned him over.

"You came?"

"I came to tell Marcel your father wants him." Benjamin put his glasses back on. His eyes flicked from side to side. "I . . ."

Marcel nodded. "In one more minute."

"You want to go straight to the Tanières?" Julien asked Benjamin softly. "See the cave?"

Pierre gave a silent whistle. "A cave?" He cut his gaze over to Benjamin. "Has he ever been up in the Tanières?"

Shut up, Pierre. "He'll know the place like the back of his hand by tomorrow night. You watch."

Benjamin said nothing. The dark circles around his eyes stood out like bruises. Nearby Marcel and the Les Chênes director were speaking of alternate plans, long-term hiding places, a village in the Ardèche. Anne was speaking to her brother; Étienne turned and Julien met his eyes, still wide in his pale face.

Julien's mind stuttered back to the gravel church courtyard beneath the gray sky, the silence of the watching people as his father and Pastor Alexandre had stood shoulder to shoulder, looking the *préfet* in the eye.

You ought not concern yourself with these foreign Jews.

We do not know any Jews, the pastor said. *Only people.*

Ten thousand people arrested. Children torn from their mothers' arms — by French police. Ten thousand people shoved into a stadium, penned like cattle in the heat for days. Then given to the Germans — those

24

who survived.

Not a word about it on the radio. But Pastor Alexandre had a letter from an eyewitness. The memory of Benjamin's face, when Papa had brought home the news, still hurt like a backhand blow. Benjamin was from Paris.

His friend hadn't spoken for two days after that. When he did, it was worse. He spoke names.

Sara Weizman. Rudy Steinmetz. The Rosenbergs. The Schneiders — no — they're citizens — I think they're citizens, Julien . . .

They hadn't done it for defiance, that protest. They hadn't done it for show. They had done it because silence was *wrong.* The truth had power, Papa said; God called those men to repent, even now. They had done it because it hadn't even been on the *radio* — as if no one in France should care, as if no one should remember Sara Weizman. Julien crushed the paper between his fingers, watching Benjamin's eyes travel the edges of the woods.

"Let's go," he said.

"Going up the old bridge road?" said Pierre. Benjamin nodded. They fell in together, walking down the long sunlit path away from the oak tree. "I have to go up that way, see a farmer. Find out if he really has a —" Pierre bit down on the word he'd been about to say and threw them both a grin.

"A what?" said Julien as the voices receded behind.

"Not really supposed to talk about it."

"Great work so far, then."

Pierre gave him a rueful glare. "Hiding's all right if you have to. Question is, why do we have to?"

Benjamin spoke in a low, dark voice. "Because we don't have *guns.*"

"Got it in one."

A chill went down Julien's spine. He glanced back toward Les Chênes. "You're looking for —"

"Someone's got to do it."

"Someone does *not* have to do it, Pierre Rostin." Julien stopped on the path and raised a stiff arm toward the children's home. "Do you need me to draw you a picture? What happens to the kids if we bring Vichy down on us by *shooting* people? What happens to —" He broke off his gesture toward Benjamin, who had gone very still.

"Well that's rich. You people and your letter, like they're gonna ask the *boches* to give those people back because somebody *disapproves —*"

Benjamin was pale, Julien saw. *Those people have names.* "We couldn't shut up about it. Let them go on thinking nobody cared —"

"Grow up, Julien. We're past that point. There's only one thing they listen to."

Julien's fist was up between them before he knew what had happened. His blood was pulsing in his ears. He stared at the fist, and put it away.

Pierre crossed his arms. "Y'know, I liked you better when you didn't think punching me was a sin."

Julien snorted. *I thought it was a sin all right. I just yielded to temptation.* "You hated me. You don't remember?"

"I remember you stood up for Benjamin. There wasn't anything wrong with that."

A corner of Benjamin's mouth turned up ironically as their eyes went to him. "No," he said. "I don't suppose there was."

"That's all we're trying to do," Pierre said. "Protect the people we care about. *All* of them. Look, I believe in God as much as you do, but some things aren't complicated. A mad dog comes onto your farm, you shoot it in the head or you run in and bar the door. You don't poke it with a stick." Benjamin was nodding. "Shooting's better. It doesn't come back."

27

"They're not dogs."

"They're traitors," Pierre snapped. He looked away into the green. When he looked back, his voice was quieter, his eyes simple as earth. "They threatened your father, Julien."

Papa had preached, the day of the letter. Preached like the schoolteacher he used to be, drily parsing the Greek words for *submit* and *obey* and the limits of a Christian's duty to the authorities. Not looking at the Vichy men in the front row. *I offered to take this one,* he'd said. *Pastor Alex doesn't trust himself. He gets carried away.*

Julien looked back along the path, a long tunnel of shifting leaf-shadow and sun, Marcel at the end of it, coming toward them. He remembered how the sun had come out strong for just ten minutes as they sat in the old stone church, the long squares of light falling sharp and brilliant from the windows, lighting heads here and there in the dimness like haloes. He remembered how small Papa looked as he passed through one of them on his way up to the pulpit, his serious face and combed brown hair exposed as in a searchlight before he walked forward into shadow. He remembered how sure his voice sounded, announcing the first hymn: "A Mighty Fortress Is Our God."

How the government men fumbled with their hymnals; how the voice of the church rang out as one.

He turned back to Pierre. "They did. He still thinks we did right. He knows what he's doing."

Marcel caught up to them, smiling. "Your father?"

Julien nodded.

"Yes. He does. Come on, you guys."

They followed him together, down the path through the shadow and light.

CHAPTER 2
A MIGHTY FORTRESS

"An *American visa*? Is this a joke?" Julien stared at the envelope on the dining-room table.

Benjamin was pale, but his face was set. "You don't understand."

It was all there: the American stamp, the address *New York, NY* written shakily below the new name of Benjamin's mother. It was real. An American visa, or the hope of one. "You could be out of here," he breathed. "You could be safe *forever* —"

"Julien." Papa's voice was gentle. Julien looked up sharply at his father. Benjamin snatched the letter from the table and made for the stairwell door. Papa watched him go. The skin of his face seemed strangely dry, the line between his eyebrows deepening.

"He doesn't want it?" Julien asked softly.

"Applying for an exit visa from France is too much of a risk," said Papa. "Even if he turns out to be still a citizen. He's afraid.

Julien — I did think of asking you to speak to him about it. But not like *that*."

Julien looked down, his chest tightening. "I'm sorry, Papa." He jerked his chin toward the big south living-room window that gave onto the downward-sloping streets and rooftops of Tanieux. His father nodded.

It had been *two weeks* since the *préfet*'s warning. He had helped Marcel with the sentry-duty roster, made sure every Scout had a bicycle when he stood watch, had them recite to each other their duties in the alert chain — their partners, their streets, all the passwords — every time they changed watch. He had stocked the cave with water and firewood, promised to guide Benjamin to it when they came. He had listened till his head ached with it, listened for the far barking of farm dogs, for the sound of engines on the high plateau roads. "Every day I think they're coming," he whispered.

"It's a hard time." Papa's brown eyes were warm when they finally met Julien's. Julien breathed deep again.

"Papa, what you said — an exit visa . . ."

"He'll have to cross a border."

Julien's belly went cold. *"How?"*

"I know some people," Papa said quietly. He raked a hand through his hair. "I believe he will come round. Given time. The visa itself isn't certain yet, but his mother has friends now . . . Don't speak to him about it again today, please."

Julien nodded.

It was a strange evening. Benjamin avoided him, of course — but so did Magali when she came home from Les Chênes. She had no Marek stories at supper, no jokes; her eyes were on her plate. When Mama softly said her name, she leapt up and almost ran to the bathroom, and came back with a fresh-washed face. Mama watched her a few seconds, then turned away. "I've been asked to go down to the L'Espoir home tonight to help with the babies," Mama said evenly. "I'll do the dishes when I get home."

Magali glanced up. Julien saw her red eyes.

The household scattered the minute the table was cleared: Benjamin up to his bedroom, Papa to his office, Mama out the door. Magali stood in the middle of the floor for a long moment, a fork forgotten in her hand. She raised her eyes to Julien's. She was weeping.

"They're emptying Rivesaltes," she whispered.

"Emptying?"

"Maybe the other internment camps too — we don't even know. They've sent the Spanish refugees away and they're — they're putting the Jews on trains to Germany."

"All of them?" Julien's mouth was dry.

"We don't know! They just keep loading trains. We heard it from a Swiss Aid worker there but they don't tell her anything — half my kids' *parents* are there, Julien —"

"Chanah — Anne — and, and Étienne?"

"Their mother's in Gurs — Marek's aunt is in Rivesaltes —"

Papa's study door opened. His eyes on Magali were dark. "Lili," he murmured, and his arms opened slightly, but Magali did not move.

"We don't have any names," she told him, ignoring the fresh tears that flowed down. "We don't know what to tell them. One of you tell Benjamin. And Mama. I can't."

"I will," said Papa heavily, and turned to the south window.

Down there the sun hung orange over the slate rooftops, filling the narrow streets and the broad *place du centre* with dusky gold. Filling the air, like that sound, that strange, low humming sound. Was that — ?

A bicycle shot across the *place.* Sylvain Barraud was on it.

Tonight's sentry.

For a moment no one breathed. Julien heard his own voice speaking — "They're here" — a strangely echoing sound in the suddenly emptied-out air. Then they all moved at once.

Papa went for his study. Julien and Magali raced for the stairwell door and reached it together. Julien jammed his shoes onto his feet, glanced up the stairs, turned to Magali, opening his mouth — "Could you — ?"

Rage flared in her red eyes. "I can't stay here and do your work for you. I've got *duties*. My kids'll be in the trees all night now and we're probably going to have to walk them to Rochepaule in the morning." She was jerking her shoes on, not even pausing to wipe the tears from her face. "Tell Papa that, if I don't come home tomorrow, all right? Bye."

She was gone. Papa came to the door, a roll of blue-lined papers in his hands. "What should I tell Benjamin?"

"I just have to check in with my alert partners. Back in ten minutes and I'll take him to the cave."

Papa nodded. Ducked into the kitchen a moment and reappeared empty-handed. "Go with God."

"You too."

Outside the air was gold with the setting sun and hummed with the unfamiliar sound of great engines. Julien saw them already parked in the *place* as he walked downhill to Gilles's house, tense hands in his pockets, forcing himself not to run as the sky caught slow fire above. A black automobile, flanked by motorcycles. And three khaki buses.

He confirmed with Gilles. He confirmed with Jérémie, who was assigned to warn the Le Puy road and was chewing his fingernails in his impatience to go.

"You boys stand up straight out there," Jérémie's mother said. "You remember to look like you're just off to visit friends."

Jérémie nodded, chewing.

They shook hands and went their assigned ways. Julien walked back up the hill, skirting the edge of the *place du centre,* unable to take his eyes off the looming buses. The sleek black automobile, the man in a police kepi who stood with one foot on the lowest of the *mairie*'s stone steps, not going up them to the mayor's office but turning back, speaking with sharp gestures to —

Pastor Alexandre. And Papa.

Julien stopped.

He couldn't help it. His body would not obey. The police chief was speaking, jabbing a finger at them each in turn.

As one bus engine shut off, then another, the hum dying down, Julien caught a single word: *list.* Then the third engine died. The hush spread like ripples in water, carrying

35

the man's last words, his angry face turning toward Papa: ". . . or will I be forced to arrest you both?"

For a moment the *place* was gone, the buses, the men. All but Papa. For a moment he stood alone under the scarlet sky, alone but for the son he did not see. His face as he answered was as Julien had never seen it, calm and utterly cold. His voice was the same, each word carved out with chill precision. "There is no list. With all due respect, monsieur, you are wasting your time."

The police chief's laugh rang sharp against the housefronts. "Time? We can comb this place faster than you can imagine. And *we* have a list." Julien saw the man's hand rise, saw him turn to the blue-uniformed men behind him; his heart stopped.

The police chief pointed down the nearest street. Two policemen started down it. Pastor Alexandre turned away, and Papa followed him.

Julien started up the *place* toward his own street, trying not to run.

He managed to keep to a walk until the heavy downstairs door of his own house closed behind him. Then he raced down the hall past the ground-floor apartment and took the stone stairs three at a time.

A dark figure barreled into him from above.

Julien grabbed the railing with a jerk that made his teeth snap. In the dimness he made out the glint of glasses, the moon-white of Benjamin's face. "What on *earth?*"

"There's someone upstairs," Benjamin gasped. "There's someone upstairs."

"But —"

"Someone came in — to the second floor — I —"

"Fine. Let's go." It couldn't possibly be the police — could it? He took Benjamin's arm and pulled him down the steps. He heard faint footsteps overhead, heard the thin voice of the old downstairs tenant talking to himself; then they were out the back door into Mama's tiny high-walled garden under a fading sky streaked with rose and gray. "All right. Hold your head high out there, look normal, you hear?"

Benjamin was shaking his head over and over, his eyes like a spooked horse's. "Not — not the cave. I can't."

"What?"

"I can't — I can't — in the *dark* —"

Julien took his friend by the shoulders and shook him. *Now you come out with this? Now?*

"The farm — your grandfather's farm —"

37

"I can't take you there," Julien hissed. "I'm assigned to warn the north road!"

"I — I —" Benjamin's breath was coming faster and faster. The sky was dim; in the east beyond the garden wall the dark was rising. Benjamin looked up sharply at some sound from a second-floor window and made to pull away from Julien toward the garden gate.

Rage rose hot in Julien's belly. He dug both thumbs into Benjamin's shoulders, brought his face within centimeters of his friend's, and ground out: *"You will come with me."* Benjamin's eyes were huge in the twilight, fixed on him. The scent of crushed mint rose sharp from beneath their feet. Benjamin nodded once. Julien took his friend's arm and pulled him into the street.

He kept his grip as they walked up the narrow streets: the Rue Emmanuel, the Rue Peyrou, the crossroads yet to come. Benjamin's steps were uneven, but he faced rigidly forward. Julien's heart was drumming, his breath coming ragged. The streets were empty, the streetlamps still dark. In the east the black crept upward, the stars lighting one by one like watching eyes.

The crest of the hill loomed up ahead, a dark bulk beneath the stars. Benjamin swallowed convulsively; Julien tightened his grasp. "We're not going to the cave," he whispered. Words came to him as he raised his head and saw the dark shapes of the last houses of Tanieux, and remembered who was assigned to the east road. "We're going *there.*"

The door he knocked on opened a crack, one eye peering through. "Madame Chaveau," Julien said, then as she flung the door wide: "is Marcel home?"

"No. Come in. Come in!"

Marcel's mother hurried them into the little living room. The lamp was lit, the shutters closed. "Does he need hiding? The basement?"

"I . . ." Hope flared in Julien. Benjamin was looking at him dark-eyed. "I . . ." He saw in his mind his father, a small far figure beneath that bloody August sunset, confronting the police with a cold eye. He saw that same sunset dying now above the north road, above the farms that hadn't been warned. "Yes," he said. "I have duties. I'll be back in an hour. Less, if I can."

Benjamin didn't speak.

Julien stood in the living-room doorway, watching his friend being led away, Madame Chaveau telling him she would bring him a cushion down there, and did he want anything to drink? Then he turned away, and

39

slipped out into the night.

The rising moon hung high above Julien when he came back to the crossroads from the north. He was sweating. On his left as he ran, woods and pastures lay thick and dark around the road to Grandpa's farm; on his right the bluff fell sharp to the gleaming river and the wild, broken land beyond. Tanieux came into view over the rise, its streetlamps still dark, and he slowed to a walk. An owl hooted. Another answered far off, and a dark shape loomed up from the road on his left. He froze.

Marcel's face came up out of the gloom. "Julien."

"Marcel? Have you —"

"I walked Benjamin to Pierre's place. Pierre'll walk him to your grandfather's."

"Thank you," Julien gasped. "Thanks." His chest hurt. He wiped his sweating palms on his shirt, seeing in his mind Benjamin's face in the lamplight, and all the faces of the farmers he had warned tonight.

"He told me how he panicked. He says you're going to kill him."

"Not me," said Julien grimly. "Too much competition."

Marcel twitched a smile, but his eyes didn't change. He thrust his hands into his pockets. "Is your father home?"

"No idea. Probably."

They walked. Marcel passed his own house without turning. Slate rooftops glinted dully under the moon. "Julien," said Marcel, "is your father still glad we wrote that letter?"

Julien turned to the Scout leader. His face was in shadow. "Is that what you want to talk to him about?"

Marcel shook his head fast. "No. Maybe." He jerked his chin upward twice as if something hurt, then spoke fast. "I was reporting to them in the church office, a policeman came in to fetch the pastor, he — he wasn't very polite, he says to your father, 'Who are you, are you anyone important?' It wouldn't have been *any* kind of lie to say no."

"And?" Julien breathed.

"And Monsieur Faure says the police chief threatened them *both* with deportation, right there in the *place* in front of —" He broke off. "I'm sorry —"

"No. I knew."

"I'm sorry, I just — I think maybe there are people who shouldn't go around defying the authorities. Witness or no witness. People whose lives other people depend on."

"What, because he's my father? Isn't that

41

my business?"

"No. I'm talking about *lives* depending on —" Marcel jerked his chin, hunched in on himself, and said in a barely audible voice, "I'm talking about his work."

"The school —" Julien started, frowning a little, and saw Marcel in the moonlight turn and stare. "He designed our alert chain," Julien said softly. "Didn't he?" No one had ever said, but it had his stamp on it somehow — so thorough.

"Yes." Marcel said it quickly. Julien could hear the wet sound of his mouth as it opened and closed. See the fear in his eyes.

Julien stopped and looked at Marcel. He heard his own voice as if from elsewhere. "You weren't talking about that, though." The blood went *swash, swash* in his ears. "Were you?" Marcel was receding from him, pulling back; Julien's hand whipped out and grabbed his friend's wrist. *"What were you talking about?"*

Marcel shook his head. "I can't," he whispered. "I gave my word. I'm sorry. I'm so sorry. I thought — I shouldn't have said anything, I'm sorry, I really am —"

"You thought I knew," said Julien heavily. At the end of the street stood his house, light spilling from the second-floor window: Mama or Papa, or both, in the kitchen mak-

42

ing tea. His throat hurt. He walked on.

They went up the stone stairs in silence. The sound of Mama singing reached Julien as he climbed: the pure, clear alto swooping through the dark with the assurance of a night-flying bird. He stopped to listen, his heart pinching, then opened the door.

Papa was hunched over a cup of herbal tea, every line of his body etched with weariness. His head came slowly up, and his face eased as he took in Julien. Then he stood abruptly. "Marcel," he said in a tone of surprise, then jerked his head toward the inside of the apartment. "My study."

Mama beckoned Julien to the table. Papa laid a hand on his shoulder in passing, not looking at him. Mama took the kettle off the wood-burning stove; the coals beneath the burner hole glowed dull red.

"Chamomile? Or mint?"

"Mint," mumbled Julien, and sank into a chair.

"Benjamin?" Mama bent over the table to pour for him. The worry lines ran like furrows above her dark-brown eyes; the crow's-feet lay dormant, ripples in the sand. He looked down.

"He's at the farm. I mean, I mean he's at Pierre's — Pierre's walking him down from there." Steam hissed up hot and fragrant, and he took a sharp breath, searching for something to say. "Did you — were you out doing —"

"We hid the L'Espoir boys. For the girls, false papers are enough. I had to rock a one-year-old to sleep on my chest and carry him down to the Thibauds' farm. That's why I'm up so late." The crow's-feet came out now, her smiling eyes warm in the lamplight. "Besides making you and your father tea, of course. Was everything all right on the north road?"

"Yeah. Yeah." *Mama, do you know — ?* Would Papa have told his wife what he hadn't told his son? He blew on his tea, blinking at the steam. Mama smiled at him, and stood to put the dishes away.

She offered Marcel tea when he came out. Marcel excused himself politely. Julien shook his hand; they didn't meet each other's eyes.

Papa strode out of his study as the stair-well door closed behind Marcel, a strip of blue-lined paper hanging unregarded from his right hand. He came to the sink to kiss Mama briefly, their free hands clasping each other a moment; then he took up his cup. "Benjamin is safe?" he asked quietly, and Julien nodded. He saw the relief spread through Papa's face, saw his head go back

44

to gulp his lukewarm tea, saw the paper sway in Papa's hand. He kept his eyes on that paper, on its neat creased-and-torn edge, till his father's hand moved just enough for it to flap gently open; and finally, as if reaching out to snatch a lizard off a sun-baked wall, he caught five words.

Need 2nd safe house Annemasse.

Then Papa set down his cup and, mildly, inattentively, not even looking at the paper in his hand, he dropped it down a burner hole into the stove. There was a brief flare. Mama sipped her tea. Julien gulped his, though it scalded his mouth, and swallowed.

Annemasse. Where's Annemasse? He looked at the stairwell door. Took another quick swallow. His parents were sharing a long, weary look.

"Julien," Papa said, "was it you I saw in the *place*?"

Julien set his cup down. After a moment he nodded.

"Did you hear what they were saying?"

He nodded.

"I want you to know it meant nothing. Men like him make threats in case they work. If he could have cowed us tonight his job would have become easy. You saw he didn't act on it. He won't."

Mama had gone still, her cup half raised

45

to her mouth. "What threats, Martin?" she asked quietly. Papa raked a hand through his hair and opened his mouth.

The hot tea burned in Julien's throat. The empty cup rattled on its saucer as he put it in the sink. They were still looking at each other. "Thanks, Mama. Good night."

As the stairwell door closed he heard Mama asking again, "What threats?" and Papa giving her an answer he couldn't hear.

He took the stairs silently, two by two. He walked softly down the hall and opened Benjamin's door. The bed was neatly made, the books lined up perfectly on the shelf. Except for the atlas, which stuck out.

He spread it open and sat cross-legged on the hard boards of his friend's floor. At least he had an idea of where to look.

He put his finger on it. Annemasse. A town of twenty-five thousand in the greater Geneva area.

Right up against the Swiss border.

He closed the atlas and put it away. He crept down the stairs, heard Mama's and Papa's soft voices behind the second-floor door as he passed it by. He opened the downstairs door and stood on the stoop in the darkness. The night wind had risen and the moon had set. A million stars stared down.

He will have to cross a border, said Papa. *Am I going to be forced to arrest you both?* said the police chief. *I know some people,* said Papa. Marcel said, *I'm talking about lives.*

He shut his mind against the voices, shut his eyes. He breathed the cool night air deep into him, letting his mind spread out into the land around his home: the shadowed silence of the woods, the farmhouses and old stone barns, the tumbled rocks of the Tanières. Feeling presences in them, like the sound of people breathing in a pitch-dark room, hundreds of people still and silent as mice inside a wall.

And the hunters, passing by.

A border. His lips shaped the words without sound. He sank down and gripped the stoop beneath him with both hands, stilling their shaking against the stone.

My father knows what he's doing, eh? he said to Marcel in his mind. Marcel did not answer. The stars looked down at him, thousands upon thousands of eyes in the dark.

CHAPTER 3
WHAT HE'S DOING

The police searched Tanieux the next morning during the church service. Motorcycles droned in the distance as Pastor Alexandre preached. One of Julien's Catholic friends — Mass ended earlier — was on the steps of the Reformed Church with the news when the doors opened: the buses on the *place* were still empty.

Tanieux held. So far.

After lunch Julien went down to the farm. He climbed first into the Tanières with his empty Scout pack; Benjamin's things were in the cave. He'd want them. Not the shiny prayer book, which he'd mostly seemed to want out of the Losiers' house, but the little bundle of clothing, the chemistry notebook, and the pens. Julien crouched in the cave mouth as he packed them, looking in: a deep slit in the dark volcanic rock of one of the ancient hills, almost high enough to stand in, with a broad ledge in front and a tiny stream visible down the rocky hillside. It even faced west, away from the road. *The safest place on this plateau.* He cast an eye around at the neat stacks of firewood and kindling, the water bottles, the fire ring; then he crawled out, slung the pack on his back, and climbed back down.

He gathered wild thyme for Mama as he came down through the Tanières, and the tender top leaves of nettles for soup. He did not think of Marcel. He felt rock and lichen under his fingers, grass around his calves, pine needles brushing him, each — in the little ravine where the sun hadn't reached — with its perfectly round drop of dew. He bent to the stream and let the cold clear water well around his hands, lifted them and drank. He made his way down to the river and waded it where it spread ankle-deep over stones; he scrambled up the short, steep slope to the pines beside the north road and walked up toward the crossroads.

On his right was the wild land he'd come from, rock and grass and twisted pine; on his left the little farms tucked into the folds of the land, pinewood and pasture and little fields brown with barley or golden with wheat. As the road climbed, the Vivarais plateau laid itself out around him wider and wider, green to the horizon beneath the huge sky. There were no words for what he felt for this place. This place he had come to as a stranger from Paris, three endless years ago now; his father's hometown he had told Papa he hated, only to find it was bred in his bones.

He looked west again, past the Tanières, away to the far green peaks of Mount Mézenc and the Vivarais range on the horizon. Ancient volcanoes grown over with grass, worn ramparts undefended by any but the weapons of the Spirit.

And whoever had sent Pierre looking for guns.

Julien had turned eighteen two months ago. Mama had served real beef that night. Jokes about men needing meat, while Julien held back from gulping his like a dog. Young man, fine young man. Jokes about shaving; Papa's hand on his shoulder, warmth in his eyes, a little smile. What did you have to do to get them to call you a man without a little smile? Eighteen. Old enough for a soldier, in a nation that no longer had an army. Old enough, by all the laws of man, to learn to kill.

That wasn't his path. He had known that a long time, and he had chosen it. Evil was resisted by the power of God, not the power of the gun. This had come down to him from his father, from his pastor, from his grandfather, and he had chosen it, in the dark of the old stone church, his soul standing up like a candle flame at Pastor Alexandre's ringing voice vowing, *We will resist them by the weapons of the Spirit.*

Witness was one of those weapons. He knew that too. He remembered, in that church courtyard, how the letter had looked like the sword of the Lord in Marcel's hand. He remembered Papa's passionate voice: *We dare not deny any man his chance at repentance, either by killing or by failing to speak out against his evil.* He looked at the road ahead, and in his mind he saw the *préfet*'s unmoved face, eyes hard and empty as gun barrels, heard the police chief's laugh ring like a blade. Was it for those men's souls his father had risked himself?

Himself, and the people who needed him and what he did.

Himself and Benjamin.

Julien stopped on the road and faced west, toward the far green peaks. You had to keep secrets, even from your family. He understood that. But keeping secrets and standing witness — protest letters and safe houses in Annemasse? Burning your notes before your son can see them and defying your enemy to his face when you don't even

51

have to?

"He knows what he's doing," he said aloud. His voice came out small and hard in the vastness, in the wind. "He knows what he's doing," he said louder. "Look what they're having him organize." He turned sharply to look behind him. But he was alone beneath the wide sky. "I wish You would tell me what to do," he whispered.

The mountains stood green and silent in the sunlight, as they had for a thousand years. The east wind from behind him blew his hair into his eyes.

After a long minute he turned, and walked on.

"Yeah. It's really good. Really hidden." Julien stood with his hands in his pockets, looking at the brush shelter Pierre had built in the woods behind the Rostins' farmhouse. It *was* good. Julien hadn't spotted it till he was ten meters from it, even with Benjamin pointing. The woods themselves felt like a shelter here, dark pines packed together, the air dim and green.

"He took me out here this morning," Benjamin said, "and dared me to find it. I think he wanted to lay an actual bet, but his mother was listening. He said if walking in circles for fifteen minutes trying to find a hideout I knew was there didn't make me feel safe, nothing would."

And do you feel safe? Julien didn't ask.

"Listen . . ." Benjamin hunched his shoulders.

Julien looked away into the evergreen shadows. "So you want me to walk you to Grandpa's or not?" he asked abruptly.

"We already talked about it, the Rostins and I. There's room for me and Gustav in the shelter, easily, and your grandfather has the Pelzinskis —"

"All right. Fine. D'you need anything else from home?"

"Julien."

"What?"

"I'm sorry."

"It's all right." Julien shrugged, seeing again that dying sunset, the dark bulk of Marcel's house against it. "We got through."

"Yeah." Benjamin scuffed at the tawny pine needles underfoot. "I — I don't know, I just couldn't *think,* I kept seeing myself getting hurt up there and then you couldn't dare bring me down. Even if you were there, and if you weren't? You told me yourself people can die of exposure if they're stuck in the rain for long enough —"

"In the *Tanières?* What did you think you were going to do, fall off a meter-high rock

53

and break your back?"

Benjamin's eyes had gone flat. "I'm probably capable of it," he said coolly. "Maybe you and Pierre should make a bet."

Julien crossed his arms and looked his friend in the eye, his jaw tightening. "I've lived with you three years now. And here's what *I* know. You're capable of a lot more than you think."

Benjamin looked away, his feet working the forest floor again. His voice, when it came, was thick. "You think I don't wish that was true? So I could stop being a burden on your family? On you?"

"You're not a burden."

"Don't lie to me," said Benjamin wearily.

"Then *don't bring it up,*" Julien growled. His tightening fist closed on the tip of a bough beside him and crushed it. The sharp scent of pine rose in the air.

Benjamin turned away.

The wind sighed in the pines. From the farmhouse came Pierre's distant voice, saying something about a harness. A thrush called somewhere nearby. Julien opened his mouth, his heart beginning to race, and said, "You could be safe forever."

Benjamin whirled on him. "Or I could be dead before the new year," he rasped. His eyes were black coals.

"That could happen *here,* Benjamin. Right here. It's only going to get worse —"

"Shut up. Just shut up!" Benjamin was trembling. "You don't know what it's like. You have *no idea.*"

"It's not my job to know what it's like. It's my job to get you out of it alive."

Benjamin gazed past Julien into the forest, such bleak fear in his face that Julien almost turned to look.

"It's not," said Benjamin softly.

"What?"

"It's not your job." Benjamin jerked his chin at the slate roof of the farmhouse barely visible through the trees. "Or theirs, or — or your father's. Listen," his voice shook slightly, "I'm grateful —"

"C'mon, Benjamin."

"Last night wasn't your fault. *I* panicked. All right?"

Julien realized his mouth was open and closed it abruptly. "Um. Sure." He looked at the ground: Benjamin's broken leather shoes, dull where they had once gleamed black; his own war shoes, canvas and wood. He lifted his head. "So you want anything from home?"

"My hat. I guess. It gets chilly out here at night."

"Sure thing," said Julien.

■ ■ ■ ■

Elisa was playing Bach when the knock came at the door. Lost in a dream of beauty and order, recalled to reality only when she touched high E or low C — both just slightly out of tune. She loved this old piano and hated it. Like a friend who tried too hard and made you feel guilty. Even six years later she still woke sometimes from dreams of playing her lost piano back in Heidelberg, her hands spread out on her covers as if on the keys.

The knock sounded again. Mama's voice came from the kitchen: "Would you answer it, Elisa?" She lifted her hands, and the music fell away; she heard the bubbling of soup, the squeak of the bed, feet shifting in the hall outside the door as she rose and went to it.

She opened it to find two policemen in uniform.

For a moment everything was still: her hand on the doorknob, her heart not beating, the men watching her with official, expressionless eyes.

She forced her lips open. "What do you need, messieurs?" Her voice betrayed her, and wavered.

"We need to speak with your parents. We need to see the papers of the entire household. Is this in fact the residence of the" — the man checked a paper — "Schulmann family?"

"Papa?" Elisa called, not taking her eyes off of the cold face, as if fascinated, a bird staring at a snake. She could hear the fear in her own voice. She could feel it jolt through the apartment, a live current through the deep water the air around her had somehow become. "Papa? It's the police."

She felt her father behind her before he spoke. It was only then, as if his warmth behind her back released her, that she made any movement backward. As she slid away from that cold gaze, Papa stepped forward and filled the doorway, looking the men in the eye. She stood looking at his back, his shoulders squared beneath his blue-collared shirt, the seam on the yoke she had mended for Mama last week. A sharp stone was in her throat. They were speaking. Asking for papers. "Élise," Papa said in French, not turning. "Please get me the document case from the bedroom." The men were pressing in on him. He did not move.

Her steps sounded strangely loud on the floorboards. In the kitchen Mama stood by

57

the cutting board, a knife poised in her hand. "Elisa, did you say the police?"

"They want papers. He wants the document case —"

"I'll get it. Elisa. Stay here."

Mama wiped her red hands on her apron carefully, took it off, and hung it on its nail. Elisa stood watching the soup simmer, hearing the hiss of Mama's slippers, the muted voices, the heavy tread of the upstairs neighbor overhead. Objects caught her eye with a strange sharpness: the black crack in the countertop, the ring of rust on the brightly scoured faucet, the orange rounds of the carrot Mama had been chopping, only a stump of it left. Abruptly she swept them into her palm and stuffed them all into her mouth. As if she'd need them. It was stupid; they had come for Papa — *my Papa.* Why should she eat? The knife lay on the cracked counter, the sharpest meat knife with the scorch mark on its handle. She stared at it; her hand moved forward. She was breathing fast. The voices at the door were growing louder. She dropped her hand, chewed and swallowed rough carrot chunks, stepped out into the hall. Mama stood straight and pale beside Papa, their shoulders touching, as they did when they sat together in the evenings. Tova stared from the bedroom doorway.

"As you can see," said Papa, "we are legal residents of France since 1936. Everything is in —"

The cold policeman waved him silent. Papa flushed dark red. The man gestured to his shorter partner, who was leafing through a thick document. "There they are. Schulmann," the partner said.

The man lifted their *cartes d'identité* out of the document case. All five of them. Elisa's heart began to race. "Schulmann, David," he said in a monotone. His partner nodded. "Schulmann, Rachel." Another nod. "Schulmann, Elisabeth. Schulmann, Brigitte. Schulmann, Karl." At each name the man holding the document gave another nod.

"That's all of them on the list," he said.

What list? Elisa thought. *What list is that?* Her feet were rooted to the floor, her mouth too dry to make a sound.

"We are under orders to detain the five of you," said the first policeman in a bloodless voice. "You may have five minutes to pack one bag. Then you will come with us."

"*I* will come with you," said Papa. "You will leave my wife and children alone. And you will tell me of what crime I am accused."

59

The man laid a hand on the gun strapped to his hip. "Be advised that we are absolutely authorized to use force."

Papa went red, then white. "You come to arrest women and children who are accused of no crime and you threaten us with violence?"

"Yes," said the man flatly. He checked his watch. "Your five minutes started thirty seconds ago."

Elisa turned and started down the hallway as her father spoke again. She had almost reached Tova when the man's voice followed her. She saw her sister's body jerk as her eyes met cold eyes behind Elisa's back. "We are not authorized to use force only against *you.*"

Heat and cold rushed through Elisa. She gripped Tova by the arm and pulled her into the bedroom. "We have to pack."

"Are they —"

"We have *five minutes* to pack!" She looked around frantically, jerked the top dresser drawer open. The dresser trembled and creaked, the pitcher clanked in the washbasin, and the front of the drawer came off on the left side, the way it did, the way it always did when Karl pulled it too hard. "Get sweaters! Socks! Karl, get up! Get the prayer book — yours, it's newer. Tova, soap, get soap, and toothbrushes —" She yanked her pillow out of its case and started filling it from the top drawer: socks, her little rosewood box of hairpins, her sewing kit, underwear for each of them. One of Tova's had a hole in it. She stood with it in her hands, cold dread finally skittering up her spine. She ran to the window, jerked it open, looked down at the bone-breaking pavement four stories below. *No escape.* Mama opened the bedroom door and set down the stiff-sided blue suitcase. Karl flew into her arms.

Elisa threw sweaters into the suitcase. Tova brought the prayer book and the soap, huge-eyed and silent. Karl clung to Mama. "Do we have to go?"

"Yes," Mama whispered. "They'll shoot us if we don't."

Karl's voice went high: "But they're not allowed to shoot us in France. You *said*!" Elisa could feel the enemy's presence like a weight, the worn hallway boards creaking at his approach. It was only when Mama turned to packing too that she dared lean over, grab an unseen handful of sheet music from the cluttered bookshelf, and stuff it into the suitcase. The creaking came nearer. The bedroom door opened. Mama shoved a last book into the suitcase; Elisa snapped it shut and stood up sharply between the officer and her siblings.

"Time to go."

Papa came down the hall for the suitcase. Mama took Tova by the hand. Elisa took Karl. The policeman gestured them forward.

They went down the stairs in silence, one policeman ahead of them and one behind, their steps echoing in the concrete stairwell like hammer taps in a mine. Outside, at the end of the street, stood a big khaki bus. The policemen walked on either side of the Schulmanns, hands on their guns.

At the door of the bus Papa turned and spoke one final time. "Where are you taking us?" There was still dignity in his straight back, in his voice.

"Get in the bus," said the policeman.

They got in the bus.

The bus took them out of Lyon to the suburb of Vénissieux, to a high blank wall topped with razor wire. A uniformed man with a machine gun passed by the window. Karl stared. Elisa took his hand.

Another armed man opened a gate. Their bus pulled through it. Elisa glimpsed rows of gray barracks. Someone at the front of the bus asked whether this was an internment camp, whether they were staying here.

"This is a sorting camp," said an impatient voice. "No one stays here."

They gripped each others' hands so hard it hurt. The gate clanged shut behind them.

CHAPTER 4
NO ONE STAYS HERE

At the other end of the courtyard someone screamed. Elisa didn't look up.

The line for the water spigot shuffled forward.

She would not watch. She would watch nothing. They were putting people on a bus over there. Or maybe another person had broken and was running hard through the camp — no way out, no way over the high, blind wall or through the gate guarded with machine guns, but you ran anyway, because you had to. You had to. She could feel it in her body, that pounding need.

She was used to denying herself.

A hand touched her arm. She whirled, fumbling and clashing the lid of the cookie tin she held. She took in the brown eyes and gapped teeth, and the breath went out of her as if Julie Altman had punched her in the stomach.

"You're here," she breathed. "Julie — I

thought . . ." She reached blindly for her friend. They grasped each other's hands. "I didn't see you at the mess hall last night, or this morning. I looked for you. I thought . . ."

"I saw you. You gave your soup to Mischa Rosen. That was kind." Elisa twitched a shoulder, shook her head. "We're not eating their food. Not till we have to. My father wants to wait . . . till we know." Julie's hand tightened on hers. "We went through the line to get whatever we could save." Elisa touched the two thin, square slices of bread in the pocket of her cotton dress. "For later."

"Elisa," Julie whispered. "I'm so scared."

"Don't. Julie, please don't."

A woman behind Julie touched her shoulder, pointed at the gap in the line ahead of them. They moved forward.

Julie spoke into Elisa's ear. "Do you know anything?"

"No one knows anything. I don't listen to rumors." She might as well say she didn't sleep on straw. *They can make you. They can put you in a place where there's nothing else you can do.* They could put you in a windowless barracks where you lay staring into pitch dark beside your brother and sister and every prayer you attempted turned to dust in your mouth.

"Madame Weider's next to us in our barracks, you know, the rabbi's niece, and she won't stop crying — they said if her little boy was under two they'd both be exempt, but he's two and a half. Elisa, everyone keeps saying the kids will be deported and the kids won't be deported and it's kids under sixteen — it's always, always kids under sixteen . . ."

Elisa took her friend's hand again. She had made Julie a new collar for her best school dress as a birthday present. Three weeks ago. Julie was wearing it.

"I'm glad you're not sixteen," Julie whispered.

"Another week," murmured Elisa.

"I was making you something. It's at home." Julie's eyes filled with tears. Elisa turned away sharply, eyes on the ground, feeling the rasp of her teeth as she clenched them. She managed to breathe without shuddering. "It's your turn," Julie said softly.

Elisa knelt and drank deep from cupped hands to fill her belly. She filled her cookie tin — the one that used to have their family photos in it, the only kosher container any of them had thought to bring — and put the lid on carefully, trying not to spill a drop. She stood and watched her friend drink, there on her knees in the bare-dust courtyard between the barracks and the wall.

When Julie stood, Elisa pulled her aside and spoke low. "You have to get away."

Julie looked up at her, brown eyes wide, and Elisa gripped her arm and went on, fast. "If they try to put you on a train or a bus or anything — run. The minute you get a chance. Even if they have guns. Better to die getting away than die from whatever they — whatever they want to —"

"Are you going to do that?" Julie's eyes were huge.

Elisa's lungs struggled to fill. The sun hung white and wavering above the razor wire, as if she saw it from fathoms deep under the sea. She blinked, but her vision didn't clear. "I don't know if I can," she whispered. "Tova — and Karl . . ."

"Elisa," Julie whispered.

They stood there together beneath the wavering sky, Julie weeping again, Elisa's mind saying over and over like a heartbeat the only prayer it still knew: *Please.*

At the other end of the courtyard, a bus engine started.

"So what's this message?" said Pierre, working the pump as Julien sank down on the stone stoop of the Rostins' farmhouse.

67

"From Marcel?"

"From my father." Julien watched the cold clear water splash into the chipped cup, and wiped sweat from his face. "Special Scout meeting tomorrow at five. He thinks the police mean to stay till they catch someone. He says we need strategies."

Pierre handed him the cup and he drank deep. It was cold from its time under the earth, and sweet.

"Your father?"

Julien lifted his head. "The instructions were all from him. Not the pastor. Found out the other night."

Pierre's eyebrows rose. "Huh."

"Yeah. Didn't even tell me. He thinks . . ." He glanced up at the stone farmhouse and barn, then out at the little field where Monsieur Rostin was still hoeing, back bent, shirt as dark with sweat as Pierre's was. "My sister took the train to Lyon this morning. Paquerette sent for her — that woman she used to travel with sometimes and bring kids here, you know? The telegram didn't say much. Besides *urgent urgent urgent* and an address. Papa thinks . . ."

Pierre looked grim. "Lyon too."

"Maybe everywhere."

Pierre shook his head, his eyes on the far hills. Julien saw them widen very slightly, a split second before he heard it himself: a long high buzz from the west — from Tanieux. Motorcycle engines.

They were coming.

Somewhere deep inside the fear there was a little space, a tiny space. Elisa found it for her brother.

Her mother was out with Tova, her father across the barracks with the rabbi and his wife. Karl slept, and she watched him from where she leaned against the barracks wall — that soft, open face, that steady breathing. She had stared into darkness all last night, meeting the whites of her parents' eyes when she tossed and turned on the straw. While Karl wandered in his dreams the halls of the old house in Heidelberg, the old sane world they'd been born in. She hoped. He blinked and stirred, opened untroubled eyes, breathed in the smell of the barracks, sharp sweat, and straw. She watched his face change. She was at his side before she knew she had moved. He looked up at her.

And then she found it. Because she had to.

"Will you pray with me?" she said.

He nodded.

"Out of the depths I have called to You, O

Lord," Elisa whispered, and the words shaped themselves to her lips this time. "O Lord, hear my voice." The words were like the handle of a door, worn and familiar to her hand, letting her in. A small space, a tiny space, within the fear. "May Your ears be attentive to the voice of my supplications," she whispered, and Karl whispered it with her. "I wait for the Lord, my soul waits."

Footsteps. They came nearer. She looked up.

A short woman with gray braids and a clipboard stood over them. "Where is your father?"

"Papa!" Elisa shouted.

She knelt there on the straw, her heart stuttering as the woman asked Papa his name. Told him she had a few questions. "More than watchmen wait for the morning," Elisa whispered. *More than watchmen wait for the morning.*

"Do you have a child under two?"

"No."

"Is your wife pregnant?"

"No."

"Are you a veteran of the French army or any Allied army?"

"No."

O Israel, hope in the Lord.

"Or" — the woman's voice lowered — "would it be possible for you to portray yourself as one?"

Elisa's head snapped up. For a moment Papa didn't move. "If I'm exempt," he breathed, "will they spare my family?"

"Yes."

From this time forth and forevermore.

"Elisa," said Papa, "get me the document case."

"Do we have your permission to search your farm, monsieur?"

Monsieur Rostin shrugged and shot disapproving glances at the policemen's neat blue uniforms and shiny motorcycles. "You're going to anyhow, aren't you?"

"We'd prefer to do it with permission," said the officer politely.

Monsieur Rostin grunted. "Well, don't throw everything around. I'm trying to get my barn in order. If you move things, put them back."

Julien watched both policemen's eyes go to the barn, and blinked. Monsieur Rostin shot him a glance. Neither looked at the woods.

"Is there another hoe, monsieur?" Julien asked the farmer in a low voice when the officers had disappeared into the barn.

Pierre was already hoeing again, head down. "In the shed. Left-hand side."

The soil was moist and loose, the weeds short and green and even; Julien moved forward steadily and fast, not looking at the barn, not looking at the woods, not looking at the wet patch on the stone stoop where he had spilled his water two minutes ago as Benjamin almost collided with him, bursting out of the barn at Pierre's sharp whistle. Or at the half footprint in it from where Gustav had followed and vanished into the woods.

Thumps from the barn. The footprint was drying, steadily drying in the sun. Voices from the hayloft. Voices from the barn's open door, dark like a mouth, which Julien did not raise his eyes to. A sudden motion from Pierre and his father, heads up and bodies gone alert as deer for an instant, then heads down and hoeing again. Pierre, incredibly, was suppressing a smile. Out of the corner of his eye Julien could see the policeman walking toward the chicken coop — walking over those dirt-encrusted boards on the ground. What were they for again, and hadn't Pierre said something about replacing — ?

There was a hollow, rotten-wood *crack,* a sudden and very undignified squeal from the policeman, and a splash.

After a few moments, a *truly* evil stench began to waft their way.

Pierre and his father stood leaning on their hoes, Pierre's mouth twitching helplessly, his father's face arranged in a look of impressively sincere concern. "Hmm. Guess we forgot to tell 'im about those," muttered Pierre. Julien barely managed to suppress his own growing grin.

"Poor man," said Monsieur Rostin. "He'll be needing some help." He strolled toward the poor man, who didn't seem to be in danger of drowning; in fact he was trying frantically to climb out, hands braced on the unbroken board, body jerking downward as his polished boots slipped, somewhere under there, on the slick sides of the cesspit. "Monsieur!" cried Pierre's father, speeding up. "Be careful! The other board is —"

There was another crack. Then another splash.

The second policeman was just coming out of the barn. Julien saw his eyes bulge.

Julien would have participated in the rescue — he really would have — if there had been room for him to get a purchase on those slimy uniform sleeves. But he did his duty: he went in to let Madame Rostin know that comfort would be needed; he came back out and hovered at a slight distance as the rescued man stripped off his uniform jacket, unspeakable *bits* falling from it to the ground, and he managed, with heroic effort, not to smile.

There were apologies, there were explanations, there was a good deal of washing up at the pump and then a great deal more. There was a huge mug for each officer of Madame Rostin's best fake coffee. It smelled awfully good. There were embarrassed thanks from the wet policeman, and another warm neighborly cup just for him.

There was no more searching.

When the sound of their motorcycles had faded in the distance, Monsieur Rostin turned to Julien and Pierre. "They won't come here again." He raised a hand. "Oh, we'll be as careful as before. But they won't come here again." He smiled, glancing toward the woods. "Let's go tell them the news."

Elisa woke slowly in the dim barracks, her body limp and heavy as dough. Karl's breath was in her face, his knee digging into her side, a red imprint of straw on his cheek. She blinked twice, and sat bolt upright.

How could she have slept? Papa was facing the sorting committee. They'd been praying for so long, her chest still ached from it . . .

Her parents sat with their backs to her, shoulders touching. Her eyes traced the worn edges of Papa's shirt collar in the dimness. Then he turned, and her stomach dropped out.

His eyes were red and dull. In his hand was half of a square, thin slice of bread. He was chewing.

"Papa." Her voice didn't sound like hers. "Papa?"

His hand clenched and the bread broke in it; his face twitched around his terrible eyes. "I thought I had protected you," he whispered. Mama put a hand on his arm. "I thought I had gotten you all to safety. But I chose France. I chose France."

Her lips shaped the words *No, Papa.* But her breath was trapped in her chest.

"Elisa?" came Tova's soft, sleepy voice from behind her. "What's happening?"

Elisa closed her eyes.

The last time she woke that night, she woke hard into pitch darkness. Someone had screamed.

Tova lay on her; Mama's hand gripped her wrist. They had slept, in the end, in a pile. You couldn't mourn forever. Not unless you preferred to die right here — right now.

Mama was scrambling to a sitting position, the whites of her eyes the one thing Elisa could see. The scream came again.

"They've come for the children!"

Mama's fingers grabbed her wrist again, tightened painfully. Elisa groped in the dark for Tova's hand, scrabbling in straw and dirt. "Tova. Karl!"

Three figures stood in the barracks doorway, flashlights making white pools of light at their feet. She stared at them, trying to make out the shape of their guns. They stepped into the barracks, and the faint shine of their flashlights on straw lit them just enough to see.

They didn't have guns. They had clipboards.

The Schulmanns were all on their feet before the man came to them. They caught words as he spoke fluent Yiddish to their neighbors: *Children under sixteen. Only chance you will have. Before morning. Sign over custody.* Elisa could feel her father trembling. When the man came toward them, Papa stepped out to meet him, and stopped.

The gleam of his flashlight lit a heavy, jowled face above a white clerical collar.

"You were in the sorting committee," said Papa after a long moment.

"Yes."

Papa's voice lowered. "I heard them threatening you."

"I have hoped to tell you how sorry I am," said the priest, "for what happened. You witnessed the *commissaire* reaching the limit of what he would accept from me and my colleagues. But there is a chance now for your children."

"Where do I sign?"

Mama stepped forward as the priest held out his clipboard. They stood shoulder to shoulder, reading. Mama raised her head.

"You will give them back?" Her voice barely shook. "If we return?"

"You have the personal pledge of Cardinal Gerlier on this."

Papa's head snapped up, his eyes blazing in the pale light of the flashlight. "I know nothing about your Cardinal Gerlier," he said. "You're the Abbé Glasberg, aren't you? Are you a convert?" With his name and his Yiddish he had to be, and a citizen as well — *or he'd be in here with the rest of us . . .*

"My parents were," the priest said quietly.

"Please. Don't tell me what you ought to say, or what your church says. Tell me, *you*, Glasberg, can we trust this Gerlier?" He

77

held the man's eyes, his voice lowering. "With our children?"

"The cardinal lent us his pledge," said Glasberg, "but it is my colleagues in the Amitié Chrétienne — the people you see here, seeking exemptions for as many as possible — they will actually take charge of your children. I would trust every one of them with my life, or anyone else's."

Papa's voice dropped further. "And with more than their lives? Can you swear to me no one will force them to become Christians?"

"You have my personal word no such wrong will be done to your family," said Glasberg, looking her father in the eye.

Papa turned to Mama. She took the pen from him without a word. Elisa stood and listened to the beating of her heart, to the tiny scratching sound as her mother, then her father, put her legally into the hands of strangers. The barracks was a shifting sea of white light and black shadow. She was breathing fast. Outside the doorway was a pale floodlit space of gravel and dust. The gray-braided woman was leading two children out into it, one of them clutching a doll. A night guard stepped toward the woman, the white light harsh on the shape of his gun. She spoke to him and passed on.

"Elisa." Papa stood by her. "Hold your pocket open." Mama was rising from beside the blue suitcase, holding her jewelry box.

A hiss and glint of tiny gold links over polished wood, a brief chink, and a small added weight to one side of her dress; her family's savings were hers. Her father took off his watch and added it. Mama was on her knees again, making a bundle. Tova was weeping silently. Karl stood over Mama, his face like pale stone in the shine of flashlights on straw. "Not me," he said. "I'm staying with you. I'll protect you."

Mama rose, her bundle in one hand, eyes blazing. Elisa didn't hear what she said, because at that moment Papa held out a worn, well-oiled leather case to her. She did not move to take it. She stood like stone, hearing nothing but the sound of her own blood beating in her ears.

"Your tefillin, Papa?" It came out as a dry whisper.

"Keep them for Karl," said Papa hoarsely. "In a year he'll be a bar mitzvah."

"You'll need them," she whispered. She was falling through nothing; the earth had let her go.

"Help him keep the Commandments,"

79

Papa whispered. "Help Tova. Help them to remember. But Elisa, eat when you must. Remember that is commanded too. Don't risk your lives."

She couldn't speak. Mama was holding Karl's head against her shoulder. A thin young man was dragging a boy through the doorway, the scratching of their shoes in the gravel the only sound.

"Take care of them," whispered Papa.

Her hands shot forward. He put the case in them, and they closed around it. The leather felt warm, almost alive. She swallowed hard through her clogged, sour throat. "I will," she said thickly and fiercely. He put his hand on her shoulder for a moment, fire flaring in his eyes.

"I know," he said. "My daughter."

It was one part fierce joy and a hundred parts pain. It would break her. She lifted a tearless face to her father. "Come back," she whispered.

His eyes in the shadows were pools of darkness. He looked away. She felt a paper pressed into her hand. "The address of my cousin in London," her father whispered.

Her fingers clenched around it. He turned away. She couldn't breathe. He was giving a paper to the priest; he was speaking: "This one is my brother. If he can't be found, contact the other."

Everything was splintered light and darkness. She was under the sea, the weight in her pocket dragging her down. A hand on her head — her mother, it was her mother's hand. She gasped a breath, saw it in her mind, the knuckles red and cracked, lying gently on her hair. They were praying. "O thou who dwellest in the covert of the Most High and abidest in the shadow of the Almighty . . ." Their voices were lifted up, a power in them. It was almost like joy. She was trembling. The words poured like water over her head. "He will deliver thee from the snare of the fowler. Thou shalt not be afraid of the terror by night. . . . It shall not come nigh thee." It seemed she could see everything now in the dark. Her father's long hands, the ink stains on his fingers, the thin white scar on his thumb. The faint sheen of sweat in the lines around her mother's closed eyes. Every pebble in the bare, lit courtyard, and the wall, and the far shapes of men with guns. "There shall no evil befall thee," her parents proclaimed, and she shivered. The priest's eyes met hers. She looked away.

The voices fell into silence; the warm hand lifted from her hair. She saw their eyes bright in the darkness, her mother and father, for a moment that slowed and stretched to eternity and was gone. They fell into darkness. The priest had turned his flashlight toward the doorway.

She felt for Karl's and Tova's hands, and held on like death. Her mother kissed her cheek, gripping her head in both hands, one last warm touch — and gone.

"Go," Mama whispered.

She went.

At the door of the barracks she turned her head one last time to see her parents there together, leaning on each other in the dark. Then she gripped her siblings' hands and led them out into the night.

CHAPTER 5
THE HANDS OF STRANGERS

Elisa sat propped against the plaster wall, a hand on each of her sleeping siblings, watching the Amitié Chrétienne workers burn addresses.

In the back corner of the great convent hall, a child wailed. It echoed against the bare walls, mingling with the sound of voices, the clacking of heels against the flagstones as the tense French women came and went around the table by the door. The table was a plank laid over two sawhorses, the only furniture in this place, nothing on it but a green ledger and an ashtray — *there,* they were doing it again. A blond woman bringing a young girl to the table, holding out a slip of paper to the tall woman behind it with her dark hair in a bun. She wrote in the ledger, as she had before: first in the back, then in the front. Then the paper in the ashtray, and the brief flare of flame.

Elisa's heart beat faster. She watched the door.

They had come through that door in the dark hour before dawn, her stomach plunging at the sight of the white marble statue of Mary standing over the lintel, a pale ghost with an upraised hand. The place turned out to be empty, echoing. They were given bedrolls and bread as the sky began to pale in the high-arched windows. Now children slept around her everywhere, motionless and open-mouthed, snail trails of tears and snot drying on their faces.

Julie Altman wasn't there.

She watched the door, her skull a space of darkness and flushed heat. The blond woman was shepherding the little girl out the door, picking a bit of straw out of her tangled hair. Another group approached the table; far down the line of bedrolls a woman walked, calling softly: "Lavandel? Is the Lavandel family here?" Tova stirred in her sleep.

London. Doors fluttered through Elisa's mind, the doors of every girl or teacher at her school who'd ever spoken decently to her, the doors of every family in her congregation who were citizens. The door of Madame Mercier's shop; a brief painful laugh escaped her. Tova stirred again. Elisa watched the dark-haired woman, the one who'd said the name *Œuvre de Secours aux Enfants.* The OSE was a Jewish organization, Papa had once told her — the Children's Aid Society. Could she — ?

Tova's eyes flew open. She grabbed Elisa's arm. "What are they doing?"

Elisa rubbed her back. There were flames reflected, very small, in her sister's eyes. "Burning addresses."

"Why?" Tova's voice went high.

"I suppose because they're coming after us," Elisa whispered. She closed her eyes. *Horse and chariot He has thrown into the sea.*

Tova turned and stared at the empty bedroll pushed up beside Karl's, where Hava and Ida Pinski had slept till half an hour ago.

"Someone came for them," Elisa told her. "Hava said to tell you goodbye. I don't have an address for her. I'm sorry."

Tears welled in Tova's eyes. "You should've woken me!"

"I tried." No more sleepovers. No more of Hava's jokes, or her joyous barking laugh. *But Tova — at least she's out . . .*

"Elisa —"

A sharp bang from the entrance. The front door had struck the wall as a woman strode in, urgent-faced. The dark-haired woman slammed the ledger closed. Elisa put a hand on Karl and shook him. His eyes stayed shut; his head wobbled.

A moment later they jumped as a shout echoed through the hall. "Your attention please! We are removing to this building's other entrance. Gather up your things. Follow your guides and stay with the group. It's a huge place and you *will* get lost. I repeat, we are removing to the other entrance immediately."

The room surged to life around them, babble rising, the sound of feet on flagstones; Karl lay limp. "Karl!" Elisa shouted into his face, and his eyes blinked open briefly. She grabbed him by his shirtfront and pulled him up, yelling at Tova, "Take the bundle! I'll catch up!" A woman's voice rose behind her, instructing someone not to know where they'd gone, no matter who asked: "Tell them to ask Gerlier, and if they ask again, say it again, understand?" Elisa slapped her brother's face and his eyes flew open. She hauled him to his feet and shouted, "The police are coming! Run! That way!"

Her words stirred a flurry of quick feet and shocked eyes, the last of the crowd speeding up toward the back door. She pulled her stumbling brother along and her sister too. A shrill high wail in Yiddish from behind them — "Put me down, put me down!" — and Tova turned, wrenching Elisa's arm.

A teenage girl with a thick black braid was struggling to keep Madame Weider's little boy in her arms as he kicked and cried for his mama. He pushed with both hands against her chest — his foot caught in her satchel strap — his head pivoted hard toward the stone floor, and she fell to her knees with a cry, barely catching him, her knuckles mashed between his skull and the stones. She roared in pain. Tova jerked her fingers out of Elisa's and in another moment was kneeling by the two, disentangling the strap.

"Tova!" Elisa snapped. "Come!"

Tova spared her a bloodshot, reproachful look. Elisa pointed at the deadly door. "You can help people when we're *out of sight of that.*"

"Here, I can —" The French girl reached for the boy then hissed through her teeth in pain, closed the bloodied hand and cradled it.

Elisa let go of Karl and knelt, her teeth clenched. Little David Weider wept silently as she gathered him up, but he didn't resist.

She stood with a grunt and shouted, "Keep up!"

The boy's head bounced as she ran. A stitch grew in her side as she pelted down the long hallway, nothing in her mind but the end of it, and the three pairs of feet clattering behind.

Also the shouting. "Hey! Hey, they're not coming this *minute*! Hey, wait for me, I know the way!"

She slowed a little. "*Who* — isn't coming — this minute?"

"The police," the girl panted. "You said. How'd you — find out?"

"Tell me what you know. Everything!"

"A priest — stole a telegram — from Vichy — new orders or something. It said — not to release you. They must've figured it out — but Madame Dreyfus says we have two hours — Hey, hey, it's all right!" The voice receded behind Elisa as she ran again. Karl's footsteps rang sharp as she dragged him along by the wrist. "Hey, I didn't mean it like that, *hey*! *Turn left*! And then right — through the colonnade and stay away from the windows, and listen —"

Elisa slacked her pace, finally; Tova was gasping.

"Listen, these people know what they're doing, I've —"

"We're leaving this building in an hour," Elisa told the French girl, "whether they've found us somewhere to go or not." She shifted David Weider to her other arm and dug in her pocket among the heavy sliding necklaces. Her father's watch read ten fifteen.

"And you'll go where, then?" The girl's black eyes flashed at her. "If you sleep on the street they'll arrest you as vagrants!"

"Karl, take the bundle." Elisa gestured forward with her chin and began to jog.

"Listen to me!" The French girl's voice cracked, and Elisa stopped short as a bloody hand grabbed her shoulder. "We have places to take you! Listen — listen, I'm from a town up on the plateau, it's a good place, everyone's on your side there and Paquerette says we can take at least ten people who don't have placements of their own — you can come. D'you want to come?"

Elisa stood staring at the guileless, blazing eyes of a girl who'd never slept on straw behind barbed wire and who thought there was a place where everyone was on her side. *I've seen how your country is on my side, girl.* What could she know, who was she — that Elisa Schulmann should lay the lives of what was left of her family on this stranger's word?

The other girl drew her hand back suddenly from Elisa, grimacing in pain. "Sorry," she murmured, gesturing. She had left a little stain of bright red blood soaking into the fabric of Elisa's blouse. Elisa stared at it, her mind empty and dark as the air of the barracks last night, the dark that would never leave her. The girl's eyes were wide on her when she looked up.

"I'll talk to Paquerette," the French girl whispered. "As soon as we get there. She can make it official for you. Will you believe me then?"

Elisa gave her a nod.

The girl nodded back. "Um. I'm Magali, by the way," she said.

Grandpa raised an earth-stained hand. "Please don't tell me."

"I'm not . . ." Julien dug his trowel hard into the soil and turned it up. "All I'm saying is, he's doing things he's not telling us about. That are dangerous."

Grandpa nodded, his weathered face sober. "It would surprise me more to hear that he wasn't, at this point." He lifted a cluster of little lettuces by the roots, worked one gently out with his broad fingers, and placed it in the hole. Julien filled in the earth around it. Far to the southeast a farm dog barked long and loud, the bark against untrusted strangers. They were searching the farms down there. "Péracs' place," Grandpa murmured, glancing up.

"I just wonder. If the other things he's doing . . . really mix well with that. The letter . . ."

Grandpa looked up, the seamed web of wrinkles coming out around his brown eyes. "He has asked himself that. He sat in my kitchen a long time speaking with me about it." His eyes rested on the far green hills. "The answer he came to was that God is faithful."

Julien dug, fingers in the earth, feeling its moist heaviness. There'd been rain last night. "Grandpa," he said finally, "did you believe in nonviolence before Pastor Alexandre came to Tanieux?"

Grandpa looked up from his lettuces. "Not exactly. Not in the way I do now."

"He brought it here. This thing about 'Don't worry about the consequences, do what's right and God will back you up.' Papa got it from him too."

"You could say that."

"Only . . ." Julien was digging his hole too deep, his fingers feverish. It shouldn't be this hard, it never was this hard to talk to Grandpa. In the distance the dog stopped barking. A hawk rode above in the blue sky. Grandpa listened. "Only if you make a mistake," he said. "About what God wants. Or if God wants us to, to be more *care-ful* . . ."

Grandpa sat back on his heels and gave Julien a long look, wiped his hands on his trousers, and stood. "Why don't you water these in," he said, "and I'll make tea."

When Julien came into the farmhouse, his sock-feet silent on the smooth flagstones of the kitchen, two mugs of mint tea were on the table. Grandpa was pulling a slim, battered book off the high shelf where the big leather-covered Bible lay, and the carving of praying hands. He laid the book gently on the table. The title read *Hymnes Huguenots.*

"We have a lot of traditions on this plateau," said Grandpa with a half smile. "Protestantism. Resisting the government. Arguing with one another. We did it constantly, in the time of the *camisards'* revolt. We'd grown so weary of persecution. Of torture and forced conversions and our pastors being sent to row galleys. We were angry. Prophets arose in the Cévennes, and even some here on the plateau, who said God wanted us to rise up and take back our freedom to worship by force of arms. Others disagreed." He flipped open the songbook, glanced at it, and looked at Julien. "One of your ancestors was a *camisard,* you know."

"You never said."

"No. I didn't. It's a short, painful story. I got it out of my grandfather just months before he died. Abdias Duvernet — he was an ancestor of my grandmother's, from Lamastre — had just come into his majority. He heard that the prophet Abraham Mazel had come north here to the Vivarais to gather men for a new uprising. Abdias wanted to go. His father forbade it. He told his father he should come too. They had heard of massacres, villages burned. The son's notion was that this had to be resisted. The father's was that they'd lose everything if they fought. Abdias called his father a coward. *Le père* Duvernet said, 'If I wasn't a coward you'd be dead.' "

"What did he mean?"

"Nobody knows. He never spoke of it again, no matter who asked. Abdias went off to join the uprising. He was killed within the week."

Julien exhaled sharply, blinking. "What's the moral?" he said harshly. " 'Don't go against your father?' "

"No," said Grandpa. "I don't know what the moral is. Except that things can be ter-

93

ribly painful between fathers and sons sometimes."

"Did you say he was one of our ancestors?"

"I misspoke. His little brother was. Pierre."

Grandpa's hand rested on the little book. Julien looked, but couldn't read the old-fashioned print upside down. "Grandpa," he said, "aren't you going to tell me what you think?"

Grandpa smiled sadly. "Not today, Julien. Maybe that is one of the morals of the story after all. There comes a time when you must let the young make their own decisions. They'll do so anyway, after all."

Julien was silent. "Why d'you bring that out?" he said after a moment.

"What you said reminded me." Grandpa slid the book gently over to Julien. Julien took it carefully, feeling its cover and its pages soft with age. He turned one, and read the title of the song, "Battle Psalm":

If God will only show Himself
In an instant we will see
The enemy scatter and flee.

"Can I borrow it?"

"Of course. You know some of them. Probably not all. But the answer isn't in there.

Just the struggles of our people, with each other as well as with their enemies." Grandpa reached across the table and turned the page back, to a hymn with a familiar title, "La Cévenole," the anthem of the Huguenots. "You're right," he said quietly, "that Pastor Alexandre brought the teaching of nonviolence to Tanieux. But there's an older tradition, one that goes back to the beginning, that may be the reason we listened to him. That's in there too. The martyrs have always been a witness that the sword does not have the last word." He raised his eyes to where beyond the window the far green mountains stood. "That's not a thing it's easy to be sure of," he said.

Julien closed the worn book as gently as Grandpa had given it. "Thank you," he said, though he was not sure what for.

The woman named Paquerette took them to another convent. A real one.

There were two other families with the Schulmanns, all children under ten. They were led through a maze of ancient clay-colored buildings, tiny alleys, streets so steep they broke into stairways; they followed, trying to believe police did not lie in wait behind every door. Then to the great hill that overlooked the city of Lyon, to climb endless steps to the church on its summit: Notre-Dame de Fourvière. Massive pillars and a great gold statue of Mary gleamed in the sun, watching Elisa with upraised hands. Elisa climbed, flushed and sweating, hearing her siblings' heavy steps, toward that golden face. She had no other choice. She sat with the others in the convent refectory, feeling eyes on her till her skin crawled, and ate the bread and thick soup, ordering her siblings with her eyes to do likewise. *Eat when you must.* They were shown to a bunkroom. It had a door they could lock.

She slept a short, hard sleep, black and hot and full of dim shapes pursuing her. She jerked awake and stared at the ceiling, checked on her siblings, checked every child in the room. She lay back down, trying not to think, trying to remember nothing, till she realized she needed a toilet, *now.*

At the door she hesitated. There were voices in the corridor outside.

"He doesn't have the addresses and he wouldn't give them if he did." That was Paquerette.

"They found his soft spot, mademoiselle. He trusts Marshal Pétain — an old friend —"

"Sister, the police are still searching

Tanieux!"

A sound behind her made her whirl. Tova stood in the middle of the floor, blinking.

"Elisa," she whispered, moving closer. "Elisa, I wanted to ask you — while Karl's asleep — do you think Mama and —"

"No. Please. Not yet, Tova. Not till we're safe."

"We're not safe?" whispered Tova.

Elisa took her sister's hand, her eyes on the opening door, and said, "No."

Mama handed Julien a jar of cooked beans and wrapped a chunk of cheese in newspaper. "Here. Pack this too. I know the telegram said today, but things can happen with the trains."

"Remember to ask Pastor Chaly to choose a family that lives far off the road," said Papa. "Tence has been searched at least once. Tell him it's for a couple of weeks at most, till the police leave. I'll find them a place in a children's home or at the school once I know their ages."

Julien glanced again at Papa's copy of the telegram. FRIENDS ARRIVING TODAY TENCE AND ST AGRÈVE. The first stop north of Tanieux and the first stop south of it on the railway line. Julien had chosen Tence; Magali was likeliest to come that

97

way. He raised his head at the sound of footsteps on the stairs.

It was Monsieur Barre, the plumber, his cloth cap in his hand, his eyes concerned. He stood on the landing, shaking his head, turning down Mama's offers of something to drink. "I just need to tell you." Papa's eyes widened slightly and flicked to his study door, but Monsieur Barre went on. "A rumor. More than a rumor. Monsieur Drac, he's been a policeman here for fifteen years and more, he says those city police've taken out a warrant for your arrest."

Julien felt rather than saw his mother behind him go still as a deer. The blood beat in his ears.

"You and *monsieur le pasteur*. Rumor is" — Monsieur Barre cleared his throat — "rumor is they plan to do it tomorrow. In church, or after."

"Thank you." Papa's voice was firm, dignified, barely louder than a whisper.

"Of course. Thought you should know. Those . . ." He trailed off, his lips twisting, then gave them all a nod. "We're with you," he said, and was gone down the stairs.

For a moment nobody spoke. Then Mama turned toward Papa, her eyes not on him but on the bedroom door, wiping her hands on her apron. "You could go into the Ardèche. Rochepaule maybe. On your bicycle you could be there by nightfall. No one would tell them."

Papa made no move to follow her. "Maria," he said hoarsely, "I need to stay."

Mama stopped dead. "Martin," she whispered.

"I *must*, Maria. I cannot abandon Tanieux. And I can't hide in half measures. They know where to find me, unless I leave Tanieux for good."

Mama was pale. "They could *deport* you, Martin."

Papa made a helpless upward gesture of his hand, broken off. "We're at a critical moment. The pressure they've begun to apply — if the people see us run at the first threat —"

"Third threat."

Julien's parents both turned to him. He stood aghast, his hand rising to his lips as if to search for why and how he'd spoken. He looked into his father's eyes. Took a breath.

But Mama spoke first. "You can stay out of this, young man." Color was returning to her cheeks, her head high, her black eyes flashing. "This is between me and your father." She pinned Papa with her gaze. "Let the people get their courage from Pastor Alexandre," she said. "*You* have work to do.

Go. Come back. It gives you a chance."

Julien licked dry lips, his eyes going to his father, to his mother, his heart speeding up.

"I have to do what God calls me to do," said Papa softly.

"You should go," Julien whispered.

They were both staring at him.

"You should go." He could barely force his voice a little louder. "And you should be more careful. You should stop — witnessing to these men. It's too dangerous. They're too dangerous." His heart was hammering. "I know what you're doing."

Papa's eyes were very wide. "How?" he said quietly.

"I looked at one of your papers. When you were burning it. I apologize."

"You're forgiven," murmured Papa. His hand gripped the back of a chair. He spoke slowly, looking into Mama's eyes. "Standing witness is not useless. It is vital. Is it worth, for a *chance,* showing Tanieux and Vichy that I do not believe God is my help?"

Mama leaned forward, not taking her gaze from him. "Martin, I am begging you."

Papa drew a deep, shaky breath, and said, "My love, I hope you can forgive me this."

There was a long, sticky silence. It was broken by Julien's mother whispering, "Julien, I think you have somewhere to go."

Go. He had to go. To Tence, for Magali, for the children, to Tence with a pack full of food in case something went wrong, wrong with the trains, in case he had to stay an extra day or — or something. Papa's face, his eyes on Mama, the lines in it deeper than they ever were, you could see where the wrinkles would be when he was seventy. If he was ever seventy. Julien picked up his pack from the scarred pine table, slid it onto his back. It was heavy. He went to his mother and looked at her till she turned to him. He kissed her goodbye, held her, her shoulder blades as tense as a staring cat's. Then his father, the wound still in his eyes, his chest thinner in Julien's arms than he remembered. But Papa held him, for one moment, so tight he couldn't breathe.

His parents' faces were a blur as he turned away.

For the first kilometer of his walk north, he barely remembered where he was going.

CHAPTER 6
ANOTHER PLACE

There was a freight train derailed between Saint-Étienne and Firminy. Karl and Tova accepted the news, and Magali's assumption that they would sleep in the train station, with exhausted meekness; Elisa did not.

"Paquerette and I slept in train stations a dozen times last year and never had any trouble with the police," Magali insisted. Elisa caught the girl's flinch and frowned. Magali lifted her chin and said with rock-solid confidence, "We *never* had any trouble with the police about where we were sleeping."

In the end there was no choice. After sending Magali out to buy food for what turned out to be a miserable attempt at a kosher picnic — she hadn't imagined raw potatoes were *that* stomach-turning — Elisa bedded her family down against a wall among a handful of other huddled families, a little flotsam of bodies and string-tied bundles left on the floor as the station emptied for the night.

She didn't sleep. She didn't even lie down.

She made up her bedding under Magali's instruction to avoid the French girl's questions, then watched the others fall asleep: Magali curled on her side, one arm cushioned with a sweater beneath her head; Karl tossing and turning till exhaustion took him; Tova on her stomach, a thin tear track still glistening on the bridge of her nose. Elisa knelt and stroked her back gently till her breathing grew deep. Then she propped herself against the wall. The hours stretched. She prayed psalms, her lips moving without sound. She put her hand in the bag and felt her prayer book and the leather case, tucked away at the bottom; she did not bring them out. She jumped, her heart knocking wildly, at the sound of a throat clearing beside her.

It was Magali, bleary-eyed, up on one elbow and staring at her. "Are you on *watch*?"

Elisa nodded slightly.

"You don't have to do that. They don't have any way of knowing we're here. I heard you last night getting up all those times, and I *know* none of you slept the night before. You must be dying."

Elisa looked at her. Inside the bag her fingertips still brushed the leather case; her fingers slid along it and wrapped themselves tight around it. She said nothing.

"I'm sorry. I'm sorry. Listen — really — you've got to sleep. Lie down. I'll keep watch."

"I don't know if I could sleep," whispered Elisa.

"After all that?"

Elisa said nothing.

Magali's shoulders slumped. "I'm sorry." She looked up at Elisa, her eyes big in the dark. "I'm so sorry about your parents," she whispered.

Shut up.

"I thought I knew, I thought I knew what this stuff was like — I used to do this, you know. Paquerette got kids out of internment camps — legally — and I used to help her bring 'em to Tanieux. They'd had a rough time, you know? But *this* — I never saw anything like this before, like what's happened to you — in just a couple of days! I . . . I'm sorry."

Elisa closed her eyes. There was something that had been floating in her mind, slipping here and there among the memories, elusive. Something Magali had said. She concentrated on forming the words. "What trouble did you have," she said slowly, "with the police?"

Magali froze. For three long heartbeats she stared at Elisa, her eyes like a cornered animal's. Then she whispered, "I got Paquerette arrested in the Valence train station."

Time spun out slowly, so slowly, as the sentence hung in the night air. Elisa's lips shaped the next word: "How?"

"Stupid heroics." Magali's voice was low and hard. "They were arresting somebody — a Jewish boy, I thought — and I pulled the fire alarm because I thought it'd give him time to get away. It didn't. They went after me. I had — had a child with me — so Paquerette took the fall. Claimed it was her. They arrested her right there."

"A child?"

"A baby," said Magali in a tiny, dry whisper. "From a camp."

"You were bringing kids from the camps? Like you said?"

"Yeah. A whole group. I had to get them home without her."

"And you did?"

"Yeah." Magali slumped against the wall. "Oh, why'd you make me tell you this? In the middle of traveling together? I shouldn't have told you. Why should *you* believe I've changed?" Her voice was anguished.

Elisa looked ahead into the darkness of the station hallway, seeing them like shadows in her mind: blue uniforms, closing in. "You know," she said slowly, "when you told me in that hallway that they weren't coming for us right away and it was all right, I thought you didn't know anything. About, about . . ." She shook her head. About walls topped with razor wire. About fear. About hard-eyed men putting their hands on their guns and telling you a second time that they are authorized to shoot your children. At lunchtime, with Mama in the kitchen doorway with her apron still on . . . "I guess you know some things," she whispered finally. "How did she get free again?"

"Someone helped her escape."

"And she's still doing this."

Magali nodded. "She had to go home to recover awhile. From . . . from the interrogation."

There was a long silence.

"You really don't think you can sleep?" said Magali.

"Maybe." Elisa looked down at her unused bedding, then up at the other girl. Magali propped herself against the wall.

"Maybe," said Elisa fuzzily, and laid her weary body down.

■ ■ ■ ■

Julien scanned the windows as the train pulled in. Her steam rose slowly in the heavy air, in the light and shadow of the shifting clouds overhead. As the ring and scrape of her brake sounded, he spotted Magali inside, and paused for a split second, his mind kilometers away in a dark church where perhaps lines of light still fell from the tall windows, fell on his father's and mother's heads sitting side by side. *She doesn't know.*

The doors were opening. Two children, flushed and weary, eyes alive with fear; a girl Magali's age, her skin badly pock-marked, her hair pulled back tightly from her face with strands escaping everywhere. In her bloodshot eyes was something that was not quite fear, something that made him look again even as Magali came down behind her saying, "It's my brother, they sent my brother." The girl stood poised protectively behind the other two, a hand on each of their shoulders, as Magali stepped up. "Julien, this is —"

"Élise," said the girl. Then with a swift glance at the other two, "And Charles and Brigitte. Where should we go?"

"This way," said Julien. "Can I carry something for you?"

The girl gripped her string-tied bundle more closely, shook her head with a tiny motion, and said to her siblings, "Let's go."

Julien led them at a good pace out of the station and down out of Tence to the Tanieux road before he paused to tell them the name of their host family and the distance to their farm. He had to speak loud; the east wind was rising. He led them jogging, watching the road, watching the line of clouds in the east, no sound but their running feet on the pavement behind him. Open country on their left, on their right pine forest and rocks. He could see the turnoff for the farm, a grassy unpaved track down to the left.

He froze.

A dog barking in the distance. A long, high buzz, getting higher.

"Into the woods!" He heard them stop in their tracks. "Into the woods! *Now!*"

Élise pushed her brother forward, and then they were all ahead of Julien, racing over the springy brown needles, blessedly silent except for the soft crash of pine boughs as they forced their way through the trees, as the buzz from the south turned to a tinny roar — a boulder loomed ahead, a great hunch of bedrock coming up through the earth, and Julien blessed them all as they went straight for it, behind it. "Down!" he hissed, and flung himself on his belly, Scout bag bouncing on his back. All down. Julien lay with his cheek against needles, the strong earth bearing him up, as the first motorcycle roared past. Then the second, close on its heels, growing and then receding, farther and smaller till it died away into the silence of the hills.

Silence. The smell of pine. Pale faces lifted from the forest floor. Julien drew a long breath. "I am so sorry," he whispered. "They don't usually come this far."

Magali sat up, shaking her head. Élise turned, her hand on her sister's back, and looked at Julien.

"If you don't want to go back on the road," said Julien, "there's another place."

"Where?" said Élise.

It was decided within seconds. Élise's eyes said a black no to the road, the same no to seeking shelter among the little sheep farms that dotted the half-wild land just north of the Tanières. No; not when there was another place. At the idea of a cave, however richly stocked with firewood and water, her sister's eyes grew round and dark, but in Élise's a little flame lit when he said, "*No *one* could find you there." She nodded.

"We'll have to go fast," said Julien. "It's almost a kilometer farther. We need to beat that storm."

Élise was on her feet before he finished.

It was less familiar country than the Tanières, but he led them through it as fast as he could find a decent path, sighting by the great hill the cave was in, trying to trace with his eyes best way to it as he stood calf-deep in the river waiting for them to get their leather shoes off and follow. They passed no farmhouses, only a ruined shepherd's shelter as they half ran single file on a narrow dirt path that curved between rocks and twisted pines and scrubby, green-fingered *genêt* bushes, sheltering them from the road. Behind him they were breathing hard. The clouds were dark and close, a gray curtain of rain beneath them. He did not slacken the pace.

The wind rose in their faces as they reached the Tanières; the storm was sweeping toward them, fast. "This hill!" Julien called above the rushing sound in the treetops. "Up this gully here, follow me!" The wind blew his hair wildly around his head as he came up into an unsheltered spot; he heard a cry and turned back, gave his hand to Brigitte where she had fallen.

110

"We're close," he shouted. "Just up there round the other side of the hill!" She nodded mutely, and began to climb again.

And the storm swept in.

The rain hit them in blinding sheets, the hiss and roar of it so loud they could hear nothing else. Julien stood stock still under the cold shock of it, then began inching back down the hill, hand held out. "Take my hand!" he screamed to Brigitte and she took it, soaked and slippery, grabbed it in a death grip that barely held. "All hold hands!" he screamed again, but Élise seemed to have the others already, and then he was leading them upward in a half-blind line, someone stumbling and slipping in the sudden mud every ten seconds, wrenching the others' arms and scrambling back up. Together they clawed their horribly slow way up the slope under the onslaught of water. Thunder rumbled. Julien crested the slope, saw the horizon wiped out in a gray seething of rain, saw the rock on his left shining wet and dark. "Here!" he shouted. The rain was slacking off just the tiniest bit; he could hear himself now. "Climb up here! It's a ledge! Be careful, it'll be slick! Hug the hillside!"

"You first!" Élise shouted to her brother. Julien gave him a leg up and kept a hand under him as Charles scrambled onto the dark gleaming rock. "Hug the hillside!" and "Away from the edge!" Élise and Julien shouted at the same moment, and the boy flinched down and to his left toward safety.

"Now wait there!" Julien called to him, and bent to help the sister, her sodden skirt flapping around her ankles as he lifted her, Élise bearing her up on the other side. Next Élise, who flung her bundle up onto the ledge and then put her muddy foot in his interlaced hands; he boosted her hard, his back and legs and shoulders braced and straining beneath her weight. Her narrow skirt wouldn't let her get a knee up, and she struggled, pulling herself up by her arms; he saw her ankles scrape on the rock as she got them up under her. Magali hoisted herself up one-handed, cradling the other; it had scabs on the knuckles. The rain and wind slacked, bright patches of white sky tumbling amid the chaos of gray, then they picked up again as Julien clawed his fingers into the handholds and scrambled up.

The wind was from the west, thank God, driving them inward toward the hillside; they shielded their faces as it lashed them, and Julien screamed, "Ten steps! Ten steps this way! Be careful!" *So close.* They crept along the ledge, the youngest ones in front,

Élise dragging her bundle by one hand, the rain running down their faces and through their soaking hair. He saw them reach the spot and see it. "Go on in! Go!" The boy disappeared, then the girl, then Élise, and he breathed a great breath. Then Magali was gone too into the hillside, and Julien crouched alone under the battering rain, looking out at the wild sky and the drowned horizon. Looking east, to where Tanieux hid from him behind the sheltering mass of the hill.

Then he bent his head, and tumbled on his knees into the warm, dark, crowded safety of his cave.

Elisa knelt on stone in the belly of the earth, in the first cave she had entered in her life, twisting her long, wet hair back up into its knot and pinning it tight. Above and behind her the deep dark; before her a small red-gold fire and a kneeling boy blowing into it, making it flare bright against the curtain of rain beyond.

She could feel the darkness like a weight, pressing on her head and shoulders: a thousand tons of rock and earth between her and the road. *No one could find you.*

"It's all soaked, Elisa, there's nothing to change into."

"Go sit by the fire," she told her sister. "It's the only way to warm up."

The boy built it higher as Tova made her awkward way toward him.

"We can't use it all," he said, gesturing to the woodpile against the dark cave wall. "If this keeps up all day —"

"We need coals," said Magali. "I've got to cook, I've got raw potatoes —"

"I've got cooked ones. And cheese and beans." The boy stared into the fire.

"They can't eat anything already cooked, they're very religious —"

"Tova," murmured Elisa. "Do we have the cookie tin?"

Within a couple of minutes she had potatoes laid on the fire to boil, the tin propped on three stones, and Karl and Tova were eating apples from the French boy's pack. She shook her head at the offer of half of Tova's and sank back on her heels, watching the rain hiss down outside the cave mouth, watching the flames dance bright and the smoke rise. There was mud all down the front of Tova's dress, gleaming wet on her torso, drying on her folded knees; there was mud in her wild hair. Karl watched the potatoes, eating his apple down to the seeds. Firelight was in his eyes. Elisa let her breath out all of a sudden; suddenly Magali laughed.

"You thought *Benjamin* could get up here?" she said to her brother.

He didn't smile. "It's easier round the south side. We didn't have time."

"Hey, you did great, Julien. C'mon. We *made* it."

Julien stared at the fire.

Magali's grin fell away. "Is Benjamin all right?" she said in a rushed half whisper.

"Benjamin's fine," Julien said to his hands. They were clenched.

"Who?" breathed Magali.

"Monsieur Barre says . . ." Julien licked his lips, started again. "Said they wanted to arrest Pastor Alexandre and — Papa." He looked up at his sister and his face was naked suddenly, terribly exposed. He said the last words in a whisper: "This morning in church."

The fire snapped and shot up sparks. In the dim blue beyond the cave mouth the rain sheeted down. Magali's hand was over her mouth. Her brother watched her. His eyes, which had been hard and focused as a soldier's as he'd run and watched over them and shouted orders, were dark and empty now. Dark as that other place, that deep, unwalled well in Elisa's mind, where kind people stood with clipboards in the gleam of flashlights on straw.

Magali was up, scrambling to get her feet under her in the cramped space. "We have to go!"

"It's noon, Magali."

"Was he going? Was he going to go to church?"

Julien nodded.

"Of course he was," said Magali. "He's — he's so *stupid!*" The last word was a scream, high and ragged from a closing throat, almost unbearable in that small space. Karl cringed.

"He's not stupid," Julien whispered. He stirred the fire with his stick. It fell apart. He scraped it together again, not looking up.

"When they're after you," said Magali fiercely, "you *run.*"

"What d'you think would happen in Tanieux if they ran?"

"Nothing worse than what'll happen now they're arrested." Magali's voice was thick.

Julien's head came up sharply at the word *arrested.* "We don't know that for sure."

"Don't know what?"

"That they went through with it."

Magali hit the cave wall with her good hand. "You think these people hold back? You think these people up and decide to

116

have some compassion? Do you have *any idea* what just happened in Lyon?"

Julien's eyes fell on Elisa. They were large and dark, the fire reflected in them. "My father told me," he whispered. "I'm so sorry."

Elisa felt Tova beside her, shivering. She turned. Tova's eyes were welling with tears.

"Are we?" Tova's voice was a thin thread. "Are we safe — enough?"

Elisa pressed her palms hard against the rough cave floor, and nodded.

"Elisa." Tova's tears streamed down. "Do you — honestly — do you think they'll come back?"

Elisa looked at her muddy knees, and pressed her hands harder into the rock. She shut her eyes, trying to open her closed throat. She heard the crackling of the fire. She shook her head.

She heard her sister's breath, tiny and trembling in the silence. She heard Karl's, sharp.

"What are you talking about?" her brother said. "You can't know that!"

She did not look at him. She reached behind her, to the bundle, felt for the smooth warm leather, drew out the case. Karl stared at it, his eyes red around the edges. "He gave me this. For you."

Tova's breath caught. Karl's eyes were getting redder. "He didn't. He *wouldn't!* He — he didn't *give* them to you!" He scrambled up and made for the cave mouth.

Julien blocked his way instantly, his face wiped clean of all emotion. "You're not going out there. Sorry. You could get hurt."

Karl whirled as if seeking an exit from a trap. "Let me *out.*" His voice cracked, and he shouted, "Let me *out!*" He made a move toward Julien.

Julien filled the cave mouth, arms out, poised. "Stay where you are."

"Do as he says," Elisa snapped.

Karl turned on her. "I hate you!"

Elisa looked her brother in the eye, and said nothing. The darkness in his pupils went down and down. *I'm sorry.* She watched him break, his face giving one twitch before he hung his head in shame.

"I'm sorry," said Elisa stiffly to Julien. He shook his head.

"But you don't know," said Karl in a low voice. "Not for sure. You *don't.*"

God help me. "I don't know." Her voice was a stranger's. Magali was looking at her; Elisa met her eyes and looked away. Julien blew into the fire. Nobody spoke.

Tova wiped her eyes on her sleeve. Flecks of dried mud fell to the rock or stuck to the

118

curve of her cheek. "Why do they want to arrest your father?" she asked Julien softly.

"He's the assistant pastor." Julien looked at his hands. "He's . . . an organizer. The police came two weeks ago and asked him and the lead pastor for a list of the Jews in town. They said no."

"That's why they're still here," said Magali, jerking her chin toward the back of the cave: eastward, to the road where the roar of motorcycles had passed them by. "They're still hoping one of these days they'll find somebody."

The fire hissed and flared as boiling water splashed over the edges of the cookie tin. The wind moaned outside. All three Schulmanns were staring.

"They caught no one?" Elisa breathed. "That's why — when Paquerette said the police — they've been doing the same thing here as in Lyon and they've arrested *no one*?"

Magali was nodding.

"I guess so," murmured Julien.

There was a strange, cold sensation in Elisa's scalp as her wet hair tried to stand on end. The darkness behind her in the cave seemed suddenly huge. "How?" she whispered. "How is that possible?"

"We had warning. We stood watch . . ."

"And what? And people just hid their neighbors? *Everyone?*"

"Yeah," said Magali. "They're mostly boarders or houseguests anyway."

Tova's hand found Elisa's. Even Karl was staring. "God brought us here," Elisa breathed in German. "Blessed is His name." She cleared her thick throat and said again in French, "God brought us here. Your father is a righteous man."

Magali's face, looking to the cave mouth, slowly hardened in the firelight. "This isn't a job for heroes," she whispered. "Heroes get themselves killed. Keeping people safe is the *only* important thing."

"That's why he couldn't run, Magali," said Julien.

"Because he's so important?"

Elisa thought she saw anger flash in Julien's eyes, but he bent to tend the fire instead of responding. Magali's shoulders slumped. Outside the rain slacked suddenly. The strange white glare of daylight brightened beyond the cave mouth, dimming the fire to a small red glow. They all looked out at it, blinking as if waking from a dream. Elisa tested one of the potatoes with a careful fingernail where it rose above the boiling water. Almost done.

"We should still go home," said Magali

quietly. "Mama will be alone."

Julien's eyes flicked up in protest, then went to the cave mouth, the fire, the bag of food, and the two water bottles stashed against the wall. He nodded. "I have to show one of you the way to the stream. That water'll be gone before tomorrow. And do you know how to tend a fire? Or make one?"

"I do," said Elisa. "In a stove."

"We'll bring you food. Julien will. Raw things, eggs — you can eat eggs, right? Grandpa has chickens — we'll find ways —"

"Can you bring a knife? I can boil it to kosher it. We don't have anything at all . . ." She was searching through her bag for the oldest piece of clothing, something to grasp the hot tin with. "These will be ready soon. Maybe you should eat what you brought. You'll need your strength."

Magali nodded, her eyes on the entrance. She shook her head, just barely, her face for a moment as naked as her brother's had been. He shifted over toward her till their shoulders touched. They crouched there in the cave mouth, dark and still against the white light of day.

"We'll pray," said Elisa. "We'll pray for your parents every day."

"And for ours," said Karl fiercely.

Elisa closed her eyes, and nodded.

■ ■ ■ ■

Julien and Magali walked down the road in silence, eating cheese. They did not watch the horizon anymore, nor listen for any distant sounds. They went steadily. The truth would come when it came. They had to walk toward it. But they couldn't — not even for Mama's sake — run.

The wind rose as they walked, and tore the last of the ragged rain clouds to pieces; the sun broke white and blinding through the clouds, and they blinked and lowered their heads against its glare. They entered Tanieux by the bridge, over brown swirling water, and took the street upward toward home. The *place* was empty, the black automobile and the mud-flecked motorcycles parked and silent. Magali's pace quickened as she passed them, her face set like stone.

They climbed the steep street to the Rue Emmanuel. It was getting harder to breathe. *Please* beat like a pulse in Julien's chest. *Look what he's done for You.* He pushed open the heavy door and they walked down the dark downstairs hallway together, hearing the brief, sharp echo of their footsteps. Magali took Julien's hand as they started up the stone stairs.

They climbed the last steps to the landing. Julien saw in his mind the empty apartment behind that door, how it would echo as they walked in. Magali put a leaden hand on the doorknob and turned it.

The door opened. There at the table, with mugs of tea in their hands, sat their mother and father.

CHAPTER 7
OUT

"You're here," said Julien. His voice stuck thickly in his throat. His father rose and let him come to him, took him by the shoulders, and kissed him formally twice on each cheek. Julien could feel Papa's hands shaking as he held him. Magali flew into Papa's arms, and he gave her four kisses as well.

"My brave children," he said.

Mama stood suddenly, the first motion she made. Julien caught one glimpse of her blank face, like a field of snow, before she turned away to put the kettle on for tea.

Elisa Schulmann turned sixteen in a cave high on the Vivarais plateau, and no one noticed except herself. She did not tell Karl or Tova. She was too tired.

Between waking in a sweat of terror in the night, sure she heard someone coming for them, and waking to Karl screaming and screaming in his deepest sleep; between holding Tova while she cried, feeling her own face grow taut and dry with brittle grief, and shaming Karl painfully into a solemn oath never to leave her sight — not even when Tova was crying — she had nothing. She had nothing left to give.

It seemed she could feel every cell in her body trembling. She barely slept. When she did, she dreamed. She saw her parents, their backs to her, following Julie Altman across a barren plain, never turning as she called and called. She never saw their faces. She woke and crawled out onto the ledge, the stars spread above her like a river of diamonds, indestructible and holy. She lay on her side, pain in her throat, pain in her chest and belly, and could not weep.

She went in, turned the wet sides of the drying sweaters toward the banked fire, and crawled in between Tova and Karl again.

The motions of survival guided her into each new day — that and the prayer book. Washing clothing in the tiny stream, gathering firewood, praying the three daily services on the ledge. Saying the prayer of supplication with Karl and Tova: *Let us fall into the hand of God.* Seeing faces in her mind, face after lost face, till the darkness behind them grew alive like a beast; then walking into it, sweeping the cave, and laying a fire. She cooked every night after sundown in the cookie tin, a thick soup and a precious egg or two to last all the next day. She had forbidden fires in the daytime. She had forbidden drying clothes outside. They lived in the scent of smoke and wet wool.

She saw herself in her mind sometimes, a cave woman crouched by her cook-fire in the smoky red light. She saw other things: their apartment in Lyon, emptied, dresser drawers dumped out on the stripped beds, kitchen cabinets gaping like mouths. Herself in that same kitchen beside Mama, slicing potatoes for Shabbos dinner; the light from the south window, the scent of frying onions, the quiet joy ringing through the house.

She pressed her forehead against the cave wall until it hurt, but still she could not weep.

Julien came with potatoes, cabbages, carrots, news: The police were still searching. No one had been arrested. His father was spared. Julien came with new papers for them, expertly made; the names beside their pictures were Élise, Brigitte, and Charles Fournier. French citizens. Julien promised them school, promised them a host family who would let them cook their own food. She ran her fingers lightly over her new name and her old picture, listening to him explain that the school had no building of its own, that her class would meet in the Bellevue Hotel, that school had started today, and she tried to imagine herself openly walking down the street in this country ever again.

She counted the days to know when Rosh Hashanah fell, and led Karl and Tova in all the prayers she could remember from the machzor. "May you be signed and sealed for a good year," she murmured through dry lips, and Karl said, "I'm sorry I said I hated you," and began to weep. She took his hand.

They prayed together every morning; every morning Karl prayed harder. Elisa turned when they were done and went into the dark to sweep out the cave and the fire ring on her knees. Seeing Mama scrubbing dust from between the living-room floorboards, her face intent and peaceful in spite of the world outside, Mama doing what she could do.

It was a housekeeping Elisa hadn't imagined, in that smelly alley in Lyon where she'd thought herself poor, but it was what she could do. The work her mother had taught her, reduced to its bare and smoky essentials: Fire. Food. Water.

Life.

In the firelight each evening she watched Tova and Karl breathe. Their chests rose and fell, their hearts beat with a rhythm she could feel in her belly. Her own heart a small, quick pulsing, a thin living flame between them and the dark. Depths moved under her, the roots of the mountain, the depths out of which one cried to God.

She watched, and counted again the days since the world shattered, trying to be sure of the date for Yom Kippur; it was then that she realized she was sixteen years old today. She stirred tomorrow's potatoes in the fire, and remembered her ninth birthday, when Papa had given her a garnet necklace. And her tenth, when they had ridden from Mannheim to Lyon in a third-class carriage, ten hours, lain down on bare mattresses in an empty apartment, and thanked God they were out. They had thought they were out.

Her throat closed, thinking of all they had given, all they had done. *For this.* This smoky cave, these beating hearts. Karl stirred and looked up at her; she saw the firelight in his eyes. She saw herself in a kitchen somewhere, years from now, a young girl in a blue dress standing beside her, saw herself slicing potatoes in the afternoon light. Saying *Your grandmother.*

Your grandfather. Saying *Never forget.*

She laid one last branch over the coals to see it catch and flare, to see the shadows retreat. The cave grew bright, the cave mouth darker. She sat watching the flames a long time before she slept.

Julien had no lack of witnesses to tell him what Sunday had been like in Tanieux — especially once school started — but his family did not speak of it. He could imagine Mama, standing by Papa as person after person clasped his hand after the service and held back tears — Mama trying to stand up straight and play the part she had been given, trying. Looking back over her shoulder through the wide church doors for the police. *I hope you can forgive me this, Maria.* Julien hadn't heard her sing since that day. Not once. The silence in the house made his shoulders hurt.

The Scouts clapped him on the back and said how glad they were. His friends at school — when he could find them in the sea of new faces crowding the hotel patio where they spent break — told him just how sure they'd been that his father would be arrested, or that he wouldn't. They sat on the patio tables and told each other that if the Germans took Stalingrad, they'd have

Russia. That they wouldn't take Stalingrad — that they would. They burned and shouted about the new law that young Frenchmen could be drafted to work in German factories, and wondered with cold in their bellies whether it would touch them someday. Magali confessed to Julien that she'd been asked to accompany Marek on a border crossing, and did he think Mama would say yes? "They won't put him on any aid group's hands without me, even the Cimade."

Julien suggested she wait a little.

Papa came home from the office late and weary, and disappeared into his study. Julien stayed up reading homework by lamplight till the moon was high in the sky. Papa came out, rubbing his lined face, and smiled at Julien. "You want some tea? Chamomile?"

Julien hated chamomile. "Sure."

Papa came back with Mama's steaming teapot, almost wetting Julien's textbook when he set it down. "Sorry. Aah. That's hot. Can't sleep without it when I work this late. What're you reading about?"

"Great War. The Christmas truce."

"Ah." Papa's eyes softened as he sank into his chair. "Do they tell how it started?"

"No. It's just a paragraph."

130

Papa made a rueful noise in his throat. "A blip. An aberration. They certainly made sure it never happened again." Julien looked up and stared when he heard the thickness in his voice. "They heard each other singing 'Silent Night.' " Papa blinked hard and reached for the teapot. "I'm working too much. It's unstringing me." He poured, the steam rising up in a white cloud.

"Papa," said Julien, then stopped as Papa looked up, his mind going blank. "I . . . I'm glad you're all right."

Papa filled Julien's cup. "It was kind of you," he said finally. "To want me to hide."

Julien shook his head. He touched the cup but it was burning hot. He remembered his father's eyes. Not the eyes of a man who had seen kindness. "Asking you to run away?"

"To be safe. You didn't see it as my calling, to be in church that morning. It's only natural you would advise the sensible thing."

Julien looked down at his textbook: the trenches, no-man's-land, a corpse tangled in barbed wire.

"I've been meaning to ask you, Julien. Marcel" — Julien glanced up sharply — "is leaving town soon, perhaps for a good while. Your troop will need a new leader. Would you be willing to take it on?"

Julien put both hands around his cup and held them there till they stung. "They want me?"

"Monsieur Astier thinks you're the best choice. With Sylvain as your second — you'd pass the sentry-duty roster on to him. Are you interested?"

"Well, yeah — yeah, of course."

"You don't have to. It's become a much heavier responsibility, I would never assume —"

"I want to," said Julien. Papa nodded, watching the steam rise in white ribbons from his cup, then lifting his bright brown eyes to Julien. "I want to," said Julien again, and Papa smiled.

The police left at midmorning on their fifth day of school. Their teachers let them out of class. They stood shoulder to shoulder on the hotel patio between the little green-painted tables; the people of Tanieux all along the street stood quiet on their stoops, watching the enemy go.

Julien got the message from Marcel within minutes: *Wait till tomorrow to give the all clear.*

Mama made an omelet that night to celebrate. But she did not sing. After dark, upstairs in their bedrooms, Julien and

Magali heard her muffled sobs coming up from below.

The next day Julien went down to the Rostins' farm to fetch Benjamin home. Benjamin was alone, and looked moodily at Julien, his hands in his pockets. "Are you assigned to this road now, or are you here to get me?"

"I already did my road. And then that family in the cave — you should've seen it, she'd made a broom out of *genêts* and she was cooking in a —"

"I'll get my things."

They walked up the road between pinewoods in silence, shafts of sunlight shattering down through the boughs. Benjamin kept his eyes on the road, even when he finally spoke.

"You might as well know. I'll be trying to cross the border in a month."

Julien opened his mouth. It closed again when he met his friend's eyes.

"My visa's on its way."

"You'll make it," said Julien softly. "America . . ."

"I told her no, get Papa out first. She told me it's already on its way. I know she's spent all her money on it."

"You wanted — ?"

"He's been in prison almost two years, Julien. They both keep telling me how safe Spain is, and meanwhile no one can offer any credible proof that place is any better than the internment camps here, *you* know, you've heard Magali's stories. He won't give me a direct answer, what he eats, how often people get sick, he just tells me to stop worrying that maybe a fascist dictatorship might not have nice clean prisons where no one ever dies of typhoid. So there we are." He thrust his hands hard into his pockets. "I'm going to America. Or somewhere anyway."

Julien grabbed his friend's arm. "*America. I'm telling you.*" Benjamin's eyes avoided his. *Pull yourself together. Don't you come from people who took a footpath through the sea?* "You think about America. It's like jumping over a stream. You look at the other bank — if you look at the water you'll f—"

Benjamin jerked his arm away. "Shut up," he whispered. "Shut up, would you?"

"But —"

"You want to tell me again what'll happen if I *get too scared*?"

Julien shut his mouth.

"Yeah," said Benjamin softly.

Then he turned and walked on between the patches of splintered sunlight, and Julien followed him.

CHAPTER 8
THROUGH THE SEA

Elisa's brother hadn't lived two weeks at the Thibauds' farmhouse before he announced he wanted to move into a dorm.

"Shh," she hissed at him, drawing the doors of the ancient cupboard-bed they shared more tightly closed. The other shuttered bed, shared by the whole Thibaud family now that the Schulmanns had moved in, was only meters away.

"But Elisa, they'd be *happy* if we moved out! Have you seen how she looks when you —"

"Shh!" Of course she'd seen Madame Thibaud wincing as Elisa served her siblings their separate and — she'd admit it — inferior food. She *cooked* beside the woman. Those anxious, bird-bright eyes, those good intentions. The light of her goodwill always shining, like a flashlight in your face.

"And *I* could eat at the dorm — I won't be a bar mitzvah till after the school year's done, and Pastor Losier *said* we could live there, and Jean-Baptiste says they play soccer every night before supper and — I just . . ."

Elisa's heart tightened, but she didn't speak. In the dark she could hear his breath come quick.

"It's just — it's so hard."

Hard? She'd seen the gentle way young Roland Thibaud and his father went about teaching Karl to hoe, and pitch hay. And shovel manure. It wasn't what any of them were used to, this ancient stone farmhouse, its heavy slate roof sheltering people and livestock separated only by a single interior wall. You could hear the mice skittering overhead in the hayloft, hear the cows shift in their stalls. *Do you understand how much worse we could have it?* She had heard stories already at school.

Tova stirred. "Elisa? What Pastor Losier said, about Switzerland . . . ?"

Elisa shook her head. "Too dangerous." They'd have to go separately, the pastor had said; the Cimade wouldn't take a sixteen-year-old. The vision was always in her mind: arriving safe on the other side and waiting for her siblings — then hearing the terrible news. In the night, every night, she heard her father whisper, *I chose France.* "It's a good place here. We can make it work." She felt Karl's gesture in the dark; she started up on one elbow and said through her teeth, "I am not risking your life on a border because you don't like farmwork and you feel awkward at the table. That's final."

She heard Tova's indrawn breath, the quiver in it. She lay feeling her heart beat, hearing tiny feet scratch on the pine boards overhead.

"I'll see what I can do about the dorm," she whispered.

It meant talking to men. But she could do it.

She had only just learned the trick she needed for it from her new school friend Nadine. Nadine, whose real name she still didn't know, who had led her and her family on Yom Kippur to a house where a tiny new congregation met in secret, who had fasted and prayed with them all that holy day. Nadine had taught her how to give the *bise,* the greeting kiss on both cheeks, to a boy or a man without actually touching him. School breaks had been so awkward till she'd learned that. She was sure she'd offended Julien no matter what Magali said — he had to have seen her avoiding him. And in spite of it all she had made friends somehow — *her,* Elisa Schulmann, making friends at school — and some of them not even Jews . . .

It had made her dizzy, the first day. The crowd spread out over the slate-tiled hotel patio, boys sitting on the chairs and the little green tables, talking, laughing, arguing. A girl with an accent she couldn't quite place, making a mixed group laugh out loud. Boys debating Christian theology with a hauntingly familiar enthusiasm while someone behind her — she never found out who — hummed a bar of a tune she knew from synagogue. Then someone else, as she turned, speaking to another girl about Mozart, giving the *z* its true German sound.

And Magali bubbling up to her to offer herself as guide. "Oh, Élise, this is so great. Did you know there's *four times* as many students as two years ago? I didn't go to school last year because of — hey, have you met Charlotte? This is Élise. She plays the piano too. Twice as many teachers too, it's the war of course, did you know Mademoiselle Schenk used to teach in an *acting* school? She's holding auditions for our first play next week. Lucie! Hey Lucie! This is Élise!"

And so she lived between the lichen-crusted farmhouse and this strange, frighteningly lovely school where not a single

138

person had yet made fun of her face. Where Czech expatriates taught physics, where she could sit at a patio table with Charlotte from Berlin arguing deliciously all through break about which was Bach's best work, where the silent conversation went on and on — expressions, gestures, the hint of an accent, eyes meeting for just an instant in acknowledgment — her people finding each other one by one. Nadine, Nicole, Jules, Sylvie, Eva, Damien. She wondered what their real names were. She wondered if she would ever have a chance to ask Nicole in private if it was true what Magali said, that she'd walked here from Austria on her crutches. She wondered what they talked about late at night in the dorm.

She understood why Karl and Tova wanted to live in the dorm.

She went to Pastor Losier. She pretended to kiss him on both cheeks. He listened gravely and told her that separate cooking in a dormitory kitchen would be extremely conspicuous. Wasn't there a provision in Jewish law for not risking life? She said there was. It didn't apply; they could stay at the farm, both safe and kosher. She knew of no provision for not risking embarrassment. He said he'd heard one place was going kosher, but it was a boardinghouse for

139

young men — La Roche, down past the south edge of town. The cook there was having a difficult time, the director had told him, with only men to consult. He smiled. "I'm sorry I can't help you more, but I suppose, if you know kosher cooking, I could direct you toward a chance to do an act of kindness."

Elisa sat up straight, her head high. "Thank you, Pastor," she said.

"But *where* are you going, Marcel?" asked Pierre with his arms crossed. The Scouts leaned in.

"To the Haute-Savoie. Now a word from your new troop leader. Guys!" He hushed them, palms down. "No more questions. Julien?"

Julien cleared his throat. "I don't have a lot to say. I'm grateful for the honor. I'll do my best. We have more important work than Scouts are usually entrusted with, and I'm proud to be with a troop that takes its work seriously. Some of you have missed class for sentry duty. Some of you have missed threshing and haying. I don't underestimate either of those sacrifices and I didn't ask for them lightly. We're the first line of defense for Tanieux and that line must not break. They're coming back. We don't know when.

But we will never mistake silence for safety, and we will *never* let down our guard. *They are coming back.*" The room finally came into focus and he faltered a moment at the wide eyes around him, then made the Scout salute. "Wolf troop holds fast!"

"Wolf troop! Wolf troop!" The room was full of eyes, of saluting hands, of young, deep voices. The Scout pledge, hand on his pounding heart. Pierre slapping him on the back and calling him "General," Sylvain taking the sentry-duty roster from him with shining eyes. Outside there was finally more air. He shook the guys' hands, the hands of the best troop in Tanieux, and walked home blinking in the light.

He saw Marcel off at the train station the next day; then September claimed him, school and harvest. The last cutting of hay, gotten in just ahead of the storms, Grandpa's seamed face watching the sky every minute. Hay dust sticking to Julien's aching limbs, blue clouds building in the west, the taste of ice-cold mint *tisane* in Grandpa's kitchen afterward, the scent of raindrops in the dust.

It poured. Julien slept and slept. The first night after the haying, he went to bed before the sun went down, and woke in the depths of night. He went down the stairs in his socks in the silent house, and stopped in the kitchen doorway staring. His parents stood by the sink in the dark, kissing: pressed together, her face upturned to his, her hand behind his head. They hadn't seen him. He backed away without a sound, and lay a long time in his bed, looking up into the dark.

The rain went on for days. He walked to school crammed under one umbrella with Benjamin and Magali; he spent break indoors with Sylvain and the other Scouts, with Magali, even with Élise, who seemed to be willing to talk to him now. Two of the new students disappeared; everyone seemed to know all about it, but quietly. "Switzerland," Magali whispered, and Julien gave her a quelling frown. Then he turned to Élise.

"Have you thought about it?" Magali asked her.

"Too risky." The calm in her eyes unsettled him. She glanced across the hotel dining room, then looked down at her homework. "Benjamin, did I plot this curve right?"

Benjamin took a sharp breath and bent over her notebook.

"A job?" said Magali, one hip perched on a patio table, staring at Elisa. *"Cooking?"*

"I worked before. I helped pay our rent." And she had never in her life worked for someone who thanked her. *All the rules and none of the recipes, that's what I'd have without you, girl,* Madame Ferron had told her, *and men looking over my shoulder all the time.* Then she'd thrown up her hands at Elisa's instructions on how to kosher a cooking pot, gone and found a blacksmith, and gotten it *done.* Elisa dropped her voice. "Charles and Brigitte will eat at La Roche with me. This way we can move into the dorms. I talked to your father. Brigitte and I will be in Les Aigles with Eva and Nicole."

"That's great! And you talked him into letting you come to school part-time?"

Elisa shrugged. "He said yes."

"Boy, if *I'd* ever asked for . . . Well, I guess they did let me — Élise, what's wrong?"

Elisa froze like a deer as the voice of the man across the patio penetrated her mind. Two hotel guests talking to each other, one on crutches: ". . . ambushed our division on the road to Leningrad. I took shrapnel in my leg, my kneecap was shattered, and I was bleeding like a pig . . ."

In purest Bavarian German.

Elisa turned, her eyes meeting Nadine's beside her. She wasn't sure, afterward, if she would have reacted as she did if Nadine

143

hadn't told her just the night before, while picking at a sore on her arm, her story of fleeing Warsaw ahead of German troops. But she was sure of the fire that shot through her at the sight of Nadine's face. A moment later she had her friend by the arm and was walking her fast toward the class-room door.

She heard Magali's high-pitched "What?" and the click of Nicole's crutches, but she didn't slack her pace. She gave the others a few seconds to follow them in and closed the door firmly behind them, thanking God that Karl's and Tova's classrooms were *not* hotels.

"They're just convalescents," Magali started, "they're billeted here —"

"I've got eyes," Elisa snapped.

"They have never done us any harm," said Nicole to Nadine. "They are only hurt soldiers. Not Gestapo. They are not here to hunt anyone."

"Have you ever seen that man before?" Elisa asked Nicole.

"No."

"Then you don't know what harm he does or doesn't do. You don't know what he's here for or who he hunts. You don't know if he's just a soldier or if he's a card-carrying Nazi and an SS. He's not in uniform. You don't know a thing about him. I know more about him than you do." She put a hand on Nadine's shoulder and felt her trembling.

Magali had paled. "What was he saying?"

"How he got injured invading Russia."

Magali recovered. "Oh, then —"

"You think that never happens to Nazis? Why didn't anyone tell us about this?" She turned to Nicole, who leaned on one crutch and wrinkled her brows worriedly at Nadine.

"I did not think to. We have gotten used to them. I'm sorry. But truly, Élise, they are only here to —"

"How long are those two staying? Does anybody know?"

"They never stay the winter," Magali put in. "Nobody wants our winter."

Elisa said to Nadine, "If you like, I'll spend break in here with you till they leave."

"Thank you," whispered Nadine. "I'm afraid of Germans."

Magali and Nicole looked at each other. Magali said gently, "*She's* German, Nadine."

"I *was* German," said Elisa. Heat was rising in her, a dark wave up her neck to the roots of her hair. "We were as German as anybody, for years, for generations, until *they* decided we weren't. They robbed us of

145

everything and forced us out, and then they turned around and hunted us. They got my parents." She lifted a finger toward Magali. "When they get —"

She stopped herself just in time. She watched the words she had not said, *When they get your parents,* strike the other three girls like a wave. Magali first. She turned white, then red. But she said nothing.

"Your parents?" murmured Nicole. "When?"

"Just before I came here," said Elisa very low.

"You never said." Nicole turned to Magali. "*You* never said."

"That stuff is private," said Magali in a thick voice. Nicole's eyebrows went up.

Elisa gripped the table edge, light-headed, her mind shocked into darkness, dark as the barracks in Vénissieux. She sat suddenly and reached for her schoolbag, rummaged blindly and brought out a book, opened it and stared until the image resolved itself into a tangent graph. She could feel the others looking at her. She tried her voice, and found that she could only whisper. "Those men out there are men who shoot people on *their* orders. That's all I was trying to say."

Nadine nodded. After a moment Nicole

146

and Magali nodded too.

October came in with high, cold winds, and Julien's mother grew silent. Magali's trip with Marek was planned for the fifth. The rain fell hard, the first real storm of autumn, touching the hills with fingers of lightning, splashing up cold clouds of water from the slate rooftops of Tanieux. Julien watched from Benjamin's little window under the eaves, his back propped against the wall beside his friend in the emptied-out bedroom. Benjamin's books and clothes would go to friends, quietly. He couldn't take a thing except the clothes on his back. And his life.

"Remember when we found the honey tree?" Benjamin said suddenly.

Julien almost laughed. "*You* found the honey tree."

"Does it count, though, when you don't know what it is?"

"You got *nine stings* getting that honey. And you never dropped your bucket. I was so proud."

Benjamin half smiled. "Julien —"

"Hey, it's —"

"No, listen. You were right. I mean, you're always right, that's what I hate about you, but I've been thinking about America."

"Oh?"

"Yeah. New York. Skyscrapers. Henry Ford, 'History is bunk' — did you know he said that? Your father wouldn't like it, but look at it from my point of view."

Julien made a soft noise in his throat.

"There's Jewish scientists there. Geniuses. I could do real work there, no one would care where I come from. Do you know how much I'd like to take my life up till now and flush it down the toilet? Except for my family, and — well. Well. And you all of course — we want to send you money after Papa's out, I've been meaning to tell you, I mean — you know." Benjamin shoved himself upward against the wall and looked down at his chemistry book. "I thought you'd like to know how right you were, I know you like that sort of thing."

"Oh, shut up," said Julien, punching his friend on the arm, as the rain poured down outside the window, and the joyful earth drank deep.

Magali left for her trip on a high, blue, windy day. Papa walked Mama home, her thin hand clasped in his, his other hand reaching out to smooth her hair. Julien led his first real Scout meeting, then went down to the farm and dug potatoes out of the

148

damp earth. Potatoes, leeks, and carrots; beets and turnips and rutabagas in great mounds. Cartloads to the train station, basket after basket into the root cellar. Bright rust and yellow flamed here and there on the hills against the green of the pines, and the sky was the high, deep blue of autumn; Grandpa's eyes drank it in, always on the horizon, where the black migrating flocks turned on the wind. Mama did her work silently, and met the train each day till Magali finally came home.

Magali's face was puffy when Mama brought her in, eyes blurred with weariness. She collapsed into a chair as Mama hurried to make tea.

"Safe?" said Julien.

Magali nodded. "It was *horrible.*"

"The crossing?"

She dropped her face in her hands. Then lifted her head and threw up her hands as if asking God why. "He didn't tell us! He didn't say a word! We said, 'Can you go through a tunnel?' and he said, 'Yes!' " She smacked a hand on the table. "He told me once that he saw soldiers kill his father. That's the only thing I know. Well guess what I just found out happened right before that?" She looked around, eyes wide and wild. "His father *hid him in a sewer.*"

Mama's hand went to her mouth.

"So we get to the drainpipe — this long drainpipe under a hill and the other end is in Switzerland — and they send him in first. Get it over with, right? I get worried. He just looked a little off, y'know? So I'm arguing with the Cimade lady under my breath, and then there's this noise like a rusty hinge again and again and it's *Marek having hysterics,* right there in the pipe! The Cimade lady goes the color of old cheese and gestures me in, and I crawl into the pipe going, 'Marek, Marek,' and the whole thing is echoing and I can only imagine who's hearing it and I put my hand on his ankle and go, 'Marek. Be quiet and you'll live.' "

Nobody breathed.

"He goes quiet. But I can feel him still having some kind of spasms. Then another kid comes up behind me because the noise stopped and the Cimade people thought it was all right. She starts to ask what's happening and I shush her, 'Just follow us when you can.' And I start coaxing Marek. 'It's all right, you'll be all right, just crawl a little. Crawl a little more.' I swear. We spent *over an hour* getting through a forty-meter pipe."

She fell back hard in her chair.

"Everybody made it?" said Julien.

"Everybody. I went with them all the way

to the safe house. That's where he told me about the sewer. I think that must be where he watched . . . watched them kill his father from." She shook her head, and the wildness and weariness and frustration fell from her face and left bare sorrow. "If anyone's got a right to hysterics, it's him."

There was a long silence around the table. "We're a little short on rights just now," said Benjamin.

"Well now Marek's —" Magali broke off. Clattering feet were coming up the stairs. Papa threw open the door, breathing hard.

"Benjamin," he said. "In my study please."

"What is it?" said Julien before he could stop himself.

"What is it?" Benjamin echoed in a fast, colorless voice.

Papa passed his eyes over the family. "There's a problem at the border," he said carefully. "It won't be possible to pass you in the Geneva area. If we don't want to let your visa expire" — he drew a breath — "it'll have to be the Alps."

It was like watching someone turn to stone. Julien was seized with a terrible impulse to jump up and slap Benjamin, strike the light back into his eyes. *Now? Now of all times? Are You playing with us?*

Benjamin gripped the chair in front of

151

him; it scraped loudly on the floor. He broke and ran for the stairwell door.

"I'll come up in fifteen minutes!" Papa called after him. "I have to send word today!"

"Lord have mercy," whispered Mama.

"Amen," said Papa, already heading for his study door. Julien followed, almost running.

"Papa." Papa was head down, rummaging in a drawer. "Papa," Julien said again, and Papa looked up, his eyes harried, and spoke quickly.

"Annemasse route's shut down. Close call, very close — our *passeur* compromised, our local allies shaken to the bone. Who knows how long till — and the second route's not up yet — a complete fiasco. And his visa's for October only — how they can justify that —"

"Papa," said Julien.

His father looked at him.

"I could go with him."

Papa's mouth opened.

"Hold his hand. One last time. It'd work. I can help him in the rough terrain. Just as far as they'll let me. Just get him, get him moving, get his courage up till he can go on — don't you think he's more likely to say yes? If he's got me?"

"Yes," said Papa slowly. "I do. I don't know if the *passeur* would allow it. These alpine guides are professionals. I suppose I could give a recommendation." He shook his head, eyes abstracted. "You just took over the Scout troop."

A flush of heat passed up through Julien's neck, his face. "Give it to Sylvain."

"What?"

"I said give it to Sylvain," said Julien more loudly.

"That probably won't be necessary, but it's — it's . . ." Papa's eyes finally met his fully, and suddenly his hand was on Julien's arm, pulling. "Let's go up and tell him."

Upstairs Papa knocked on Benjamin's door. Silence. He knocked again.

"You said fifteen minutes," said a low, dark voice through the door.

"We have something to tell you."

The door was flung open. Benjamin's lightless eyes were very still in his thin face. "Yes?"

"I could go with you," Julien said.

Benjamin's shoulders rose slightly. The life that came back into his eyes looked mostly like pain.

"What do you think?" said Papa.

Benjamin closed his eyes, his lips parting. He forced out the words with a visible effort. "I'll go."

Then he sank down on the bed. Put his face in his hands, raised his head, and whispered, "Can you leave me alone a little while now?"

"Of course," murmured Papa. Julien got one last glimpse of his friend as his father shut the door: his eyes looking at nothing, his head in his hands.

One more day.

Julien slipped Grandpa's slim little songbook into his Scout bag, alongside the shaving kit Papa gave him. *If God will only show Himself. Oh, show Yourself. I believe.* It was intended — his father sending Julien to lead his best friend to safety — it was right. The time came toward him like a cold and rushing headwind, bracing him, lifting up his wings. Like a promise. He felt Papa's warm eyes on him sometimes, and met them when he turned around.

On his last afternoon he walked down to the La Roche boardinghouse after lunch, with a letter from Papa to the director. The sky was deep blue and very high as he walked south out of town. The wind rippled the long grass of hayfields gone to pale fluffy seed. He wondered if he would see Élise, whether she would want to talk to him.

He'd thought about telling her privately where he was going. Maybe offering to tell her more about the border when he came back.

He walked up the La Roche driveway and knocked, then walked in. He saw the director's name on one of the pigeonholes along the lobby wall, but kept going. Was she here? Silence as he walked on through the foyer; a male voice somewhere up on the stairs.

As he stepped through the doorway of the common room, the music struck him like a storm.

It rolled and climbed and built itself higher, deeper, hanging and towering like a thunderhead in the sky. *She* built it. He stood transfixed, watching her. Her hair was up in its tight bun; a stained apron hung limp on the piano bench beside her; her sleeves were wet. Her face was hard and luminous, like a diamond. Like a diamond cutting glass. She bent to her work, shoulders tense, her eyes barely glancing at her twining, flying fingers; seeing nothing but the thing itself, in her mind, the music. She searched, her eyes seeking something beyond, something neither of them could see. She struck a false note, a dissonance that went through her like an arrow; she froze, trembling, as if someone had flung a curse in her face.

The silence lasted one eternal second. Then slowly, with a breath that shook and then smoothed out, she bent to the piano again, touching it gently, building the thunderhead again, higher, deeper, her eyes on something beyond as if in prayer. He dug his fingernails into his palms, not breathing. She slowed, she paused, she crouched like a tiger for a moment over the keys. Then her hands flashed out and struck them again like lightning, and the air was filled with the anger of angels, and the light in her face made his body tremble.

He stood rooted as the music washed over him, wave after wave. He stood till it slowed, till a voice was heard from the kitchen; till Élise's fire began to dim, and a swift side glance of her eyes made him afraid. She hadn't seen him. But she would. What on earth would he say to her?

He faded backward into the shadow of the doorway, turned on silent feet, slipped Papa's letter into the right pigeonhole, and fled.

CHAPTER 9
PROMISED

"See the house?" Julien murmured. "Number twenty-five, shed with a green roof."

Benjamin nodded, barely glancing up. He had made eye contact with no one on their two-day journey, except a gendarme who had demanded his papers. He had answered to the name Charles Béranger with a stony face and given the name of the bombed-out northern village he was supposed to be from, and gone on expressionless till the safe house door closed behind them in Saint-Étienne. Then he'd started gasping for breath while Julien told him how excellent he'd been, and the kind old lady hosting them plied him with tea. The tea worked, eventually.

Here in Annecy he did better. When the door shut and Madame Cantal ushered them through the little wood-paneled foyer into the dining room, he merely sank into one of the oak chairs, leaning his head against the high back and closing his eyes. Madame Cantal looked him over with brisk compassion, said, "Coffee will be ready in a minute," and bustled out. Julien turned at the sound of feet coming down the stairs, opened his mouth, and forgot to close it again.

"Hello," said Marcel. "I'm Jean-Pierre. Nice to meet you."

Benjamin opened his eyes. They widened a little, then closed again. Marcel shot him a worried look as he and Julien shook hands, and asked quietly, "How was Lyon?"

"Better than Saint-Étienne. It was scary, but nobody stopped us." The Lyon station had been like a night forest full of eyes, the uniforms everywhere seeming to watch them through the crowd: the blue of gendarmes, the gray-green of soldiers with their hooded German helmets.

"You were lucky. Lyon's the worst. You got stopped in Saint-Étienne?"

"Just a *contrôle*. Benjamin was amazing. And his papers —"

"I wasn't *amazing,* Julien." Benjamin glared at him.

"You were! You were stone-cold like a —"

"Please. You don't have to praise me for not wetting myself with fright. If he'd decided to investigate it wouldn't have mattered how much I moved my facial muscles —"

"I'm not —"

Marcel cleared his throat loudly. A young man and woman in dark clothes stood in the doorway, watching them warily. Julien gave them an apologetic nod. "This is Jean and Marie," Marcel said. "The rest of our group. They don't speak French. Charles, I've been told you speak Yiddish?"

Benjamin straightened slowly, meeting the man's eyes and then the woman's. He spoke politely. The young man answered with something about Krakow.

"I have some instructions for you all," Marcel said to Benjamin. "Do you think you can —" He broke off as Madame Cantal came in with a pot of coffee. "I'm sorry, you just got here."

Benjamin sat bolt upright now, his eyes pinning Marcel. "It's fine," he said. "Let's hear it."

Julien spoke only once to Benjamin, in the silence of their guest room that night: "You'll be in Switzerland tomorrow." Benjamin said nothing. The next morning, he was already dressed when Julien woke. In another hour they were on a train to Chamonix.

159

The Alps were a revelation.

Julien had seen them before on the far horizon, cloudy blue masses sharp-peaked against the sky. The young mountains. Not like the green and gentle peaks of the plateau, smooth-sloped volcanoes dead and harmless for millennia, grown over with sweet grass. He loved those soft green mountains with all his heart, but he felt no awe. The feeling that rose in his chest as the train pulled toward Chamonix and the Alps rose up to their true height before him — this was something new.

They grew and grew as the train rushed toward them, and he could not take his eyes off them. Huge, jagged shoulders and spires of rock thrust up from steep slopes mantled with dark pines, rising and rising toward heaven till they reached it, till the great snow-crowned peaks that soared above them gleamed whiter than white in the young morning sun, blinding as angels. Immensity that stopped his breath, that made his heart lift out of him and fly. He had never known there was so much sky before, fathoms and fathoms up into the blue — except once or twice, caught out on the road home from Grandpa's as a summer storm built up to breaking, the thunderhead rising like a towering castle in the sky, and him

160

small and running for home beneath it, wide-eyed and silent with fear and joy. Music rose in his mind as the mountains drew closer, music that built up and towered, that broke like thunder, like angels surging up with lightning in their eyes, and then a girl's face blazing with intensity, with a sharp and single-minded love. And suddenly his eyes were shut and he was shaking. *You have other things to think about. Other things.* As if this of all times was the time to stop and stare like a fool, to forget everything because he had seen beauty.

He took short breaths until his heart slowed. Then he opened his eyes and looked up at the great snowcapped walls between Benjamin and safety as the train pulled in to Chamonix.

It was chilly. They huddled down into their layered clothes and followed Marcel's Scout uniform through the air brilliant with white light from the snowfields above. There were no police. Marcel stood at the bus stop watching people get off, then turned away as if in disappointment. Julien led Benjamin and the Polish couple onto the bus.

It climbed a long valley between steep mountain walls, its engine laboring; it stopped at clusters of houses, built of rough gray granite or polished wood, steep-roofed against the heavy winter snows. Down on their left a swift clear river ran, boiling over rocks. A bearded young man in a mended wool coat walked up the aisle, swaying easily with the motion of the bus. "You'll drop me at my brother's house today, Monsieur Chellet?"

It was the signal Pastor Cantal had given them. Julien waited till the next stop after the *passeur* descended, then led the others down.

Huge clouds hung above the mountains, unbelievably bright. It was colder here, almost freezing. He found the little footpath Marcel had described and took it, hearing the others breathe behind him, the skin of his back crawling with imagined eyes. They reached the forest, dark as an old stone church under the canopy of the pines, and stopped at the fallen log. The silence of the place sank heavy and soft around them. No one broke it.

Not even the *passeur.* The bearded young man came up the path without a sound, pulled a pack from the hollow of the log, and beckoned them on.

Up and up the tiny, winding path, legs laboring, breathing deep of the thin, cold air. Julien scanned around them, but there was no one, no presence but the rocks thrusting up through the hard earth, humps and jags and boulders crowned with emerald moss that glowed where the rare shafts of sunlight struck it. After a while the sound of water broke the deep cathedral hush, and they came to a swift rocky stream. The *passeur* crossed it first and made fast a rope to a tree on the far bank, then stretched it very taut over the stream and spoke his first words to them: "Use this to keep your balance. Don't slip. Water's even colder than you think." They stepped cautiously from rock to shaky rock, Jean helping Marie, Julien helping Benjamin. "That was the easy one," said the *passeur*, coiling up the rope.

An hour later the others' pace was faltering, and even Julien's legs ached. The sound of white water, growing and growing, rose to a roar as they stepped into bright light beyond the trees and saw the river, its surface gnarled as muscle from the rocks hiding under its flow, wet boulders casting blue shadows on the foam. "This is the hard one," murmured the *passeur*, and slipped the rope out of his pack. But Julien had eyes for nothing but the waterfall upstream.

The pounding water, the water flinging itself over the edge, the weight and the weightlessness of its fall. It stopped Julien's breath with a strange deep clenching. Then

163

Benjamin gasped.

The *passeur* had leapt across the white water, rope in hand; he clung to a great boulder. A scramble, another lithe, practiced leap. The blood was draining from Benjamin's face. The *passeur* was making the rope fast to a rock somehow. Another leap, and he was on the far bank tying it to a tree. Then the return, swift and smooth. Benjamin was fish-belly white.

"One at a time," said the *passeur.* "Rope won't hold two."

Julien had to ask Benjamin twice to translate for the others.

Marie crossed first. Jean watched her, his hands clenched by his sides. Then Jean crossed, almost falling once, jerking hard on the rope. He reached Marie, safe on the riverbank, and they gripped each other.

Benjamin's turn.

"In one minute you'll be over there," whispered Julien. Benjamin stepped forward, grasped the rope, looked at the ledge, and at his feet, and at the water. Then he leapt.

A cry burst from Julien as Benjamin's right foot missed the rock and splashed in the water, one hand grasping the rope white-knuckled, the other scrabbling at the boulder as he fell to one knee on the little ledge, his face striking the rock.

"Stand up!" shouted the *passeur,* his calm dropped like a mask. *"Stand up!"*

Benjamin pulled himself up, a scrape showing shocking scarlet against his white face. He paused, gasping, his hand tight on the rope, as the *passeur* held out palm-down hands. *Calm now.*

Then he started to climb.

Up that boulder, hauling on the rope, slipping, regaining, tearing his trousers, *doing it.* He stood panting on the boulder, then straightened, flinging his head back, hand on the rope — and swung into the second leap. He landed two-footed on the midstream stone, crossed it and jumped again, wide across the deadly water, and fell to his knees and hands on the grassy bank beyond. From across the torrent Julien could see him breathing like a bellows.

"Thirty seconds," he murmured, and smiled.

"He's lucky I brought extra socks," muttered the *passeur.*

They walked on, their pace flagging and strengthening, crossing the rare open places at a run. Benjamin panted and stumbled. They crossed a road once, after the *passeur* scanned the valley with field glasses; they walked slowly, looking straight ahead, the *passeur*'s hand going up once in an acknowledging wave to some unseen villager. The forest, when they entered it again, was like a mother's arms.

There was no path now. The slope was very steep. At the ridge's crest the trees opened out, and they went on hands and knees on the short, tough grass, between sharp-scented evergreen bushes and tawny, fading heather. They stood when the *passeur* did, and followed him up a steep, dry gully between great ridges of rock. Julien's thighs were burning now; Benjamin and the Poles were in a bad way, gasping for breath in the thin, freezing air, Benjamin leaning often on Julien. The *passeur* motioned them to sit and climbed out of the gully. Benjamin sank down and watched dull-eyed, shivering in the cold shade.

"Clear," said the *passeur,* returning. He dug in his pack. "Eat."

They shared bread and cheese and water. Benjamin stopped shivering. Julien looked up as he ate, at the deep blue sky and the brilliant white clouds that flowed through it, at a hawk riding the air currents, turning in wide circles, flashing his intricate cream-and-brown markings in the sun. When the *passeur* called them to go on, Benjamin rose with gritted teeth and pain lines in his face. Julien put a hand on his friend's shoulder and asked the *passeur,* "How far now?"

"About a kilometer to the pass. That's the border. You're the Scout?"

"Yeah."

"Stay with us till the pass." The *passeur* asked Benjamin, "Can you translate again?" Benjamin nodded. The young man turned to the group. "After the pass," he said, "you're all right. But I'm not. If the Swiss border patrol picks us up, you get your visas stamped for entry and I go to jail." He shrugged. "That's how it works. So please be careful on the other side too. Understand?"

They understood.

He gave them a nod and led them out onto the heights.

The world widened to hugeness around them, the sun high overhead in the deep, dark blue, great gulfs of air between the grassy uplands where they stood and the massive peaks rising like islands to east and west. Joy welled up in Julien as he walked, fresh strength flowing into his legs. They climbed slopes of grass and lichen-crusted granite, using hands as well as feet, Julien staying below Benjamin to brace him. They climbed between jagged boulders thrust up out of the earth like broken bones, now and then catching sight of the pass itself, up beyond hillcrests of rust-red heather and tawny winter grass: the gates to freedom. The image rose in Julien despite himself, the image he had repressed since the day he undertook this journey, for fear of rejoicing too soon: standing in a high pass in the mountains, watching from far away as his friend walked down and down. Already safe, already free, walking into the green valley: into the promised land.

The *passeur* motioned them down, and Julien went flat on his belly. *Too soon.* The man scanned the length of the heights with his field glasses, then beckoned and led them on without a word. The hawk called once, shrilly, piercing Julien's heart with longing. They walked on, the *passeur* stopping every few minutes to scan the far passes. The fourth time, crouching on a flat rock, he swore softly.

"Someone's there," he murmured. "Could be nothing. I can't tell." He stuffed the glasses in his pack. "This way." He moved off downward.

They avoided the heights now, taking pathless ways among clumps of grass and jutting rocks, the ground rising so steeply on one side that they could lean and touch it as they walked, and dropping just as sharply on the other side. They walked in tight single file; Julien brought up the rear. Once Marie stumbled; Jean caught her as she fell to her knees. Julien kept his eyes on Benjamin's feet, his muscles tense, hands ready.

It didn't matter, when it came.

High above in the blue, the hawk screamed again. There was a swift movement in the corner of his eye, a crunch of rock on rock, and a short sharp cry.

And Benjamin was gone.

It happened so fast. It happened so agonizingly slow. Julien saw the rock fall from the slope above, the moment before it struck the side of Benjamin's foot; he saw Benjamin's heel struck out from under him, his body falling sideways, and knew that in a moment it would be too late, he would be gone. And in a moment he was, and the whole terrible story had been nothing but a split second, and Julien was only beginning to reach out his hand. It closed on air. A scream came from below.

Benjamin was tumbling down the slope. Julien cried out, staring down at the drop-off, the fathoms of air; he saw his friend strike a spur of rock, saw the angle of his foot go suddenly *wrong,* heard Benjamin scream again, true agony this time.

Saw him stop, splayed against the rock.

"Wait here." It was the *passeur.* "Wait." He was looping a rope round a rock, testing its fastness, then off down the slope within seconds, scrambling in a swift, careful zigzag to the place where Benjamin lay. Julien crouched useless by the fallen stone — it was still there, the stone that had done this — and prayed, gathering up the shattered promise with hot hands, a child insisting shards meant nothing, time meant nothing, the beloved thing could be fixed. *Oh God, the promised land. Oh God, I watched him fall.*

The *passeur* began the climb back up. Alone.

The man's face was pale as he reached Julien. "Broken ankle. We can't bring him up." He gestured to the Polish couple who crouched watching him. "I have to take them on."

Julien nodded. His head seemed no longer to belong to him, floating somewhere in the cold, sunny air.

"I've anchored him to the rock and put three blankets on him. I'll tell you where to go and who to ask for. Listen." The man's voice lowered, and for the first time he looked Julien directly in the eye. "You have to come back for him no matter what happens. You get caught, you tell them where he is. He won't live the night on this mountain. They're predicting snow."

Julien nodded mutely.

The *passeur* gave him landmarks, distances, names. He repeated every word twice. "Clément. Ask for Clément." Then the young man looked him in the eyes again and said, "It's my fault. I chose bad terrain."

Julien looked at him, at Jean and Marie. "I hope you make it."

"Same to you," said the *passeur*. He beckoned the others, and they stood. The *passeur* raised a hand to him and led them away, upward.

Julien looked down at his friend's white face and raised one fist: *Hold on. Please. Please hold on.* It was all he could give him.

Then he turned back and took the downward path, away from the promised land.

CHAPTER 10
THE HOUSE OF LIFE

Elisa stood by the head of La Roche's table, a match in her hand. The white tablecloth glowed rosy in the sunset light; thirty young men turned their faces to her where she stood behind the two tall candles. Chaim Maslowitz, former rabbinical student from Prague, nodded respectfully to her to begin as Karl watched him admiringly. She struck her match, a small, fierce flare, and lit one candle, then the other, looking up to meet Tova's steady gaze. Elisa drew her hands three times over the candles, laid them over her eyes, and said the blessing her mother had said before her, in Heidelberg, in Lyon, every week of her life, faithful as the sunrise. *Mama.* "Blessed art Thou, Lord our God, King of the universe . . ." In the deep hush that followed, the time for silent prayer, her mind emptied out into darkness: *Oh God, help those in danger. Help them.* The afterimage of the two small flames trembled against her eyelids. She opened her eyes and took a deep breath.

"Good Shabbos," she said.

Madame Ferron set a huge tureen of soup on the table, and threw Elisa a wink. The painfully thin young man beside Tova — Joseph, was it? — stared at the soup with his face working. Tova, who hadn't seen him, began to tell Elisa about a carnival planned by her dorm and the skits her friends were writing. She had too many friends to keep track of now, including one sweet girl from Lithuania who had sworn to be her best friend forever. Tova took the bowl that was passed to her, still talking, then broke off when she saw Joseph's face.

"Would you like some of mine?" she said softly. "I'm not very hungry."

"No!" He shook his head vehemently. "No. Thank you. I — I'm not sure I can even eat this. Day before yesterday I vomited what I ate. I couldn't stand to waste this, this . . ." Tears were in his eyes. Tova almost put a hand on his arm.

"I'm sorry," she whispered. "Did you just get here?"

"I was in the Rivesaltes internment camp till last week." Everyone was listening now; Joseph lifted his head and spoke clearer, unembarrassed tears still in his eyes. "So was Rudy." He nodded at the young man sitting opposite him. "We were out hiking during the roundup in Grenoble. When we found out, we took a train for Saint-Gingolph by the border, we knew some people there. But the French border guards were waiting for us on the Swiss side, I still don't know why. They sent us straight to Rivesaltes. There was hardly anything to eat and what they did give us was rotten. People were being deported every day." He kept shaking his head.

"We're lucky to be alive," said Rudy in a deep voice. His soup lay untouched in his bowl.

Elisa's eyes went to Tova, to Karl. She closed them. Then opened them again to the circle of faces, solemn and candlelit, and to the flames reflected in the windows, shutting out the dark.

Julien crouched behind pine branches, still as a rabbit in cover, watching the patrol.

Three uniformed men, one with a fresh scrape across his face, cradling his wrist, another supporting him, the third dressing him down in a disgusted undertone as they went: "Of all the stupidity I've ever witnessed in this job, *that* was —"

"I'm sorry!"

174

"You'll be sorrier when I've told Perraud, you unspeakable moron . . ."

Julien forced himself not to shiver in the freezing air as they moved away. *Help me.* As their voices faded he pulled his coat around him. He closed his eyes and counted to sixty: sixty times the rock from nowhere, sixty times Benjamin's scream. *We would be at the pass by now.* No sound but the cold wind rising in the pines. *They're predicting snow.* Julien stood.

He stayed off the path, moving fast, listening. He came to the landmark, the rock with letters etched in the lichen: M ♡ D. He took the turn and found the little green valley spread below him, and the cluster of stone houses. He stopped.

Far down on the path to the nearest house were three uniformed men.

He hissed almost soundlessly and slipped back behind the rock. The sun was gone; a thin band of bright turquoise sky glowed above the mountains ahead. Clouds massed in the east, gold now in the slanting light and deadly.

He stepped out and scanned the valley again.

At the tree line near the road, a man put an axe to a pine. Down in the hamlet a man and woman stood at their door speaking to the patrol. In the green beyond the houses, small white-and-brown figures of goats clustered, a lanky child walking behind them, herding them with a stick. If he skirted the valley and kept to the trees . . .

The patrol vanished into a house, and he ran. He kept in cover, branches slapping his face, fox-colored needles blurring beneath him, twisted roots standing out to his leaping feet. He froze, gasping, gripping a tree, looking down at the stretch of open grass in the evening light that lay between him and his hope. The herder boy stood by a stone trough, watching his beasts jostle each other for a drink, now and then giving one of their rumps a little sting with the stick. "Bad girl," he said, his words carried clear and small through the thin air. Julien drew in a breath and whistled like a blackbird.

The boy looked up sharply. *You don't have blackbirds up here, do you?* Heart pounding, Julien whistled again, and let his face show for a moment between the trees. *Here. Here I am.*

When the boy came into the forest, Julien was kneeling on the pine needles waiting, sick with hope. The young goatherd gave him one swift look like a bird turning its head, sharp and canny.

"Clément," Julien whispered.

"He's away. Bergers are home. You need help?"

"I have to get someone off the mountain with a broken ankle. And hide him."

The boy's lips shaped a silent whistle. "You wait. I'll get 'em."

An hour later the western sky flamed scarlet and rose, the zenith a deep royal blue above Julien where he stood on the grassy uplands again. Below, Benjamin's face showed ghostly in the gathering dusk. "Wait here," said Jeannette Berger as she and her brother Maurice clipped onto their lines and started down. Julien knelt gripping the scrubby grass, listening. *Oh God,* he prayed. *Oh God.* He found no other words.

The sky was still lit when they reached him, Benjamin strapped down on a home-made stretcher, swathed in blankets, tears shining in his eyes under the bloody sky. Julien bent to him. "They're allies," he murmured. "They're *passeurs.* You're safe." The tears spilled over and streamed down Benjamin's face, reflecting rose-red streaks of light. He opened his mouth, but his teeth chattered too hard for him to speak.

The Bergers coiled their ropes and stood, lit ruddy in the last light of that endless day. Him with his squashed and broken nose; her with her figure broad and ungraceful in thick men's trousers, her neck and chin and smiling mouth too big. He had never seen such beautiful people. They knelt and took the handles of the stretcher. "You walk beside us on the downhill side," Maurice said. "Steady him."

Jeannette grinned at him. "You also get to be the cushion if we fall."

"Where are you taking me?" Benjamin asked.

"To my mother's house," said Jeannette, and smiled.

It was a hard walk back, but not so hard as Julien feared. In the dying light they didn't try to hide, but walked the crests of the gentlest hills, on dry dirt paths between the rocks and heather. And the last of the light died very slowly, held by the great snowy peaks that glowed a warm rose against the fading sky. The line of shadow crept slowly upward, till only the highest summits were lit; the light winked out, and the world darkened, and still they could see the path. Nothing in the world but the pale ghost of the path before them, the warm, dark, breathing bulk of each other, and the peaks, still the peaks, now glowing an unearthly ice-blue. Julien walked beside his friend, his eyes watchful, his heart stunned into silence.

Somewhere deep in a valley the promise lay shattered on the rocks; in another a goatherd boy went home whistling, swinging his stick; within Julien's reach his friend lay breathing in the impossible light. *God, God,* the word sang itself in his head. *What is this? What is this?* The Alps stood sentinel around them, guarding and lighting them, the Alps that had nearly killed Benjamin, and they did not answer.

They descended into forest darkness, down and down, Julien straining to keep watch. They came out onto the short soft grass, the stars overhead, above the eastern peaks a silver half moon showing bright-edged against the black. Ahead of them the cluster of stone houses, their windows golden; in one of them a red blanket hung, lamplight behind it making it glow like a living heart, the signal: *all clear.* Before they could knock, a wrinkled woman in an apron threw the door wide. Inside was warmth, and a scarred pine table, a worn brown sofa by the old stone fireplace, and a blazing fire.

Julien followed the Bergers as they carried Benjamin into the house of life.

Julien opened the attic shutters the next morning to find the sun high and fresh snow on the ground. Benjamin slept deep as a child, breathing evenly, the fresh-made cast showing bulky under the blanket. Soft voices floated up from downstairs as Julien felt his friend's cool forehead. Then a sudden shout of laughter, and loud shushing. He came down the attic stairs in his socks.

A fire danced in the stone hearth; Maurice and Jeannette and a stranger sat around the pine table with mugs, Jeannette shuffling a pack of cards. She smiled at him. "You're awake! Join us, have some coffee. It's fake, but it's hot. And there's milk. And tell us what you're called, so I don't have to call you 'you' anymore. Officially, of course." She fluttered her fingers in a *you-know* gesture.

Julien smiled. "I'm Julien. Officially."

Jeannette poured him a cup from a dented coffeepot and added milk from a stoneware jug. She pointed with her chin at the stranger. "This's Clément. He's very curious who you were crossing with, but you won't know that."

Julien warmed his hands on his mug. "He was young . . . had a beard . . ."

Jeannette grinned at Clément. "I win."

"I didn't really think —" began Clément.

"Then why on earth d'you take my bet?"

"Because bragging rights look so good on you."

Jeannette threw back her head and roared with laughter. Both the men grinned.

"We'll find out," said Clément. "Has to be someone we know."

"That, or your reputation's getting out of hand."

"How's your friend, Julien?"

"No fever. And he has more color now."

"Poor boy," said Maurice. "He looked half dead. Listen, you are both welcome here for as long —"

"But you are in a border zone," said Clément, "so don't leave the house, and *my* recommendation —"

"Jean-Baptiste said two weeks, Clem." Jeannette leaned over the table. "At least two weeks."

"The doctor?" said Julien. He tried to recall last night. Benjamin laid out on the table, a bottle of something, a young man in a black coat. In the morning light it all seemed like a firelit dream.

Jeannette threw her head back and laughed again. "I'm sorry," she said, wiping her eyes. "You tell him."

Maurice gave her a patient look and turned to Julien. "He knows what he's doing. And he's safe. The doctor — well, the doctor's down in Argentière anyhow, we just sent that patroller down to him." He rubbed his chin. "Jean-Baptiste is a, uh, very experienced vet."

Julien didn't know just what kind of look crossed his face. But Jeannette, naturally, laughed at it.

The beams in the Bergers' house were rough pine, blackened with woodsmoke; the walls were granite outside, plaster inside, and cold. The faces were warm and open as the fire in the open hearth, filling the house with light and life. The past and the future stayed outside with the wind and the snow. For those few days there was peace.

Long slow mornings waking and dozing again, feeling his friend's warmth beside him under the blankets, sliding back into the blessed soft darkness where it was enough to be alive. The song of enough sang its rich harmonies all through his body; when he felt the questions behind him, he did not turn, and in the end they went away.

Long slow mornings in the attic; quiet afternoons downstairs by the fire, bringing tea up to Benjamin. His friend slept and slept, woke and watched the slow dance of dust in the slanting sunlight with a strange calm on his face. It was three days before they spoke of anything more than food, or tea, or whether Benjamin was warm enough or in pain. Till the day Julien came up to find his friend propped against the wall with tears slipping silently down his face. He froze, but Benjamin turned.

"Julien, do you think there's anything I could do to help your father?"

Julien gaped.

"I know I'm not good at much." The wet brown eyes were steady. "But if I could do anything at all?"

Julien gathered his wits. "Translate. You speak Yiddish and French and German."

"You think that would help?"

"Of course."

The tears slid down again. "Why didn't he ever ask?" Benjamin whispered. "No. I know why he didn't ask. I was never that kind of person. Julien, I thought, out there on the mountain, I thought —"

"Look —"

"I was always going to be someone different. Later. It wasn't all stupid, I had reasons, I wasn't made for this, Julien. You know. I was made for a lab somewhere, running experiments with particles while someone else keeps the animals out. Not like you — when I see you do this stuff — it's like seeing one of *them*."

Julien frowned. "Who?"

"I don't mean . . . That hawk, did you see

it, yesterday? It was up there for hours. This perfect circle over and over, I could see every feather on its wings when the light hit it from the side and it was so — smooth, all this . . . precisely applied power, like, like I don't know what. Like you. Climbing something." He wiped his tears with the back of his hand. "It's no use even envying that, you know? I've got to be a man in my own way. Do something for my neighbor. Not — not *give in*."

"Benjamin . . ."

"I was angry. Because I can never, ever pay you back. As if that was any good. I'm making some changes. Do you know, I really believe? I didn't have reasons for not doing the things I'm supposed to, I just didn't do them. That's no way to live. If I make it back to Tanieux I'm getting my prayer book back from Damien, and I'm going to keep the Sabbath, and I'm writing to my mother, and . . . Well." He fell silent.

"Are you all right, Benjamin?" The casual way his friend had said "If I make it" made Julien's belly clench. *Who* are *you*?

"Yes. Really, Julien. I'm well. I . . ." The tears started again. "I want to know who I *am* next time I die."

Julien took a deep, slow breath, staring at

his friend. "Maybe," he said, "you won't die."

"Maybe. But if I do, I don't want this again. I want something better."

Julien shook his head. *Benjamin Keller.* Élise's fierce eyes flashed into his mind. Before he could stop himself, he blurted, "D'you have to eat kosher now?"

Benjamin threw back his head like Jeannette Berger and laughed aloud. "Not out of a cookie tin. It's actually not that complicated, the way I was raised." He smiled. "Your mother'll be fine."

CHAPTER 11
A LITTLE DOOR

Benjamin sank down onto a bench, chalk-white with pain, as Julien scanned the Annecy train station. Five police. Benjamin didn't even notice. He must be in agony.

Traveling so soon had been a mistake. Julien had known that hours ago. Yet if Clément was right — ? This was better than arrest.

"I've done something to it. I can tell. It hurts *so much.*"

"If we make it, it wasn't for nothing. Shh now — wait. All right, they're gone."

Benjamin did not ask who.

The one-kilometer walk from the station to the safe house took over an hour, Benjamin sweating and trembling every time he moved the bad leg. In the foyer Julien had to hold him up as Madame Cantal went for her husband; the three of them carried him to bed. A doctor gave Benjamin painkillers and a very stern lecture Julien couldn't seem to focus on. "A *vet*?" and "two weeks' complete rest" were the only words he heard.

Benjamin slept deep; Julien woke twice, starting up at some blind fear and hearing his friend's slow breathing. The peace of the Bergers' house was gone. The world pressed in around the windows, the street sounds reminding and reminding him how far safety lay. Around his shut lids that night, many nights, questions gathered like ants.

Marcel came and went, sleeping in his little guest room, often leaving at first light. Benjamin slept and slept. Julien paced. Switched on the radio and heard that in Stalingrad the Russians were holding on by their teeth, their backs to the Volga under heavy machine-gun fire. He switched it off, and slipped Grandpa's slim songbook out of his pack.

The Battle Psalm spoke of God carried on the wings of the storm. "He frees the captive from his fetters, He seizes the proud man and drives him from the city." "La Cévenole," in praise of persecuted *camisards* and martyrs, had phrases in it like "hunted from peak to peak" and images of bones lying hidden in deep valleys till judgment day. Julien let the worn page fall from his fingers.

The songwriter called the *camisards* "lions," and the martyrs "sublime." You could tell who the man preferred right there. Did anyone actually want to be sublime?

Had they wanted that? Surely not more than they wanted to protect their families, their villages? *If God will only show Himself.* They had lost their battles. Or had they believed, somehow, that they had won?

Benjamin prayed propped up in bed, murmuring phrases in Hebrew, admitting to Julien afterward that he'd forgotten most of something called the Shemoneh Esrei. Julien knelt and prayed when Benjamin did, rose when he saw that his friend was done. *Help,* he prayed; he asked no questions. Marcel brought a refugee to Benjamin for translation; the man stayed for hours, talking softly in Yiddish and writing down prayers for Benjamin in a tiny script of strange letters.

When they were alone Julien gestured at the paper. "You're not going to . . . ?"

"I'm going to hide it under the carpet. And memorize and burn it before we go." Benjamin pulled out a blank sheet and stared at it, rolling his pen between his fingers. "What did you say again, in the telegram to my mother?"

"Injury prevents travel, safe and recovering."

Benjamin uncapped the pen. "She'll have to listen to me this time."

"About getting your father out?"

Benjamin nodded.

"Do you know how long that'll take?"

"Of course, I know Franco's government like the back of my hand. What are you talking about, Julien?"

"About trying again when it's possible. In the spring."

Benjamin gave him a hard stare.

"Papa says we'll be safer in deep winter. It's so hard to get vehicles up onto the plateau then. And by spring you'll be well —"

"Well enough to do that again? Thank you for asking what my plans are, Julien. I'll tell you. I plan to stay in Tanieux and not waste any more of my family's money on breaking my bones."

"You almost made it. You didn't — it was a *rock*. It wasn't you at all, it was . . ."

It was God.

Julien's blood beat in his ears. His friend's eyes were chips of ice. Benjamin said in a slow and measured voice, "She can get me a visa. You can get me a *passeur*. But you can't put me on a train, because I will not go. Consider this your warning and don't waste your time."

Julien licked dry lips, his sinuses aching. "Benjamin," he said, "it's your *life.*"

"It is," said Benjamin. "Mine. Now if you don't mind, I have a letter to write."

It was God.

It almost seemed true.

A door had opened in his mind, a little door that would not close. Behind it the rock fell, over and over again, for eternity. Benjamin lay broken on the mountainside; Élise hid in the dark of a cave. Heads bowed in the church; bones lay mute beneath the valley grass; men with guns herded families into buses. The rock fell, and fell, and fell.

The next morning, kneeling beside his bed while his friend prayed, Julien found himself not saying *Please.* Only, *What would it have cost You?* He had kept his mouth shut all this time; he had never asked God why. Not when tanks rolled over his country, not when children had to start changing their names. He knew the answers; he had known them from childhood. God's plan behind it all. The infinite preciousness of man's free will. God had His reasons for not stopping the Nazis, that was what it meant. *But this?*

What would it have cost You to stop this? A rock!

Julien dropped his head into his hands, seeing in his mind Benjamin's face go cold at the mention of trying again, seeing Élise shake her head no, dark curly wisps of hair escaping her bun, a terrible calm in her eyes. *God brought us here,* she had said months ago, in the cave.

His response welled up within him, impossible now to force down. The door was open.

Are you sure?

Behind his closed eyelids he saw her: that diamond-hard light in her eyes, that intense, wary grace. Would she go quietly, when they took her away?

What would it have cost You?

He rose from his knees and walked away, ignoring Benjamin's stare.

Elisa sat on a sofa in the common room of her dorm, Nadine's feet tucked under her leg for warmth as they read a Molière play to each other. From the other couch Eva laughed at one of the lines, and Nadine grinned shyly. From the open door they caught a few words from a boy standing out on the stoop: ". . . need to ask Madame Mireille — madame, do you have any milk that you could spare?"

191

The alert. They were on their feet in an instant, Madame Mireille calling after them as they flew up the stairs: "Alexandra and Marie should come too! And dress warm!"

Alexandra seemed annoyed at being revealed to be Jewish, offering Elisa a tight-lipped frown.

"It's a *raid,*" Elisa snapped.

"I'm French, I don't need to hide!"

"Downstairs. Two minutes." Elisa stalked out.

Elisa and Tova were the first downstairs; Elisa gripped her sister's hand as Madame Mireille thrust girls at her and the other leaders. Tova — Nicole — Eva — Alexandra. *Just my luck.* "No talking," Elisa hissed to her group as the cook filled her satchel.

The sky was blue, the wind cold in the treetops. She knew the landmarks by heart. The little path, the rock, twenty paces after the burned tree. Nicole was quiet on her crutches. The low shelter of pine boughs was as hard to see as Elisa remembered, and as small. She spread the blankets from her pack over the other girls, crawled in between Tova and Eva, and prayed.

For Karl, for themselves, for every soul in hiding today, breathing quiet as the hunter passed. In the green shade she studied the tiny stitches in the gloves Julie Altman had made her, and asked God silently if there was a chance for her friend. Farm dogs barked in the distance. She prayed all the psalms she knew, then all of them again.

She woke with a start. The light was slanting. Nicole was up on her elbow, looking eastward. "They've stopped barking," she murmured.

Elisa frowned, but Eva made a tiny gesture at the empty woods. "They can't hear us." They all listened for the all clear, a song called "Compère Guilleri." A silly little song about a hunting mishap, but every verse ended with *"te laisseras-tu mouri' "*: *Will you let yourself die?* Someone hadn't thought. Or had thought far too much.

"You ever think about going, Élise?" whispered Eva.

"No. Do you?"

"Damien heard Benjamin Keller went. Heard he got through."

"He heard wrong," said Nicole.

Some tiny creature rustled among the pine needles. "What do you know?" whispered Elisa.

"Nothing. Only Magali would have looked different when I said his name yesterday. If she had good news."

Elisa felt the long slow breath go out of

193

Eva. Tova huddled closer.

The wind whined in the pines. High in the small, cold patch of sky she could see from where she lay, a scrap of cloud turned to gold, then darkened into orange. A single bird was singing, over and over. Alexandra stirred suddenly and said, as if anyone had asked her, "They won't arrest citizens."

There was a short, hard silence, the air above Elisa humming with heat. "Wait a month or two. They will."

"You'd like that, would you?"

Elisa raised herself on her elbow, but her sister was up and speaking low through her teeth.

"No she *wouldn't*. She protects people. Even when they're being — *stupid* like you. Our parents thought it was safe in France and now they're deported and my sister — my sister's always . . ."

Tova broke off, breathily. Elisa's mouth had opened, drinking in the chill evening air, eyelids blinking against the welling in her eyes. Here in the woods between Tova and Eva, here under orders to keep the rest safe — this was no place to weep. Tova gripped her hand. She closed her eyes and felt the tears spill down. In the shadows she could only hope that no one saw.

Silence. Then Alexandra's soft, daunted

voice. "Sorry."

Elisa didn't move. Tova shivered. Elisa pulled the blanket up higher over all of them. When Elisa opened her eyes, Alexandra looked away.

The bird had fallen silent. You could feel the long slow dimming begin, in the cold golden light. There was a rustle under the shelter as heads turned suddenly. Away down on the road a young rough voice was singing that a little man named Guilleri had gone hunting partridges. Elisa let out a hard breath and sat up, pushing the blanket off, working her toes to get the blood flowing.

"Good," she said. "Let's go home."

Two days after the Allies invaded North Africa, Julien and Benjamin made it from Annecy to Saint-Étienne without injury. At the *contrôle* Benjamin was calm, presented his papers, and told the gendarme, "I fell down a hill and hit it on a rock." They took a good night's sleep at the safe house in Saint-Étienne and woke early; the sun was just climbing above the slag heaps, the streets almost empty as they walked to the tram stop. As they waited for the tram a man walked by, straight down the middle of the street, uttering a low and continual stream of curses. Two teenage girls beside them gave the man a superior smile. The tram pulled up, its bell dinging, and they climbed aboard.

Two stops later, Julien was on his feet, staring out the window. The hair on the back of his neck had risen, and he wasn't sure why. Little knots of people talking on the sidewalk, gesturing, an intensity between them that felt eerily out of place in the quiet early-morning air. A man spoke to a woman and she grabbed her child, went into her house, and slammed the door while he hurried on. Another man walked down the sidewalk weeping openly. *They've done a roundup, they are right now doing a roundup, we have to get out of this tram* —

"What's that noise?" said Benjamin, struggling to his feet.

"What?"

A far-off mechanical roaring from the north, like the sound of engines bigger than Julien had ever seen. Buses? *Must be dozens of them. I have to get him out of here* — *no. Stay on the tram. Make for the station.* They'd be knocking on doors; they'd have a list. Should he send Benjamin on? Stay and try to warn people?

The tram lurched to a stop. The driver bit off a curse, then fell silent. Somewhere in the streets ahead, the roaring grew. People crowded up against the windows, trying to see; whispers spread back through the tram; then shock in a palpable wave.

Two soldiers in gray-green and hooded German helmets, bright metal plaques on their chests, blocked the street with a barricade between them. Julien's mouth shaped the word *What?*

And in the boulevard beyond, the tanks rolled into view.

Julien watched open-mouthed, his bones turning to water, as the sight he had feared for so long came down the streets of Saint-Étienne. The sight he'd watched and waited for, the year he was sixteen, the year his country fell. It hadn't come then. *The armistice — they're breaking the armistice.*

The massive war machines roared past, their huge treads almost as tall as a man, filling the street with deafening thunder. Stiff-backed soldiers standing up in the gun turrets stared coolly around, secure in their power, expecting no counterattack. There could be none. There was no army anymore, not to speak of — only the unarmed people silent on the sidewalk. The people turning their faces away.

The conquerors had come.

"You'll have to get out," said the conductor in a flat voice. Benjamin drew a sharp breath. Julien looked out on the final defeat of his country, thanked God this was not a roundup, and took his friend's arm.

"Train station," he said. "As fast as we can."

By the time the station was in sight, Julien was frantic. There'd been troops after the tanks, rank upon rank of men singing in German, marching between them and safety. When the field police had let them through, the crowd surged around them till he had to protect Benjamin with his body. They faced two checkpoints, walked straight past their first SS in a crowd of evicted hotel guests spilling off a sidewalk under the calm eyes of gray-uniformed officers. They saw armed Germans forcing their way into houses, watching with long rifles from high windows. None of these things scared Julien as much as the thought that grew in him with every click of his friend's crutches.

They might be stopping the trains. They might have stopped them already.

The shriek of a train whistle was almost drowned by the roar from behind them, distant engines drawing nearer. He urged Benjamin on, though the sweat stood out on his friend's pale forehead. On either side of the station door stood two German field police. Benjamin stopped.

"Today," Julien murmured, not looking at him, "is the safest you will ever be in this city. They're not looking for you."

He thought he felt Benjamin nod.

"We are going to get on a train."

The two field police checked an old woman's papers; a third officer spoke to a Frenchman in a station security uniform, who stood with his fists clenched by his sides, his face stiff and pale. "When they come," the Frenchman said, and the German answered, "*Now.* Go in and tell them." The Frenchman turned on his heel and walked into the station. Julien pulled Benjamin forward.

"Papers." One of the Germans took Julien's papers, frowned at them. "Coat off. Hands on the wall."

Julien's heart pounded. He turned to obey — and saw Benjamin lurch against the doorframe as a German pulled one of his crutches away. Every nerve in his body screamed at him to strike out, to run to his friend's side. *No. You obey.* He put his hands against the wall. The German felt his body all over, patting methodically, as he stood looking straight ahead, trembling with rage. Then with horror as the German picked up his coat to search it.

Benjamin's coat had his papers sewn into the lining.

The other German was prodding and probing at Benjamin's cast as he clutched the doorframe and tried not to cry out.

"He has a broken ankle, monsieur," said Julien in a voice he didn't recognize, wholly empty of the fury and fear in his body. "Please be careful."

"And why is he traveling on that?"

"We're just trying to get home, monsieur."

One of them picked up Benjamin's coat and went through the pockets. He said something in German. Julien's heart paused. The man dropped it and gestured Benjamin onward. Julien knelt to gather up the crutches and the coat, fumbling beneath the scowls of the Germans. He got Benjamin onto the crutches, head bent as the Germans ordered them to hurry up, and shepherded his friend into the station.

"I'm sorry," he murmured. Benjamin didn't seem to hear.

He saw no Germans inside the station. A train stood at the nearest platform; Julien quelled a blind impulse to run toward it. "The train to Dunières?" he asked a man in coveralls. "To Annonay via Firminy and Dunières? Is it still running?"

The man turned blank eyes to him.

"Maybe. That's the one over there. You get on it, I don't know. Maybe they'll let it leave."

The click of Benjamin's crutches was like the tick of a clock, fast, automatic, dead. The railroad worker let them into a packed passenger car where people sat silent, some of them weeping, all staring out the windows. Someone stood to give Benjamin a seat; he managed to whisper his thanks. Shouts were coming from outside the train, an argument. A loud string of curses.

They felt their train car vibrate as the engine roared to life.

The sensation of escaping through the jaws of a trap, Julien reminded himself all through the journey home, was an illusion. They were fish swimming away from the net at blind and desperate speed. Away and away, inward and inward, because they could not swim out.

"They won't come to Tanieux," he whispered once to Benjamin, after they changed at Dunières to the plateau train, and in his heart he cursed himself for being a liar. They would not come with tanks. It didn't matter.

They would come with a list.

Snow lay on the Vivarais mountains as the

train climbed to the plateau, snow on the hills around Tanieux, the whole land hushed and gentle. Gentle and helpless.

He could not bear to look at his friend as the train pulled into Tanieux.

CHAPTER 12
THE HUNTER

It was two days before Christmas, walking out into the crystalline air on a sentry roster errand, that Julien saw his first Gestapo in Tanieux.

He hadn't dreamed it would take so long. He had watched hard, almost glad to have his old duties back and to leave the troop in Sylvain's hands. What mattered now, after all, but standing watch — with the sheltering forest deep and hushed with snow, a tracker's dream, and a cast on Benjamin's leg? Yet the snow was not their enemy, lying in great drifts over the roads down off the plateau. It was the wall of a city under siege. There had been one raid only, during a thaw.

And they'd had warning.

A voice on Pastor Alexandre's telephone: *Watch out! Watch out tomorrow!* Then silence. They had a friend, it seemed. The police — the French police — came the next day, and found no one. But Julien had not relaxed his vigilance.

And still they came when he did not expect them.

Snow blew over the frozen river, settling into little curves and ridges with the eddies of the snow-wind they called the *burle;* he hunched down into his patched coat as he crossed the stone bridge. Along the narrow-dug path up the street into town a Scout came in sight and hailed him urgently. Julien ran to meet him.

Benjamin was out there, at some unknown house, translating some nameless person's instructions: *Follow your guide twenty meters behind. Remember you don't know him.* It was his third translation this week. He'd begged to go.

"Soft alert," murmured the Scout. "Two Gestapo off the train a couple minutes ago, headed for the *place du centre.*" He walked off singing "A La Volette."

Julien threaded the streets toward his assigned route, singing it too.

Benjamin was who knew where. Élise was at her dorm. Right on the Rue de la Gare, the Gestapo would pass by it, why had she moved into town? Julien stopped at Gilles's house to pass on the alert, then took a route that would take him past Élise's dorm to start his own streets. "The branch was dry and it broke," he sang, and saw faces turn to him from behind a window, and a young girl retreat from the room. "My little bird, where are you hurt?" he sang, remembering the one and only time — till yesterday — that Élise had set foot inside his house. She came with others from school to hear Benjamin's full story in private; Julien made a fool of himself, asking her why she wouldn't drink the tea. The next day on Benjamin's advice he had gone down to La Roche to ask a rabbinical student known as Jacques Marlot how to make a teacup kosher, then ransacked the attic for his old tin cup, rejected it twice as too ugly, and brought it down to be boiled fully immersed at a rolling boil. And looked away when Mama called him a considerate young man, trying to silence the mocking voice in his mind: *Why don't you boil yourself at a rolling boil, stupid? Still won't make* you *kosher. Why don't you just stop?*

He had tried to stop. He couldn't. His first day back at school after returning from the Alps, she had walked in and seen him and Benjamin, taken them in with the slightest widening of her eyes, and stood perfectly still a few seconds, breathing carefully. It was clear she had understood everything.

How could a mere moment's pause, a slow, careful step, have such heartbreaking courage shining through them like a lamp? She had lost so much. She stood to lose everything. And yet she moved through the world with such self-possession. Those attentive eyes, that mind behind them poised and watchful as a hunting cat. Hunting and hunted. She was so young. Was everyone's soul that beautiful? Was he seeing reality as it was for the very first time?

Or was he losing his mind?

It was her face he saw, and only her face, as he climbed the streets, as he came to the intersection. Her face, and the hard light in her eyes, and the softening of it as she held out her hands to take the steaming cup from Mama, his cup, just yesterday. Her face, and still her face, as he walked out into the *place du centre* singing, within sudden sight of the enemy. Her face, and the high black boots, the black coats and blood-red armbands bearing their twisted cross. Her face, and the proud eyes sizing up the quiet people like cattle too thin to buy.

"You, boy!" A black-clad arm beckoned.

Julien forced his gaze upward, past the impossibly broad chest of the blond man to the chiseled face of the other, the one who had spoken, with his straight, sure shoulders, his bright cold eyes. He thought of the word *noble,* the word *warrior.* Anyone would have thought of them. He felt sick.

"Do you know where the pastors live?"

Julien cursed the *s* in that question, his face like stone, still as old gray-white ice. He nodded.

"Tell them they're wanted at the *mairie.*" The man turned on his heel and walked on.

Julien did as he was told.

He kept singing. He passed the alert to Philippe; he sent a boy to find Pastor Alexandre. He thought of the hiding place they'd made in the attic for Benjamin. He thought of Mama. He took the way to his own street.

He delivered his message, looking past his parents to the kitchen window. Papa stood without a word. Mama closed her eyes.

Julien turned away. "I have to finish the alert."

"Sit down, Mama." Magali's flat voice came from behind him as he watched his father walk down the stairs to go where he'd been summoned. "I'll make you some tea."

Two hours later Julien climbed up to the landing, stripping off his gloves, put his chilled hands under his armpits for a minute to warm them, and opened the door. Papa sat at the kitchen table drinking warmed-over *mélisse* tea, its lemon scent spreading faintly through the air. Mama was wiping the same spot on the table over and over. Before Julien could speak she lifted her head and said to Papa, "And what *would* make you?"

"If it became clear it was what God wanted . . ."

Mama squeezed out the dishrag hard and splashed fresh water onto it.

Julien closed the door. "What happened?"

"It was a warning," said Papa. A look passed between him and Mama. "That fellow wanted to . . . introduce himself. Kriminalkomissar Haas. He's the regional head based in Le Puy. He came to let us know we're in his jurisdiction."

Mama turned a steady, slightly chilly gaze on her husband. "And what else did he say?"

Papa sighed. "He said, 'The French police have done excellent service, and are still handling most matters, as you may have noticed. We don't wish this to make you forget we are here. Anger us, and we will jog your memory.' "

Mama turned fully away, wiping at the clean edge of the sink, her head high and her back very straight. You almost couldn't see her shake.

■ ■ ■ ■

They held their quiet Christmas — a young pine hung with candles, a hushed service in the candlelit church. A hand-knit sweater for each of them, made from the yarn unraveled from their old ones. Papa read the Christmas story aloud; at the quote "Get up, take your wife and the child, and flee to Egypt," Mama turned her face for a moment toward the wall.

On the twenty-sixth they invited Élise and her siblings. For tea, and sweet wrinkled apples from Grandpa's root cellar; for a chance at Élise's rare smile. For the sober way she talked to Papa, like a woman grown and older than Julien already; for the way she stood behind her sister's chair, that silent watchfulness in her eyes and hands. He could see how she would look, how she would watch, with a child of her own. He escaped into the bathroom and pressed his hands against his eyes until they hurt, until he saw red and white in the dark behind his lids. *Stop. Stop. There's nothing in this for you but pain.*

He couldn't stop.

He started spending breaks in the hotel dining room, where students daunted by the plateau's cold kept to one side away from the hotel's handful of winter guests. Élise sat with Nicole, their dark heads bent low together, talking quietly. They cast a wary eye now and then at the hotel guests.

Except the new guest, who came the second week of January. He rated a long, slow, covert stare. Julien saw both their mouths open, breathing him in, and his own mouth tightened.

He tried to see what they were seeing. Soft, wavy brown hair, he supposed. Broad shoulders and strong arms, and a catlike sureness in the man's body as he sauntered up to the bar. In his smile, in his bright brown eyes glancing about the room. Who did he think he was?

The young man ordered, tapped a cigarette out of a full pack on the bar, returned the pack to his fine shirt's pocket, and lit up. A rich guy. No one smoked anymore, especially brand-new cigarettes, except Germans and black-market fat cats. *And which are you?*

The girls whispered together, and turned their chairs a little inward, toward the wall.

"I know what he is," Pierre said at Scouts. "Antoine Duval. He's an informer."

"What?" breathed Julien.

210

His friend's face was stony, that boastful Pierre grin nowhere to be seen. "Or an inspector or something. Monsieur Pérac thinks he's actually police himself." He lowered his voice. "He offered the Péracs eight hundred francs and ten extra ration tickets if they'd point him to one foreign Jew. A thousand five hundred for a *résistant,* two thousand if a weapon was found during the arrest."

Nobody spoke.

"They said no," said Pierre.

Sylvain made a small rough sound in his throat. "Nobody would. Not in Tanieux."

"Never," said Julien, but his stomach tightened. You could buy a heifer with that kind of money. People were hungry. *Not in Tanieux.*

The man was everywhere. In the street, the bookstore, the café. In the post office, mailing a fat package to some police address in Vichy, in front of God and everybody, returning an easy, courteous nod to the postmistress's grim stare. Everywhere, but especially in the hotel dining room. Smiling. Leaning back in his chair and lighting up with smooth, leisured grace. Élise and Nicole weren't there anymore for those bright eyes to light on; Julien had told them the instant he knew. He'd told everyone

211

what the man was. A traitor to his nation in the pay of Vichy, a sniffing hound for the Nazis. Every stitch he put on his self-sure shoulders bought with blood.

On a bitter night in late January Julien walked past his parents' bedroom door and saw Mama sitting on the bed with her hand pressed against her mouth, tears running down her face. An open suitcase lay beside her. Her other hand clutched one of Papa's shirts.

Julien froze. She turned away from him. "I'm sorry," he murmured, making to go.

But he couldn't tear his eyes off that shirt.

"I'm sorry," said Mama. "I should have —"

"Did something — is there — ?"

"He packed it. In case. In case they —" A sharp sob shook her, and she covered her mouth again. "I'm sorry," she said finally. "I've tried, Julien, so hard. He deserves for me to support him — all he's doing, all he's done — he packed it himself to spare me. He forgot to pack *socks*. I've tried so hard, but . . ." She raised her eyes, red around the edges, coal-black in the center, and her voice went low and hard. "I'm done."

Julien opened his mouth, but no sound came out.

"I'm sorry." She wiped her eyes with the

back of one hand. "Parents are supposed to be strong." She laid the shirt down on the bed and refolded it carefully, smoothing out the wrinkles she had made. She put it in the suitcase, her movements neat and controlled, and he almost jumped when the next words out of her mouth, in that dark voice again, were, "Parents die like anyone else when they're shot."

Mama. He couldn't get the word out. *Mama, what? Mama, stop.*

"And so do heroes." She closed the suitcase. Tears were streaming down her face. "I'm sorry," she whispered. "You should go."

He tried one more time to find his voice; then he turned, and went.

Chapter 13
Anyone Else

On a black night in late January Benjamin came home staring, limping worse than he had since he'd had his cast off. "It's nothing. Slipped on some ice. Really Julien, it's nothing at all. Listen. Listen to me." Benjamin's pupils were wide. "I . . . The police. I got the police — interested in me." He sank onto the couch.

"Interested?" Julien said. Papa came out of his study and nodded at Benjamin to go on.

"I got called away from translating. They needed me at the train station right away — two young guys, they were getting agitated in German and wouldn't go with their guide. One of them had lost his papers on the train. There was nothing we could do, the train was gone, I said he had to come away. Then we heard an engine, it didn't sound like Monsieur Faure's auto, so F— the guide had me hide them in a shed.

There wasn't room for us. There wasn't any time to run. We just walked down the alley like we were supposed to be there, right into the headlights. They checked our papers. They were checking everyone."

Julien chewed on a knuckle.

"They looked at mine a long time." Benjamin's voice was dropping. "They said I wasn't on their list but my status was very 'unclear.' "

Julien hissed through his teeth.

Papa stared at the fire. "We'll have to move you."

Benjamin sat up straight. "What do you mean?"

"Likely to a very isolated farm. Not my father's place, I think. I could delegate Madame Thiers so that we truthfully won't know where —"

"No."

Papa looked up.

"I can't stop working. Protecting me isn't the only thing. I saved two people's lives tonight!"

"Benjamin, there are other interpreters —"

"And why do you call on me so often if there's so many?"

Papa sighed. "Because you are young, and the young are more often ignored. And because I believed your French citizenship protected you."

"If I *am* still a citizen."

"Indeed."

There was a brief silence. Benjamin looked up at Papa with dark eyes, his breath coming fast. "Let me keep working, Monsieur Losier. Please."

"Benjamin . . ." Papa raked a hand through his hair, eyes uncertain.

"I'm not a child anymore. This is my choice. If it's a bad choice, I'll be responsible. Only me."

"That is not how your parents will approach the matter."

"I'll tell them I defied you and wouldn't go. I already defied them."

"You put so much in your letters, Benjamin?"

"We have a code. We worked it out in one of the letters you sent the safe way. *Bad dream* means a raid — *Marseille* means Switzerland. Monsieur . . ." Benjamin looked Papa in the eye for a long, intent moment. "You know, Monsieur Losier. You're staying too."

Papa covered his face with one hand. A log in the fire cracked loud in the silence.

After a while Papa nodded.

■ ■ ■ ■

The gray-white cold of February set in. The cold of death.

People huddled deep into their coats, walking between walls of crusted snow, between drifts the *burle* swirled into dune-like curves, dry glittering snow dancing like knives in the air. Julien worked after school with the other Scouts, delivering emergency firewood to the households that needed it most. The cold touched exposed skin like an enemy, moment by moment stealing more warmth. More life. It seeped in through the cracks, relentless, through the thin windowpanes, gathering, waiting for the fire's blaze to falter. In the mornings it was a presence in Julien's room, watching with cold eyes as he fled down the stairs to where Mama built up the fire.

Mama moved through the days with steady hands and lost eyes: wood on the fire, sheets on the beds, potatoes in the pot, all done without seeming to look at them. There was a silence between her and Papa, at mealtimes, that made Julien shiver and Magali hunch in on herself.

Papa took his shortwave radio out of the attic and sent Julien to hide it at Grandpa's farm. Julien put it in the root cellar under a heavy stack of potato crates, wrapped in a burlap sack. Then he loaded his sled with turnips and trudged home.

The next day he saw the Gestapo again.

Not the same men. Two new ones, striding through the bright cold air in their black coats and high black boots. Julien watched them, heart pounding. They turned away from the *place,* toward the train station.

He got to school early and walked straight into Élise's classroom, to the corner where she and Magali sat.

Magali looked up as he came in. "I saw them too."

"They went to the café and the *mairie.*" said Élise. "Louis told us. Then they watched the people get off the train and asked the stationmaster questions. They didn't arrest anybody."

"And Monsieur Bernard told them he was sure he would have noticed anything illegal going on in *his* station," said Magali, her eyes lit.

"Louis says they laughed," added Élise.

Through the open classroom door they heard a shout. A flurry of voices, exclamations. Magali sprang to her feet, but at that moment Mademoiselle Combe strode through the door, stripping off her gloves, face flushed and eyes shining.

"The Germans have surrendered at Stalingrad," she said.

Magali froze, her mouth open.

"Surrendered?" Élise's voice was calm and even, but in her eyes was a flame.

"Hitler tried to make them fight to the last man. Win at any price. But the Russians would not give up their city. Sit down, class. I couldn't possibly teach today. I'm going to read to you from the *Iliad.* Hector's farewell. Yes. In their honor."

Julien watched Élise, wishing he could stay. Her eyes had turned dark at the word *farewell,* and she sat very still. She raised them, and they met his for a long moment, like the dark surface of an untouched well.

"Clawing up to the heights," quoted Mademoiselle Combe, "headlong pride crashes down the abyss — to its doom."

In Élise's eyes the fire lit again.

The Gestapo did not return.

Duval came to church.

He sat in the far-left side of a middle row, near one of the side doors. He had a notebook. He sat there twiddling his pen and burning a hole in Julien's brain, as Pastor Alexandre proclaimed that the worshippers of force believed their power stronger than

God's, and that great would be their fall. "The meek shall inherit the earth," he thundered, and Julien watched, out of the corner of his eye, the slightest sideways movement of Duval's head. "How is this possible? Is it not clear that the world belongs to the strong? To those who have the biggest guns, and the ruthlessness to use them? And yet we have the witness of our Lord Himself to the contrary: the meek shall inherit the earth. Brethren, it *is* possible, by the power of God. And by the power of God," his voice dropped, tightened, focused in quiet power, "it is sure."

Duval made a note.

Julien went to Pastor Alexandre. It was the only thing he could think of. Going to Papa was no good.

"I know," said the pastor mildly. His blue eyes seemed to go right through Julien. "I've been told. To be frank I would be surprised if he *didn't* take notes."

"What are you going to do about it, pastor?"

"We cannot muzzle the Word of God on account of this man. God is faithful."

Julien looked down at the pastor's scarred desk, and raised his head slowly. "Of course He's faithful. What would make you say He isn't? If you're trying to say we'll be all right, it doesn't exactly follow."

"I know you are concerned for your father, Julien. We are being careful. There is a reason he hasn't preached since August. At the same time, his administrative skills are desperately needed here." The pastor's blue eyes met Julien's where they were this time instead of piercing to the back of his skull. "He has made his decision freely. I'm afraid that is all I can tell you."

The conversation seemed to be over. Julien felt small, shrunken; he studied the dry, chapped skin on the backs of his folded hands, then shifted finally in his chair and stood. "Thank you, *monsieur le pasteur,*" he said, his voice seeming to come from far away.

He walked home in the bitter darkness, hunched in his scarf, the stars like holes in the cold black sky.

Julien shoveled snow, brought in wood for Mama. In the mornings he whispered a quick Lord's Prayer and fled downstairs to the fire. He watched the meek go by in the streets of Tanieux; he watched the meek get off the train and melt into the alleys in the cold half dusk, following some Scout with a sled. He watched the strong stride across

221

the *place* in their uniforms — blue for Vichy or black for Hitler, they came, and they came again. He hid Benjamin in the attic and whisked the ladder away to hide it. He went back out and watched the strong walk the streets, and tried to tell himself what he believed, but his tongue tangled, and in his throat was silence.

Benjamin came down when they were gone and shut himself in his room. Julien heard him chanting in Hebrew. His throat tightened and burned. He did not know why.

Benjamin watched Mama. Showed up in the kitchen when she cooked, set the table for her, carried the soup pot. She gave him a rare smile as he set it on the table. Papa came out of his study and smiled back at her. "It smells delicious, Maria."

It did. Leeks and potatoes in real chicken broth. The sweet, hot steam of it rising into the evening light defied the dead world outside. With that warmth in their bellies they could, for a moment, look each other in the eyes.

"We had some good news today," said Papa, scraping the bottom of his bowl. Then looked up quickly at the sound of boots on the stairs. Benjamin stood and vanished silently into Papa's study. Mama gathered up his place setting in both hands and shoved it all into the icebox. Papa opened the door.

A stranger in a blue police uniform stood on the stoop. His eyes were red. They fixed on Papa and did not leave him.

No one moved or spoke. The air had become a thick, viscous thing Julien had to force into his lungs. It filled his chest painfully and hardened there. A second policeman came up behind the first. Mama's eyes stood out black in her bloodless face. Papa was a statue, staring at the policeman.

The stranger's eyes dropped first. "I'm very sorry, monsieur. I'm under orders to arrest you."

If you're sorry — if you're sorry — The thought wouldn't finish itself.

"Do you need —" The man's voice stuck in his throat. "To pack a bag?"

Mama rose without a word and walked into the bedroom. She brought the suitcase out and gave it to Papa.

"Where're you taking him?" Magali was on her feet, hands flat on the table, leaning forward.

The policeman dipped his head. "To headquarters in Le Puy, mademoiselle. Those are my orders."

"And then? And then where?"

"I don't know, mademoiselle."

Julien saw the muscles by his father's jawline shift. Saw him swallow.

The sound of voices in the stairwell. The policemen stepped aside. Madame Rostin entered in her worn gray dress, jaw set and eyes a little frightened, a newspaper-wrapped package in her hand. "We heard," she said, and pressed it into Papa's hands. "For you."

Mama was looking at Papa, dry-eyed. Her face seemed brittle somehow, her skin suddenly thin. Had the shape of her skull always been so visible?

"They're waiting," murmured the second policeman. The first one gave Papa the slightest nod. "The car is down in the *place*," he said. "Please come with me."

Julien stood. His father turned slightly; he could see his face working, as if not to collapse, as he looked from Mama to the policeman, to Magali, to Julien.

To the door.

"You must come," said the policeman, his voice still soft, but with a certainty in it. He was sorry. But he had no plans to be a hero today.

After all, heroes died like anyone else when they were —

Julien's fingernails bit into his palms. He

could hear the swash of the blood beating in his ears, that stupid, primitive song: *Run, run. Fight, fight.* Useless, powerless, hopeless, in a time when the only safety was to hide or bow. *My father. They're taking my —*

"I'm so sorry, Maria," Papa whispered. She was in his arms. Trembling. Then she was half out of them, giving him a long, gentle kiss. The policemen looked away. Julien's heart turned over at the bright, painful vision that flashed through his mind, the image of his parents young and in love. *One last kiss.* Mama broke off. Turned away. Papa's face was like a stranger's. A man afraid for his life. He took Magali by the shoulders and kissed her four times. Then Julien, Papa's rough cheek against his own, Papa's hands gripping his shoulders, Papa still here with him in this kitchen for another moment, and another, and another. *The last time I saw my father.* Élise didn't know where her parents had been taken, didn't even know — *Those are my orders.*

Papa bent his head, and stepped over the threshold. His hands trembled as he set down the suitcase and pulled on his coat. His hat, his scarf. So cold out there, so cold.

Papa picked up the suitcase and started down the stairs.

CHAPTER 14
THE MEEK

They sang "A Mighty Fortress" as the black police automobile pulled away.

The people of Tanieux sang it together, their voices echoing thin yet strong against the housefronts as they stood shoulder to shoulder in the *place* watching their beloved Pastor Alexandre go. *And two others.* Julien hunched down in his coat to hide his unmoving lips, seeking only a last glimpse of his father's face, his father's hand, blurred through glass, eclipsed by the bulky form of the third man — Monsieur Astier, arrested for forgery — and then gone. The bright trail of the taillights vanishing round the corner lingered in Julien's vision as the sure voices rose around him:

The Prince of Darkness grim
we tremble not for him . . .

Mama's eyes were like black pebbles in

her face.

The walk home. The people surrounding his family, protecting them, too late. His mother shaking her head rigidly at their offers of help. Benjamin at the door. Julien didn't know what he said to him, whether he spoke. Mama gathering them all up suddenly, shaking like a piece of clockwork wound too tight, saying, "I can't." Then she was gone into the bedroom, locking the door.

The table with the dirty dishes still on it. One spoonful of soup still in Papa's bowl.

The silence, worse than sound, from Mama's room.

Magali running the dishwater, the good plashing sound of it in the basin, the home sound. Magali's half whisper, telling them where to put the plates away, and the breadboard — Julien heaping precious wood on the fire, anything to keep the cold and the dark at bay. The lost eyes in the others' faces, watching that fire dance its hardest, watching it believe and believe: a flame of hope against the night, flaring and living and warming its world. Flickering. Falling.

Going out.

The hours in the dark with the cold seeping in. The pictures his mind could not keep out, any more than his thin bedroom windows could keep out the frost. His thoughts turning in circles, like a wolf pacing its cage. *Fools. The meek shall inherit the earth. The meek shall inherit the scorched, frozen earth, ringed with barbed wire. The strong shall inherit the guard towers.*

The slow, disconsolate creeping of the pale morning light.

He dressed slowly, letting the cold take bites out of his flesh. He took the stairs down to the back door and brought up wood, found Magali ahead of him, lighting the fire. "Thanks," she whispered as he set his load on hers. Mama's bedroom door was still closed. "You could go down to the *boulangerie.*"

Papa had bought the bread every morning since they moved to Tanieux. Julien nodded and went to put on his coat.

The *boulanger* gave him his bread for free.

Mama did not come out. They ate a hushed breakfast and left the dishes in the sink. Built the fire high and went out together into the icy wind.

At school there was a prayer meeting. Voluntary, but the Jewish kids stayed. They sang "A Mighty Fortress Is Our God" again:

But still our ancient foe

doth seek to work us woe;
his craft and power are great,
and armed with cruel hate,
on earth is not his equal.

The cold had crept in behind Julien's eyes and made a numbness there, a dim and cloudy space. His friends came around him, but he couldn't quite make out their words.

When they came home Mama was putting lunch on the table. Potato *galette* and cooked carrots. She laid five place settings, then took one away. They sat and looked at each other.

Papa had always said grace.

Finally Julien cleared his throat. "We could sing *'Pour ce repas, pour toute joie.'*"

Mama opened her mouth, but her voice was inaudible. Without her they limped through the song. They ate, the scrape of forks loud on their plates, till Mama spoke.

"Your grandfather."

"Yes?" asked Magali after a pause.

"Monsieur Raissac said he'd tell him. He should have come." Mama rubbed her thumb along the edge of her plate. "I don't."

A longer pause.

"You don't what?" said Magali, tilting her head.

"He's not *here.*"

"Do you want me to go get him this afternoon?" said Julien.

"No. Go to school. That's what your father wants."

"Are you sure, Mama?"

"You should do what your father wants." Her voice was harsh.

He went to school.

It was when he came home that he understood.

They came in from the landing together, Julien and Benjamin, taking off their snow-dusted boots. Magali had stopped at the café where her friend Rosa worked. Mama's door was open.

On the bed lay a suitcase, half packed.

Mama turned from the closet and laid hard, determined eyes on them. "There you are. I'm going. I'm sorry. Your grandfather can help you with your meals and all. I've got to take the five-thirty train."

"Mama?"

"It must be illegal. She's not even of age. I'll stay with Madame Astier's cousin in Le Puy and I won't come home till they release her. Pastor Alexandre would know who to talk to. But he's gone. We can't rely on Pastor Alexandre anymore." She put two skirts in the suitcase. "I won't let them have her."

"Have *who*?"

She stared at him, aghast, then spoke in a harsh, clipped voice as if he'd committed an unforgivable fault. "Your *sister,* Julien."

"Mama — what?"

Benjamin had turned pale. "Madame Losier," he said carefully, "Magali is at the café."

Mama lowered her hands, staring. "They arrested her last night."

Julien's body went slack. There was such assurance in her angry face. She really thought — could she be — ? How could he imagine such a thing of his mother? It was him, it was *him* that was going . . .

Mad.

"Madame," Benjamin was saying, "they arrested your husband —"

"Do you think I don't know that?" snapped Mama, turning red. "What's happened to you two? If he was here I'd ask him to do it! But he's *not.* I don't know how to talk to those men, I may be nothing but a *paysanne* with no education, but I'm not going to sit here and let them have my *baby* —" a sharp sob wrenched out of her, and she put her face in her hands and wept.

Julien broke from his paralysis and murmured to Benjamin, "Run and get her."

Benjamin ran.

Julien took one step closer to his mother. Then he turned back as Benjamin reached the door, and cried out suddenly in a voice he hardly recognized, it was so high, so nakedly afraid: *"And don't tell anyone!"*

Benjamin shook his head, his face gone pale. The door closed behind him.

Julien took another step toward his mother, then another. "She's coming home," he said softly. "She'll be here in a few minutes, you'll see."

Mama raised a tear-wet face. "What are you *talking about?*"

"She's — she's at the café, Mama. She's coming —"

"What is this *nonsense?*" She blazed with anger. She was like she had been when he was small, when Magali pulled his hair and he hit her — he felt six years old, looking into those righteous black eyes. "I saw them take her away with my own eyes, Julien! I don't have time for this — whatever this is." She wiped her tears away and slid the suitcase off the bed. "It's five ten."

Julien swallowed and squared his shoulders in the doorway. "Please wait just —"

She was coming toward him. His soul cringed back from her, but he didn't move. She came up almost against him, the top of her head level with his nose, and looked up at him, her eyes terrible in her livid face. Her voice dropped to a harsh, trembling whisper that chilled him to the bone. "Get out of my way."

"I'm sorry, Mama —"

"Get out of my way this instant!" she shouted into his face, and he recoiled, sharp pain starting in his chest and throat.

He put up a shaking hand as she blazed at him, and his voice cracked: "She's at the café! I swear she is!" He grabbed the doorframe with both hands as she pushed at him. "It's not real, she's at the café, she's coming, just wait two minutes and you'll see, she's at the café, Mama, she's at —"

She pushed him again, and he staggered. Her dark betrayed eyes were centimeters from his. "Please trust me, Mama," he whispered, and saw her lips part and her teeth bare in fury.

Behind him he heard footsteps on the stairs.

He heard the door open. Mama's eyes went wide. The joy in her face hurt to see.

He stepped aside, and she ran to her daughter.

Julien slumped against the doorframe as Mama wept on Magali. Magali gave him a hunted, pleading look.

He backed away to where Benjamin stood,

his heart hammering as if he'd just faced a gun.

"I didn't tell anyone," Benjamin whispered. "Is your grandfather coming?"

Night was falling deep blue outside the window. Surely he'd have started as soon as he heard. "I don't know."

It was not over.

Grandpa didn't come. Mama didn't cook. She started to lay a fire in the stove then walked away from it. Julien found her in the bedroom, packing again.

There was a tip-off from Monsieur Faure this time. So she said. A man from some Resistance or Maquis group had warned him their whole family was in danger. They would take the train to Saint-Agrève and then walk into the Ardèche. She was sorry she had let her fear for Magali confuse her. Julien listened to this last with his mouth open, then asked when Monsieur Faure had spoken to her.

"Julien, you were standing right there."

"I must not have heard," he mumbled, and fled.

Ten minutes later she came out of the bedroom believing Magali had been arrested.

The lost look on Mama's face, as she wept and held her daughter's rigid shoulders, was too much for Julien. He fled into the kitchen and found Benjamin there sitting in the dark. It was deep night outside, and none of them had eaten. He stepped back into the living room, and quailed as Mama snapped, "Of course he did! Julien! Tell her!"

"Monsieur Faure . . . ?" Magali asked him in a voice that quavered.

He gave his head a tiny shake, his eyes on Magali's. Mama saw.

He stood still beneath her anger, shutting his eyelids tight against the face of a mother when her own children turned on her. She said, *"Look at me,"* and he looked at her. Magali said something he didn't hear, then pulled back suddenly as Mama reached for her. He ran into the bathroom and stood with his hands pressed against his face, breathing raggedly.

After a while the voices moved off into the bedroom.

He walked into the kitchen, light-headed, and flipped the switch. The glare off the night windows hurt his eyes. He dug shakily through the icebox: turnips, beets, carrots, a single egg. A stub of bread left on the breadboard. The voices from the bedroom were growing shriller. Benjamin opened cupboards and closed them, his eyes lost. Julien found a pot and ran some water.

Boiled potatoes, you put them in boiling water and they boil, right? He had never felt so useless in his life. He had just bent to put more sticks in the stove when the knock came at the door.

He froze.

It came again, light and firm. Benjamin gestured to the living-room window. "I saw Élise go in the downstairs door."

Julien's heart caught. "Alone?"

Benjamin nodded.

Julien looked at the dishes in the sink, the cold pot of water on the cold stove. Magali's voice from the bedroom rose high and desperate, "Mama, I swear! It's *not real*!"

Julien went to the door and opened it.

Élise stood on the landing, a scarf wrapped around her dark hair. Her eyes went to Julien then swiftly past him, as the opening door let the sound come through to her, the sound of helplessness and fear. Julien bent his head.

"Please come in," he said.

CHAPTER 15
IF GOD WILL ONLY
SHOW HIMSELF

Élise walked in like a miracle. A living, breathing miracle of God.

She stood in the doorway as Julien cringed at the voices coming through the bedroom door; stood there flicking her eyes between the dirty dishes in the sink and the tangled mess of beets and carrots on the table, one side of her lip caught between her teeth. Then she spoke.

"Have you eaten?"

Julien shook his head.

She pulled off her scarf. "Is that your pantry?" Then hesitated. "Is it all right if I —"

"Yes." The word leapt out of Julien.

It was as though the kitchen filled with warm wind: finally, a sure voice to follow. "The fire first — smallest wood you have — get it to coals as fast as you can. Does your mother have a grater? Benjamin, would you peel these potatoes? Is that a meat knife —

wait, never mind. Do you have any oil or lard?"

Ten minutes later Mama emerged from the bedroom, drawn perhaps by the mouth-watering scent of the first potato pancake. Julien could take his eyes off it only because *she* stood at the stove, her face calm, her deep brown eyes lifting to meet his mother's.

"You . . ." Mama made an aborted gesture, staring.

Élise ducked her head apologetically. "Won't you please sit down, madame? You've had such a hard time. Here." She pulled out a chair and served the pancake onto a plate. "They're called latkes. My mother taught me to make them."

Mama sank into the chair. "You shouldn't be here. It's not safe for you."

"Julien, some water in the glasses? I'll go home very soon, madame." She put another latke in the pan. Julien nudged a fork toward Mama.

He had never known what food meant. Not in the worst days of the first shortages after the invasion, when he'd dreamed of it constantly. He had never known how much was in it, in the fire that warmed it, the hands that offered; he had never seen the light that wove around it, setting the twisted

238

world straight again. He had been an utter fool.

Élise gave him the second latke.

He should have passed it on to Benjamin or Magali. He didn't. She had given it to him with her own hands. He sat gazing at it, at the calm in Élise's gestures as she served the next one onto Magali's plate, a calm that imprinted itself on the air, the miracle turning round and round them unseen like a gentle wind. The scent of fried potato filled his nostrils. He drew it into the depths of his lungs, feeling that he hadn't drawn a single breath since yesterday.

When she had served the last one, the others looked at him. He bowed his head and began to sing *"Pour ce repas." For this food, and for all joy, we praise you, Lord.* He picked up his fork, then looked up at Élise. She stood smiling at them all, a smile suddenly false, painted-on, wrong as the dissonant note that had filled her with such frozen fury at the piano the day he had seen her soul. He put down his fork and stood abruptly. Filled the kettle and put it on the stove. Took her kosher cup out of the cupboard and filled it with water from the tap. He set the cup in front of Papa's chair, and looked at her.

She pulled Papa's chair out with hesitant

hands and sat, wrapping her fingers around the cup as if it could warm her. Her eyes met his, brown and clear as a pool with oak leaves at the bottom.

"Thank you," she said, and drank.

"I want you all to go up and pack as soon as the table's cleared," said Mama. The morning sun shone through the kitchen window on her neatly brushed hair. Magali stared at her red-eyed. They had shared a bed last night. "When I've done the dishes I'll go ask Madame Thiers about a hiding place for us." Mama took her plate to the kitchen sink.

Julien slipped out onto the landing and put on his boots, tying the knee flaps as high as they would go. Magali came out and shut the door and stood watching him.

"I'll go," she said suddenly.

Julien looked up. "You can't. You know what she'll do."

"Am I quitting school now, then?"

"I don't know, Magali —"

"And staying with her all day and night? Do you have any idea what that was like?" Tears were streaming down her face unheeded. "And are you gonna feed this family while I do that or" — she fluttered a hand down the stairs — "go do *important man things* out of the house? Cause I can't put three meals on the table and keep her from walking out the door at the same time by myself. You got a girl to rescue you last night, but she's got a *job.* Cooking. Every noon and night except her Sabbath, and you know she's not breaking *that* for you —"

"I have to go get Grandpa!"

"I'm just wondering what else you're going to have to do." Her tear-streaked face was like granite. "And how often."

Julien tightened his jaw and put on his coat.

The door opened, and Benjamin slipped out. "I'll go."

They looked at him. "We could hear some of that," he added. "She wants to talk to you, Julien."

Julien stood for a long moment looking down the stairs.

Then he began taking off his coat.

"I'm sorry, Mama," said Julien, his eyes on the table.

"Sorry has nothing to do with it," his mother snapped. "Your father is gone. I'm responsible for this family's safety. You will explain why you are making plans behind my back to keep me in the house. And you will stop it *immediately.* I am working my hardest to overlook your disrespect, believe me. Because this is an emergency. Look at me, Julien."

He gathered a breath and wrenched his eyes up to hers. They were hard and sharp and determined. They didn't look mad at all.

"Tell me you're going to obey me."

His eyes flew to the window behind her, to the fire, to the door.

"I may not be him, but I'm all you have left, Julien. You will look at me and promise to do as I say."

His throat tightened painfully. His eyes found hers again though his vision wavered, and he forced the words out. "I can't."

Her eyes were black and rimmed with red, tears flowing down her face. "You never respected me like you did him. I accepted it. I never even finished school, I was never his equal — but I didn't expect *this.*"

"I respect you, Mama." His voice was a croak. "It's not that. It's got nothing to do with Papa, or you not finishing school, I swear."

"Then tell me what on earth is going on!"

He tried to square his shoulders. He had never felt smaller. He looked her in the eye and forced his lips open, and told her shakily how she had told him Magali was arrested when he'd seen her five minutes before in the café. "Normally I would obey you, Mama, I give you my word. But I think the — the shock must have turned your mind somehow. I can't make you any promises — because — because I don't know what you're going to do next."

Mama stared at him, blank with shock. She turned slowly to Magali. "Tell your brother."

"You mean . . . ?"

"How you were arrested."

"I was never arrested, Mama." Magali's voice dropped to a whisper. "What he said — that's what happened."

"How could you," Mama murmured, eyes unmoored. "How could you *both* have gone mad?" She laid her palms flat on the table, bowed her head, and took a long breath. "We'll get through this," she said evenly. "Never mind the dishes. I need to see Madame Thiers."

Julien looked at Magali, her eyes reflecting the gray light in his own. They moved together, between their mother and the doorway.

"No, Mama," said Julien.

When it was over Julien sat slumped in his chair, a dirty plate still in front of him, listening to his mother's sobs from behind her bedroom door. Magali was pacing, clenching her fists and unclenching them.

He had faced it. He hadn't run off to Grandpa's. He had stayed and faced his mother and he had told her the truth.

For all the good it had done anyone.

She hadn't even struck him when he blocked her way out with his body. He almost wished she had.

Magali stopped in her tracks. "We'll have to manage her," she whispered. "Pretend we believe her. Make up reasons we shouldn't go, or shouldn't talk to anyone about it, or —"

"Lie to her."

"Yeah."

Julien said nothing.

Benjamin came in the door at ten, stripping off his snow-caked scarf and kicking off his boots, breathing hard, more physically sure of himself in his rush than Julien had ever seen him. "It's *so cold*," he panted, making straight for the fire.

Grandpa wasn't with him.

"He's sick in bed. A bad cold. He says he's very sorry, and we should ask one of the women in town. Madame Raissac maybe."

A single hard shudder went through Julien. Magali said in a low, passionate voice, "Is he *joking*? *Tell* everyone?"

"There's no shame in needing help," said Benjamin slowly, watching their faces.

Julien looked away.

The day became a labyrinth of time, coiling continually back on itself. They packed under Mama's direction, promising over and over not to forget their socks. They unpacked frantically when her back was turned. Then packed again as she repeated Monsieur Faure's tip-off word for word, filling the suitcases they had just emptied, like Penelope hopelessly weaving. Magali lied to her barefaced, claiming the train wasn't running. Mama tried to leave the house to check.

When the shouting was over Magali fled to her room.

Ten minutes later Julien came up to get her. Her eyes were bloodshot and despairing. "She has to see you," he whispered. "I'm sorry."

As Mama wept on her, he slipped into Papa's study. Papa's Bible was gone; a few gaps showed in the bookshelf. On the desk beside the pad of blue-lined paper lay a letter: *Dear Madame Jones, Please accept our*

profoundest gratitude for your generous dona-
tion to our school. I believe you know —

Papa's neat handwriting broke off there.
His pen lay capped beside it.

Julien walked back out.

Julien and Benjamin cooked haphazardly
that night with the aid of hurried directions
from Magali, boiling lentils and potatoes
and choking them down unseasoned. Élise
came after dark, accepted a cup of tea, and
asked Mama if she might speak with her in
private. To ask her advice.

Twenty minutes later she slipped out of
the bedroom and whispered, "I think she'll
sleep soon. She just" — her eyes lit on Julien, a little rueful — "wants me to check
that you packed socks." Her gaze turned to
a stare as the tears rose in Julien's eyes; they
both looked quickly away.

In another ten minutes she came out and
said Mama was asleep. "If she wakes up —
are you planning to have someone stay
down here?"

Julien glanced at Magali. The slightest
glance. Magali broke down sobbing.

Élise rubbed her back and Julien brought
her water as she tried to get her wildly heaving breath back under control. "I'll do it,"
Julien whispered. "I'll sleep on the couch."

Magali almost started crying again. He could feel Élise's eyes on him, warm. But in the pit of his belly, coldness lay curled.

But Mama didn't ask for Magali that night. She woke at three in a panic instead, convinced the Gestapo were at the door.

Julien went down to check, over protests about the risk that must have woken the others on the third floor. The cold was bitter, earth and sky like iron, the stars like diamonds overhead, glittering and hard. He looked out at it all, feeling the touch of the air suck the warmth from his skin. If you stayed out here long enough your blood would freeze, starting just beneath the skin and working inward. Freeze and freeze, till you were as hard as the earth out here, a statue that would bruise any flesh that struck it. Out there among those hard, bright stars, he'd read, it was colder. A frail island of warmth and life swimming in a sea of death, and somehow they still expected things to hold together. Whole families to survive intact. Fools.

He took a deep breath of the killing air, and went back upstairs to tell his mother the Gestapo weren't there.

He was still awake when Magali came down, just as the stars were beginning to fade. She whispered to him, "I figured out a story."

"Story?"

"The tip-off is a trap. The police are watching and we mustn't leave the house. Monsieur Faure told you. You can say he told you when you bought the bread this morning. But it has to be you. She'll believe you."

His stomach felt strange. "Papa wouldn't."

"*You* would," hissed Magali. "Because you *have* to."

He said nothing.

He went out to get the bread. On the street in front of the *boulangerie,* Pastor Alexandre's young son hailed him.

"We got a telegram from the police. They're at Saint Paul d'Eyjeaux. It's a, a *political reeducation camp.* They're staying there."

"They're in France?"

"Yeah. Mama says it's near Limoges. That's all I know."

"They're in France," Julien whispered, and closed his eyes against the blinding line of sunrise in the east: just one long white-gold line between the frozen hills and the heavy sky.

■ ■ ■ ■

They could not make her believe the news. How could she, when they wouldn't let her leave the house?

A whispered brother-sister argument produced no decision — both of them started to breathe much too fast when they got anywhere near the idea of Mama and competent, curious Madame Alexandre in the same room. *She'd get us help. And it would be all over town by tomorrow.* They heard a wavering note in Mama's voice and looked up.

"Even if it's true, Benjamin, you know what those people are. They could deport him anytime."

"Madame Losier," said Benjamin earnestly, "it's a political reeducation camp. That must mean it has a purpose internal to France."

Her voice dropped to a breath. "Don't. Don't try to give me hope." She turned away.

The weather softened outside under deep clouds; the harsh cold eased and the air filled with snow. It fell and fell; after an hour no one expected the trains to run.

Mama hid Magali and Benjamin in the attic.

Downstairs again, she paced. Julien no longer heard the things she said. Till she looked up with fear in her eyes and asked where Magali was.

Upstairs they found Magali sneaking out of her bedroom, a book in her hand.

Mama clasped her daughter to her heart and wept, then grabbed her by the shoulders and demanded to know why she had left her hiding place. The Gestapo might be at the door at this very moment!

"I was going to the toilet," Magali said whitely.

"I left you a chamber pot. Back in the attic. Now."

Magali fought her.

Julien had never seen his sister's face like that. Not since the day she'd found a neighbor boy in Paris tormenting a stray kitten, nine years ago, and she scratched him hard enough to draw blood. She tried to jerk her arm out of Mama's grip; they both staggered. Julien tried to set himself between them. Mama screamed at him.

Julien ran.

He took the stairs three by three at such a speed he nearly fell. Outside, the snow was swirling thick and drifted already against the door. He counted to thirty, his heart hammering, and ran in again. When he reached the top, thighs burning, Magali was on the bottom rung of the attic, still struggling, screaming, "I can't! *I can't!*" as Mama raged at her about trying to throw her life away and Benjamin's too —

"Mama!" Julien shouted. "Monsieur Faure! I saw him in the street." He grabbed her arm and babbled into her face: "You were right, I'm sorry I didn't believe, Monsieur Faure says he did tell you those things but he found out it's a trap — a planted rumor — Antoine Duval — it's not real." He looked into his mother's stunned eyes and gasped out in one breath: "He says we mustn't leave the house."

"In the street, Julien? Why didn't he come in?"

"He came during the storm for secrecy! They're *watching* us!"

"Lord have mercy," murmured Mama. She let go of Magali. Magali stood hunched on the ladder, her chest heaving, looking at Julien with bloodshot eyes. "Lord have mercy," said Mama. "They've grown so clever as that."

Magali closed her eyes. Julien swallowed against the sour taste in his mouth.

"Let's go downstairs," said Mama, stand-

ing back to let Magali past her, gently patting her arm. "I'll make you some tea."

CHAPTER 16
THE OTHER SIDE OF THE BARBED WIRE

Julien lied to his mother two more times that day, with Magali and Benjamin backing him up. Still at suppertime Mama was upstairs stripping Benjamin's room. Meanwhile her red-eyed daughter stood in the kitchen giving orders in a heavy, colorless voice — "Uh, make a fire please, and I guess . . . get potatoes, Benjamin" — punctuated by long moments of pressing her fists against her bowed forehead, standing completely still.

Then Élise knocked.

The sky outside was deep blue, the streetlamps lighting spheres of white and swirling snow. There was snow all over her boots and skirt to above the knee; her scarf was white with it. She shook it out and looked at them.

"You came," said Julien.

She nodded.

"Élise," he said, "would you teach me to make latkes?"

253

They weren't magic. They didn't make Mama well. Most of them were burned on one side. But to stand in the kitchen and listen to Élise, to chop onions under her level, considering gaze, salved something in his heart. To put food on a plate and set it down in front of Magali, of Mama. There was some hot shame in him that he couldn't find the source of, but it eased around that table, no sound but the scrape of forks, the snap of a log in the fire, the constant swish of wind and snow. The faces and the light. Mama ate, calm and weary.

After supper she went to bed.

Magali dropped her face into her hands the moment the bedroom door closed. Élise sat warming her hands around her tin cup. It was deep dark outside, but she made no move to go.

"Are you going to get in trouble?" Julien said softly. "At the dorm?"

Élise shrugged.

Magali walked over to the farthest chair in the living room, dropped into it, and closed her eyes. Then opened one again. "It's freezing in here," she mumbled, not moving. "The fire's almost out." The others came to her; Benjamin laid wood over the coals.

Julien crouched and blew the fire gently

into life. Then turned to Magali. "Do you think . . . we should ask for help? After all?"

"Do whatever you like. I'm going to Élise's dorm and staying there."

"Um —"

Magali opened her eyes. "I don't know if you *noticed,* but I had a *bit* of a hard day, Julien. You want to sleep in my room, Élise? It's probably neck-deep out there by now."

Élise half smiled and pulled up a chair. "Thanks."

Magali turned red eyes on her brother. "If she was a Les Chênes kid she'd be on the urgent list for Switzerland. Like Marek. I dunno. Switzerland's starting to sound pretty good. I didn't mean *you*" — she scowled at Benjamin, who had made some random gesture.

I did. Julien did not look up. The fire was a mouth, eating.

"He should've listened to her. He should've listened to her while she still knew a Maquis tip-off from a hole in the ground. Now it's too late."

"We pray for him," said Élise suddenly. "All of us."

Julien's eyes began to sting. *Don't try to give me hope.* He didn't want to say it to Élise. To say anything that might close those lips. He would take any gift she chose to

give, even if his hands bled around it.
"Thank you," he whispered. "Thank you
for coming here —" He caught her dark
eyes looking at him, and stopped breathing.
*Thank you for staying. Thank you for talking
to me. Thank you for being.* He tore his eyes
off her.

Nobody spoke.

A pit of shame opened up beneath him.
They had all seen. They were all thinking
the same thing now. He was a fool. He'd
made a fool of himself to her. *We're finally
friends and now you've scared her off.*

Into the silence Benjamin spoke. Slowly,
as if deep in thought. "There's a thing I
imagine sometimes. When I can't sleep. I
imagine getting to America — and it's the
same. They're fighting Hitler but they hate
us too. Or they get a new president or
something, and he wants to get rid of us."

"*That's* what you think about when you
can't sleep?" said Magali.

"Not on purpose." Benjamin's smile
twisted.

"It won't be like that. In America!"

Benjamin and Élise were looking at each
other.

"I didn't say it would. It's just, I don't
know, a feeling." Benjamin's face was all
planes and angles in the light and shadow

256

of the fire. "That nowhere's safe. Hitler didn't start this, you know."

Élise was nodding. "It seemed like he did. It felt safe for us, you know — in Germany. It was Poland you heard the bad stories about. My mother's grandfather was Polish. She said when Papa bought our house in Heidelberg, her mother said, 'Don't get too attached.' When we left, my parents' friends were saying it couldn't last, the German people would vote him out soon. But they didn't." She looked at Benjamin. "They didn't want to."

Benjamin nodded. "My parents . . . knew people like that too."

"How is your father?" Élise asked him.

"We don't know yet. They might be . . . We don't know yet."

Blue flames crawled over the coals. Julien watched Élise's face, still as earth in the firelight. *None of us have suffered as much as you.* She turned toward Benjamin and Julien, eyes down, one finger picking at a pockmark on her face, and said in a low voice, "I'm sorry I was rude. For so long. At school."

"What?" said Julien. "You weren't —"

"I didn't know I was going to be going to a coed school," said Élise. "I never went to one before, except yeshiva, in Heidelberg, and that was . . . different. All our families knew each other, it was different. The way I grew up, we weren't just friends with boys — not on our own." She stared into the fire again as the words *on our own* spread out into the silence, like ripples from a tossed stone. "It's been a lot to get used to."

"No, really?" Magali muttered wryly.

Tears sprang into Élise's eyes. He saw the glint of them. She said nothing.

"You haven't done anything wrong," said Julien, his voice falling too loud in the silence. The fire crackled. "It's been so hard for you," he said more quietly.

Élise's tears spilled down her cheeks in two shining tracks. Her eyes rose to meet his, brilliant with firelit tears, and he drew in a sharp, silent breath. "I didn't want you to know what it's like," she said in a rush. "I didn't. I prayed for your father last summer and I was so glad for you." She looked down. "But there was something. I don't know." She touched her heart. Her voice hardened a little. "Envy, I guess."

"Fair enough," said Julien in a low, rough voice.

Élise shook her head. "Envy's wrong. It's the evil eye. Wishing harm on another. I don't wish . . ." Fresh tears flowed down. "I could never wish what's happened to you.

258

But — I don't know how to explain it, how it feels — envy. It's almost like anger. It actually feels like you're in the right."

Benjamin was nodding, his face turned away. He wiped it with the back of his hand.

"Maybe that's just how it is," said Magali. "Maybe it happens to everyone that way."

"I don't know. It can't be right. But it's like there's a wall, and you can't take it down. There's just no way to tell someone." Élise looked right at Julien. "You know? How different the barbed wire looks. When you're on the other side."

"Yeah," breathed Julien. "Yeah."

It was cold in Magali's room when Elisa woke. She slipped quietly out of the shared warmth of the blankets and began to dress.

Magali stirred and went up on one elbow, eyes unfocused, listening. "She's not up yet." Down in the street a shovel scraped and muted voices called.

"D'you need my help this morning?"

"Are you going to get in trouble? D'you need to sneak in?"

"I was stranded. I'll tell them so."

"You've helped us so much."

"I just cooked a couple of times."

Magali shook her head. "No. Julien —" She broke off.

Elisa's eyes met hers for a split second. They looked away from each other.

"I'm only saying," Magali whispered, "him learning to cook — cook *anything . . .*"

Elisa tied her sash on, keeping her eyes on her fingers as they made a neat, tight double knot.

"Well, anything that's not on a campfire," conceded Magali. "Listen, I'm sorry. I know. I mean, he knows. He's not going to — you know —"

"I really don't want to talk about him, Magali," Elisa whispered.

"I'm sorry, Élise. I just — all I really wanted to say was thank you. A lot."

Elisa nodded. She pinned up her hair, looking at the door. Magali went and opened it. "You're welcome," said Elisa. "Always." She gave her friend the *bise,* holding her tight around the shoulders, then slipped out the door and down the stairs. She walked home slowly between the high banks of snow, despite the cold, watching her breath steam upward, pale gold in the winter dawn.

The next day they were discovered.

Julien wasn't home when it happened. Magali and Benjamin had agreed he should stand his sentry duty. Mama had woken calmer that day, less sure of her fears when challenged. They felt they could handle her. *I'm sorry,* Benjamin mouthed as Julien came back in the door that day. *Nothing we could do.*

A casserole lay forgotten on the table as Madame Faure and Madame Raissac comforted his weeping mother.

Madame Faure pulled him aside and told him gently that Mama was having a nervous breakdown. He bit his tongue like a good boy and asked if someone could be sent to check on his grandfather. Then he slipped up to his room.

He should be grateful. He understood that.

The house was full that evening, but no one looked at him; he didn't know where to stand. Ladies talked in hushed voices of "suffering for the Lord" and "a purpose in it we can't know." When Élise knocked on the door, Madame Alexandre opened it; Élise stood blinking, and made a small backward motion before Julien went and firmly pulled the door the rest of the way open, said, "Please come in," and put the kettle on.

"What happened?" she murmured, following him when he went to feed the fire.

"Someone came to visit. Should've seen it

coming. Now they're in charge."

The next evening Grandpa came. It wasn't till he saw his face that Julien remembered the obvious. *Papa's his son.*

Grandpa held them each against his heart, a long time. Mama longest. He took her by the shoulders, and she looked at him, her eyes strangely young.

"Can you bear to pray for him, Maria? Together?"

She nodded.

Grandpa led them into the living room and knelt on the thin carpet. They knelt with him. He didn't read from the Bible; he barely spoke. "We ask for Your help, O Lord. You know our need." Then nothing but the sound of five people breathing close together, and Julien's mind going down into emptiness, groping through dark rooms and endless corridors, groping for God. *Show Yourself. Please.* He had said it so often. He said it again. *Please. Please. Please.* Till it no longer sounded like it meant anything. Till it was only a sound.

Monsieur Faure came; he and Grandpa spoke long with Mama, and she looked up with a flicker of doubt in her eyes and asked Monsieur Faure if he was sure. It was strange, she said, her eyes soft and willing as Julien hadn't seen them for days.

Weeks.

The next morning Julien came down to find her crying in the kitchen as Grandpa fetched wood.

She gave him a wavering smile. "Julien, what's been happening to me? Do you know . . . what this is?"

He stood with his mouth open for five long heartbeats. "Is it over?" he whispered.

Mama began to cry again. He laid a hand on her shoulder and stood tongue-tied till he heard Grandpa's feet on the stairs, and let Grandpa answer.

A spell, Grandpa called it. His aunt had taken one once, when he was young. For a week she'd believed the neighbors were trying to poison her family, then she'd come back to herself. It had never returned.

"Never?" whispered Julien. "You're sure?"

"She was like anyone else for the rest of her life." Grandpa smiled. "A lovely woman."

Julien closed his eyes.

That night Élise did not come.

A young boy knocked on the door instead, and said that his mother needed to borrow two turnips. Benjamin started up wide-eyed at the words. "Tell them I'm coming." He came home very late.

They went to school. Julien didn't speak of his mother, and nobody seemed to dare ask. Friends told him the news: the Germans had revived their old plan of drafting French young men to work in their factories. They were taking every twenty- to twenty-three-year-old they could find. Some guys who were of age had already gone into hiding by slipping off to join the armed Maquis groups organizing in the countryside.

Pierre was one of them.

Mama spent two days at the kitchen table making tea for Madame Raissac and Grandpa, saying things like "They were going to take them all away from me" and "It seemed so real." She told Julien how much he reminded her of her oldest brother, the one who'd been killed in the Great War, and started crying again. She cooked supper. She talked with Magali for hours in her bedroom; he heard their voices quietly rise and fall. Magali sat looking out the window a long time after she came out.

"She told me stuff she never told me before," she whispered. "I guess it makes more sense now." Her mouth quirked. "If it ever happens again, though, I'm running away from home, so be ready."

Julien huffed out a painful laugh.

Grandpa stayed, sleeping downstairs on the couch, deep silence all through the dark house. Safe in his own bed each night, Julien slept less and less. Sometimes at midnight he woke in fear, and it was hours before he slept again. Once he woke weeping.

A letter came from Papa.

They gathered so close around it they could feel each other breathe. Mama drew it out of its envelope, crackling like onion skin, black with Papa's small handwriting. He sent his deepest love. He was well. The food was adequate, the barracks clean. Most of the other inmates were French Communists. *A comradely group,* he wrote, and even Mama smiled. *Very interested in debating religion with us. We've asked permission to lead services.* Julien could almost see Papa's eyes. He thanked them for their prayers. *We sense them. Please don't be afraid for me, Maria. This place is bearable, and we feel God may even be giving us work to do here. There has been no talk of deportation.*

No talk of deportation.

He signed himself *Martin* and added the word *Papa* in parentheses. Julien reached out a finger and touched it before Mama gently folded the thin paper. He stayed in the kitchen long after the others had gone, looking across the table at the empty chair.

Two days after Grandpa left, a knock came at the door. Julien rose swiftly, pulled Élise's kosher cup from the cupboard, and went to open it.

Two men. One with a folder in his hand.

"Forgive us for disturbing you, monsieur, madame, mademoiselle."

The accent was French. No uniforms. Yet cold brushed the back of Julien's neck.

"A matter regarding your lodger."

Julien opened his mouth. Mama's voice came from behind him. "Do come in and sit down. Have some tea — there's sugar in the pantry, Magali — or if you prefer there's a lovely *sirop de myrtilles* my father-in-law makes. Fetch that too, Magali." He heard the clink of the kosher cup going back in the cupboard.

He heard Magali whistling the alert song. Piercingly.

"And the *sablé* cookies, Magali," Mama called.

"I can't find them."

"Oh dear, they're downstairs. Would you?"

"We really don't need . . ." began the younger man, his eyes resting brightly on

266

the dark bottle Magali was putting on the table.

His colleague flopped the folder down and opened it. "Benjamin Keller. I believe that's his name?"

Magali went out the stairwell door. Mama filled the glasses, the dark blueberry swirling as she mixed in the water. The leader took a sip and raised his eyebrows. "This is excellent." He took another long sip, then cleared his throat reluctantly and went on.

A bureaucratic error. Most regrettable. It was their job to regularize such matters. They now had a document proving Monsieur Keller's French citizenship — was he home?

You came all this way — ? "No," said Julien.

"We could certainly give them to him next time we see him," Mama put in.

The leader pulled his folder a little toward himself. "As you are not his family members . . ."

Julien's heart was pounding. "He left. He went to Le Puy to look for work. I could —"

"And his address there?"

"He didn't leave one. It was kind of sudden. We had a — disagreement. About money."

The two men looked at each other. The younger one took his last sip of *sirop*. The other readjusted his half-full glass by a centimeter, and laid a hand on the table.

"If you don't mind my saying so, Monsieur Losier, we are surprised to learn this. We were not under the impression that your lodger was, shall we say, prone to taking such initiative. You won't mind, of course, if we verify whether what you are telling us is the truth." He glanced toward the stairwell door.

Nausea crept up Julien's throat. Mama leaned forward. "You came," she said slowly, "to deliver a *carte d'identité* — and you want to search my house?"

The older officer gave a small, cold smile and rose. He picked up his glass, tossed its contents back, and said, "The bedrooms are upstairs, I take it?"

For a moment no one spoke. "Yes," said Julien. His voice seemed to come from elsewhere.

The younger officer stood too.

On the top landing all was quiet. Julien did not, even for a split second, look upward.

"Whose room is this?"

"Mine," Julien said. The closet was ajar.

"And this?"

"That was his room till he left us, yes."

The bed was unmade except for a blank sheet, two folded blankets. Science books stood in one neat row on the bookshelf. One of the officers opened the top dresser drawer.

Empty.

Nothing in the closets, nothing under the beds. When all the bedrooms were searched, one man turned to go downstairs. The other looked up. "Is that your attic trapdoor?"

Julien's heart stopped.

"Yes," said Mama. "Please feel free."

Julien watched from the kitchen window as the two men disappeared down the street, then collapsed into a chair, holding his head. "Where on earth is he?"

"Down in the root cellar," said Magali. Her face was slack. "We bundled everything into his sheets — went down the stairs in our socks. We thought they would hear us if we tried to get the ladder out."

"You were *amazing*," said Julien.

"They would have heard everything." Mama looked sideways at Magali. "Did you find the *sablé* cookies?"

Magali gaped. "That's why you asked —"

"Yes."

Magali sat down.

■ ■ ■ ■

"I don't think you should go to school tomorrow," said Julien.

Benjamin sat on a potato crate, his back against shelves half full of jars. Two bulging bundles were wedged into the narrow space with him. His face was still bloodless to the lips. "I'm not going back to that school. Ever."

"You figured it out too, huh?"

Benjamin looked away, at a bag of garlic on a shelf a handbreadth from his face. "They knew that much about me."

"That rat," whispered Julien.

Benjamin gave him a flat, cold look, a faint glimmer of tears in his eyes. "It would be all right with me if you didn't use that word. Antoine Duval isn't the one getting called that in the newspapers." His voice lowered. "He's not the one hiding in a cellar."

The walls pressed in around Julien, walls of shelves lined with food by the careful work of his mother's hands, now gaping with holes like a moth-eaten coat. "This has to end. Now."

Benjamin looked at him, and said nothing.

"Are you ready to go up?"

"Are you kidding?"

"We'll have to take you to Grandpa's farm."

"After dark."

"Just before first light maybe. Fewer people around."

"I'm not spending the night, Julien."

"If you like." Julien took a deep breath, and looked at his friend. "I want you to apply for another visa."

The air was very still, as if holding its breath before the force gathering in Benjamin's eyes. His voice was quiet and even, and frightened Julien. "Who do you think you are?" Benjamin bared his teeth, then cursed softly. Julien drew back against the narrow door. "Is that an *order*? *Who do you think you are?*" Benjamin hissed, almost in his face.

Julien cringed, then flared at him. "Someone who doesn't want you to die."

Benjamin took a shuddering breath. "If you don't want me to die, don't send me on that road."

"*Benjamin.* They came for you today —"

"I was wrong. You still don't have the faintest idea what it's like."

"And *you* were supposed to have changed. I don't *want* to know what it's like to be — be someone who doesn't understand that

271

the only way out of the fire is through the fire."

"Why don't you just say it, Julien." Benjamin's eyes were bleak and cold, his voice a weary whisper.

Julien stared at his friend, feeling his molars grind against each other, tasting bile. He turned the handle behind him.

"Hide till you rot," he hissed. "If that's what you choose."

And he stepped out and slammed the root-cellar door.

They walked down to Grandpa's farm in silence together beneath the cold hard stars, long after dark.

CHAPTER 17
TRUTH

They felt their way blind into this new life, as though clambering out of a marsh on a moonless night. Walking with arms outstretched, thanking God for their lives, feeling for soft ground with freshening terror. Fear was Mama's voice rising as she asked where Magali was, or a too-wild look in her eye; a blue or black uniform in the street; that moment with your hand on the doorknob, after the knock. Fear was the envelope in your hand before you turned it over, Papa's neat handwriting looking up at you, the return address still unread. That moment before you were sure he was in the same camp still, eating decent food, leading services with Pastor Alexandre, standing room only.

Hatred was Duval's eyes.

The sight of the man, the smell of his smoke, was a daily nausea to Julien. Every week he was in church. The Sunday after

Papa's arrest, Pastor Chaly from Tence had preached a dry, history-laden sermon on Herod and John the Baptist, saying not a phrase that would make a decent anti-fascist quote, while the people's fury against tyrants rose like waves of heat in the old stone church. Fury and silence. Yes, you saw a black uniform sometimes in the street, like glimpsing a wolf in the woods. But the snake in your house, that was another thing. *Show Yourself,* Julien prayed. *And strike him down.*

Victory was nothing more than another day without disaster. Power was standing by the Le Puy road wrapped up against the *burle,* knowing they could not get past without your seeing. Pain was knowing just how much you could lose anyway, if a man in an office chose. Pain was hearing, even still, his mother weep at night.

Joy was Élise's quiet knock, and her face behind the door.

He could have kissed her feet in gratitude the first time she came. She came to invite them to La Roche. She would be playing for her friends there, and did they want to come? She looked at Mama as she said it.

Awe. That was the music.

The storm, the calm, joy and pain twisted together into one bright thread. Her face, her seeking face, eyes open to something nobody could see. "She has a gift," Mama murmured. All the way home that night under the cold stars, Mama sang softly and sweetly as she hadn't done in months.

And Élise came again.

It was a miracle. She came, of her own free will, up dark, icy streets after cooking and serving supper to thirty people, and knocked on his door. She came while his mother was out at her sewing circle, and sat at the table by lamplight with him and Magali. She sat across from him drinking tea from his old tin cup, and he looked at her and away, like looking at the sun. The calm of her face, like deep still water, and the light. He tried to keep his hand from trembling where it lay on the tablecloth a handspan or two from hers. Even at that distance he could feel the warmth rising from her skin, a fierce denial of the dark of death around them. He was with her inside a sphere of glass, fire-warm and radiant, their backs to the cold and the dark and the void. He was with her, although she didn't know.

He hoped to God she didn't know.

And yet he hoped to God she did. In spite of all he could say to himself about the folly of it. He would have given a chunk out of his flesh, and willingly — even if they never touched, even if none of his wild wishes could ever be — for one flash of those deep eyes *seeing* him.

Seeing him as he saw her.

It was impossible. But he thought of it as he lay awake hearing Mama sob in her bed. He remembered his parents kissing in the kitchen in the dead of night; he imagined them young and hungry-hearted, their soft hands meeting for the first time. He envied them so much. Even now, after police at the door who didn't know where they were taking his father.

They've had twenty years. I'll have nothing.

He ground his face into his pillow, and ordered his body to forget her, and heard behind his back the voice of nothing, the cold and the darkness, laughing at him.

Fear came in and in with the first spring thaws, the dripping from the roofs, the white drifts sagging down into dense ice-blue mounds — warmth and light and fear. *How long?* Julien's mind whispered. *How long?*

The softening ground held every footprint on the day he went down to the farm with a letter for Benjamin. Benjamin walked into his bedroom, already ripping it open, and shut the door, but a moment later he was out again. "They still don't know. They *still* don't know if they can get him released." Julien looked at him and opened his mouth. Saw his friend's eyes harden. He went home with clenched fists in his pockets and nothing to strike.

At break Élise stood out on the patio with the others, and Duval walked past them, smoking, casting a sidelong glance. Julien wanted to reach out and grab him by the collar, throw him against the wall. He watched empty-handed as the betrayer passed by, watched empty-handed down the Le Puy road for the buses that were sure to come. *Vigilance,* he preached to the Scouts, but he no longer called them *the first line of defense.* He watched empty-handed, and thought of Pierre and the people he was training with, somewhere in the hills. The only people in all this land who had guns and were not pointing them at the innocent.

It's wrong, his mind reminded him. *Do not resist an evil man. Turn the other cheek.* In church they sang about the power of God, they read Psalms about how He protected the poor and the righteous. In church Papa and Pastor Alexandre were heroes, imprisoned for the cause; their deportation and their deaths would only strengthen their people's faith. At Saint Paul d'Eyjeaux they were witnesses, holding prayer meetings with the Communists, preaching to the lost in prison. It was in the house that things unraveled. In the house where the ghosts remained in every doorway, sick reverberations in the air: screams, sobs, accusations. Lies. *The lies worked best, Papa. Magali told me to, and she was right. You should have seen their eyes, Papa. But you didn't, did you? You weren't there.*

The truth has power. But what was the truth? He'd believed and believed in the things his father told him. Now he sat in church and cringed when he heard, "The mighty arm of the Lord has been revealed. The Lord has thrown down our enemies. Horse and chariot he has thrown into the sea."

Have you seen the chariots? I've seen them. They're in fine condition, Papa. That's *the truth.*

He sat among the praying people, and wondered if it was time to start believing his eyes.

On the twenty-fourth of March there was a knock on the door as the Losiers finished supper.

It was Monsieur Astier, who'd been arrested with Papa.

Suddenly there was no air in the room. Julien stared at the man, his travel-rumpled clothes, the sheer presence of him. He watched Mama open her mouth to ask.

Saw the little warning shake of Astier's head.

"Did you escape?" breathed Magali.

Astier shook his head again. "No. No. I was released. We . . ." He looked at Mama with dark, apologetic eyes, and Julien's heart knotted. "Madame, your husband and Pastor Alexandre are still in the camp. I thought I should tell you personally."

"Go on," said Mama whitely.

"They — they announced our release. The other inmates congratulated us. At the *poste de commande* we were given a document to sign. I've been a government employee for years, God knows I've signed so many things." He sat awkwardly in the empty chair across from Mama. "Your husband read it very carefully. He's a meticulous man."

Julien's mouth was growing dry.

"He pointed out to *monsieur le pasteur* that it contained a promise of loyalty and obedience to the orders of Marshal Pétain."

Mama's right hand was over her face.

"They refused to sign. They said they couldn't swear to a lie."

279

The silence in the room had a thick, viscous quality to it, like glue. Astier didn't seem to know where to put his eyes. His voice fell into that silence like a struggling fly. "I'm ashamed. I offered to stay with them but they told me to go and I do confess —"

"Because he didn't want to lie?" breathed Magali. "That's why?" Her voice rose. *"That's why he's not here?"*

"Magali," muttered Julien reflexively.

She turned and looked right through him with burning black eyes. "He . . ." she said with a jerky, helpless gesture. "Didn't . . ." She turned to the door, her hand trembling.

"It's just like him," said Mama in a ghost of a voice. "It's exactly what he would do." She looked at the door as well. Her shoulders were curving forward, a hollow jar around her heart.

Julien said nothing.

The silence thickened. Hardened. Monsieur Astier cleared his throat twice, vigorously, as if to keep from choking. Nobody spoke. It was the moment when someone ought to have finally offered him something to drink, now or never, so he would know he was a welcome guest in their home and they weren't just waiting for him to leave.

Nobody spoke.

Monsieur Astier stood, gave them all a quick nod. "I thought you should hear it from me. The whole story. Not a rumor." He ducked his head again. "I'm sorry I didn't have better news to bring you, madame. I admire your husband very much."

And he was gone, the door closing behind him. His footsteps echoed in the stone stairwell.

"Of course you do," murmured Mama tonelessly. She stood and made her way blindly toward the bedroom. Tears were streaming down Magali's face.

"He could've been released," said Julien. His voice came out mechanically. He seemed to be floating a meter above his own head. Everything was very clear, the air like crystal, reality laid out before him like a map. He was the son of a man who had thrown his life away for an ideal. It had happened before, and it would happen again. A footnote in the terrible story of the world.

He could have been released.

But he wasn't.

Julien stood and walked away from the table, going he didn't quite know where.

Chapter 18
Since the World Began

Julien slept deep that night and had no dreams. When he woke the light was coming in his window. He lay a minute looking at it, then rose and dressed and knelt by his bed. He prayed the Lord's Prayer. The wood floor was hard against his knees. He looked up into the brightness and whispered, "You don't want us to be stupid, do You?"

Then he stood and went downstairs.

He watched Mama carefully, that morning. Her movements had a slow hopelessness to them. But she knew what had happened and what hadn't. Her mind was clear.

Like Julien's.

Everything was vivid to him, that day. The light on the remains of the snow was harsh white, the bare trees etched precisely against the sky. He felt grieved and alive and new. New in a new world, one where you believed your eyes, where the clear and simple reasons were the true ones. There was a

God, but He didn't stop wars, and hadn't Julien always known that? If a rock fell in the mountains, it was because it was loose. If a man had a gun and chose to shoot you, or take you away, he could. The Germans had conquered France because they had so many tanks, and they knew how to use them. Maybe the Russians would beat them and be the new masters. Maybe not. In the meantime the Nazis were enslaving and probably murdering innocent people. They had to be stopped somehow.

And telling them murder was wrong didn't seem to be working.

It was hard to hear the teachers over the clatter of rearranging in his head. It was like a housecleaning. All that trying and trying to make sense of it all, he tossed into the fire like a hopeless tangle of string. *Enough.* Sweep the floor, open all the windows; it's time to face the truth.

The truth had power, all right.

Word hadn't gotten around yet. It wouldn't be long. But for now, he and Magali stood on the patio shoulder to shoulder with Élise and told her in low voices. She nodded gravely, and looked out at the broken, white-and-gray horizon. "I'm sorry," she said.

■ ■ ■ ■

The next day, when he and Magali came home for lunch, Mama opened the door for them wide-eyed. "He's been released," she said.

Julien's throat closed. *She's gone again.* He held out both hands in a suppressing gesture. "Mama —"

"Look," Mama snapped. She snatched something up from the kitchen table and thrust it into his hands. *"Look."*

It was a telegram.

RELEASED STOP EXPECT US AFTERNOON TRAIN TOMORROW STOP MARTIN LOSIER

Julien stood like stone.

The station's platform was packed, the streets lined with people all the way back to the *place du centre.* They parted silently for the Losiers, nodding respectfully, light in their eyes. Madame Alexandre and her children already stood on the platform.

Ten paces beyond them, under the eaves of the station house, stood two Gestapo.

The crowd shifted quietly, like grass beneath a breeze. Heads turned. The black coats of the enemy swung as they followed the people's gaze toward the sound: a faint far whistle, away between the hills.

Mama gripped Julien's hand. He gripped back.

The white steam flashing up into the cold blue sky; the shriek and grind of the brake on the track; the engineer staring. Then there was no sound in all that place but the creak of the passenger doors as they opened.

Pastor Alexandre stepped down out of the train.

A sound went up from the crowd, a sort of collective sigh. Then a drawing of breath. Faces turned. The Gestapo did not move. Julien watched the train.

Mama started forward the instant she saw him, tears streaming down her cheeks. Papa came to her, tall and thin and smiling, took her face between his hands and kissed her briefly, then folded her into an embrace. There was such joy in his eyes. He took Julien by the shoulders and gave him the *bise*, again, again. *You're here.* The hands on his shoulders were real, the stubble on Papa's face, the fog of his breath in the cold moist air, it was real, he was here. Julien's head swam. He glanced at the Gestapo again. Watched them watching. The hush and rustle of a hundred people standing in taut silence was around them, palpable as the sea.

Tanieux was watching too.

Julien's heart beat harder, higher, like a battle-drum. *Give them nothing.* These people knew. The enemy could stand there with their hunters' eyes on the prey, but these people knew now. Never break the stare. Never turn your back. Never say a word. Give them nothing.

It was almost eerie, the silence in which the people walked with them down the street away from the station. It was bare and reassuring, like a wall. It was not broken till they were on the *place,* most of the crowd turning off toward the parsonage with the pastor and his wife.

Even then it was broken for no one but Julien.

The face flashed out of the alley for the merest second, eyes on him, a look like an arrow in a hard-bent bow — then gone. Julien checked, then kept walking, watching the alley; he was already peeling off from his family with a casual nod, as if they knew what his errand was, when the face showed again, a quick hand beckoning. Julien went up into the alley without a glance at the figure pressed against the wall, till they were both out of sight of the *place.* Then he turned.

It *was* him. "Pierre."

Pierre's chest was heaving. "Alert," he panted. "Get your alert chain going. They're searching the farms on the south road." He wiped a sleeve across his sweating forehead. "They've got your sentry in their car."

Manuel staggered in the La Roche kitchen door holding his side, gasping, "Raid. Raid."

It took Elisa a moment to understand. She dropped her pan with a bang on the stove and dashed into the common room. "Raid! *Raid!*"

The room erupted. She ran to Karl, grabbed his arm, looked round frantically for Tova till she saw short-bearded Paul Maier towing her sister toward her. The doorways were packed — Rudy leapt smoothly out a window, one hand on the sill — she pulled her siblings back the way she'd come and out the kitchen door.

They pelted through the kitchen garden, up into the woods. Boots on the path behind them — someone grabbed her sleeve. It was Édouard. "Follow me. Place. Place for them."

The pinewoods deepened, rocks jutting before their flying feet. Dark stones loomed ahead, gray-starred with lichen, a great hunched boulder like a sleeping bear, a crack showing black beneath it. "Under there," Édouard panted. "Room for two."

She mounded pine needles against the crack once Tova and Karl were in, for camouflage and warmth. Édouard was gathering fallen pine boughs, piling them over a space between two rocks; he motioned to her. She wedged herself in, the dark rock rough and cold through her apron and sweater.

Footsteps sounded on the path below. Then Manuel's wheeze. Heat surged through her. *Nobody helped him?* She shot out, scraping her arm on the rock, and hauled him in. There was room, barely room, for three. They'd need more boughs; there were no fallen ones; she plunged into a pine and began wrenching at a half-broken branch, tearing with her fingernails at the shreds where the green wood split. She glanced back, saw Édouard go into the crack, beckoning to her, saw him hunch down under the boughs — heard boots on the trail again.

From above.

She froze, twigs digging into her skin. Through the lattice of green she could see the figure approaching, blond and slender, using its tall walking stick carefully to clamber down between the rocks, keeping its balance so neatly despite the right arm in a sling. Cold spread through her belly.

She had seen the man yesterday, at the Bellevue Hotel.

She didn't know his name. But she knew he was one of the convalescents. She had heard him say he missed the Black Forest. And she knew the Resistance had given him that wound.

She kept utterly still. He moved cautiously, easily down the path, singing softly to himself in German, swinging down to one knee beside a hollow stump, lifting the leaf litter out of it and breathing in the scent. A high sharp squeak; a tiny brown body darted up out of the stump and into a sheltering mound of pine needles.

The mound at the base of the boulder.

The world slowed around Elisa, her blood congealing in her veins, as she waited for what would come.

A higher, panicked squeak. The wood mouse fled again. The blond German turned, eyes widening.

Elisa stood.

Then let herself fall to her knees, hard pine twigs gouging and scratching her, drawing a sharp cry from her throat. She crouched on all fours in her green cage, hair falling across her face, staring out at him. *Look, fox. A bird with a broken wing. Leave that nest, fox. It's not there.* He had turned. His eyes met hers through the pine boughs. *A bleeding girl in an apron, hiding in a pine tree. What could* that *possibly mean?* Bitter triumph was on her tongue, and under it cold fear. Far down near the house was the sound of an engine shutting off, and voices.

The man stared. Then stood smoothly, slowly, leaning on his stick.

And went on down the path toward the house.

She crouched like a mouse in a hole, watching his back, her mind racing. When he was well gone she rose and made a dash. She plunged under the skirts of another pine tree, a larger one, its branches fuller.

She did not dare hide somewhere where she could not stand guard.

She pinned her hair up, fast and tight. She worked a green stick off a branch, split as sharp as she could make it. The Talmud said, *If a man comes to kill you, get up and kill him first.* She had no hope of that. Still she might keep their eyes off that boulder — if she went for the face.

Help me. Out of the depths I cry to You.

O Lord, hear my voice.

She knelt in the pine needles, eyes on the downward path, hand white around her weapon, and waited for her time.

■ ■ ■ ■

Julien's side ached with running, but he didn't slow. Three whole hours he'd been, managing frightened children separated from their handlers. Anything could have happened. *Élise. Benjamin . . .*

At the first house at the edge of Tanieux a young girl stood behind a window. He tapped gently on the glass, and she opened it.

"They — catch — anyone?"

She nodded. "Papa said —"

"How many? Who?"

"He said they got a few people. I don't know who."

He ran.

Faces flashed through his mind. *They're getting smarter.* To come today, to finger Jérémie as a sentry — could they have arrested Jérémie? *They'll find the way in one of these days. Find where the fault lines are. Crack us like a nut.* Faces and faces flashed through him as he ran.

Benjamin. Élise. Jérémie. Eva. Nicole. Samuel. Charles. Brigitte. Élise.

He burst out onto the *place* and saw the bus, and Monsieur Thibaud coming up to the back window. His heart compressed.

The back of the bus was filled. He ran forward looking frantically for Élise — she wasn't there. Six, seven, eight people — strangers. An old lady with her hands over her face, a young man with his arm around her shoulder. A middle-aged man in a battered hat — Julien did know him, Monsieur Heckel, the Thibauds' houseguest since last fall. Monsieur Heckel, tears in his eyes, taking the package Monsieur Thibaud was handing him. Luc Marceau was coming up to the window too, holding something up. A bar of imitation chocolate. As Julien saw Julie Pérac start across the *place* with a determined step — as he thought of the apples in the root cellar at home, and the last three little jars of honey from last year — he stopped in his tracks.

Antoine Duval stood in the mouth of an alley, writing in a notebook.

Julien's heart sped up. He slipped into the narrow street nearest to him. He knew the back ways of Tanieux. In a minute he was behind Duval, walking toward him. Every nerve in his body told him to be silent, to set his wooden soles down with the slow precision of a hunting cat, but that was folly. He walked steadily, openly, watching the notebook. The man was still writing. Julien's eyes strained: *response to first arrests . . .*

several young people . . .

Names. There it was: the word *Pérac.*

Duval glanced up. Smiled his confident smile. "Hello."

"Hi." On impulse, Julien thrust his hands into his pockets and stood looking out at the scene beside his enemy, as if casually. He nodded at the bus, where three more people now waited in line. "Eight people. Wonder how they did it."

"In the usual way. Or so I hear."

"While the rest of us were in town welcoming the pastors back." He tried to keep the hard, black edge out of his voice, and failed.

Duval said nothing. He closed his notebook around his pen, as if he'd been sketching. He gave Julien an ironic, half-smiling side-long glance, took out a pack of cigarettes, and shook one out. Julien watched as he flicked a lighter to its tip, his own hands shaking in his coat pockets with the effort of not knocking the thing out of Duval's fingers and into the dirty slush.

Finally he could stand it no longer. He pointed his chin at the bus. There was a crowd around it now. "Happy?" he said in a low, dangerous voice.

Duval inhaled and blew out a thin stream of smoke. "The sun is shining. Spring is coming. Yes, I'm happy."

"About *that.*"

Duval pursed his lips. "Doesn't look like they'll lack for anything on the way."

You're going to hell. He almost said it. His heart was beating wildly, currents of heat running through his body. "Why do you do it?" he bit out. "How do you sleep?"

Duval turned fully to him this time, his eyebrows rising. "Do *you* sleep well?"

Julien simply looked at him, his eyes burning.

"It's a hard time, my friend. A man has to survive in one way or another." Duval opened his coat and tucked his notebook into an inside pocket. "People find ways. That's how it has been since the world began."

And he turned and walked off down the alley.

Julien stood for a long moment, watching the people of Tanieux gathered around the bus, thinking of guns, and broken rocks, and hell. He still believed that, he found: that God did justice, that there was justice in the end. It wasn't enough. But it was something.

Finally he turned, and walked away down the alley too.

Jérémie was at his house. "They just asked me to get in the car," he said, his eyes begging Julien for mercy. "I didn't know what to do."

"There wasn't anything you could do. They'd have followed you."

"I was just getting on the bicycle when they got to me —"

"Jérémie. There was *nothing* you could do." Julien held Jérémie's eyes till he nodded.

Then he looked north toward Élise's dorm.

The dorm mother said Élise hadn't come home from La Roche yet. She must be all right, she said, or they would have heard. She gave him a hard stare, as if to ask what business it was of his, and why he was running around drawing attention. *Go home.* The police were still in the *place.* He knew she was right.

He went home.

Magali and Mama were at the table, Magali eating her share of their cold supper. She looked up and he said, "Élise?" The name came out of his mouth like a bird taking flight: nothing he had planned, nothing he could have stopped. "Did you see her? Hear anything? She's all right?"

"She was at La Roche. I saw Madame Ferron. She said they searched it hard and didn't find anybody. They had ten minutes' warning from the Maquis guys coming up the south road."

Julien sank into a chair. "She must be all right then."

Mama gave him a long look. He turned away from her to stare out the window. *Don't you start.* He was surprised at the bitterness the words took on in his mind.

"Your father is already in bed," said Mama. "Have some supper."

In the last light of the dying sunset Elisa crouched under her tree, shivering uncontrollably, her teeth clenched hard to keep them silent. Her stick was in her hand. The rocks stood like hunched old trolls in the green gloom. She blinked the fog of exhaustion from her eyes, forcing herself to keep watch. *You never know.* It was so cold. Tiny rustlings in the forest floor around her. A sound from down below. She froze. A voice from the road, a young man's voice; a song rolling up through the dusk, carefree and fast.

"*Ti ti carabi, to to carabo, Compère*

Guilleri . . . te laiss'ras-tu, te laiss'ras-tu, te laiss'ras-tu mouri'?"

"I guess not then," murmured Elisa Schulmann, and sank to her knees.

CHAPTER 19
WHO I AM

"I don't believe you," said Édouard to Elisa. "You're not stupid."

Elisa glanced round the empty street and lowered her voice. "I did cry out because I scratched my arms. I scratched them on purpose. He was about to look under the rock. Don't tell them, all right?"

"Now that," said Édouard, "I believe."

"Promise me."

"I promise. You're those children's mother, aren't you?"

Her eyes stung. She looked away.

"I'm sorry. I think you're very brave."

"I didn't have a choice."

"People always have a choice. That's what my father used to say." Édouard squinted at the sun in the washed-out sky. "He said it all the time when I was younger. I hated it." His mouth turned up in a sad half smile.

She did not ask where his father was.

A woman leaned out a window above,

shaking out a sheet. Two men came round the corner, and Elisa's breath flattened out of her; Édouard's eyes cut swiftly to her as she froze, but she herself looked straight ahead. And yet the two figures burned themselves into her mind's eye: the thin blond one with his arm in a sling, moving as neatly on a sidewalk as he had in the woods, his face upturned with awe as the other man spoke. The thick-chested one, some battle-scarred war hero, one side of his face an angry mess of pink and red, the familiar cadences of German on his tongue. Her feet carried her forward; there was nowhere to run.

She felt rather than saw it — a pause in the young man's step, his grace arrested for a split second. She did not turn. And yet she saw him clear as his eyes swept smoothly over her and into the middle distance behind her head, as he offered her — she knew it was her — a tiny, barely perceptible nod.

She didn't breathe. The scarred one didn't even glance her way. She heard a single sentence of his story as they passed on the sidewalk centimeters apart: "And then we came over the hill." Then they passed behind her, out of sight.

She walked on, filling her lungs deep with

the clear plateau air.

When Julien woke it was raining: the first rain of spring, cold and shining. His father and mother were in their bed together, or downstairs at the kitchen table. Papa was home, home, home. Maybe if he said it enough times he would believe it. Papa was home.

He was thinner, tired-looking. He sat at the table and smiled and smiled, and told them that he and Alex had been suddenly released, no questions asked, nothing to sign. No explanation. He met Mama's eyes across the table, inched his chair closer to hers, took up her hand and kissed it. They smiled at each other, tears in their eyes, till Julien and Magali looked away.

The rain came on, and the world turned to mud, slick and fresh-smelling. Élise was at school, the short dark hairs around her hairline curling with the damp. She told him how she had almost been caught. He forced himself not to touch her arm or shoulder, and asked if she would keep working at La Roche. Yes, she said. But she wouldn't bring her siblings there anymore.

She looked at him with those eyes so deep you could lose yourself in them, down and down to the center of the earth, and he understood that it was useless to ask if she was sure. He stood watching the rain with her, smelling the damp earth, and his fingers a few centimeters from her hand tingled with life and blood. What it would be like to touch that wrist, the sculpted curves of bone and skin and vein, the tiny soft hairs that stood out in the rain-light, the blood held close like a treasure inside. Just to put his fingers on it once, to hold it and feel the warm pulse of life, life, life within, to feel it and swear on his life and his honor and his death never to let it stop. Oh God, if only he could, if he could swear that and know that he could carry it through. Know that his blood would be enough against time and chance and cold-eyed men with guns. You couldn't go swearing things like that. Not on the little they had. The alert chain, and barns, and watchfulness, and a God who might or might not be listening. Who might or might not have freed his father. Who might or might not have sent eight people to the slaughter instead.

Papa prayed for them after family devotions every night.

Mama sang softly as she cooked. Papa sat at the table and told them stories of the men he had met in the camp, grizzled Communists who wanted to help the poor and

spoke the word *Revolution* always with a
capital R, who argued about Stalin and
Trotsky and Karl Marx, who asked Pastor
Alex whether the salvation he wanted so
much to tell them about was for this world,
or was it simply pie in the sky? " 'I've never
seen Heaven.' That's what Alex told them.
'But in this world I have seen the salvation
of God.' "

Julien looked at his plate and scraped up
the last fragments of potato.

Papa took him aside the next day and said
it must have been very difficult for him,
"how it was with your mother, in the first
few days."

Julien looked at his hands and nodded,
his tongue feeling thick in his mouth.

"Magali says she was very grateful for your
help."

Julien glanced up at him and then away.

A letter came from New York. From Benjamin's *father* in New York. Julien gave Papa
one look over the envelope, and Papa nodded. "Go on down. I'll tell your teachers
you're excused."

Julien ran most of the way.

Benjamin flushed dark as he read the
envelope, and excused himself to his room
without a single word that could be understood. He came out almost half an hour

later, red-eyed. Julien opened his mouth and Benjamin began to weep again. Grandpa gave them tea, and they drank together, and Julien walked home through the misting rain, rain veiling the hills and the town.

The rain came on. The police came back. Pastor Alexandre had warning again this time, thank God, a stranger's voice crackling at the other end of the telephone line. Scouts scattered along the gleaming-wet roads, bringing the alert. The river brimmed its banks, brown and foaming, as police in rain gear walked in and out of the houses, leaving slick brown footprints on the floors. As Scouts hurried through the rain, and wet refugee children shivered in haystacks and barns. No one was caught.

This time.

Élise brought her siblings to La Roche once, for Passover. Julien stood guard on the south road that evening, listening to the pine trees drip, glancing back now and then at the lighted windows.

The sun came out. The mud dried slowly. Papa worked long hours at his desk, came out of his study pale and rubbing his face. At the table there were silences, Mama's eyes on Papa, a shy smile between them that faded more and more on Mama's face, grew more and more sorry on Papa's.

Their lights burned late into the night, Papa working, Julien studying for exams. Magali making up homework after long days at Les Chênes training children to answer to false names, to be silent for hours, never to say a word aloud in their mother tongues. "I never know their real names anymore," she told Julien. "Some of them I don't find out their names at all. We have kids who're only here for a week sometimes, waiting for someone to take them farther." She pointed east with her chin, her shoulders straightening. "A lot of kids have made it across. A lot."

"How many?" Julien sat straighter too.

"I don't know." Magali shook her head. "But there's always someone more. Always." She closed her eyes.

The day after the Allies defeated Rommel in North Africa, Julien ran into Pierre in the street, come to town to buy things for his unit. They were moving out of winter quarters, Pierre said, starting to train in the field. They had guns. Pierre smiled to himself when he spoke of his, shaping his hand into an imagined grip on it, then admitted he only took turns with it. But he hoped to see action before summer was done.

"What action?" said Julien.

Pierre only smiled. "Secret. Captain's orders." His smile twisted a little. "Tell you the truth, I'm not sure."

Julien looked at his friend. "You'll come see me again? When you're in town?"

"Sure thing."

The sun shone. The wet brown grass grew dry, and the new green blades came up through it, piercing the earth, life advancing again into the hollows death had left behind. The deep emerald-green of young nettles beside the road was like a shout of joy, like Élise's rare, bright laughter, precious beyond words. Julien picked them and brought them to Mama for soup. He brought some to Grandpa and Benjamin at the farm. Grandpa let Julien try his hand at plowing, then sent him home, saying he had studying to do and next spring was time enough to learn. Next spring. The thought sent a shiver down his spine. From day to day he could hope for a life still unshattered. But for a year? He did not want to look down that span of days. He did not want the voice of time in his ear, telling him how much he could lose.

The police came back, and back. It was only a matter of time.

Papa came in from work early one evening,

taking off his jacket and coming to kiss Mama where she stood at the counter shredding sorrel leaves with a weary, unsmiling face. He sank down in a chair. "There was an arrest at La Roche today."

Julien's head snapped up.

"A man named Paul Maier. Not Jewish. A German anti-fascist — a political arrest. I don't like it. Antoine Duval has been visiting there. Apparently he tried to chat up the cook yesterday on her way home."

Julien's chair scraped loudly on the floor as he stood. "The cook? You mean — you mean Madame Ferron?"

"Yes, that's her name," said Papa mildly, blinking at him.

"Why would he talk to her?"

"Hoping she'll let something slip, I'm sure. I don't like it."

Julien walked toward the door. Magali said to him quietly, across the space of the dining room, "She's there right now, cooking. They'll have told her."

Julien stopped. They were all looking at him. He kept his face as still as he could, feeling naked.

"Who is 'she'?" said Papa carefully.

"Élise Fournier," said Magali instantly and calmly. "The cook's assistant. You know her, Papa, you got her the job at La Roche because her family has to eat kosher. I'm good friends with her, and she helped us a lot while you were gone. You could say she's a family friend now."

Mama was nodding, but her eyes were still on Julien. Papa hesitated and seemed about to speak. Julien turned, trying to keep his face still. "Sorry. I forgot how soon supper is." He sat down. Took a breath. "She's a good friend. I wish she would try to cross the border. Everyone I know seems to think they might as well try swimming the Atlantic." He looked up suddenly, feeling a small fierce flame rise up in him. "Have you thought about going into hiding yourself, Papa? Have you considered that?"

"After being released —"

"Before being arrested would've been better." He couldn't believe he said it. His heart was hammering.

Mama turned slowly and looked at him.

"I have thought about it," said Papa heavily. "I don't believe it is the right thing at this time."

Now the eyes were on *him.*

"There is still work to do. And God has been faithful. He has gone over and above. When they summoned us that second time . . ." Papa shook his head.

You knew you'd done the right thing. Your

faith was rewarded. Your life made sense.
Some people were shot in the head by the Germans for no reason at all. Some people were released by the French with their beloved integrity intact. Some people were deported because they'd been out on the road at the wrong time. Was it God who chose who? How did He do it? How did He sleep?

Mama watched Papa for a long moment, her face seeming carved out of white stone. Then turned away.

That night after supper Julien went out the door without speaking to anyone, put on his jacket, and went down to Élise's dorm.

She was downstairs in the common room, sitting by Nicole on the sofa reading homework together. She looked up at him, and he looked at her, ashamed. He should have brought Magali. He didn't want to embarrass her. He hadn't thought.

"Is your family all right?" she said.

Julien swallowed, not wanting to lie to her.

She saved him. She said, "I can come over," and stood. He waited silently as she got her jacket from its hook, and didn't speak till they walked out into the chilly spring night together, the streetlights mak-

308

ing pools of light around them.

"I'm sorry," he said. "It's not about my family. It's — my father told me about, about the arrest at La Roche."

Her face went still.

He looked at her helplessly. "It's none of my business — but . . . I wanted to ask you."

"Ask me?" She was standing in the dark with him on a street corner. Did she want to be seen like that? She did not move.

"Are you going to keep going there?" he blurted.

"They're my friends," she said. "If I should quit, they should . . ." She made a little scattering motion with her hands.

"Are they going to? Disband the house?"

Élise shook her head. "They wouldn't have anywhere to go. A lot of them are sleeping in the woods tonight. But they're on waiting lists for visas, or for —" she pointed east with her chin, and did not say *Switzerland.* "Two of them are leaving next week." She glanced around. "I think we should walk."

"Yeah. Yeah." He took the way toward his house, and she followed, walking between pools of light. The darkness was better for speaking somehow. As they turned the corner he asked, very low: "Have you thought about trying it?"

She walked without speaking, straight-backed, gathered in on herself. Finally she spoke so low Julien could barely hear. "I have. They strip-search boys, you know. It would be over, that minute."

They walked down his street in silence. Away in the woods an owl hooted, and another answered. High above them clouds sped over the moon. Finally Julien whispered, "It could happen here too."

She stopped, a low flame in her eyes. "I know of ten people who were arrested on the border," she said. "That's two more than here."

"Not if you count my father."

"That's true."

"I didn't know — ten people?" He looked east. The wind rose, and Élise pulled her jacket closer around her. Julien faced into it, heart knocking in his chest. *Don't send me on that road,* Benjamin had said.

"Édouard at La Roche is friends with a *passeur.* He gets news."

They were past the last streetlight now on the north road. The wind had uncovered the moon, and the forest was moving. He turned to Élise, and the curve of her cheek, the planes and shadows of her moonlit face made him tremble. He looked and looked at her, at those dark eyes that had seen the barbed wire from the inside and still held a hard, bright flame in the depths of them, at that body whose heart beat moment by moment, that heart that one day, no matter what, would stop. Cold flesh, and silence. In seventy years, in thirty — in a year, a month, a week —

"I'm so afraid for you," he whispered.

"Don't." The word was like a bullet. Something came out from her, some intensity, and struck him like a wave. "Don't." Her fists were clenched, the tendons in her wrists standing out like cords. She turned on him a face like a falcon's. "And don't tell me you can't help it, Julien. This is war. This is life. People *have* to help it."

"I can help it." He was looking straight ahead now. Her voice saying his name rang in his mind like a bell, a clear, far, angry music. He glanced at her. "I'm not — whatever you're thinking."

She spoke in a low, dark voice. "I know."

There was silence.

After a moment she started walking again. "Do you know the last thing my parents said to me?" she said in the same voice, not looking at him. "They said 'Help them keep the Commandments.' We were in the barracks at Vénissieux. The aid workers had come to get us. My parents had been denied their exemption, they were going to take them away in the morning, it was a few hours before dawn. It was pitch-dark — the Amitié Chrétienne workers came in with flashlights, they came for *us*. The kids. They said we could get out if they signed us away." Her voice was trembling. "You know what my parents were afraid of? The one thing that made them hesitate? That if they left us with Christians they'd force us to convert."

Julien stared at her.

She stopped and looked him full in the face, her eyes like dark pools, reflecting nothing. "You people have been wonderful. No one's said a word to us. Your pastor lets us use the church annex for prayers. I didn't know what to expect, and you've been as respectful as . . ." She shook her head. "We're here — at your mercy. You could . . ."

Julien opened his mouth hotly, and she held up a hand.

"I know you don't see it that way. It never occurred to you, and I'm glad. But put yourself in my shoes for a minute. We *are*."

Julien looked at her. She looked back. He lowered his head. "I'm sorry," he whispered. "I'm sorry." He turned back toward Tanieux.

She stood where she was. "I don't know

where they are," she whispered. "I don't know if they're alive. I don't know — if they're dead —" Her voice thickened, but she went on. "I don't know if the dead can see us, or if they know — but *God* sees, and *I* see, and I'm going to do what I swore to them." Her face was all lines and angles in the moonlight now, straining. "I'm going to protect my brother and sister with my life. And I'm going to help them keep the Commandments. And I'm going to keep what's left of who I am." Her gaze focused suddenly and held his, hard. "I don't betray people. And I don't think you do either."

He lifted his eyes to hers, terrified that in a moment he would feel tears in them. He had never seen anything as beautiful as her dark shining hair and pale face in the moonlight, her whole soul burning in her eyes. His lips shaped the word slowly. He forced his breath through his throat. "No," he whispered.

"That's what I thought," she whispered back, her eyes still locked with his. He saw the edges of them fill suddenly with tears. One instant, the moonlight turning them to silver; one instant, and she tore her gaze away from him, and turned aside. He swallowed, heart hammering, his whole body singing with joy and longing and pain.

He turned aside too. They began to walk back, two silent figures beneath the wide sky, their steps keeping perfect time.

At the turnoff to his street, she paused and turned, whispered, "See you at school." He nodded mutely, and watched her as she went on down the sidewalk, through the darkness and the pools of pale light, alone. He stood breathing in the spring night air and watching her, till she was almost gone. He couldn't help it. Then he took two deep, harsh breaths, and turned away.

He did not sleep half that night, for remembering the fire and silver in her eyes.

CHAPTER 20
DREAM

He came wide awake in an instant next morning, his heart racing, her face in his mind.

And her voice saying, "They're my friends."

She wasn't going to quit. She was going to keep spending hours every day in a house where young Jewish men were afraid to sleep. Why hadn't he *made* her —

He rolled over and pushed his face into the pillow, remembering why. That look in her eyes, hard and bright as a sword. He was a fool. Trying to push these people around — people who looked their own deaths in the face every day and made calculations about them . . .

At school he nodded to her respectfully and went into his classroom. Then he slipped out of class and quietly tailed Duval to the café.

At the door Duval turned and gave him a

long, cold look. He went back to school.

He pumped Magali, whose best friend's parents owned the café; Duval had sat by Marc Fraysse from La Roche and offered him cigarettes he didn't take. Magali promised to tell Élise.

He would have told her himself. But he was trying to prove to her that he could keep a promise. He hadn't spoken to her alone since that night.

He hadn't spent a night nor a morning without lying in bed with the sight of her eyes filling his mind. It hurt. It hurt gloriously. A no — *that* no — from her. He wouldn't have traded it for a yes from any other girl in the world. *She saw me. She looked at me and saw me — like* that.

She was right. She shouldn't have had to tell him — oh, thank God she had had to tell him. But she was right. What kind of future could they have? He belonged here, and she belonged —

Gone.

The pressure built in his throat and his head. Gone. One way or the other. *Oh God, God, God.*

He slipped out of bed, the hard boards of the floor under his knees. He clasped his hands together, gripping the blanket, his mind breathing words again and again, filling him, muffled as if deep below the sea: *Get her out. Get her out.*

Please.

The word caught in his throat like a stone. In his mind was the darkness of a barracks, the faint gleam of flashlights reflected in the tears on Élise's face. *Help them keep the Commandments.* That was what they'd wanted to tell her, before men with guns took them away. That was what was on their minds.

God.

And surely — *surely* — they were not the only ones.

Please, he prayed one more time. Then he lifted his head, his chest filling, the pain in his throat sharpening. He said in a steady voice, "People say that to You every day."

He rose from his knees and walked evenly over to his closet to get his clothes for the day, without finishing the thought aloud.

And then they die.

On Thursday afternoon he went down to the farm, alone. He ought to be studying. But he needed to breathe the same air as his grandfather, even just for an hour. And he wanted to see Benjamin.

Spring was in full cry around him, the chestnut trees in thick, polleny bloom, the little birds twittering their happy loves from every tree. The grass was lush and green, ankle-high in the pastures, the cows and goats turned out on it tearing and munching busily, their mouths stained with green, their calves and kids at their heels, or butting against udders bulging with milk. It wasn't a rich country, this cold plateau, but it seemed so, always, at the end of May. He passed beneath an apple tree laden with pink and white blossoms slowly, sweetly opening to the sun; the scent made him shudder. He stood under it, breathing in; he closed his eyes and prayed for her. He saw himself standing in a sunlit mountain pass, watching through the thin, deep air as far below she and her brother and sister took step after sure step into the valley. Into the future. And him on the height, his heart singing and breaking: *Goodbye.*

Losing her. That was his unattainable dream.

He took one more breath of the heady scent, looked up and heard the gentle buzz of bees as they crawled in and out. He swallowed, and made himself start walking again.

Grandpa and Benjamin were planting, Grandpa sowing and Benjamin putting each seed precisely in its place. Grandpa raised an eyebrow and brushed the seed-dust from his hands. "Thought I forbade you to help. Or didn't you know I'd be planting?" There were crinkles around his eyes.

"Sorry." Julien shrugged. Of course Grandpa was planting. Everyone was. He looked over at Benjamin.

"Take a break," said Grandpa over his shoulder. "Pick some mint on your way in, and have yourselves some tea."

It was a wonderful thing, tea. It let you do something with your hands and with your mouth a dozen times before you had to say anything. And it was warm. Julien put his wind-chilled hands around his cup and blew on it, avoiding Benjamin's eyes.

"Y'know," he said finally, abruptly. "It's your life."

Grandpa's clock ticked.

"I do know that," said Benjamin quietly.

"I shouldn't have —"

"I wrote to my mother last week and asked her to apply for me." Julien's head jerked up; Benjamin's lips twisted oddly at Julien's uncertain stare. "For another visa."

Julien looked at him for two long heart-beats before saying, "That's not a joke."

"Would I joke about that?"

A painful laugh escaped him. "No."

Benjamin took a sip. Looking at his cup,

he said, very fast, "Will you come with me?"

"Anytime," said Julien roughly.

They both watched the steam rise from the teapot. "So," said Benjamin. "How is everybody?"

When Grandpa came in, leaving his earth-stained boots at the door, he smiled to find Benjamin explaining to Julien that milking was all in the wrist. "He's taken it over completely while I'm planting. Julien, did you know Pierre is at home? I'd catch him quick if you want to see him."

"Yeah," said Benjamin. "He never stays long."

When Julien knocked on the Rostins' door, Monsieur Rostin opened it a crack, then flung it wide. "It's Julien!" he called down the hall.

Pierre sat cross-legged on his bedroom floor, whittling. Short sticks and small carved cylinders lay among the shavings on the floor. He took one up and blew into it, bright eyes on Julien. A hoarse twitter came out, surprisingly like a thrush.

"My father taught me how," Pierre told him. "Listen again." He blew a swift pattern of twitters, three short, three long, and three short again. "Ever hear a thrush do that?"

Julien blinked at him. "Not that I've noticed."

"That's Morse code. Captain taught us. It's our signal. You hear that, you go to the place and be ready for anything."

Julien knelt and nodded. "Useful."

"Want one?"

Julien's pulse jumped slightly. "Why would I need one?" he asked carefully. Pierre just looked at him. Julien lowered his voice. "Are you actually thinking your people would shoot at the police?"

"If they're coming here to arrest us and our friends? They're traitors." Pierre's face was grim.

"They'd come back in more force."

"You let us worry about that, Julien. Because we're *willing.*" Pierre bit off the word with a snap, then met Julien's eyes. "Look at it this way: it's got nothing to do with you. We're your enemies. Tell 'em that if you want, I don't mind. They're not gonna know what this thing is. Just" — he held out the whistle again — "*take* it. Please. Favor to me. I don't want to see my friends deported any more than you do, Julien. And we're not just going to show up shooting. Someone gets hurt, out in the woods . . ." he shrugged. "We can help. We patrol, y'know. You don't see us." He grinned suddenly. "But we're there."

Julien stretched out his hand.

The thing fit inside his fist, tiny; he blew the signal into it once, to Pierre's brief, half-shy grin, then tucked it into his pocket.

"So c'mon." Pierre brushed the shavings off a space across from him on the floor. "Tell me the news."

He told Pierre about everything but Élise. Mama's "spell," Benjamin's brush with the police. Pierre whistled through his teeth at the story of the fight in the root cellar. "I knew he was mad at you about something, but he wouldn't say what."

"Did you ever tell him he should go?"

"Me? No."

The news about La Roche brought up the name Duval, at which Pierre bared his teeth so bitterly that Julien pulled back a little. "Yeah." Pierre called Duval something unprintable. "You hear what he did to *us*?"

"No."

"Last week. Two of our guys, they'd been going into town too much. Visiting some girls. Last time they went — police were waiting for them."

"No."

"Yeah." Pierre's jaw was hard, a fierce light in his eye. "No idea where they took them. Nothing. We spent all week moving our camp since then. All new signals. That's why I'm here." His voice dropped. "You can keep a secret now, right?"

"C'mon. I never ratted on you. Not even that time to your mother."

Pierre's jaw loosened into a wolf's grin. "We were such kids. I thought I was so tough."

"You were. I had that black eye for a month."

Pierre laughed. The light was still in his eye. He leaned forward and said very softly, "Captain says Duval has to go."

Julien did not move. He watched Pierre's eyes. After a moment Pierre, looking back at him, made a small gesture with his finger across his throat.

"Thought you'd want to know," Pierre murmured. "Benjamin told me — y'know — about the girl."

Julien flushed hot. *"Benjamin —"* He snapped his mouth shut.

Pierre laughed out loud, throwing his head back.

"Does *everybody* know my business?" Julien growled.

Pierre gave him a rueful grin. "No, no, he didn't even really tell me. I just got the idea." Pierre turned one of the whistles in his palm, his face sobering. "I mean, I get it. I've been seeing somebody, and if she was Jewish . . ." He shook his head. "It's got to be hell."

Julien put a hand to his pocket, felt the small hard shape of the whistle. Outside the open window a blackbird sang. "So," he said, a slow smile breaking out, slow as sunrise, and backed by almost as much light. *Duval. Go.* He sat back. "Seeing somebody, eh?"

CHAPTER 21
NOTHING TO DO WITH YOU

Elisa stood on the bridge, resting the dish she carried on the stone parapet as she gazed down into the water. She was very weary.

There had been no time to think for a week. La Roche was like a kicked anthill. Édouard and Philippe sleeping in the woods, returning only for meals; Chaim due for a border crossing in a week; Joseph and Rudy and Theo wavering daily over going too. Manuel had sat outside in the sun with her after Paul Maier's arrest and asked her with tears in his eyes whether he should go back to Spain. She'd looked at the place where she'd last seen Paul — his back against the stone wall, legs sprawled out in front of him, playing on his accordion, a jaunty, haunting tune — and said yes. "Better the devil you know, that's what they say, eh?" said Manuel with a painful smile.

She breathed in the scent of the running

water and bowed her head. The dish between her hands held only her own meal; four young men had missed supper last night, and she'd brought Tova and Karl all the leftovers. For the space of one small hour no one needed her. The sound of the water eased her a little; the grass on the bank looked soft as a bed.

She turned aside onto the riverbank. The June sun shone bright on the water, glowed green through the young leaves of a chestnut she passed under. She remembered moonlight, and a young man's empty hands, stilled, making no claim. His open, solemn face, taking in her words like precious counted coins, nothing discarded. The gifts that had passed from hand to hand, not touching, more costly than silver, more silent than snow. There are promises not made under a canopy, she thought. There is fidelity. *I don't have words for it. It's holy too.*

From the bridge behind her came the shouts of children and high laughter. She walked on. She had told him her parents' last words. Why had she told him? The darkness had been alive in her again since then; she could feel it move. The place inside her, at the dead center, the dark and the sheen of flashlights on straw. The place where she had left them, and walked away. She could not see them out of it, could see no faces in her mind. Only eyes looking out at her in the darkness, and a voice saying, "Go." Her lips shaped the words *Where are you?* but no breath came through them. Around the dish her hands felt numb.

There were dark patches in the lush green grass, wet wads of last year's leaves. She set down her dish and took one up, tossed it in the water. The old leaves spun and crumbled as the current carried them away. She found her jaw clenching so tightly that it hurt. She looked down and saw the flattened grass, pale yellow, exposed now to the light. The tears that welled in her eyes shocked her, and she bent to pick up her dish again and began to walk fast. Not here. Not here where anyone could see her from a window, where voices called behind her from the road. Round the bend in the river lay a broad, deep place, sheltered from the town, where the young men sometimes swam. She heard no voices from there now. Alone. She walked in a blur of green and light. A sound made her look up. A splash in the water.

She stopped, her chest tightening, her tears cut off. She wasn't alone. She was with some bare-chested man out there in the water, some man swimming in a river on a bright June day. Her breathing slowed, then stopped as her eyes focused in on him, as she understood what she was seeing.

He wasn't swimming.

He was doubled over in the water, listing to one side, his legs not moving. One arm splashed up, an oddly small sound, and the half-submerged face rose fully out for a few seconds. The sound of his gasping breath came to her over the quiet water. For a moment she didn't move.

Time became strange, in the gap between one breath and another. There seemed to be hours, and yet her body moved so slow. She had dropped the dish and was running forward at top speed, step after endless step, thinking and thinking. She couldn't swim. There was a short, steep grassy bank here, with clusters of trees. He was a good ten meters out or more — a tree branch, was there one long enough? He lifted his face out of the water again and she froze.

It was the man with the burn. The one she'd seen in the street. The war hero.

Time stopped. She stood like stone on the bank, her hand on the tall hazel branch she'd been about to break off, watching one of *them* struggle with death in the water.

Watching one of them, and the fear in his eyes.

Heat rose up through her body in a swift,

sharp wave. She saw faces dark with fury, chanting beneath banners. The flat eyes of the man who had entered her home with a hand on his gun. She saw herself, in the darkness of the barracks, turning and walking away.

The drowning man rose out of the water and gasped in another breath. His eyes were on her now, on her face seeking kindness. *Kindness.* She felt her teeth grate; the sound went down her spine like the rasp of steel on steel.

Justice. Who had he killed? Who would he kill, if he went on breathing this day? Who did he think he was, that she should help him do so? *I have no idea who you are, you son of Amalek. I have no idea what you've done. I only know if you were ordered to, you would shoot me in the head.* Her hand was white around the hazel branch, white the thin scar on her wrist where a pine branch had scratched her months ago in the cold woods. *I have a right.*

His eyes on her had changed now. A memory rose in her whole and alive from her childhood in Heidelberg, the eyes of a wild scarred tomcat someone had drowned in a cage. Its hair on end, spine bent, face distorted in a hissing snarl. Then the change. The pupils going wide and dark, the ears flattening utterly. The unmistakable, unendurable look of eyes that saw death. She'd been seven.

She had seen it in other eyes since then.

She stood still for a dizzying moment, within that darkness at the center of her soul.

Then she began to wrench the hazel branch back and forth.

Five strong wrenches and a long bark-stripping pull, and it parted from the tree. It wasn't long enough. She looked up. He had drifted half a meter downstream. She ran stumblingly over the uneven ground, ran for a place where pine roots jutted from the bank. She climbed down them, the hem of her skirt trailing in the water, and stretched herself out, holding the branch out to him. With a flail of one arm he reached jerkily out to it and fell short, bobbing in the water. Not enough.

She gripped the last pine root with one hand, prayed he was not SS, and plunged in.

She drew in a hissing breath from the shock of cold; panic shot through her as her feet felt for the bottom, down and down, then found it, slippery muck. She held on to the pine root for her life, took a cautious step outward with one foot, and reached the hazel rod as far as she could toward him. His face was underwater — he wasn't even looking. "Here!" she screamed, and he lurched upward — one last time? — his hand reaching out, not far enough.

She let go of the pine root and took another step out into the water, her foot reaching for ground she could not see.

She found the bottom, far below. The water rose to her chin. She felt a sudden tug and gripped the hazel rod hard. She prayed, a sharp, deep, silent prayer in time to the hammering of her heart, wedged her back foot as deep as she could into the mud of the bottom, and pulled very, very gently. She could feel how little force would slide her backward and down into the muck, the waters closing over her head. He was coming toward her, slow and steady. She took a careful, slow step backward, her heart in her throat. Her foot found the bottom. She reached behind her, fingertips brushing against the pine root. She reached farther, felt the deadly slide begin, and with a cry and a splash fell backward, catching the root in her right hand.

She pulled herself up out of the water again, pulled him swiftly toward her now, a strange, heavy lump in the water, still doubled up, his face gray, eyes stunned, his hand still gripping. She found firm footing in the shallows, the pine root bracing her, caught his wrist as he came near and pulled awkwardly, lifting his face fully out of the water. He was naked from the waist up, wearing black shorts, and impossibly heavy. His skin was slippery; she couldn't get a grip under his arms; his legs seemed to be locked. She had to put one shoulder under his armpit and shove upward to lift his arms and torso up onto the bank, his legs still in the water. He clung to the grass with both hands, gasping in air, his bare back heaving. She climbed up beside him, cold, muddy water streaming from her clothes. His wet dark hair gleamed in the June sunlight. The burned side of his face lay uppermost, his mouth open, one eye on her. His face convulsed suddenly, his fingers digging into the earth, and he began to drag himself upward, turning his body to bring his locked knees up over the bank, his teeth gritted, eyes fierce. She didn't help him. She didn't know where on his body to put her hands. Suddenly she didn't quite understand how she had failed to notice she was grabbing at a half-naked man. He came up and up, and fell on his side on the grass, taking huge breaths.

She was shaking. With cold, with the

memory of that water lapping at her chin, with the sight of that hard light of will in his eyes. *Who are you? Who are you? Oh God, who have I killed today?*

"I didn't know — it would be — so cold," he gasped. In German.

She climbed to her feet, her eyes on him. Telling herself he was in shock, telling herself it was no deep instinct that made him address her in the right language, telling herself — *Who, who, who have I killed today?*

"*Danke,*" he breathed, and she ran.

"What," said Mademoiselle Combe, "was the crucial wrong that sparked the miners' riot in *Germinal?*"

Someone raised a hand. Julien looked aside out the classroom door. He should know this. He'd done the reading. Awful reading. Élise hadn't come to school this afternoon — where was she? Mademoiselle Combe was listing atrocities on the board. Papa said it was all true, that Zola had been the first to write it like it was. *People don't like to face these things,* he'd said.

Did that take courage? Julien wondered, staring through the doorway — and where was she? His heart jittered in his chest, and he closed his eyes, drawing in a long, bitter breath, ashamed.

He'd slept well the last three nights, and why? Because someone with a gun had decided his enemy had to go.

He'd woken before dawn this morning, his mind clear and empty. The house silent as death. He'd lain there and looked at the dim lines of light that sketched the edges of the shutters outside his window, and heard Pierre's kind voice saying, *Thought you'd want to know.*

Yes. I wanted to know.

He hadn't opened his mind to anyone in months. He couldn't remember the last time. He wasn't at all certain what he would have said, if he had.

He leaned back in his chair and watched Mademoiselle Combe underline *Deceit by mine owners,* imagining, just hypothetically, what Papa would say if he joined the Maquis.

A figure flashed by the door. The silhouette, the head with its dark hair pinned back — it was Élise. He craned his neck to follow her, but she was gone. He shut his eyes and felt it spread through him like rain through the soil: *Still alive. Still free.*

He saw her again at break, in a tight knot with Nicole and Magali, their heads bent together. When class let out at five she came to him, catching his eye across the hotel dining room as their two classes filed out.

"Julien, would you do something for me? Does your f—" Élise inhaled sharply, her eyes sweeping the room, and pressed her lips together. She jerked her head onward and he followed her out the door and across the patio, looking straight ahead, feeling Duval's eyes on them like the small blank eye of a rifle. Duval at his usual table, sipping coffee, idly glancing up from his paper with a small smile at the poor fools filing past.

They went down the patio steps in silence, down past two streetlamps before she turned to him. Something in her face made his heart leap, some hardness of decision. *She's going.* He controlled his breathing, wrestled his mind down. "Yes?" he said.

"Could you ask your father to come down to" — her voice dropped — "La Roche? Two of my friends — have some questions. About going. But they don't want to come into town."

Julien swallowed and gave her the answer she wanted. "Of course. I'll ask him to come tomorrow. If it has to be later I'll send you a message."

"Thank you." She gave him a single nod. "I'll tell them."

His hand flashed out of its own accord; he almost touched her arm. "Have you thought about it?" he said, very low.

Her face was carven wood. "I told you. I think about it all the time."

His eyes dropped. "I'm sorry."

"Don't be sorry." She didn't look at him as she said it. "For anything." She murmured, "I need to go." Then walked away from him, her steps not quite steady, without giving him another glance, without giving him the *bise* to say goodbye. Thank God. He could not have stood even the chance brush of her skin against his. Not now.

Not ever again.

He stood and watched her go. Then he took the Rue Vaillet, walking aimlessly, feeling the rush of blood in his ears, thinking of the moment he had believed. Of course she wasn't going. He was such a fool. *Don't be sorry. For anything.* He turned onto the Rue de l'Étang, looking down along its sloping length as if it were a tunnel that would lead him down and then up into some other place, some great, good land where everything happens for a reason, where there are no walls and no barbed wire, where not even animals hide from the hunter or are herded onto the slaughtering floor. A place of childhood and of hope, a place people tell their children is true because they are not strong enough yet to face the horror of the world. To face the fact that the meek are eaten and the strong survive. For one long moment he could see it, golden in the slanting afternoon light.

Then he blinked, and saw that Pierre was coming up the street at a hard jog, and that he carried a gun.

He was sure it was a gun. Not because he could see it — it was only a bulge at his right hip, under his jacket — but because of how Pierre wore it. The way his hand strayed to it as he jogged, as if to check that it was still there; the way he carried himself when he slowed, when his ranging eyes met Julien's and brightened suddenly with purpose. Julien understood, watching him come: a man walks differently when he has a gun.

He was a few steps away now, his eyes trained on Julien, his face hard and bright. He closed the distance between them swiftly, without any greeting, and asked in a low fast voice, "Is he still at his hotel?"

Julien's heart seemed to slow, lumping in his chest. The sun on the puddles blinded him; the lines of Monsieur Chastain's empty hay wagon going down the street ahead of him stood out etched like a woodcut. A little girl ran into a house; a young woman with a basket greeted an old man. It was spring, and the sun was shining, and Pierre was continuing breathlessly, "I got delayed. Bicycle chain." There was black grease on his fingers. He glanced swiftly behind him, lowered his voice. "They'll be there any minute, I'm supposed to be there ahead. I just need to know if he's still there, Julien. That's all. It's nothing to do with you."

Please, his eyes said.

It's everything to do with me, Julien's eyes said back, and just as Pierre's face began to move back away from his, narrowing into bitterness, Julien opened his mouth.

"On the patio," he said. "Reading a paper. Right-hand side."

CHAPTER 22
THE HEART OF LIFE

He tried to stay away. He couldn't.

He was walking up the Rue des Genêts when the news reached him. He had already seen three men on bicycles go by. First a young man Pierre had once mentioned as a fellow soldier in the Maquis, then two strangers, hard, weathered faces under their cloth caps, impassive, eyes front. At the sight of them a tightness struck down through his chest: *This is real.* He didn't stare after them; he turned onto a side street, and began to make his way home.

But he couldn't.

Élise would be at her dorm by now. Everyone would be home or at the park or the café chatting with their friends, the Hotel Bellevue patio would be almost empty. He could see it so vividly: the single broad step up to the slate-tiled patio, the cast-iron railing along one end, the round green tables with their flaking paint, the steam of Duval's coffee and his cigarette smoke mingling in the warm, sunlit air.

The four men, approaching.

He was already taking the Rue Vaillet back toward the hotel when little Frédéric Comte dashed by, shouting: "They've shot Duval! They just *shot* him!" Julien quickened his pace. At the corner of the Rue Peyrou there was a jostling on the sidewalk behind him; he stepped aside and Pastor Alexandre passed him by, almost running, limping slightly from his bad back, flanked by Frédéric and Monsieur Faure. Julien looked instinctively behind them, but his father wasn't there. He followed, almost running himself now.

They came out of the Rue Vaillet into a small crowd that was edging backward before the fierce face and gestures of Madame Flory, the Bellevue owner. Behind her on the patio two men knelt over a prone figure. "Let them work, and mind your own business, can't you? Can't do an honest day's work without people walking in and firing off *revolvers* in my hallway —"

"He deserved it," a male voice growled.

"And they had to shoot him in *my* hotel?"

"You had to put him up in your hotel?"

Madame Flory rolled her eyes and threw up her hands as if this were the stupidest question imaginable. Pastor Alexandre reached the front of the crowd then and said something to her as he stepped up onto the patio. She lowered her hands and nodded *of course, of course,* ushering him past. Julien pushed his way desperately up to the patio railing, the place he had stood so many sunny days with Sylvain, with Magali, with Élise. Then along the railing on its lower side, a place where he could stand down beside the raised patio rather than on it, his face level with the tabletops. He could see Duval clearly now, in profile, gray-white, the skin and muscles of his face seeming stretched over bone, deep lines Julien had never seen before around his staring eyes. A man bent over him with some bright metal instrument, his face intent and his shirtfront wet and shockingly scarlet, the cloth's check pattern still showing in a crisscross of dark-red lines. The man muttered a curse and shook his head. Duval's shirt was open, the thin cloth lying heavily on the stones, slick and shiny with blood. His chest looked like lumped, half-charred sausage meat except for the blood that welled up at steady intervals, as if from a squeezed sponge, and spilled out over the stones: blood, and then pause, and then again blood. He could smell it. It smelled like slaughtering time. He remembered Monsieur Thibaud bent over a pig; Grandpa murmuring, "There, it'll be quick now" to the old rooster as he laid his head out on a stump.

Pastor Alexandre knelt beside the man. The medic glanced at him briefly and muttered something Julien couldn't hear.

"Monsieur Duval," the pastor said, and Julien could hear him fine. "You have done great wrong, and you've paid dearly for it. God will forgive you this moment if you repent."

The head turned slightly on its trembling neck, not toward Pastor Alexandre, but away. The white lips drew back. Duval's eyes stared out for one last moment with a look of wounded reproach; then he closed them, slowly, his lips still twitching between pain and contempt. Julien saw Pastor Alexandre's face fall, like a hillside slowly giving way in a flood, heard his sigh, and the medic's muttered curse, then the pastor's grunt of pain as he heaved himself back to his feet. Julien realized he was clinging with one hand to one of the uprights of the railing, that he was light-headed from not breathing, that he was not alone.

"Come away, Julien," said his father, not taking his eyes off Duval.

Julien swallowed. " 'We dare not deny any

man his chance at repentance.' You said that."

"I did."

"They don't want it." His voice rasped deep in his chest.

"Some of them do."

"Have you *seen* them?"

Papa said nothing. The blood was welling more slowly now from the ruin of Duval's chest. His face no longer straining. Slack, the muscles lying beneath the skin like stretched-out elastic, a worn object, no human expression on it at all. Another smell rose from the man now, like the smell of Monsieur Rostin's cesspit on that day so long ago. So long ago. The medic, hand spread on Duval's chest, called up to his comrade in a flat voice: "Dead."

Julien turned from the corpse to his father, looking him full in the face. "He was a murderer."

"Yes."

"They kill every day. How on earth do you think we're going to survive if we aren't allowed to shoot one murderer?"

Papa's voice was very quiet. "You know what I think, Julien."

Julien looked at the deep lines in his father's face, at his eyes like deep pools of water. Then at the patio he and his friends had stood on every day at break, the ash-colored face of the corpse lying between the little green tables, the scarlet pool staining the stones. Madame Flory came out the front door grim-faced, with a bucket and a mop.

"It's not going to work," Julien said heavily, and turned away from his father to begin the long walk home.

He saw it when he closed his eyes. Behind his lids there was crimson, wherever he looked. School was canceled the day after the shooting. After Papa left for La Roche, Julien walked out the door and took the road to Grandpa's farm, and climbed the ridge north of town instead to sit on a boulder and shut his eyes and turn his face to the sun. Red pulsed around his eyes, the glow of the living blood in his body, the secret at the heart of life. A secret spilled over and over. Often enough that people should know. Wasn't it in the Old Testament? Wasn't that the reason the Jews weren't supposed to eat blood?

This is life. This red stuff here. If you let it out, it doesn't go back in.

If you dare, you can change the world forever.

With this.

He still remembered how Pierre had walked. The weight of it somehow, the gravity — you could feel the world bending around the thing at his hip. The hard purpose in his eyes, cutting like a knife through the months and years of helpless rage and fear; making a path.

Pierre, on his way to change the future.

Julien wondered what he had paid for it.

Pierre hadn't done it himself. Julien understood that. They'd sent experienced men for that, men who had killed before. But you didn't have to pull the trigger to be part of it. Part of taking a human being out of the world.

He understood that too.

He had almost told his father what he'd done. He'd meant to. He didn't intend to be a coward anymore. He had looked at Papa across the supper table, between questions from Magali about what it was like and quelling looks from Mama, and he had seen the questions in Papa's eyes. He had pictured himself going into Papa's study with him, sitting across the desk from him, looking him in the eye.

Then his mind had run along the paths his story might take, and every single one had run headlong into Pierre.

"He just turned away and closed his eyes,"

Papa told Magali soberly. "A minute later he was dead." He glanced up at Julien. "It's a terrible thing to watch. I'm sorry you had to see it."

I'm not.

It was right. It was right that he'd had to see it. To see blood whenever he closed his eyes. To understand in his body that a man wasn't so different from a chicken or a hog, not in that way — that a breathing human being could turn in the space of seconds into meat. That it could happen to him. It was right that he should see that and know that. He had been a part of it. He had chosen to.

And Duval would never betray anyone again.

"We did it," he whispered, the rock warm against his back, the sun a crimson glow through his eyelids. "You didn't do it, but we did. How do they know You didn't want us to? How do they know?"

Shadows of clouds moved between him and the glow, dark red and bright in turn. The rock was rough behind his head. He had done it, and he had meant to do it. The knowledge was like a smooth stone in his hand, turned over and over in his fingers, heavy and real. It wasn't something someone could give you, this weight. It was something you found, after searching and searching. Alone.

He bowed his head, and in the sudden darkness behind his eyes he saw Élise. She was at the piano, her wet apron lying limp on the piano bench beside her, her face hard and bright and painful with longing, the music rising up from her hands like flame. He saw her in a long black dress, her hair braided into a crown, pearls on her neck, faces in the dark beyond her watching in wonder: the same face, the same hands, the same naked joy.

He took a long, careful breath, and let himself dare to hope.

CHAPTER 23
A LITTLE WHILE

The Gestapo came the next day.

They marched into the *mairie,* kicked the mayor's assistant out of his office, and took it over, piling up papers and tossing them onto the hallway floor. By midday the rumor was three people had gone in "for questioning" and hadn't yet come out.

When class let out at five, the word was that they'd come out. And Pastor Alexandre and Papa had gone in.

Julien walked down to the *place du centre* with his school satchel still on his back. He couldn't help it. He stood looking at the *mairie,* remembering Haas, the Gestapo chief: the classic profile, the eyes that owned everything they saw, the way the man had called him boy and told him to fetch his father.

He wanted to stand and stare at that door for hours, not leave till he saw his father's face again. He wasn't stupid.

He went home.

At home Mama and Magali moved silently around the kitchen, pulling potatoes from the pantry and greens from the icebox. "Soup," Mama said. "We can keep it warm." Her eyes going to the south window down into town. Silence. A clink as Mama took a knife from the drawer.

Magali drew a glass of water from the tap, put it in front of Julien's chair. He sat. "Did Élise tell you why she was late the other day?" she said abruptly.

Julien shook his head.

"She was rescuing a *boche* from drowning in the river."

"What?"

"One of those convalescents. I guess he didn't know how cold that water is."

"She can swim?"

Magali shook her head. "She used a long branch. It was a mess, she said. She almost got swamped herself."

Julien's heart beat hot. *If she had . . .* It swept through him in a wave. *For one of* them.

"She told me she stood there a moment and had to make up her mind."

"Of course."

"Not about whether she could."

"Of course not," he whispered.

Papa came home at eight, his share of soup still simmering on the stove. His face was gray and lined. "I'm all right," he said, sinking into his chair. Mama put a bowl of soup in front of him, and a cup of coffee. He sipped it and looked up at her, his face weary and open. They had asked him the same questions over and over, he said. They wanted to know who had done the shooting. But he believed it was clear to them by now that the pastors simply didn't know. Julien looked out the window.

"I'm not certain of my German but I think one of them may have shouted, *They're not lying.* Very angrily, you know. As if that were truly offensive." Papa's lips twitched into a small smile. "Can you imagine?"

"Eat," said Mama, pushing his spoon at him.

He ate.

The next day Papa took Julien aside and asked him if they could take a walk together before school. "I wanted to ask you," Papa said, "whether you really meant what you said the other day, or whether it was the emotion of the moment."

"When?"

His father turned to him, grave-eyed, and said nothing.

Julien's jaw clenched. "I meant it."

"You believe it was right for them to kill him?"

"I do."

Papa studied his face. "Did someone make the case to you, or . . . ?"

"Yeah. *He* did." It welled up out of him suddenly, whole and lightening in its truth. "Duval did."

"I don't know exactly what you mean."

That's how it has been since the world began. For a moment Julien saw paintings on dark cave walls, heard the cries of women and children, smelled campfire smoke and blood. The blood of the meek, soaking the earth. Grinning men behind them who had everything they wanted. "He got you arrested," he said. "He almost got Benjamin arrested. He was a threat to everyone, everyone I love. For *money.* And he didn't care. If he'd ever managed to face who he really was he would've hanged himself. And you saw. You saw what he did with his chance at repentance. You really think *witness* is going to stop these people? Guns stop them. Period. You really think God wants us to die?"

Under the eaves of the slate roofs above them, mourning doves cooed. "God wants us to be willing to die," Papa said quietly.

"God does not ask less of us than the Maquis."

"But for a *reason*. Not just because someone decided to kill us. Jesus said turn the other cheek. If he'd meant, 'Let them murder you,' maybe he would've said so."

Papa stopped on the sidewalk, his face working suddenly. "He *did* so, Julien. He did so, and in that act the power of God was made perfect more than in any before or since — the hinge itself of history — why does no one ever understand?" His voice went high.

"Papa — are you all right?"

"They've emptied the St. Paul d'Eyjeaux camp," Papa whispered. "We just heard. They deported everyone."

"Deported? When?"

"Two weeks after they released us." His eyes were like caverns. "All those men . . ."

Julien's lips shaped words, but they didn't come out. *Two weeks.*

"Just hold on to God, Julien. Please hold on to God."

Julien looked up at his father and nodded wordlessly at the tears in his tired eyes. Papa gripped his shoulder for a moment, then let his weak hand fall.

They went on down the street in silence together, beneath the spring sun.

■ ■ ■ ■

Elisa grunted, applying more pressure, and the chicken bone snapped between her hands. Mama had taught her long ago: for the most nourishing broth, every bone must be opened to the marrow. They needed every bit they could get. It wasn't every week she could get *two* chickens, even now that she'd found a kosher slaughterer Chaim approved. She smiled, remembering Karl's eyes when he'd seen the portion she brought him yesterday.

She put down the bone-sawing knife and picked up the short butcher knife to start on the second carcass, tested its blade, and reached into a drawer for the whetstone. She drew the blade down the stone to the rhythm of the thought that was always with her now: *Who have I killed? Who have I killed?* She had not told Karl what she had done. She had told Tova, who said she had done right. Tova always thought mercy was right.

It had been a week now. She'd woken this morning thinking of it again. Of the way the young German in the street had hung on his every word, of the fierce will in his eyes as he clambered up the bank with only his arms, legs still locked in a cramp. Even that heavy face of his, so careless of its scarring, spoke of power. *Who have I killed?* She'd woken hard in the darkness, her heart beating that rhythm, no hope of falling back to sleep. She'd walked down here before dawn to start the day's work. Might as well. The broth was better if it simmered all day. She drew the sharp knife down the stone, praying again for mercy, for justice, for no more death. Outside the windows of the quiet kitchen, dawn was pale behind the trees. A movement caught her eye in the woods. She froze, one hand on her knife.

There was a knock on the door.

In the dark stone church the sunlight fell bright as Élise's eyes, between shadows dark as her hair. Julien's father was preaching for the first time in many months, and something in the rise and fall of Papa's hoarse voice held him, something that made the shadows stir in the corners and the hair stand up on his arms. Papa did not sound like a teacher now.

" '. . . and in His word do I hope.' Our hope is real, brethren . . ."

There had been Gestapo in the street again on Friday. No one knew why. Gestapo in the street, and a stain on the hallway wall by their classroom door despite all Madame Flory's scrubbing, and a place on the patio the students silently stepped around as they filed into class. There was a whistle in his inner jacket pocket, always, and a place on his hip that his foolish hand drifted to when he saw one of their uniforms. An empty place, and useless.

She hadn't come to school on Friday. Midmorning Nicole had slipped him a note, *She's fine,* and he'd bowed his head in relief and wished he could sink into the floor. Wished he could keep watch by her side always.

He sat in his pew hearing his father declare the word of the Lord and seeing nothing but her, her pale face and fierce dark eyes in the moonlight. Seeing the world he wanted to promise her, and the world she was given instead. He stared at the pew ahead of him, one finger tracing the grain of the wood, and heard Papa's voice rise, ringing into the final psalm, phrases coming out to him between his broken thoughts: *The Lord is my light and my salvation. Whom shall I fear? He will hide me in the day of trouble.* He looked up at his father in the high, shadowed pulpit, his face cut out sharp against the darkness behind. *I would have lost heart if I had not believed I would see the goodness of the Lord in the land of the living.*

Julien almost stood up that instant. Something seized him, the muscles of his belly and chest all clenching painfully at once. He couldn't sit there another second. He rose unsteadily, not looking at Mama and Magali. The faces turned toward him were a blur as he walked slowly out of the church. The June sunlight hit him like a blow.

He walked up the Rue du Verger, past the *mairie* where his father had been questioned. Across the *place* where Monsieur Heckel and seven strangers had sat in their bus waiting to be deported. Past the alley where he had seen Duval writing down names. Where Duval had told him flatly that this was the way of the world. He stood on the corner by the Rue des Genêts, where a black automobile had taken his father away for what could so easily have been the last time. He tried to breathe, his lips shaping words he couldn't say. *The land of the living. A little while yet.* A fist was gripping his heart and lungs, painfully. He felt dizzy. He was going mad. It ran in families. He threw his head up toward the sky, the pressure in his chest so tight that the upward movement felt like tearing, and tried to force his gritted teeth apart, the words barely escaping through them: *You have a little while yet, to show Yourself.* He lowered his head and stood there breathing hard, though he had been walking very slow.

After a minute he raised his head again. In the bright morning sun someone was coming toward him across the *place* at a loping, uneven pace. Someone panting, his legs unsteady from running. Roland Thibaud.

"Julien," he gasped. "Julien. The Gestapo are at La Roche. They're arresting everybody."

Julien's hand shot out, his fingers digging into Roland's arm. "Élise? Élise Fournier?" He didn't recognize his own voice. She was there. It was eleven — she was there.

Roland took a ragged breath, his eyes large and dark. "Everybody," he said.

CHAPTER 24
A PROMISE OR A LIE

Julien stood very still as the world staggered around him. When he opened his eyes he still stood on the corner, but the place had changed: the stone houses around the *place du centre* with their empty, staring windows; the wilderness of cobblestones stretching out before him; the dark maw of the *mairie* door under its lying colors, the blue, white, and red that should have been taken down and burned three years ago now —

"How many?" he said.

"I told you. Everyone."

"How many *Gestapo*?" He realized his hand was on his right hip. On his empty right hip pocket. He pulled it away forcibly and thrust it into his light jacket, where it found the small, hard shape of the whistle.

Roland gaped at him. "I saw three outside — with machine guns. Must be more inside. Julien, what on *earth* . . .?"

His mind sketched the encounter for him

in brief, bright lines, from the Maquis patrol's discovery of the odds stacked against them — and swift retreat — to Pierre's demotion for giving him the whistle. His nerveless fingers dropped it back into its hidden pocket. "Sorry," he murmured. "I've gone mad." His other hand touched his lips, as if he could hold the words in front of his eyes and stare at them. Roland looked disturbed. "I'm all right," said Julien tonelessly. He was a city on fire, the bombs falling in waves, screams muffled by the massive, almost soundless shock of explosion. He looked at his hands again, at his feet, intact. He could walk down to La Roche. Walk down to La Roche and scream, *Take me instead.* He could see their laughing faces.

He could walk down to La Roche and say goodbye.

The power of the truth turned his knees to water, and he put a hand on the wall beside him to keep from stumbling. Roland was watching him. "Thank you," Julien got out. He pointed the way to the church with his chin. "You'll tell them too?"

"You're going down there?"

Julien nodded, his mind spinning out wild things for him to say. *Maybe I can get them to shoot me. That'd be good. Quicker. That's*

359

how this ends, you know. Me. You. Her . . .
"Yeah," he whispered hoarsely, remembering Élise's face as they stood together in the street — *Don't be sorry. For anything* — so bright, like the sun, even his mind's eye could barely look at it. She had pulled a German soldier out of the river that same day, and he hadn't even known it. The day he had betrayed Duval. Was it better to go down that way? he wondered as Roland walked away from him — *with your innocence whole, nothing on your soul but an act of mercy* — if you were going down anyway? *I did it for you. I would've shot him for you.* He grudged her nothing. She deserved everything, everything but what she was doomed to. And those swine with no idea of what they owed her —

"Roland!" Julien roared, the name echoing loud against the housefronts, and ran. Within seconds he caught up to him, took him by the shoulders and babbled into his face: "Do you know? She pulled a *boche* out of the river, a convalescent, she saved his life, do you know? Did you hear? Do you have any idea who he is?"

Roland was shaking his head. "I never heard that. She did that?"

"Yes! Yes! She did that!" He realized he was shouting, but he couldn't stop. He let

360

go of Roland's shoulders, turning. "Magali — Magali knows!"

"Julien, what —"

Julien barely heard him. He was racing for the church, as fast as his feet could go.

Almost an hour later he was knocking on the door of Les Genêts — "that fancy little guesthouse down by the river," Madame Flory had called it — sweat beading on his forehead, a deep ache in his chest. He tried to slow his shuddering breath, to summon tact, politeness, any kind of thought at all — what if the man himself answered the door? — but his heart could only hammer, *What if they're gone? What if they're gone?* Papa had gone down to tell them what Élise had done, to tell them he was coming with evidence, with this man — Lord willing — this man he had lost so much time finding.

Silence. He knocked again. A sparrow landed on the wrought-iron balcony railing above and twittered at him. Geraniums in window boxes raised their blood-red petals innocently to the sun. He started at a sound from inside. The door opened on a woman his mother's age with a calm, lined face. The scent of roasting meat from somewhere inside made his stomach twinge.

"Bonjour," the woman said, her eyebrows

going up a touch.

"*Bonjour, madame.* Madame Delaure?"

"That is me."

He swallowed. "I was told there's a German staying here who has, er —" His hand came up and brushed one side of his face.

"Scarring, I suppose you mean? Major Albrecht is on the terrace out back. I ought to ask what you want with him," she added, laying thoughtful eyes on him.

"It's a — a personal matter, madame."

Her mouth quirked. She stood aside, gesturing toward the French windows at the back of the little oak-paneled sitting room. He wiped his feet on the mat and walked in past the umbrella stand and between the spotless sofas, the rug deep and soft beneath his feet, the sour taste of terror in his mouth. Outside were two wrought-iron tables in the shade of a spreading tree; at one of them, leaning back in his chair, a man smoking. He turned at the sound of the glass doors opening, and Julien saw his face, the whole left side a ridged and melted mass of pink and red. His eyes fixed on Julien, who swallowed and started forward.

Did she tell you anything at all that could identify him? he'd asked Magali.

Yeah, she'd said.

"*Bonjour, monsieur.*" He ducked his head,

362

forcing the words through his tight throat. "Forgive me for disturbing you . . ." He looked up into the piercing gaze, and suddenly he was speaking fast and clear. "I'm told a young woman saved your life in the river last week. She's just been arrested by the Gestapo." His hands came up and clasped in front of him; he couldn't take his eyes off the man's eyes. "I'm here to beg you to save her life."

Albrecht rose to his feet. "The girl?" he murmured. His lips moved stiffly, the skin of the burned side stretching oddly as he spoke again, louder. "You tell me you know who she is? How do you know?"

"She told my sister, the day after she did it. She's a family friend."

"Family friend, eh?" The man examined the glowing tip of his cigarette, his ravaged face unreadable. "And how were you able to find out who I was?"

Julien took a breath, looked down. His hand went up to one side of his face. He glanced up to see the German's lip twisted upward on the intact side.

"Naturally." The man looked at his cigarette again, exhaled slowly, then put it to his lips and took a drag. "And you really think that I can save her?"

"If anyone can, sir."

"I am an army officer. I have nothing to do with security. Nothing to do with those men."

"Surely they must think your life is worth something, sir."

The lips quirked up again. "One would hope." He ground out his cigarette in the ashtray. "Where is she?"

"At a boardinghouse called La Roche, just a little ways down the road from here, out of town. The Gestapo are there right now making arrests. Will you come, monsieur?"

The man nodded, and turned toward the house. His first step forward showed a slight limp. At the door he paused, and called in, "Madame Delaure! We would like to borrow two bicycles, if you please."

"Of course, major." The woman's voice came again a moment later, calling, "Murielle!"

As a girl came down the hallway to her, the major turned again to Julien and said quietly, "Now listen. I can ask them to produce her, and if I recognize her as the one, I can tell them what she has done and ask for her release as a personal favor. That is what I can do."

"Yes, monsieur."

"I have no authority over these men."

"I understand, monsieur."

"See that you remember it." He limped across the living room and through the foyer. Out front the girl was just bringing up a second bicycle. Julien stood politely, his stomach roiling, and mounted his bicycle at the same time Albrecht did. "Lead on," the German said, and Julien did, spinning down through the streets and over the bridge. *I'm coming, Élise, I'm coming.* The light played lovely on the water, wind in the hayfields, the whole world a promise or a lie. Sweet the sun's light, bright and terrible the last bend in the road before La Roche came into view. Their wheels took them round it unwavering, and Julien let out a hoarse, inarticulate cry.

The place was deserted.

Papa's haggard face lifted out of his hands. "They were already in the bus. The men wouldn't speak to me — wouldn't acknowledge me at all. I tried, Julien . . ."

At the far end of the La Roche common room, someone was weeping. Another young man sat by him, staring. In the corner a broken suitcase spilled shirts, a toothbrush, a pair of glasses. Dirty dishes lay here and there on the long table; Madame Ferron turned toward him, a plate in her hand. "They wouldn't let any of us leave," she

365

said. "I kept her in the kitchen, I told them she was only a cook. She was the last one they questioned — she had that little bit of an accent . . ."

Julien held up a hand just as Albrecht stepped through the door behind him. The man's eyes swept the room. "They'll be taking them to headquarters," Albrecht said.

"In Le Puy?" said Papa.

Albrecht nodded.

Julien turned to him, his stomach rising up sick with hope and fear. "I'll buy you a train ticket. I'll — I'll give you a tour of the town — there's some beautiful places. All I ask is that you try — once."

Albrecht's eye studied him out of its angry scar, his ruined jaw set. Julien watched him, not breathing.

"You can fetch me for the morning train tomorrow," said Albrecht. He gestured out the door. "And bring back that bicycle when you're finished here. Madame Delaure would not like to lose it."

And he turned on his heel and strode out.

"It's not *crazy.*" Magali was leaning forward over the table, passion in her voice. "It's a *chance* — she deserves a chance!"

"Let your brother speak for himself, Magali."

Julien lifted his head out of his hands, elbows on the familiar wood of the kitchen table, throat too tight to speak. A whole afternoon. A whole night. Why was there no late train on Sunday? Monsieur Faure was out of town with his automobile. Julien shook his head to clear the mad vision behind his eyes: Albrecht in a farm cart, bouncing as Julien whipped the horse to a gallop . . .

"Contrary to your immediate assumption, young lady," Papa was saying, "I absolutely believe this ought to be done. What I don't believe is that this senior German officer needs a French eighteen-year-old to accompany him —"

"He doesn't even know her name —"

"*I* know her name!" shouted Papa.

Julien looked up. Across the table, Mama sat up slowly and very straight, her eyes on her husband.

"And I should go," said Papa, with weight.

"*No!*" Mama shouted, her voice like a whip. Everyone jumped. "No, Martin! If you dare —" She raised a hand. She didn't move from her seat, but she actually raised a hand to him. She spoke between her teeth, and Papa pulled back from her. "You maniac, you troublemaker, you *pastor,* have you truly forgotten where you were three months ago? *I* haven't. They haven't. You'll go present yourself at Gestapo headquarters over my dead body."

"You'd rather have your son go?" Papa's voice cracked.

Mama sat very straight and still. After a moment she said quietly, "I'd rather go myself."

Julien started up from his seat.

Magali dropped her forehead into her hand and muttered, "No, me. *I'll* go."

Mama stared at her, mouth open. A strangled bark of laughter escaped Julien's throat.

Mama drew herself up. "I'd rather go myself," she said to Papa, lifting her chin. "But I don't fool myself about my chances of leaving him here. I don't know if you've heard, but our son doesn't answer to me anymore. He's made that quite clear. You could try and see, if you like, whether he still answers to you."

There was a moment of shocked silence. Julien still stood, leaning forward with his hands on the table; he stared and stared into his mother's sane eyes. Papa said nothing.

"Mama," said Magali a little shakily, "are you . . . all right?"

"I am perfectly well," snapped Mama.

Julien spoke at last, hearing his own voice like a bell struck once and hard in clear mountain air. "He told me to fetch him for the morning train. I'm going to do exactly what he said."

No one said a word. Julien sat down. *I have spoken,* he thought, and felt a bubble of strange, bleak laughter rise up in his throat.

Then he put his head down, and returned to trying to rein in the carthorse galloping in his mind.

CHAPTER 25
THE MOUTH OF THE BEAST

They prayed that evening, the whole family, down on their knees as the dark came on. Begging a God they had never set eyes on to show His goodness here, now, tomorrow, before it was too late. It was already too late for hundreds, thousands; it was too late for Jacques Marlot and Édouard and all the guys at La Roche who had never pulled anyone out of a river — anyone German. *Who do you think you're fooling? It's too late.* He wanted to leap up and beg his family to shut up about hope, to go away and let him scream himself to sleep. He begged God instead, for mercy, for *her,* though his heart ached like a broken bone with the pain of it, like the broken leg of a man running for his life.

The prayer ended. The eyes opened on him, too many eyes. Mama caught him as he rose on shaky legs, and steered him to the kitchen where she gave him two sips out of a small blue bottle she said was tincture of valerian she'd grown herself. It smelled like damp earth, and burned going down. "Now bed. Go. I'll be up in ten minutes." He was too tired to tell her not to. Did he really want her not to? He didn't see her when she came, only felt a second blanket laid over him where he shivered under his, and heard her low voice. "You're not a child anymore. Don't think I don't know that. But just for a minute, pretend." Her low, sweet voice singing in Italian, the lullaby she had sung to them always in the long, soft nights of childhood, that time that would never come again. *Stella, stellina.* Then the kind darkness took him, for a while.

Albrecht came to the door of Les Genêts in full dress uniform, a row of medals shining on the right side of his thick chest. The good side of his mouth went up at Julien's stare. "You like them?" he murmured, his sharp eyes at the same time running up and down Julien. After a moment he gave a firm nod. "Let us go."

The stares in the street were just what he might have expected. Julien ignored them. Albrecht's eyes swept the street, narrowed and casual, missing nothing. On the platform Julien paid for their tickets, returning the stationmaster's gaze without flinching, then turned toward the hills at the sudden far cry of the train whistle, feeling relief and terror.

La Galoche was on time.

The seats in the passenger cars were only long benches where people sat facing inward; Albrecht took his place in a corner, his back to both windows and wall. He returned the brief stares of the handful of French country people in the car unwaveringly, and continued to watch them after they looked away. They all sat in silence, feeling the rattle of the train on its rails as the green hills passed by — till Tence, where two of the other passengers got off and the other two seized the chance to quietly switch cars. In the suddenly empty train car Albrecht shifted his weight, leaned back against the wall, and lifted his chin at Julien. "Sit there, boy," he said. "Where I can see you."

Julien moved down the bench to the spot he'd been ordered to, and sat still as Albrecht's eyes ran over him again. Albrecht reached into his pocket and brought out a silver cigarette case, took one out, then leaned forward and held the open case out to Julien.

Julien stared at it.

"Cigarette?" said Albrecht. "Really. Feel free."

"I, uh — don't smoke. But — uh — thank you, monsieur." Julien looked down at the mended knees of his trousers as Albrecht snapped the gleaming cigarette case closed.

"Wise man." The German smiled, fished out a heavy silver lighter, flicked it open, and lit up. He inhaled deeply, his eyes going suddenly inward, and let out a long sigh. "I have to say, though" — he drew again — "there's nothing like one after battle."

Julien looked away.

"Perhaps it would relieve your mind, boy" — Albrecht's voice was touched with irony — "if I told you these bits of metal on my chest were won on the eastern front? A wise choice on the part of high command, as you can see by my fluency in the local language." Julien looked at him. The man's lopsided mouth went very wry. "I don't speak Russian. Nor Polish, nor any of the other tongue-twisting languages the Slavs have seen fit to inflict on Europe. French, on the other hand, I've studied since I was six. My mother had a sort of love affair with France." He drew on his cigarette again. "But she's dead." He glanced out the window. The peak of Lizieux stood in the distance, ancient and green.

"Now," said Albrecht suddenly. Julien jumped. The German was looking at his watch. "We have an hour, presumably alone. So. Tell me more about this girl of yours." He settled back in his seat and folded his arms.

Julien's mind was blank with panic. "She's not — not really mine, sir," he said.

Albrecht's eyebrows went up. "Truly?" His eyes went sharp on Julien's face. "What's the obstacle? You're easy enough on the eyes."

"Looks aren't everything," Julien got out, looking down at his shoes.

"Someone ought to have told the girls back home." Albrecht's tone was so edged that Julien looked sharply up at him. The German barked a laugh. "What? Did you think you were looking at the ruin of a formerly handsome man? Look again."

Julien looked, but saw nothing. "Monsieur," he said, "I — I don't . . ."

"My face is not the part of me you're interested in? Indeed. This is usually the case. I'm quite a useful man." He inhaled and blew smoke away from Julien. "Once I became an officer, even the girls looked at me." He studied the glowing tip of his cigarette morosely. "I have a wife at home."

Julien watched him in the short silence that followed, watched his dark-brown eyes as they lifted to the far hills. The glow of the cigarette as he drew on it again looked strange so near the red wreck of his cheek and jaw.

"So. I'm to understand the objection is on her part? Is this correct?"

"Yes, monsieur."

"And it's what?"

His heart stuttered. "She didn't say exactly, monsieur."

"Hmm. So tell me what she's like. Her name. How old is she?"

"Sixteen, sir. Her name is Élise. Élise Fournier." He tried to breathe evenly as the man's eyes studied his face. "She turned sixteen last September. She plays the piano. She's really good. You should hear it, she — she . . ." he looked up into the man's expressionless face and faltered, then lifted his chin, his voice coming out almost angry. "The music is alive when she plays it. It has a soul."

Albrecht's eyebrows went up, slowly. "And where did she come from, this musician?"

"Lyon," said Julien, trying to keep his eyes on the officer's, his heart pounding.

"Is that so." Albrecht drew on his cigarette. "Does she have any family?"

The clouds over the northern hills were like towers, snow-white and huge beyond measure, unmoved by anything beneath. Julien spoke through his dry throat. "She lost both her parents last year."

There was a brief silence. The sickness rocking in Julien's belly subsided slowly, second by second, as Albrecht did not ask.

"Tell me what you like so much about her, then," Albrecht said finally. "Looks, as you say, are not everything. What is she? Sweet and kind? Charming and witty? Brave and loyal?"

"Brave and loyal."

Albrecht was nodding. "That was my impression too," he murmured. "What else?" he said abruptly. "What did you see in her? What was she doing when you first realized she was the moon and stars and assorted celestial bodies?" He gave his lopsided smile and gestured vaguely with his cigarette, trailing smoke. "I was young once too, you know. So? What was she doing?"

"Playing the piano."

"A true music lover! Should she keep you away from concerts played by women?"

"It wasn't the music." He looked out the window, his stomach coiling in on itself. The clouds were white blurs. "It was her face. The look on her face. Like — like she saw something other people couldn't see. Just for a moment. Something real. Like that was what she played the music for, to chase after — whatever it was. Is."

"The sun above the clouds," said Albrecht's soft voice, and Julien turned and stared at him. The cigarette was dangling forgotten between his fingers; his eyes in his ruined face were like dark earth. The instant their eyes met they both looked away.

"You've never been up in an aeroplane, have you, boy?" said Albrecht in a loud voice. "It's quite a sight." He took a drag on his cigarette and leaned forward. "That fellow we spoke to at La Roche, who is he? What does he do?"

"He's the assistant pastor of the Reformed church, monsieur."

"And is he anything to you?"

"My father."

"Hmm." Albrecht inhaled twice before speaking again. "You know, I like your town. It's my habit to be on my guard and I don't plan to change that, but you've got a good record in spite of the other week." The right side of his mouth quirked up. "You understand, from my point of view, the idea that the local church instructs people not to shoot me is quite pleasant. A state of affairs one takes for granted till it is suddenly not the case." His eyes flicked for a split second to Julien's right hip, and it went through Julien in a belated flash what those quick eyes had been looking for all this time. *That wasn't my plan, sir.* "Beyond that, though, I see the wisdom in it. Truly salutary, in your position. Men keep their pride, order is maintained, all without useless loss of life on both sides."

Julien drew himself up. "That's not the idea, sir," he said in a low voice.

"Don't growl at me, boy. I know it's not. It doesn't work if you don't believe in it. But listen." He stabbed his cigarette in the air, his eyes gone hard. "When I'm at the front, I hold the lives of over five hundred men in my hands every day. I make decisions that mean life or death to them, again and again. That's what a leader does. Don't you wave your hand and dismiss strategy. It's what keeps my men's blood in their veins. It's what cost you your country. Maybe your father does believe in all that. Tell me he doesn't, I'll say he's a good officer, and he has my respect." He took a sharp drag on his cigarette. "This girl. Is she in your church?"

Julien stopped breathing.

"The truth now, boy. I *hate* liars."

"No, monsieur." Try as he might, he

couldn't get above a whisper. The words *She's Catholic* battered at his shut teeth, trying to get out. He swallowed them.

There was a long silence, Albrecht pulling slowly on his cigarette, his eyes all over Julien's face. Finally he spoke, quietly and plainly.

"I like you, boy," he said. "You're a loyal man. You might be officer material, even. It's a loyal thing you're doing. A risk like this, for a girl who won't have you. You know she probably still won't, even if it works?"

"She definitely won't," said Julien tightly.

Albrecht sighed, and nodded. "What you're doing, I understand. But her. Can you tell me" — the brown eyes met his now, direct and clear — "do you know why this Élise did what she did for me?"

Julien looked back at him. "The truth is I don't know, sir. She never even told me she'd done it. I only heard it from my sister."

"Hmm." Albrecht studied the end of his cigarette. "I don't understand it. She had no kind of duty toward me." His eyes flicked to Julien, sharp and considering. "Quite the reverse would be my guess, though you've been very careful not to say."

Julien drew a slow breath.

"It was my guess before I met you, boy.

379

She never spoke a word to me. Pulled me out of that river, at no small risk to herself, and then ran." Albrecht looked out the window. "It was my guess even before that," he murmured, half to himself. "You should have seen her eyes."

Her eyes. Julien kept his eyes on the far high clouds, and gripped the bench beneath him till his hands hurt.

Albrecht looked at his cigarette for a long moment, shook his head, and lifted his eyes slowly to Julien's. "Both her parents, you say."

Julien nodded.

Albrecht shook his head again. There was silence, and the rattle of the train.

"I wouldn't have done it," the German said finally. "No one would do it." He looked at Julien. "Would you?"

Julien opened his mouth, his mind gone white.

"Don't answer that, boy. I only asked it to see the fear in your eyes." Albrecht's lips drew back from his teeth, and he crushed out the stub of his cigarette savagely on the wooden bench beside him. "You see? That's the way things are. People *like* power. If you knew. If you knew what it feels like when you win." He took a deep, slightly ragged breath, and sat suddenly poised again, his

380

calm, piercing eyes meeting Julien's. "Listen. If there's any way I can, I'm going to protect your girl. She saved me from a very stupid death, though I don't know why, and when she did that she made herself one of mine. I do right by my own. You have my word on this."

Julien looked at him, his heart lifting slowly, very slowly, as if drifting up from fathoms deep under the sea. "Thank you, sir," he said.

"I've commanded men in battle," said Albrecht. "I know people. You live with your illusions till you come up against death. And then you learn to deal in reality. You learn that sweetness and mercy won't protect your own from the horrors. Everyone who's faced the gun knows this."

"Yeah," breathed Julien.

Albrecht looked him in the eye. His mouth quirked up, but his eyes were dark again, earth under stone. "You'd like to know why she did it too," he said. "Wouldn't you, boy?"

Julien closed his eyes, and tried to breathe, and nodded.

"Yes," said Albrecht. "We'll see what we can do."

The Gestapo headquarters was a blank-faced box on the Rue Saint-Pierre, Nazi flags laid over its windows like coins on a corpse's eyes. Albrecht fell silent when they came round the corner and saw it. Julien's stomach contracted. A young woman hurrying down the other sidewalk gave them a swift stare, her face twisting for a moment with loathing before she turned sharply away. His right fist clenched. She must have thought she was seeing Duval, seeing what he'd seen in Duval. Till the end, when he'd seen blood and meat. The swastikas crawled above him. Albrecht rang the bell.

Albrecht turned to him. "Don't speak unless you're spoken to. I'm hoping we won't need your testimony at all. If they ask questions, don't lie, and whatever you do don't claim she's Aryan. They won't take that well if they know otherwise."

Julien nodded. The door opened.

A huge blond man in an ink-black uniform, a man Julien had once seen on the street in Tanieux. The officer looked him over from head to foot, listening to Albrecht's swift German, then motioned Julien to put his hands against the wall. He submitted to the search, taking shallow breaths, looking away into the narrow hallway beyond — straight-backed chairs along the wall, office doors, the foot of a flight of stone stairs, a dark stain on the lowest one; beyond it a dark space, the other stairs, down. He caught a faint whiff as if from a sewer as the Gestapo officer pointed them to two chairs and walked into an office. They sat.

In the silence that fell then, he began to hear it, the sound that had been lurking in his mind since entering this hallway. It was coming from below, quiet but constant.

Footsteps. The squeak of a shoe or the creak of a chair on a concrete floor, here and then there. A hollow knock on a pipe. A muffled voice, two voices, more. A sharper, deeper voice, and silence.

There were people down there.

The stairs moved and shifted before Julien's eyes, shadows in the woods, beasts crouching. Up and up they went, and down, down into the dark. Faces came to him, and he shut his eyes. Jacques, Édouard, Rudy. *You can't save them. They are beyond your power.* He could not even think her name. He couldn't dare.

The office door opened, and they were beckoned in.

The two men shook hands over the broad oak desk: Albrecht in his gray uniform, his medals swinging a little, and the cold-eyed one in black with the swastika on his arm.

He heard them, as if in a dream, say "Anton Albrecht" and "Gerhard Haas." Was he really here? He was sweating. At Albrecht's gesture he sat. There was no window. There was a picture of Hitler on the wall. There was nothing he could bear to look at. Haas's armband, his hunter's eyes, the file cabinets, full of names. His stomach churned. Albrecht was speaking.

Julien caught the word *Tanieux,* the German for *life, river, ask.* Albrecht's voice was slow and measured, polite; his head dipped every now and then, just a fraction. Haas asked a question, then another. Julien lost the thread, saw only that Haas's eyebrows went up; that a small smile appeared on his carved face; that Albrecht went on smoothly till Haas interrupted him with a question like a lash.

Somewhere below them someone cried out.

Albrecht answered, and the calm power in his eyes made Julien breathe again. Haas smiled on, and made some airy remark with the word *girl* in it. Albrecht's eyes turned cold, and he repeated himself, slowly and quietly.

Haas asked a question.

"Élise Fournier," said Albrecht.

Haas's face tightened. He gestured at Julien, asking something, shrugged at the reply. Then said something brief, shuffled some papers on his desk, looked at the door.

Albrecht leaned forward, his eyes not leaving Haas's for a moment, and asked a question. Haas snapped out a reply.

Albrecht sank back in his chair. He opened his mouth, and said nothing.

The room shifted around them. Ending was in the air. *Danke,* and some courteous phrase, and Albrecht shifting his weight to stand. The air was thick as blood, the weight of stone above Julien pinned him, struggling like a roach underfoot. The room smelled like death; he was breathing it in. From below him came the voices of the dead. He opened his mouth, and Albrecht's hand closed over his wrist in a crushing grip. He closed his mouth. Wrenched himself upward and out of his chair. He did not feel his feet carrying him to the door. Haas's eyes were on him, calm, cat's eyes. *If I had a gun you'd be Duval. Blood and meat. If I had a gun I couldn't save her, not even then. Not from the lords of creation. But I'd see* you *in hell.* Albrecht still had him by the arm. They were walking past the staircase, that dark mouth. The front door was open, sunlight falling on the stoop. He almost recoiled. Albrecht dragged him, step by step, out into the free and choking air.

The door closed behind them. Julien almost fell to his knees on the stoop, nausea rising in his belly, but Albrecht did not loosen his grip, and they staggered on together. Five or six numb paces, the hand on his arm like a vise. Then Albrecht bent down to him, his eyes blazing in his ruined face. "They cannot release her," he whispered, "because she has escaped."

CHAPTER 26
GRASS

"That paper-pusher," said Albrecht. The train wheels rattled under them. Julien stared out the window, straining to catch a glimpse of the Le Puy road. "Trying to twit me about being rescued by a girl. Ten minutes at Stalingrad and he'd have soiled himself."

"What else did he say about her, monsieur?" He'd go to her dorm first. Of course if she'd walked into town, *everyone* would know. But if she hadn't . . . ?

"I've told you all of it. 'We cannot release her because she has escaped. She disappeared in transit.' That's it." Albrecht shook his head. "He asked me questions. Wanted to know how long I'd been in town, whether I knew any of the people. I don't like him. Wouldn't be surprised if he's opening a dossier on me right now."

"I'm sorry, sir."

Albrecht waved a dismissive hand, his

dark-brown eyes fixed on the distance. After a few moments he said, "Thought we had a chance. By his uniform he's not SS. But he thinks like one. Party member, maybe." He turned and looked Julien in the eye. "You watch out for him. Tell the girl to watch out for him, if you find her. He has his eye on your town."

"Yes, sir."

"I'd be grateful to hear that she's all right," Albrecht murmured. "I will not ask you where she lives, but — if she would come down to Les Genêts and speak with me one time, if she is willing . . . I will understand if she doesn't wish to."

"I'll tell her, sir."

Albrecht bared his teeth a little, the scarred side of his face twisting oddly. "He thinks he's such a German hero. You know what it means, *Haas*? It means rabbit."

Julien looked at him. *What are we then? Grass?* "That's a last name?"

"They used to call rabbit hunters that."

Julien nodded. Of course they did.

"Julien," said his father carefully, "you are quite sure they weren't lying?"

"The one with me wasn't. He doesn't." Julien sat in a kitchen chair as Mama banged packets and bottles into his Scout

388

bag. No one at her dorm had known anything. The dorm mother had accused him of cruel jokes. *The Gestapo told me themselves* was a sentence his mouth hadn't known how to make. "He thought the Gestapo officer wasn't lying to him. I have to look."

"Of course you have to look." Papa stood. "Magali. You go and find Sylvain and tell him to get the other Scouts together, whoever he can find. Tell him what's happened, tell him it's a request from me. Get your friends on it too if they're free."

"And we search south of town? You're sure they took the Le Puy road, Papa?"

"I saw them drive away."

"Julien, here," said Mama. "Look at these. The brown one slows bleeding. Dosage is written here." The labels on the little bottles were worn, written in a crabbed hand. "The clear one strengthens the body to fight infection. There's disinfectant here, and bandages. Did they teach you how to make a splint?"

He nodded.

"There's potatoes and cheese and water. We'll be praying."

"Thank you," whispered Julien.

It was two when he started, and four o'clock

when he dropped to a crouch, sweating, and took his first bite of lunch and swig of water. Another minute and he was up again, his heart lashing him onward, his mind full of her face twisted in pain, of blood slowly soaking into the forest floor. He had crisscrossed the woods south of the river all this time, working his way steadily, checking every bush, every stone. He couldn't do otherwise. His heart howled for the open road, to run down it at speed till he found her, but she was no fool. She would not be on the road.

He had sent Sylvain and his Scouts onward to search two by two. They would each leave a blaze on a tree where they started so that when he found the first blaze he could run on till he met them, then search beyond them on and on toward Le Puy. He would come to the first one soon, he was sure — but she could be here, she might be here, even so close to Tanieux. He knew her. She would come to her brother and sister like a homing bird. A bird that flew in cover.

She knew the paths down here; she had hidden here once, Magali had said. These open woods around the Les Chênes treehouse, roots knotted underfoot and spreading limbs above, seemed to hold no secrets; there were almost two dozen places now where if you had a rope to throw over a branch you could clamber up and strap yourself in, unseen and held. If you had a rope.

There was only one place, if you had none. He was almost there.

A narrow path, almost a deer path, slipped like a swift brown thread through the green sunlit woods, curving around trees and old stones this way and that. He gave up beating every bush in this open place and sped up, hope springing up in him like a weed. Could she have gone to ground for a while before daring the town? The treehouse was fifty meters on from here, past two bends. *Please.* He came around the first one — and stopped, his heart choking, a low, inarticulate sound coming from somewhere in his chest.

She lay facedown on the path.

Her right arm was flung out; her torn skirt clung wetly to her left leg, red and brown with blood. Her face was bone-white, her dark hair spilling across it. A black bruise bloomed on her temple, crusted with blood. Her eyes were closed.

He steeled himself, his heart contracting painfully in his chest. *You are going to walk forward.* His right hand was out and reaching already, fingertips ready to take her wrist in a wordless plea for one last mercy — but he could not move. *You are going to do it now.*

Her fingers twitched, the dirty fingernails brushing the earth. Julien covered the space between them in a heartbeat and fell to his knees beside her, his mouth opening and all his breath coming out, a silent scream of hope: *You. Here.* Élise, here on the forest floor in the land of the living.

His hand reached for her wrist, dared to touch her skin; the pulse beat warm and strong as ever he had dreamed. The other hand brushed hair out of her face. Two dark crusted lines of blood traced down to her jawline. "Élise," he whispered. "Élise." Tentatively he took her shoulder and shook it. Her eyelids fluttered. They were so pale. Her eyes opened. "You're alive."

She raised her head very slowly and looked at him.

"Élise, oh God — can you walk? We could get you to Les Chênes — I'll carry you —"

"I —" She broke off, and got her hands under her, and pushed herself up to all fours, hissing through her teeth in pain when the bloody leg moved. She stared down at it, then up at him. "How did I get here? Is this real? Julien, where are Karl and Tova? Are they safe?"

He knelt open-mouthed a moment, understanding who she must mean, understanding just how shaken she must be to use their real names. "Yes! Yes. Let me help you —"

She took his hand and staggered to her feet, her left hand feeling the bad leg. "It's not broken," she whispered.

"We'll go —" He froze.

It was as if his mind had gone out into the woods around them, now for the first time since he'd seen her lying there. He did not know what he had heard or felt, but his hackles rose like a dog's. He turned down the path he had come up and stared hard through the trees, Élise's hand still on his shoulder, and the sickness of what he should have known bloomed in his belly as he caught a far glimpse of blond hair.

Fool. You fool. Haas's eyes on him after telling the truth to Albrecht, eyes like a stalking cat . . .

Her eyes caught fear from his as he whirled to face her. He spoke without breath, so fast his words almost tripped over each other. "Go on up the path there till you find a rope ladder. Climb it and pull it up after you. I'll hold them off. Go."

She did not ask who. Her eyes and her bruise were dark against her white face as she reached into the deep pocket of her skirt, pulled out a short, gleaming butcher knife, and held the handle out to him.

He stared at it for a moment, his mind alive with readiness and fear. With the woods behind him, and the woods around him, and the shadows that might be moving in them, and the one man — he only heard one man — behind him on the path. His hand was already in his jacket, grasping the whistle. He saw Duval's meat-ground flesh, saw Albrecht's dark eyes above his rueful mouth. He saw Élise standing before him, bruised and filthy, shining like the sun above the clouds. He saw the dark mouth of that staircase, and his throat closed at the thought of what he was about to do.

"Keep it," he whispered, pulling the whistle out and stuffing it into the palm of her hand. "Blow this if you have any trouble up there. Go."

Then he turned back on the path.

He heard her go, behind him, her steady, almost silent run. He looked down the path like a tunnel of green and gold light, descending into darkness, then up for a split second into glowing leaves, the last time he must look upward in these woods today. A wordless prayer like a beggar's burning eyes: *Give or I die.* He bent suddenly, and threw leaves over the small dark patch of blood on the forest floor.

Then he ran downhill and away from the path she'd taken, down into soft ground, going heavily to make sure he left a trail. He ran, listening for the boots on the path behind him, slowing a little. He couldn't afford to be missed. The boots drew nearer. The man came over the rise behind him: blue shirt, blond hair, hard and focused face, the barrel of a pistol pointed straight at Julien. "Halt!"

Julien halted.

The man came toward him, the blond giant who had opened the door to him in Le Puy today, whose eyes and pistol did not leave him for an instant now. Julien turned at bay, his empty hands outstretched by his sides, and looked his enemy in the eye in silence.

"Where is she?"

"Who?" asked Julien quietly.

"I *heard* her." In another moment Julien was on the ground with the man's knee on his back, his face in the dead leaves. Cold metal pressed against the base of his skull. "Where is she?" the German said softly into his ear.

Julien closed his eyes. "I don't know," he said thickly. He could not stop his trembling. "I was looking for her."

"I heard her." The barrel pressed harder for a moment as the man raised his head. "Élise Fournier!" he called out in a ringing voice that carried through the woods. *"Zeige dich oder ich erschiesse deinen Freund."* Then in French, "Show yourself or I will shoot your friend."

There was earth in his mouth, cool and gritty against his tongue. The leaves were rustling overhead. The breeze was warm. His death was cold against the back of his neck as he lay with his face in the dirt and prayed for silence.

He waited for the next sound, and did not breathe.

CHAPTER 27
THE STRANGEST THING

The next sound was a muttered curse in German.

The pistol left Julien's neck. There was one moment of joy, like a sweet wind barely rising, before rough hands flipped him over and his breath left him with a cry. The man's knee pressed painfully into his stomach, a snarl on the cold face above him as the German grabbed him by the throat. "You little French coward," the man hissed, and his huge fist struck Julien just beside his left eye, snapping his head sideways in a flash of pain and splintered light. Julien's hands spasmed upward, going for the man's arms unbidden as if this were a fight, and the hand on his windpipe cut off his breath. His fingers locked weakly around the man's hard left forearm as, on the other side, the pistol pointed at him again. His knees jerked; white terror filled his mind as he struggled for air. The Gestapo man leaned down, teeth bared, and whispered, "I'll teach you to fear your betters."

The hand let go of his throat. He drew in one long, gasping breath, seeing the exultant face above him with its wolf's grin, blond head haloed in the green and golden light. Then he cried out as the man backhanded him on the same place he'd struck before. In one fluid motion the German jumped to his feet, dragging Julien up by the arm.

"Run!" he snapped, aiming the pistol at Julien and dragging him along. Julien stumbled with him up the false trail he had laid and onto the treehouse path.

They were almost twenty meters closer to Élise before he gathered air and wits enough to dig in his heels. The German was looking back and forth, searching the woods, his pistol gripped firmly but not quite pointing at Julien, and Julien managed to snatch him a little off-balance in the sudden stop. The man cursed him and jerked him forward so hard he almost fell, then pulled him along ten more paces before Julien managed to stop him again, diving to his knees and skidding in the leaves.

They had come over the rise, in sight of the treehouse oak. The rope ladder was gone.

He did not look at the oak. He looked at

the ground in front of him, gasping for breath. A boot hit him in the belly, and he doubled over. A hard hand grabbed his right arm; he felt something cold against his wrist and heard a click. He was hauled upward, and the handcuff on his wrist pulled suddenly tight as the Gestapo man locked the other side of it around the lowest limb of a young chestnut above him. The man's blue eyes blazed at him; he raised his hand to strike again, and Julien flinched. The man smiled slowly, showing his teeth, then put his hands on him and searched him swiftly for weapons, smiled again, and went on down the path at a swift jog, looking left and right through the open woods. Julien stood tethered and sick with fear, his cuffed hand raised in a parody of defiance, forcing himself to look at the ground as his enemy approached the oak.

After twenty seconds he looked up again.

The man had gone past.

Julien stood shaking, taking in deep gulps of air as the broad back receded. His free hand came up to touch his throat, then the tender left side of his face. *That was nothing. Nothing. Don't you know what they do?* He'd known nothing.

The foot of that dark staircase filled his mind. *Now you will learn.*

He couldn't fall to his knees. He turned and pressed his face against the smooth trunk of the young tree. He was shaking uncontrollably. *Please. Please.* Heat and cold washed through his body. *Please. I've been a fool. Please. Please.*

He tried to pull himself together, to slow his breathing. He couldn't. He shut his eyes tight and saw Élise in the treehouse, Élise, her blood and bruises and her living eyes, Élise. He opened his eyes and the light of the afternoon woods smote him, a rich, glowing patchwork of sun and green shade, leaf-shadow and gold, shifting gently as the leaves moved in the wind: utterly, achingly beautiful.

Please. Keep her safe. Anything, if You'll keep her safe.

Help me face this. Please.

Leaves rustled. The German was returning, off the path. As the man came in sight, his head went up like a dog's at a sound from the road. An engine. He pulled a whistle from his pocket and blew it, loud and shrill. Julien heard the engine drawing nearer along the Le Puy road, then, unmistakably, turning into the Les Chênes driveway.

Turning off.

The German continued to search as the

sound of an automobile door slamming came through the quiet woods, as boots came down the path. He turned at the sight of a black uniform, hailing his colleague with an upraised hand and a call, then stared and converted his wave to a salute.

Down the path came Haas himself.

Haas glanced from side to side, eyes sweeping the woods, strode up and looked Julien over, then turned a cold eye on his subordinate. He snapped out a few questions, the blond one answering with lowered head. Haas's eyes narrowed. He took up a position in front of Julien, their faces very close, looking into his eyes. Julien tried to keep still.

"Where is the girl?" Haas said in French.

"I don't know, monsieur."

"You will address me as Kriminalkomissar. Why did you look for her here rather than elsewhere?"

"I've just been searching all the woods, Kri— Kriminalkomissar."

Haas's mouth tightened and he glanced away, saying in the same level voice, "Why was she armed?"

Julien's breath stopped. *Armed?* A strange detached part of him wondered what she had done as he tried to look blank.

Haas stood watching him, eyes narrow,

face utterly still. Then half turned on his heel and spoke to the blond one, scanning the woods. The blond one stepped off the path where Haas pointed; Haas went the other way, scuffing the deep leaf mold with his boots as if to find any hollow where a girl might lie hidden. Neither of them looked up. Julien did not look up. His throat was utterly dry. They would run out of places so soon, in these woods.

"God's going to strike you down," he croaked suddenly. It was pathetic. It was all he had. "You must know that. How do you keep going?" He swallowed, and his voice grew louder. "Knowing how it'll end? Is it worth it? Being on top for a little while? And then going to *hell*?"

The blond one laughed, and did not turn. Haas shot Julien a glance and smiled. They went on.

"You think you're secure in your power. You have the guns and that's the end of it. God is not mocked!" shouted Julien. "God comes to judge the earth! He has heard the cries of His people! There's going to be *fire*!" His voice went shrill. His handcuffed hand was an upraised fist, his other clenched in front of him. His left eye and cheekbone throbbed, unnaturally warm. He must look such a fool. Haas glanced at him again, and he drew breath. "Stop now," he said. "Turn around. Change your ways. There's still time." Something knotted behind his breastbone as he spoke the words, and his hand strained against the steel that bound his wrist. "You're not damned yet," he said, and his voice shocked him, deep and guttural with rage. "I wish you were, I wish to *God* you were, I'd see you rot in hell before I'd give you a speck of the kingdom. They say the truth has power, well *that's* the truth if you like. But *God* forgives. So you still have a chance. So here's what I'm saying to you!" He was roaring now, almost hanging by his handcuffed hand as he half lunged forward with each shout. "Take it! Take it while you can! I hate you but God will take you in and I will stand by and salute Him because He's *better* than me! I'll do this God's way and my father's way because it's not your way and I *loathe* your —" He broke off in shock.

Haas had turned and was staring at him.

"Your father?" the man said, as quietly as if they were together in a small room. He paced toward Julien, slowly and precisely, the bright eyes fixed on him. Julien stood straight now and very still. Haas's voice dropped, speaking into Julien's face. "You are the pastor's son?"

Julien met his eyes, breathing shallowly. "No — Kriminalkomissar," he got out. His lips felt like chunks of clay.

"Who is your father?"

"The assistant pastor."

"Ah yes. The quiet one. Kahler!" he shouted, his eyes still on Julien. "*Verhör. Noch keinen Drück ausüben. Stehen Sie wache.*" The blond Kahler unholstered his gun and took up a watch position as Haas stepped close to Julien again, the chiseled face softening as he looked into Julien's eyes. "Listen," Haas said quietly. "I am sure your friend must not be here. Otherwise she would certainly have responded in order to save your life, *n'est-ce pas?* Or" — the eyebrows were touched with pity — "she is not so much your friend as you believe. But listen. I came here to find her. But I also came to find the answers to a few questions. Let us make an agreement. You talk to me. Some very small questions only. And Kahler here does not search. Are we agreed?"

Julien looked at him and said nothing.

"Ah. A further agreement. You tell the truth, and I ask for no names. Agreed?"

Julien said nothing, his heart knocking in his chest. Somewhere to the south, at the Thibauds' farm perhaps, a rooster crowed.

"How did you feel," said Haas, "when

404

they arrested your father?"

Julien said nothing, but the tears didn't care. They welled up in his eyes, betraying.

"Kahler," said Haas. "Search."

"Terrible," Julien whispered. "I thought I'd never see him again."

Haas made a palm-down gesture, and Kahler took up his guard position again. "They found people to take over for him and the lead pastor, I suppose, while they were gone?"

You said no names. But if he wanted *those* names he could find them in public records.

"Yes. Some guest preachers, and an interim director for the school."

Haas glanced away. "And for their other work?"

Julien's breath paused. "I don't know what you mean, Kriminalkomissar."

Haas smiled. "Naturally. Now, the arrest of your father. I can only imagine what a difficult day that is for a young man. I want you simply to tell me about it. Begin at the beginning. What were you doing when you learned the police had come?"

"We were finishing supper. They knocked on the door."

With a patient voice and listening eyes Haas drew the details from him, strand by strand. The gifts. The policeman's red eyes.

The policemen not knowing where they were taking him. What Papa and Mama said to each other, what Papa looked like as he turned to go. Julien did not want to let the story catch him and carry him onward; he did not want to admit he had seen Papa's fear. He saw Haas see it anyway, felt it pass between them like a current, the German's eyes darkening, his face suddenly, shockingly human. Julien dropped his eyes, and Haas took his chin and gently raised it. "And then?"

"He got in. They drove away. Everyone sang — sang 'A Mighty Fortress.' "

"Did you sing?"

"No."

"Why?" breathed Haas, looking into his eyes.

"I didn't — believe. They were all together like that and I — I couldn't."

Haas's mouth went wry. "You were the one whose father was arrested."

"It wasn't only that. We've been so . . . You understand, I was still a Christian. I just didn't believe — that God would help us. That God has anything to do with this world. I thought the world belonged to . . ."

In the tree above him a blackbird sang. The light poured down green and gold onto Julien's handcuffed hand, onto the listening man with the gun at his hip and the swastika on his arm. "To you," said Julien.

Haas drew back an instant. His eyes went to the handcuff, then followed Julien's to the gun. They darkened again, and from that kind look Julien turned his face away. "You still believe that?" said Haas quietly.

The silence above him was the wind waiting. The silence above him was Élise. He did not look up, only felt it all breathe above his head: the young green leaves that brushed his aching hand, the clouds beginning to catch fire, the vast great sky above it all, the depth and depth of it beyond his sight, the hidden stars. He felt the muscles of his face shift quietly beneath his skin.

"No," he said.

Haas looked deep into his eyes, put a hand to his belt, and drew his pistol. Julien watched it come up, its small blank eye watching him. Haas pressed it to Julien's forehead and smiled.

"Really?" he said gently, and cocked it.

The click vibrated through his skull, down into his bones. He saw the blur of the dark barrel, Haas's finger caressing the trigger, terribly near, the exaltation in Haas's face as the man's shoulders settled back and his other hand came up around the grip. Julien closed his eyes. The steel against his head was a live thing, dense with power. He could feel how it would knock him backward, how he would dangle like a rabbit in a snare. His guts shifted inside him. He could not breathe. He could not even tremble.

It came slowly, like water seeping upward in the dark. Like a spring fed by blind caves, cold and pure and shocking; like an artesian well. It went down and down: he could not find the end of it. It was the strangest thing he had ever felt.

It was joy.

He opened his eyes. The two men were outlined sharp as crystal, every leaf on the trees behind them, the etched lines of the gun. The finger on the trigger. His heart was beating faster than it ever had in his life. He looked into the bright elation of Haas's eyes and said, "Really."

Haas's lips drew back from his teeth. *"Verdammte Märtyrer,"* he spat. His eyes blazed into Julien's for one more moment, every hair on Julien's head standing up, Haas's chiseled face hardening back into stone. He pulled the gun away from Julien's forehead and holstered it in a swift gesture, drew back his fist and, without changing expression, hit the bruised side of Julien's face with all his strength.

The world exploded with pain. Julien staggered and fell, the handcuff cutting into his wrist; as his free hand caught the tree to pull himself up, the second blow landed on his jaw from the other side. He tasted blood. The world was red and white and green and sickening pain, and under it a strange laughter bubbling up from the core of him. The light and the air seemed alive around him, the faces of his enemies weirdly beautiful. There were brown and green flecks in Haas's eyes. The tree beneath his clutching hand felt almost warm, the life within it pulsing like Élise's wrist when he'd taken it in his fingers, there on the forest floor, just there . . . He leaned against the tree, wincing as the left side of his head touched it. Haas grabbed him by the hair and slammed his head against it.

His ears rang, and he felt the crunch of a breaking tooth. He blinked at Haas, his vision blurring, as Haas stepped up with their faces so close he could feel his breath, and kneed him with force in the groin.

Julien screamed. He doubled up reflexively and was brought up with a jerk by his wrist, sharp pain shooting down the bones of his arm. He stood in a half crouch, half hanging by the handcuff, gasping in agony. Haas squatted beside him and looked up into his face, smiling a little. After a moment the man began to speak, each word soft and precise.

"You are right," he said. "God does not help you. But He does involve Himself in this world. Look around you, and you will see whom it is God helps." Julien gasped, and Haas leaned in closer. "You think we are privileged, you think we were born to power. You are wrong. It is in the struggle that strength is born. You French sat on what you took from us and grew soft, while we learned what it is to be men. We learned it in fighting the Jew." The eyes had gone gentle again. "We came here to help you. Your people still have your farms, your little pastures, your apple trees. The Jew took that from us. He will do it to you too. He is a creature who can stand on the wet earth in springtime looking at apple trees in bloom and see only firewood, and cold little coins. A creature who can see women and children turned out to slave in factories or starve and feel no pity. Do you understand? He will do it to you too, unless you let us help you. Unless you open your eyes, and place yourself on God's side." Haas laid a hand on his gun. "He comes to judge the earth indeed. And we come with Him."

There was a flavorless trickle in the back of Julien's throat. "And deport children?"

he whispered, watching Haas's hand.

The hand didn't move. Haas gave a weary sigh, and stood. "It's in their blood," he said. "You're all like children. When we have made Europe clean of them, you will see what we have done for you. But first," he said indifferently, turning to Kahler, "you will see whom it is God helps."

In the west the sun was red between the leaves. Night was coming. The pain throbbed upward into Julien's body as he stood, and the core of him trembled as he saw again the darkness of those stairs. Somewhere in his belly, deep in the dark, *please, please* beat like a pulse; it had been there for years, beating day after terrible day. It had a counterpoint now, almost too faint to hear but solid somehow, like a sound made by roots beneath the earth.

Yes.

He knew what to do. What *she'd* done. Risk anything to escape. If they shot him they'd have nothing from him —

"What's so important about that girl?" said Haas.

That girl. Above him in the green, just *there* where he did not look, the rising wind touching her pale face where she lay. That girl —

"She is infinitely precious to God," he

said, looking into Haas's eyes. *You will know. Someday you will know.*

Haas backhanded him across the face. "Tell the truth!" he shouted as Julien cringed backward, his free hand coming up to shield his stinging eyes. Haas grabbed Julien's chin in one hand and held it, his thumb digging into the soft flesh beneath. *"What's so important about that girl?"*

That girl. Her eyes in the moonlight, her sorrow, her courage, her hands on her sister's shoulders. Her hands on the keys, her eyes hard and bright, making, seeking, finding — the sun above the clouds —

"I love her," he said. The tears spilled down his face. Haas let go of him with a jerk. Kahler threw his head back and roared with laughter.

"Beherrschen Sie sich," hissed Haas, and Kahler shut up. Haas's lip curled as if he smelled rotting meat. "Don't you know they're *different* from us?" he said. "A dog-faced little *Judenweib* like that. You're an Aryan, boy. Have some self-respect." He turned to Kahler. "Search."

Haas and Kahler turned aside from each other, and began to search the forest floor again in the evening light. This hollow of leaves and roots, that rock. Julien stood praying, his roots in the earth, one bloody hand toward heaven. From down away from the oak he heard a shot, looked up to see Haas looking down some burrow. Haas turned from it and came toward him, and with a considering eye on Julien's face aimed his pistol upward, into a young chestnut with branches low enough to climb, and fired. Julien's pulse beat low and dark, the pain moving through him like water through the roots beneath the earth, the terror mute and slow as shifting rock. Haas fired into a second tree, another low one, still watching him.

Then he holstered his gun, turned away, and rejoined Kahler in the search.

At some point Kahler began to laugh again.

Before the sun touched the far hills beyond the trees, they finished and walked back to where Julien stood.

They were speaking in German. Kahler gestured at Julien, his voice going high in surprise. Haas shook his head and smiled at Julien. *"Das ist nicht nötig. Ich hab' jetzt die Lösung."*

Kahler's eyebrows went up. Haas gestured to Julien's handcuff. Frowning, Kahler unlocked it. Julien stared at him, his hand going unheeded to his bloody wrist, as Kahler muttered fiercely, "You stand right where you are till you can't see us anymore. Move and I'll shoot you."

Julien nodded mutely.

Haas turned away. With a last dark glance at Julien, Kahler followed.

Julien stood and watched in wonder as the two men walked away through the dimming woods. His pulse beat in his ears like the sea. They walked under the treehouse oak. They walked on down the path. Every now and then Kahler glanced behind, a hand on his gun. They walked out of sight.

Julien swayed suddenly and gripped the tree for support. He leaned against it, breathing, staring into the trees.

In the distance near Les Chênes, an engine started.

Julien snapped upright, a wild strength shooting through him. He took two steps and looked up, trembling. *No.* He dare not. In another moment he was running as fast as his legs would take him toward Les Chênes, ignoring the pain that shot through him at each step, his feet finding the path as if they knew it in their bones. He broke out of the trees and shouted at the young woman he saw, "Did they both get in the car?"

"Julien!" It was Claudine, one of Magali's colleagues, he saw dazedly. "What's happened to you?"

He had a sudden vision of himself, dirty and wild-eyed and beaten bloody. *"Did they both get in the car?"* he shouted, his voice cracking.

"Yes!"

"Which way did they go?"

"That way!" She pointed out of town. He turned and dashed down the driveway, a high, desperate energy running through his body, drowning out the pain, drowning whatever she shouted after him. He ran on the road, openly, his lungs working like a bellows, listening with all his might to the receding sound of the engine: not stopping, not turning. Still going away. As he neared the turnoff to the Thibauds' farm he slowed and scanned the verges of the road as far as the eye could see, searching the rocks and *genêt* bushes.

He was alone.

The Thibauds' stone farmhouse stood like a humble slate-roofed fortress, a glory to see. Madame Thibaud stared at his face as Claudine had, and Monsieur Thibaud and Roland came up behind, and he didn't hear a word they said as he gasped, "Élise. Élise Fournier. She's in the Les Chênes treehouse."

■ ■ ■ ■

He begged Madame Thibaud as she daubed ointment onto his bruises — those she could see — to go get the doctor, to go get someone who knew German. *"Lösung,"* he said. "I need to know what it means. He says he has it. *Ich hab' jetzt* means 'I have now.' I need to know what it means, madame, I have to —"

"Hold still," snapped Madame Thibaud. Julien surged up from his chair and leaned on the table, tottering.

She got him paper and a pen.

The word lay coiled in his memory like a snake he did not quite recognize. He spelled it as best he could. <u>WHAT DOES IT MEAN</u>, he wrote, and underlined it. The black words swam before his eyes.

"Bed," said Madame Thibaud.

She put him in a cupboard-bed, but he fought her silently when she tried to close its doors. After a few moments the farmwife huffed and left him there, propped against the wall, looking out the window to the farmyard, to the road Élise would come down.

His head was dropping with weariness,

416

but he kept watch until they brought her in, and he saw that she was breathing.

CHAPTER 28
THE LAND OF THE LIVING

When Elisa came to herself the scent of hay was in her nostrils, its soft prickle under her back. Her head throbbed and her left hip ached. The fingers of her right hand were clenched hard around something buried in the hay. She opened gluey eyes, blinked at the dim sun-shot space above her and the rough pine beams of the Thibauds' hayloft attic, and pulled the object out. A wooden handle, the rest of the tool wrapped in rags and string.

Her knife.

Pain lanced through her skull as she shot upright. *Karl. Tova.* She almost leapt to her feet, but stopped, her mouth clamped tight. She was in hiding. She dared not leave her shelter. *Karl. Tova.* She saw in a blur the circle of faces in the light of the Shabbos candles, the circle broken once again. She saw the man come out of the woods with the machine gun, come toward the kitchen

418

door. She saw her friends lined up against the common room wall; she searched frantically for her brother's and sister's faces among them. She didn't find them. And yet they seemed to have been with her. She had heard their voices in the dark — she could feel it beating in her still, the pull of them like a string stretched so tight it would snap, calling her, pulling her home. *Home.* She lay down and took a deep, slow breath, trying to still her hammering heart. Her mind threw up images, like the memory of a dream: the dark, the trees whipping past, branches striking her in her headlong flight. A fall, the rough edges of rocks against her skin, her hands and knees in shallow water. A black, wet space she slid into on her belly, cold water and thin slime beneath her fingers. The void behind her and the terror, the need to burrow and hide; the blind, frantic certainty that death was seeking her.

And before that, nothing.

There was a gap in her mind, like the space left by a missing tooth. Sitting in a crowded bus in broad daylight, meeting Chaim's or Joseph's bleak eyes and then looking away, her belly cramped with fear. Running through the woods in a blind panic in the night. Between the two, a space of darkness. A shudder went through her. She rose on one elbow and unwound the rags that wrapped the knife.

It was clean. Had they washed it? She felt the edge. It was dull.

She did not know what she had done.

She closed her eyes and the common room flashed in on her again, Chaim and Rudy and Édouard and Manuel lined up against the wall by armed men; her mind flinched away. She remembered Roland's face coming up over the edge of the tree-house. His gentle voice, promising to give her knife back when she reached the bottom of the rope ladder. Telling her she was safe. She'd been carried. She had begged to know where Karl and Tova were. They would come after she slept, they'd told her. Promised her. After she slept.

The sound of footsteps from below; she sat up sharply. Then someone whistling a swift, high little tune: *"Compère Guilleri,"* all clear. The ladder — the far one, up from the living room — shifted, and a low voice said, "Élise?"

Julien. She looked down at herself, still in her blood-crusted clothes, and saw for the first time the bandages on her legs. She pinned her loosened hair up as quickly as she could, made sure her ragged skirt covered her, and called, "Come in." More memories flooded in on her as Julien's face came up into sight: light through green leaves overhead, rough wood beneath her cheek, the sound of Julien's voice below, and the nightmare voice. Julien's scream. He had two black eyes and a bandage on one cheek, and his movements spoke of pain.

"Élise." He spoke low, his eyes searching hers. "How do you feel?" He knelt near her by the great mound of hay, slowly, with a wince. Then an uncertain glance at the ladder hole, as if he would go if she wanted.

"I'm all right." She kept her voice low as well. "Julien, where are Karl — Charles and Brigitte? Are they all right?"

"I haven't seen them. I — I've been here. Downstairs. Roland went to get them, I think they'll come soon." He swallowed. "Did you see the paper? Do you know what it means?"

"Paper?"

He unfolded a slip of paper and held it out to her. "This. He said this. At the end. I might have spelled it wrong — what does this word mean — *Lösung*?"

"It means 'solution.' 'I have the solution now.'" She sat back. "He did say that. I heard it. They . . . Did they almost arrest you?"

Julien was staring at something she couldn't see, his pupils wide and dark. "What have I done?" he whispered.

She shivered. She did not know what he had done. She did not know what she had done. So many of her friends in that bus, and her running through the woods alone. In the common room, when they'd finally stood her up against the wall with the others, Chaim walked over to stand beside her, holding his head high against the back-handed blow he got for it. She remembered a fierce German voice in the sunlit woods shouting *"Élise Fournier!"* and her slow, floating mind telling her that was not her name.

"I must have given them something — somehow," Julien said.

Elisa swallowed and opened her mouth. "Someone said he'd shoot you if I didn't come down. Did that happen? Was that real?"

"Yeah."

"It feels like I dreamed it." Her hand came to her mouth. There was another moment — like a dream — not in a bus, in an army truck with canvas sides, an armed Gestapo man at the back — Chaim . . . "He could have shot you."

"He didn't."

Julien looked down. Dust motes moved in

slow patterns in the thin sunbeams. The mound of hay behind him crouched like some waiting beast. She remembered standing very still in the La Roche kitchen, looking at the machine gun, tucking that knife into her waistband with no idea of what she meant to do.

"How did you escape?"

She shook her head, slowly. It hurt. "I still can't remember. I remember running through the woods in the dark — walking home — I could barely see." Had Karl's and Tova's voices really guided her? She must have been half delirious. How had she found her way? "I found a sign — at dawn — a sign for Tanieux, I remember that . . ." She put a hand into the hay and slid the knife out, scraping it against the planks. "I had this. But I don't know how I used it. If I used it. I suppose it's not kosher," she murmured, "now I don't know where it's been." The tears sprang to her eyes, and she turned away from him.

"I'm so sorry," whispered Julien.

"They must have come before dawn," she whispered. "When they knocked they already had us surrounded — Julien, they must have been there in the woods when I came in the door. I was going to make broth . . ." She closed her eyes. "They made me serve them food — at our own dinner table . . . They were taking the others into a little room — one by one." She drew a harsh breath. "The others would barely look at me. Except some of them slipped me messages when I went past them, if the Gestapo weren't looking. They must have thought I wasn't going to be taken, right up to the end . . ."

"Why did they take you?"

"I don't know exactly why. They asked me questions." She opened her eyes. "You. You said they followed you. Why on earth did they follow you?"

Julien spoke fast in a hoarse whisper, not quite looking at her. "I went to them. I found the soldier you pulled out of the river and asked for his help and we went to them together to beg them to release you. He's a major. I thought it might work." He bowed his head; she could see the quivering tension in his neck. "They followed me back to you instead."

Went to them. Her breath came shallow and fast. "You went to the Gestapo headquarters?"

He nodded.

"Did you see them? The others?"

He shook his head. He was very pale. "I

424

heard people moving around — down-stairs."

She closed her eyes again and saw them. Saw them whole now, and themselves. Rudy's bruised face and hard, frightened eyes. Édouard dashing out the La Roche door for the woods, till the man with the machine gun came out of the trees. Chaim taking the blow for her, his eyes on hers saying nothing but *I'm so sorry.* Joseph at the kitchen door, asking her to write to his girlfriend and tell her. Manuel's sad smile as he said, "Better the devil you know." She covered her face with her hands. *They're gone.* Gone where her parents had gone, and Julie, and Julie's parents, and Mischa Rosen, and all his family, and Madame Weider, and so many, so many. Gone where she had thought she was going. Chaim and Manuel, Édouard and Joseph, Rudy and Theo and Isaac. Philippe and David, Friedrich and Marc, all of them. The tears gathering behind her eyes sent sharp pain through her skull. They deserved her tears. They deserved everything. She had left them behind. They were gone, and she was here.

"I was such a fool," Julien whispered, and she looked up. "I'm sorry. I *led* them to you. I thought I had to do something for you, and I made it worse."

She shook her head. The tears were streaming down her face now. "You did something."

"What?"

"I don't know." She heard his voice in the sunlit green, and the voice of the other, the soft German voice that made the hair stand up on her neck. He had gone to them. To tell them they owed her for what she had done. She was reaching for something, reaching within the darkness in her mind. "I don't know how to say it."

He looked up at the high loft window, a small square of blue. "Yeah," he breathed. "I don't know if I'm ever going to be able to explain it. They can tell you what it's like a hundred times and you'd never know."

"What what's like?"

He shivered. "Life. Everything. Death. The other side of the barbed wire, why did you say I understood? I didn't."

"You sort of did."

He snorted.

There was a moment of silence, the hay dust dancing in the beams as slow as time, dancing as if it had eternity to dance in. "And then," said Julien in a low voice, "there's something more. You come to the end and there's something more. And it's part of the end. It's both at once exactly, you can't separate them, it's like . . ." He grasped at the air in front of him and shook his head. "I saw a waterfall in the mountains once. There was something about it, the way it fell, I never could explain it. It fell so fast and so — slowly at the same time. No. That's stupid. I don't know how to say it. It just pours itself over the edge, and the whole time it's falling to the rocks it's like it's floating, like it's *weightless* . . ."

"I jumped," said Elisa, and began to tremble.

She could feel it. She could not see it. It was in the dark. She could feel that moment, suspended — nothing else. Nothing but the strange, quiet sensation under the terror, the accepting: *I am going to die.* Nothing but the air around her.

"I jumped," she whispered. "The knife. I cut, cut the canvas." She clasped her arms around herself as her body remembered the rattling of the truck, the guard and his gun, her arm bent painfully, hiding the knife. "We were in an army truck, with canvas sides. The bus stopped somewhere, we were there for hours, they came back with more prisoners and put some of us into a couple of those trucks. I was up near the cab, away from the guard. I cut — very slowly." The knife lay on the rough boards beside her;

427

her fingers shaped themselves tightly to that remembered grip. "Later," she whispered thickly, "I started cutting very fast." She put her head in her hands and spoke through them. "They were beating Chaim." A bird's wings whirred in the little window, and she parted her hands. "I remember — a flapping noise, the wind must have got into the cut — it must have been then that I jumped, or I wouldn't be here. It's, it's *unbelievable* that I'm here." The pressure of held-in weeping in her head was agony. The tears began to flow again. "I think," she whispered, "I was hoping at least one of them could jump too." For a moment there was silence. The light above her wavered like sunlight on the water, above the drowned. "They're all gone, Julien."

His eyes were like dark wells in the dim light. "I'm so sorry. If we had —"

"It wasn't your fault."

He looked down, and nodded. She nodded too. It didn't matter that it wasn't his fault. It didn't matter that it wasn't her fault. If they had disbanded the house — if she'd cut faster — if Chaim had fled here, to this hayloft — if Manuel had decided two weeks sooner to go back to the devil he knew — if the canvas hadn't flapped so loud, so loud she knew she didn't have a second to lose . . .

She drew in a sharp breath, feeling it again in all her limbs. Suspended, falling toward the earth. "I had to get back to Karl and Tova. They were all I could think about. Julien, I heard them, I heard their voices telling me the way back to Tanieux. I remember it as clearly as anything." She put a hand up to her aching temple. "I suppose I hit my head."

Julien let out a soft breath that was very like a laugh. "I suppose so."

"It was like you said. That's exactly what it's like. You're falling and you're flying and you know you're going to die. And, and you're *lifted.*" She looked up into the sunbeams; gold and darkness danced above her. "I don't remember landing. It's still like that for me, like it was when I did it." She turned to him. "You just jump," she said. "Into nothing."

"Because there's nothing else you can do," said Julien.

"Because you have to."

There was a long moment of silence. His eyes were on hers, his thin face utterly still. She drew a sharp breath and looked down at her hands. Somewhere in the hay they could hear a mouse scratching. Julien moved away from her a little, toward the ladder. He said quietly, looking straight in front of him, "I don't know what else you heard up there, but you should probably forget it."

"No," murmured Elisa.

He turned sharply to her.

"I — I don't . . ." She looked at her knees. *It's not that.* She raised her head. "You don't deserve to be forgotten."

His eyes were wells, the dusty gold light of the loft trembling on the surface. He closed them. "Thank you," he whispered. She could see one hand gripping the seam of his trouser leg, stretching the worn cloth. After a moment he said, "Albrecht — the man you saved. He asked me to tell you he'd like to talk with you if you're willing. He stays down at Les Genêts."

She shivered. "What is he, Julien?"

"A major."

"Of what?"

"Army. He was on the eastern front."

She let out the long breath she had been holding, then drew it in again. *It doesn't mean you didn't kill anyone just because they're in Russia.* "And you're sure he wasn't SS?"

"Yeah. He said — Yeah, I'm sure."

She sat back in the hay, filling her lungs with the scented air. A breeze was blowing in the little window under the eaves. "Julien," she said, "when you see your father, I have a message for him. I want my siblings taken to Switzerland. And me. But they can travel without me, by the Cimade or the OSE, if he thinks it's safer for them." She sat up. "As soon as possible. Make sure and say that."

"Élise," he said after a long moment, *"thank God."*

"It's not over yet."

"I know," he breathed.

"I'm so afraid," she said. "But we have to. There's nothing else we can do."

"You're here," he said. "Élise, you escaped from the Gestapo."

She felt her mouth twist slowly into a painful smile. "I did. Didn't I?"

"Yeah." His eyes were warm on her, a smile creeping over his own face too.

The far sound of voices came in through the little window. Elisa sat still a moment, breathing them in. *Yes.* Then she was on her knees by the window, ignoring the pain and the dizziness, drinking in the sight of them down below: the dark heads of her brother and sister, Tova's face upturned for a moment, Karl's voice raised up in some question, then passing out of sight into the house, their bodies moving easily and whole. Julien was watching her. "They're here," she whispered, and he nodded.

"I'll go."

Then their voices already at the bottom of the ladder. Julien went for the other ladder as Tova's face came into sight, already streaming with tears. "Elisa. I thought —"

"Shh, shh. I'm here. I'm here." Her sister came to her arms, and she held her against her heart.

"I told you she'd come back," said Karl's gruff, cracking voice. Elisa opened her eyes and stared.

After a moment Julien's voice came from the top of the far ladder: "You *did*?" It cracked too.

And then they were laughing, and Karl came into her arms, all of them laughing and Julien laughing too, even as he slipped quietly down out of sight, leaving her holding tight and warm to what was left of her family.

Julien climbed down the ladder into the barn side of the ancient stone farmhouse. The cow stalls stood empty, each with its trapdoor for hay above it. The air was dim, fragrant with hay and the rich, familiar stink of manure. The low sound of laughter and voices from upstairs mingled with the clucking of chickens just beyond the wall. He closed his eyes for a long moment, listening. Then he turned away.

He let himself through the door to the living room and blinked, blinded by morning light on plastered walls. Through the window he could see Roland and Monsieur Thibaud out in the near hayfield, their scythes swinging in unison. It was quiet in the house, no one there except, sitting at the table with a glass of water, the person he had known must have brought the children to Élise.

"Good morning," he said hoarsely, and his father turned.

Papa's eyes did not go to his bandage, or to the stiff and careful way he moved. They went to his eyes, and he nodded very slightly. "Julien," he murmured, and stood, scraping his chair raggedly on the floor. He held out his hands for Julien's shoulders, stared at his bandage, drew in a breath, and turned away two steps to Madame Thibaud's kitchen, returning with a pitcher and glass. "Here. Sit. Julien." He poured him water, overfilling it, spilling some on the pine table. Julien saw him suddenly in a barracks full of listening men, his eyes dark and calm, his upraised hand trembling a little as he said, *God is my help.* Saw him going to bed and waking up behind barbed wire.

"Papa," he said. Papa handed him the glass, and he drank deep.

"Tell me," his father said, and sat.

And so Julien sat at the Thibauds' table, hearing the faint, glad voices in the hayloft overhead, and told his father everything, every word he could remember. Even the parts he wanted to tell no one yet, until he had gone up to the cave and stared at the stream for a while, until he had slept alone and woken alone and found at least a few words to put to the things inside him. Words that someone would understand who hadn't lately leapt from a Gestapo truck in the dark. But he owed Papa this.

And Papa needed to know.

He did not watch his father's face. He looked at his hands on the table in front of him and didn't glance up for a moment as he forced himself to say the words, "And then he put the gun to my head." Hearing his father's breathing change was bad enough. He did not leave out what he had said about Élise. He didn't look up until he had repeated the German phrase and Élise's translation. Then he looked his father in the eye.

"Do you have any guess, Papa? As to what he meant?"

Papa had one knuckle over his mouth. He straightened, not taking his eyes off Julien. He lowered his hand and said softly, "You didn't do anything wrong."

Julien gripped the table, sudden fury rising in him. "But did I do anything that will *hurt* someone?"

"I'm not a prophet," said Papa with almost equal vehemence, then quieted. "But I don't think so, Julien. I don't see how."

"But there was *something*. He smiled."

Papa nodded soberly. "I'll talk to Alex. There may be some way for us to find out more." He looked Julien in the eye. "You did a very brave thing, and a good thing. I do not believe evil will come of it."

"I hope you're right," said Julien.

Élise's faint, low laughter came from above. Julien saw his father watching his face, and looked straight back at him. "She wants to go to Switzerland. She says you can send Charles and Brigitte by the Cimade or the OSE if you think that's best."

"She's doing the right thing."

Julien nodded.

"You've acted honorably toward her, from what I can see."

Julien looked away. "Acting honorably hurts."

"A great deal, sometimes," said Papa.

"Like many of the things most worth doing. It's a clean break, Julien. It will heal well and strong."

Julien blinked and kept his face still. His father's brown eyes were warm and sad. For a moment neither spoke. Then Papa said, "Where would you like to go now?"

He touched the bandage on his face. "Somewhere quiet."

Papa nodded. "I'll be glad to walk you to my father's farm," he said.

Grandpa put ointment on his cuts and bruises, sat him down at the kitchen table with bitter tea laced with wild honey, then moved around the kitchen making lunch in perfect silence. The clock ticked; the kettle hissed. They could hear the wind in the trees outside. They ate together at the kitchen table, Julien and Grandpa and Benjamin; they asked no questions but how he felt. He felt very tired. He slept the afternoon away, a blanket mounded behind him so he couldn't roll over. He woke to a breeze on his face and in the sunlit curtains, and Benjamin hesitating at his half-open door.

"Your grandfather sent me to see if you needed anything."

"Thanks. I'm thirsty."

Benjamin brought him water and stood

by the foot of his bed. "Your father said the Gestapo beat you," he said.

Julien nodded, drinking.

There was a long silence. Benjamin was looking at his bandage.

"I owe you an apology," said Julien finally. "You were right. I had absolutely no idea what it's like."

Benjamin let out a sharp breath that was almost a snort. "Being beaten by the Gestapo?"

"No. That was nothing. I thought they were going to take me in."

They looked at each other for a long moment. Finally Benjamin nodded, exhaling again, and sat on the bed. "My new visa's supposed to come any day," he said very quietly. "I don't know how I'm going to do it."

"But you are."

Benjamin looked out the window for a long time. Then he nodded, very slightly.

CHAPTER 29
AT THE END

It was two days later, after his pain had started to ease, after Mama and Magali had come to visit and Mama and Grandpa had agreed he was healing well, that Julien told Grandpa he wanted to go to the cave for a day or two. It was good here. But something in him was turning over and over like a rolling boil, waking him in the night. He had to sit for a while and see for kilometers. He had to wake in the presence of rocks and trees, until the boiling calmed somehow.

Roland had brought his Scout bag, found in the dirt in the woods near Les Chênes, potato skins and mouse droppings scattered among Mama's medicine bottles. Grandpa washed it and packed it with potatoes again, and a jar of cooked beans. He loaned Julien a blanket, and asked him if he was sure. Julien said yes, and tied the blanket on underneath, and slung the pack on his shoulders.

It was midmorning; they stood on the porch together, watching Benjamin pitch fresh straw from a wheelbarrow over the floor of the cow's stall. He did it pretty well. Julien spoke suddenly, unsure until the last moment whether he would.

"The day Antoine Duval was shot," he said, "someone from the Maquis asked me if he was at his hotel. I told him. I told him exactly where he was. I wanted him dead."

Grandpa was silent.

"I'd prefer you didn't tell Papa, but if you decide to, I don't want him asking me who it was."

Grandpa nodded. Benjamin wheeled his wheelbarrow back out of the barn, and they both watched him. Grandpa said, "Do you feel that it was the right thing?"

"It wasn't and it was. I don't know how to say it. I don't know yet." He settled his pack on his shoulders. "I just wanted someone to know."

Grandpa nodded, and held out a hand. Julien shook it goodbye, and started off.

It was July. In the hills the crickets sang; the little stream up near the cave ran shallow. He sat on the ledge in the sunlight for hours and did not move, his life tumbling and churning in his head. The gun at Pierre's hip, the gun in Haas's hand. The terror of it, that loosening in his guts; his body preparing for death. He did not start trembling till he recalled the joy.

There's something more, he had said to Élise. *It's part of the end. It's both at once exactly.*

I never felt anything like that before, he said to God. *That's where You are? At the end of the gun?*

He closed his eyes and tilted his head up. The sun was a red glow through his eyelids, red with his own living blood. The secret at the heart of life, spilled again and again. He trembled and bowed his head, fingering the healing scabs around his wrist. A silence beneath silence hushed his mind, and he sat a long time with his eyes closed.

Then he opened them. Away in the distance the worn green ramparts of the Vivarais range stood as they had for centuries, and sunlight lay on them.

He sat on the ledge for hours, and neither moved nor thought. Rabbits wandered and browsed in the tufted grass below. Lizards ran up the rocks and sunned themselves. A hawk floated in the blue above, and the rabbits disappeared into cover.

A doe stepped out of the woods, silent as an image, not looking at him. The lines and movements of her body were fluid and soft and utterly strange to him, who had never before seen a deer unafraid. She glanced from left to right, easily, flicking her ears; her eyes almost touched the place where he sat, but she walked on, placing each hoof lightly and precisely, apparently at peace. She walked like a creature in another world, some far earth that did not know him: a place she had inherited long ago.

He began to weep.

He wept a long time, there in the sunlight. The doe browsed and went; he heard her hooves splash in the stream. When he was finished he stood, and climbed down to gather firewood.

He boiled potatoes under the ragged red sunset and ate them with salt. Then he unrolled Grandpa's blanket and slept out on the ledge in the cool summer night. He woke once and saw the stars overhead in their billions, their brilliance making the shreds of cloud glow pearly white, and heard the sharp bark of a fox somewhere down in the woods. He passed from waking back into sleep without knowing it, and woke again to find the dew in his hair and on his blanket, and got up to wash. He spent most of the day on the ledge again, looking at the far hills, motionless, holding something he could not quite name inside him like a brimming cup too precious to spill. He remembered the knowledge he had found after Duval's death, the sure and solid weight of it, like a stone in his hand. The thing that could not be given, only found in the seeking, and alone.

But this, this was another thing. It had no weight. He couldn't grasp it. It was not his.

But it was real.

He ate all that was left of his food that evening. Before bedding down he searched through his pack and set a rabbit snare, the way Roland had taught him. At dawn the next day as he laid his small campfire, the branch started jerking, down below the ledge in the growing light; he scrambled down as fast as he could with his Scout knife out. He held the rabbit by the ears and found himself whispering, "I'm sorry" as he drew the blade swiftly across its throat. He watched its red blood pour out into the earth, wondering if that made it kosher, wishing he could feed her, put the blood back in her white face. "Thank you," he whispered, and took it up to the ledge to skin it. He cut off a haunch for breakfast and wrapped the rest in newspaper, carefully, a gift for his mother.

He was holding the spit and blowing on

the roasted meat to cool it when Pierre appeared.

His face came up over the rim of the ledge, and a smile broke out on it. Julien found his own smile answering, and without another word Pierre took a handhold and swung himself up, moving easily. He was leaner now, dirty and tanned. Julien held out the spit to him, and his eyes lit. He squatted and tore off a couple of slivers for himself, juggling and blowing on them before he bit into one. Julien grinned and started to unwrap the rabbit again.

Pierre sat back on his heels, watching Julien cut off the second haunch and spit it over the fire. "Heard you saw some action."

"In a way."

"Boy, this is good."

"More?"

"Yeah. Mmm." There was a minute of silence, until they had both licked the juices from their fingers. Then Pierre settled himself. "Listen, I want to hear all about it, but I should probably give you my message first."

Julien almost leapt to his feet that moment. *Lösung. I have the solution now.* "Something happen? Down in town?"

"No! No. Nothing happened. Least I don't think so. I haven't been there."

Julien relaxed. "What?"

"I have a message from my captain. To you."

"He knows who I am?"

"He *wants* you. For our unit. We heard about the incident, he figured you might like to leave town. He's always thought you'd be an asset. He'd like to train you as a junior officer." Pierre grinned and gestured to Julien and his Scout pack and pallet back in the cave. "Come as you are."

Julien sat back looking at his friend.

"C'mon," said Pierre, then his grin sobered as he looked into Julien's face. He spoke more quietly and seriously than Julien had ever heard him speak. "I'd be proud to fight with you."

"I'd be proud to fight with you too," said Julien, and looked into the little fire. "Tell him I'm honored. But no."

The fire crackled in the silence. "I thought you were over that stuff," said Pierre finally.

"I was."

"Should I — I mean," Pierre gestured at his shredding bandage, "it takes awhile, after you see your first action, I mean I *know.* Should I ask again . . . later?"

Julien's sudden laugh rang through the valley. Down in the grass below a rabbit ran wildly into cover. Pierre stared at him.

"No," Julien said. "Sorry, I didn't mean — it's . . ." He poked the fire, then looked up at his friend. "It's kind of a long story."

"Yeah? Tell it to me sometime."

"I will. You still hungry?"

"Are you kidding?"

They ate the second haunch in silence, looking out over their hills.

It was midmorning when he started down toward Tanieux. He took the short way, down the little ravine and across the shallow river, glancing north toward the steep slope he'd scrambled up in the driving rain with Élise and the others, in that storm they'd fled ahead of and not quite escaped. He remembered Élise's driven, bloodshot eyes. He stopped for a moment on the north road, remembering the sound of motorcycle engines, and prayed.

Then he walked on down toward his town, singing "A Mighty Fortress" softly under his breath.

At the corner of the Rue Peyrou, just three houses into town, he paused and looked twice at a figure sitting on the stoop of the Chaveaus' house, whittling on a stick. It was Marcel. He walked over to him, and Marcel rose.

"You're home," Julien said as they shook hands.

"And you," said Marcel, gesturing to his face. "Your father told me that was the Gestapo."

"Yeah," said Julien. "You on a break?"

Marcel shook his head. "I'm home. I got compromised. I'm off the job."

"Arrested?"

"Almost. The person I was guiding got caught. Then the police came looking for me. She'd told them I could testify she wasn't Jewish." He looked away. "I always wondered if that would happen if it came to the point. I testified, not that it was likely to be any use. Our train was leaving that minute. They asked for my papers, I saw one of them going for his handcuffs, I ran and jumped onto the moving train. I was lucky."

"And her?"

Marcel shook his head, and looked down at his knife. After a moment he said, "That's my story. Trade."

Julien watched the knife peeling bark for a few seconds, and finally said, "I tried to get someone back from them. She'd rescued a *boche* officer who was drowning in the river and I thought they might release her. They told me she'd escaped and sent me home, and like an idiot I almost led them to her, down in the woods by Les Chênes. She hid in the treehouse and I tried to throw them off the trail and they beat me up. They didn't find her."

"That treehouse."

"You were right to put on the canvas covers."

"It seems like so long ago."

"Yeah," said Julien.

He went on down the familiar streets, nodding to someone every now and then, ignoring curious glances. The Rue Emmanuel still looked the same, though he didn't know why this should surprise him. The heavy downstairs door of his house still made the same rising creak when he pushed it open; the hallway and stairwell were dark and cool, the old stone steps worn in all the places he remembered. As he climbed, his mother's singing came down to him in the dark, pure and clear as falling water. He knocked, and Mama opened to him, letting light in from the dining-room windows to shine on the tears welling in her eyes.

She didn't hug him. She took both his hands and looked into his face. She said, "My son," and shook her head. She kissed him on each cheek, carefully, then did it again. He slung his pack off his back and fished in it for the package of meat, the layers of newspaper slightly bloody now, and held it out to her.

"Oh, Julien!" She took it from his hands with both of hers, her eyes shining, and turned toward the stove. "I'll lay a fire right away."

"Isn't Magali at Les Chênes? Shouldn't we wait for supper so she — ?"

Mama's laugh rang clear. "You stew a rabbit for hours, Julien. At least if you want a good flavor. Yes, we'll all have supper together, and celebrate."

He blinked at her, thinking, *Roasted for minutes tasted fine to me.* Thinking, *So happy.* "Sorry it's missing the legs. I was only going to eat one, but Pierre showed up."

Mama gave him a long look, sobering. "That's all right, Julien," she said. "Your father wants to talk to you. He's in his study. Why don't you go see him while I get this started?"

Papa's study was also the same. The pitted surface of the desk, the straight-backed chairs, the file cabinet, the pens, the scarred blotter, the pad of blue-lined paper in the lower left-hand corner. Papa stood to give him the *bise* and sat back down with a small, rueful smile. Julien sat in the right-hand chair as he always had, and looked at his father across the desk.

"We've had news," said Papa.

Julien waited. Even the sick tightening of his stomach was familiar, and the sudden rush of his pulse. He watched his father's eyes.

"We've found out what the Gestapo chief meant. I was able to learn — well, we believe they have new plans regarding Alex and me." Papa picked up a pen. "They're taking steps to hire French criminals to have us quietly murdered, with no provable connection to themselves."

Julien put his hands on the desk and leaned toward his father, but before he could open his mouth Papa was speaking again.

"If anything was decided the day of your encounter with them I am certain it was this. We believe their reasoning is that with the eastern front going so badly for Germany it's no time to arouse outrage here in France, nor" — he stabbed his pen into the blotter — "to make martyrs." He looked up at Julien and spoke quickly. "We got the news yesterday. I've thought and prayed about it all night. There is no witness in being murdered, no possible good to others.

And I've heard of cases like this. These gangs they hire — bystanders have been killed." His eyes fell to the pen in his hands. "Family members." He laid it down and sat up straight, putting both hands flat on the desk. "I'll be leaving Tanieux as soon as I've made arrangements that can't be traced. I'm almost certain Alex will do the same." He met Julien's eyes with the ghost of a smile. "I've asked your mother to come with me."

His mother. She had laughed like a girl. *So that's it. This. This is it.* When he glanced down he saw he was gripping the edge of the desk. He looked out the window then, to where a high hawk floated in the blue, and said so softly he could barely hear himself, "I think I might be afraid to be happy anymore."

"It's a hard time. A hard time God chose for you to become a man in."

Julien turned back to his father, saw his eyes like dark earth. After a moment Papa said, "I've been wondering about you. Whether you want to stay in Tanieux now or not." He looked down at his desk again, picked up the pen. He cleared his throat and said, "I hear you've had an offer from the Maquis."

"You heard about that?"

Papa's mouth went wry. "Well, the rumor was you were out in the hills already, training for an officer, but I didn't credit that."

Julien snorted. "I guess Pierre's still got that mouth."

Papa nodded, looking at his pen.

"I turned that down."

Papa's head came up. His eyes searched Julien's, his face strangely soft, the lines of it washed clean by wonder, as if the face of the young man looked out for a moment from the old. "You did," he murmured.

Julien nodded. Shrugged. "I'm not doing that."

Papa kept the pen in his hands, rolling it very gently between his fingers, still looking at Julien.

"I ran into Marcel Chaveau on the way in," said Julien.

The pen stopped rolling; Papa motioned with his head for Julien to go on.

"Did you find a replacement for him yet?"

Papa shook his head. "Not yet."

Julien sat back in his chair and looked into his father's eyes. "Well, then . . ."

Papa's eyes did not leave him as his hand went to the pad of blue-lined paper, slowly. "Well, then," he said.

CHAPTER 30
THE OTHER SIDE

Julien was still mending his night-crossing shirt when the knock came.

They were early. The rooftops of Annecy gleamed wet and pale in the dawn light; it couldn't be six thirty yet. But it was the signal. *Knock, pause, knock knock knock.* Through the open guest room window he heard the voice of his nameless counterpart, high and courteous: "A parcel for you, monsieur," and Pastor Cantal's low voice replying. He pushed the needle into the black cloth and pricked his finger. He heard the door close, and the other guide going away. *Five minutes,* he told his suddenly racing heart. *More if they're smart. Finish your seam.*

The stitches crisscrossed drunkenly; Magali would have laughed. Magali wasn't here. It was only the second time he'd mended anything. The first had also been this shirt. He couldn't really tell himself he had to be more careful. When you heard boots you went in the ditch. You got used to it, he had heard. He wasn't yet.

This part, though. He would never get used to this part. Not till the day he was waiting for.

He made the last stitch and tried to remember how Mama and Magali would have tied it off. He should have paid more attention. Too late now. He attempted a double knot and tested the resulting snarl for fastness. He stood up and with trembling hands began to change into his Scout uniform. He did not allow himself to go to the window. He prayed, though not with words. God knew. He saw in a brief flash his home as he'd last seen it: the bedrooms stripped and made up for strangers, Papa's study gutted. The spot on the kitchen table where Mama's Bible had always lain, glaring empty like the gap of a missing tooth. The low rumble of a nameless ally's automobile down in the street, like a great purring cat in the night. He remembered Magali taking his hand in the dark, as the taillights moved slowly away.

He tied his kerchief on, pulled on his socks. He folded the black night-crossing shirt, tucked it into the bottom of his Scout bag, and started the check. Full change of clothes. Money. First aid kit. Papers. He glanced at the clock. He walked slowly over to the window, keeping his breathing steady, and looked down into the street, finally, to see whether his group was there yet, and whether one of the people he was waiting for was in it.

Next moment he had both hands pressed flat against the glass, breathing shallowly.

They both were.

He knew Benjamin's clothes like his own. He knew his walk. He knew Élise's — everything, he knew her hair, the set of her shoulders, the lift of her head, he could feel his soul go out to her like a shining thread strung between them, feel the tension in her body as his own. A third person walked behind them — Tova? No, it was a stranger. She'd come alone. He didn't ask himself what that could mean; she would answer that. He only thought: *Both of them. Tonight.* And leaned his forehead against the window, praying.

Then he went down.

He stood on the bottom step of the stairs, listening for their knock, eyeing the dining-room table where the parcel had been opened and left: a copy of Calvin's *Institutes*. It would be Collonges then, without the monks and their ladder to do the crucial last two minutes' work for him. Collonges, where he would lift up the barbed wire for his friends himself. His mouth was dry. Pastor Cantal was in the doorway of his study, stepping forward as soon as the knock came. And there they were.

Three young people in dark clothes, empty-handed, eerily alike for the fear in their faces. Élise came in last, dark wisps of hair curling out of her bun, her eyes like the others'. Pastor Cantal closed the door. Julien stepped off the bottom stair, and they saw him. Benjamin came to him with a hand held out, and he shook it silently.

Élise said, "Karl and Tova are in Switzerland."

He let out his breath. "When?"

"A week ago. The OSE."

"Thank God."

The third girl stood silent and stared at him.

"He's the *passeur*," Benjamin said to her in German, his voice coming out hoarse.

"Come into the kitchen and eat something," said Pastor Cantal. "My wife is making breakfast. You'll have two or three hours here. Eat and rest."

Benjamin looked at him, but Julien said, "I've eaten. I have to go out and see someone. To get the go-ahead. I'll be back."

The girl was still looking at him. So were the other two.

"You'll be in Switzerland tomorrow," he said.

Confirmed. The priest was ready for them, the right bus driver was on duty, all was ready. At the Cantals' table when he opened his mouth to give the others their instructions, it was the *passeur*'s voice that came out. Even and calm. The core of a pear lay on Élise's plate, beside the breadcrumbs on the others'. When they got to the rectory he would ask the priest's housekeeper to make something she could eat.

The sun was bright in the deep August sky as they went out of the house to the bus stop, Julien in his Scout uniform twenty paces ahead. He was a boy, hands in his pockets, a Scout going up to Collonges to help a priest for a few days. He did not know the people boarding the bus behind him, though he felt them in the pulse of his blood. There were no police, no patrols. He sat and watched the houses go by, and the trees; he rang the bell for his stop and stood, swaying with the motion of the bus.

He heard them get down behind him. He did not turn.

He did not turn as he went down the path,

footsteps behind him. He did not turn till he had knocked, and given the priest the signal, and gone into the house.

They were all there.

He didn't follow them up the attic ladder. He spoke with the priest about the patrols — still consistent, still twenty minutes apart — then with the housekeeper about roasting potatoes in hot coals to keep them kosher. He thanked them both and went out. It was only his fourth crossing here. He couldn't afford mistakes. The wind had risen in the west, carrying clouds; the poplars on the Swiss side swayed. The barbed wire did not move. He noted the crossing place and its landmarks, the little house, the ditch, the spot where the wire was loosest. The French barbed wire, then the Swiss. He walked on, his hands in his Scout uniform pockets, and nodded to the patrol he passed.

He climbed back to the attic. Élise sat on a blanket, her legs folded under her, between dusty boxes; the nameless girl lay on the worn-out couch that lined the south wall, very pale. Benjamin sat on the floor at her feet. "She came from Mulhouse a week ago," he told Julien softly. "Stuttgart before that. Her name —" Benjamin broke off and shook his head. The girl looked up with

457

bloodshot eyes, her head turning wearily toward Julien. Benjamin's eyes went to hers, then tore themselves away. "She thinks her sister might be in Switzerland. She's not sure."

"We'll be here till nightfall," Julien told him. "She should try to get some sleep. You all should." They turned to him with a look he knew well. "It can be done," he said. "I've seen it."

They ate the lunch the housekeeper brought, the woman's face brightening at Élise's thanks for the blackened potatoes. He gathered them by the little east window and gave them their instructions, showed them the place. "There are Swiss soldiers just behind those trees," he told them. "They're there to keep the enemy out, not you. Go toward them, show them your hands, and tell them who you are. Don't turn back for any reason, ever. If there's any trouble on this side, just run."

They looked at him. It hurt to see their eyes. "There's never been trouble yet," he said.

He laid out blankets for them, told them to close their eyes for a while at least. The girl from Stuttgart slept, her mouth open, her breathing deep and even. He believed Élise slept too. He drifted awhile as the slanting light entered through the west window and lengthened. When he came to himself Élise was beside him, knees drawn up beneath her skirt, propped against the east wall.

As he sat up she met his eyes and said nothing, but drew a small object out of her pocket and held it out to him in the palm of her hand. It was his whistle.

"Are you giving it back?"

"If you want it."

He shook his head.

"I thought . . . if you didn't . . . I could keep it. To remember you by."

He waited till he could trust his voice. "Please."

She looked at his empty hands resting on his knees. "I don't have anything for you. They didn't let us pack — I don't have anything."

"It's all right," he whispered.

"No." The light from the west window fell on her neck, her mouth, as she shook her head. Tiny dark curls escaped from her bun. "The — the Thibauds have my knife, if you want it — I — do you have a knife with you, Julien?"

He gave her his Scout knife, handle first. She took it and laid it beside her on the floor, and reached both hands up behind her head to unpin her hair.

It fell in a dark cloud around her face and shoulders, half in sunlight, half in shadow. He did not breathe. Her eyes met his as she lifted the knife to the crown of her head and carefully sawed off a long dark lock near the roots. "Here," she whispered. It was soft in his fingers, in his fingers that did not quite touch hers. The slanting gold light was on all her face now; he could see all the browns in her eyes, colors from deep in the earth where the roots drank water. It was more than he could bear. Her soul lay on her face like sunlight on a field, and he sat with her gift in his hand, the other hand digging its fingernails into the bare pine boards beneath him, because it was all he could do.

She turned away, looking down at the floor. He remembered her turning, that spring night under the moon, walking away from him under the streetlamps alone. Her hand lay on the boards five centimeters from his; stray strands of her hair brushed his shoulder. He remembered brushing it out of her face; he remembered taking that wrist in his fingers for one brief moment: the softness, the warm beat of life within. He could still feel it. She was looking at his hand too. He was shaking.

"That officer," she whispered thickly. "I got his address. From Madame Delaure at Les Genêts."

"You did?" He tried to breathe slowly, to still the blood pounding in his ears.

"I couldn't go and talk to him," she whispered. "But maybe someday."

"Élise," he said, "why did you save him?"

She was silent so long he thought she would not answer. "He didn't come to kill me."

"I don't understand."

"I don't either. Not really. Julien . . ."

"Yes?"

"Thank you," she whispered.

His voice was so low and hoarse he could barely hear it. "Anytime."

Their gaze broke. He followed her eyes to the west window. The sinking sun had touched the hills. He drew in a long breath and straightened, as she twisted her dark hair back up and pushed the pins in, one by one.

It was like the other crossings, more and more, as the night came on. The same fog of fear, filling the attic, seeming to curl out through the cracks in the little window frames like smoke; thickening with the setting of the sun.

461

They sat together, backs against the wall, as the clouds rolled over the sun, their edges turning the color of gold and blood. They ate together, when supper came, almost in silence; there was so little left to say. Even between him and Benjamin. *How are your parents? I don't know.* After a while the girl from Stuttgart put her face in her hands, and Benjamin whispered to her in German. The attic was dimming, the clouds edged in paling rose and yellow. Night was coming. He sat next to Élise. Even through the air between them he could feel how taut she was, like a bowstring. She lifted her head, her lips moving silently, and he looked where she was looking, up into the darkness between the rafters. Behind him, outside the window, he heard the rain begin. He got up on the balls of his feet to look out; it fell softly and steadily, on France, on Switzerland, on the narrow space between. "Rain," he said quietly but aloud. "It's good. Rain is safer." He saw them all turn to him in the near dark.

They sat in silence after that. He knew this moment. He felt them winding tighter and tighter, growing brittle and agonized with fear. Like the last group. Like the next. He listened as their breathing grew shallower and quicker in the dark. Felt the rough boards under him with his fingertips and prayed, soundlessly, wordlessly, a thin thread of pleading rising up fragile as a bird lifted on the wind. He heard the wind rise in the trees, and the rain come harder. He checked his watch and buttoned the sleeves of his black shirt. He heard the downstairs door open quietly and close. He checked his watch again, took it off and slipped it into the Scout pack beside him, and rose. Three shadowed faces looked up, breaths drawing in at the same instant. "Downstairs now," he whispered. "When the priest comes back, we go."

They stood to follow him, unsteady on their legs. The housekeeper had the ladder up for them; Julien took it first and stood below Benjamin as he came down. In the sudden light downstairs his friend's face showed pale, almost greenish. As Benjamin reached the bottom of the ladder he turned and whispered urgently to Julien, "I want you to send me through last." He grabbed Julien's wrist as he hesitated. "Say you will."

Julien nodded.

He put the others by the wall as the housekeeper put the ladder away, and stood at the window watching. Through the rain at the top of the path he could just see the dark figure of the priest returning; the first patrol had passed. *Now.* He beckoned the others and they started forward, staring. The housekeeper turned out the lights. He opened the door, and together they slipped out into the night.

The rain was steady, blurring the darkness and the lights of the few houses, the sprawling lights of Geneva in the distance ahead. The others were right on his heels as he came down the path carefully, quietly, listening for boots ahead on the paved road, scanning the watery dark, hearing the footfalls behind him clumsy with fear. The wet road shone palely; no figures moved on it to the east or to the west. All clear. "In the ditch," he whispered, taking Élise by the arm and pointing. "Lie flat."

He crouched in the wet grass as they went down one by one, the road still clear at both ends, his heart going like a snare drum. Then he slid in himself, belly in the mud and water. Breathing softly through his mouth, listening. He could hear only the rain. He felt it running through his hair, soaking the back of his neck, he could feel the wet night all around him for a kilometer in every direction, he could almost feel the slow approach of the second patrol. There: boots on the road to the east, a far and rhythmic sound. He prayed silence, silence, not a muscle in his body moving, his heart hammering as the boots came closer; he could feel the thud, thud, thud down the back of his neck. Closer, closer, right beside them, steady, steady, not a pause. The sound receding, step by endless step, away down the Collonges-Annemasse road.

When it was fully gone, he stood.

In silence he reached down to them, each of them, and pulled them up, scrambling out of weeds and mud. On the other side of the road the barbed wire gleamed in pale lines and points, the tall shapes of the poplars behind it silhouetted against the far lights of Geneva. They crossed the road; they crossed the other ditch; he crouched by the barbed wire and lifted it as high as he could, beckoning.

The girl from Stuttgart came first, the whites of her eyes in the darkness huge with fear. Down on her belly, crawling with her elbows, agonizingly slow. He watched the east, he watched the west. Nothing. She was through. Benjamin was pushing Élise forward. He saw her eyes for one split second as she went down, then she was squirming her way through. He strained against the barbed wire, lifting it higher for her as she came up to hands and knees to make the last centimeters. Benjamin was right on her heels, face almost in the dirt, belly-crawling frantically. The road was still clear in both directions. Élise had turned and was holding up the barbed wire with him, looking at him. Then Benjamin was through and Julien swung himself under sideways, quick as he could. The lights of freedom ahead were blinding as they crossed the narrow no-man's-land, as he knelt to lift the Swiss barbed wire.

The girl from Stuttgart, down and crawling. Through. Silence on the road behind, and dark. Élise, Élise, down in the mud and crawling for her life, and through. Benjamin, last of the three, eyes flashing wild for a moment in his wet white face, down and inching his desperate way forward as Julien hauled the wire up as high as it could go.

And through.

"Go," he whispered, "go!" And he was already turning away, the road was clear, clear to the east, clear to the west, and he was back across the no-man's-land and taking the wire in one hand, doing the swift sideways roll under it that Marcel had taught him, feeling it catch and tear the shirt again, coming up on his hands and knees back in France. He could hear nothing but his own rustling in the grass, intolerably loud; he flung himself down in the ditch.

He was panting for breath, his heart stuttering; he was trembling all over. He thought he heard boots to the east.

He lay still and heard them coming, eyes open to the dark, one cheek in the muddy water, the beating of his heart so loud anyone could hear it. He lay still and listened, listened, till he heard, louder than the far boots, another sound. From the other side, where the far lights blazed, a sound he had heard before: the Swiss soldiers behind the trees, calling out challenge and welcome to those who had been saved, and voices answering.

He closed his eyes.

He lay in the ditch and breathed as the patrol passed by. *Thank You,* he breathed, *thank You.* The rain ran down his face, dripped from his hair, and he listened to the boots passing, and thought of them there, saw in his mind their faces, their eyes staring at each other, just barely beginning to believe. *It's real. It's done.* He saw Élise, her black hair shining in the rain, walking away through the darkness and the pale pools of light, not turning back.

The boots receded into silence. He pulled himself up out of the ditch and crouched a moment by the empty road, looking at Switzerland. Then he turned away. The rain fell and fell as he walked, watering the earth, soaking deep into the thirsty roots on both sides of the barbed wire, and between. It wasn't till he'd reached the house that he realized they had never said goodbye.

HISTORICAL NOTE

A great deal of this really happened.

Julien, Elisa, Benjamin, and Magali are fictional; their stories, their choices, are invented. But many of the events surrounding them are real. Tanieux is based on a real town; Pastor Alexandre and Julien's father are based on real people.

I'm going to do something unusual in this historical note. I'm going to let the town and the pastors keep their aliases. I have reasons for this. One is that I've given the assistant pastor's wife an *extremely* fictional episode of brief reactive psychosis, and I don't want that associated with the name of the steadfast woman she stands in for in the novel.

But the other is this.

This story has been told before, and it's been told wrong. Or at least in a way that distorts important truths. It's been told as the story of an exceptional French village

469

and the heroic pastor who led his people in hiding Jews. But that's not how the story went, when it was happening.

It was never the story of one town, and it was never the story of one man.

In south central France there is a high, cold plateau, a hard place to farm, a hard place to keep warm through the long, bitter winters. Hundreds of years ago the Huguenots — French Protestants fiercely persecuted by Catholic kings — fled to that cold plateau and made it their own, built their homes out of the rocks, and learned to till the stony soil. For hundreds of years their descendants kept their traditions: their worship, their independence, their distrust of the government. Their memory of persecution.

And then France fell to the Nazis, and the new French government in Vichy began arresting Jews.

Writers still debate why the people of the Vivarais-Lignon plateau hid so many Jews during World War II, but one thing is clear: they did, and it seemed normal to them. It's said by people with memory of that time that there was a Jewish refugee in every farmhouse. They saved thousands of lives at the risk of their own, saying afterward that it was only the decent thing to do. And

470

across the plateau, in its eleven villages, a network of pastors worked with each other and with their congregations and their neighbors to welcome refugees, hide them, feed them, provide them with false papers, and eventually (with the aid of allies Catholic, Protestant, and Jewish, French and Swiss) smuggle many of them across the border into Switzerland. The real Tanieux was among those villages. The real Pastors Alexandre and Losier were among those pastors.

Here are the parts of *Flame in the Night* that are real.

- The story of the protest letter handed to a Vichy official (the Vichy Secretary of Youth) is real; so is the *préfet*'s threat in answer. That *préfet*, Robert Bach, was later considered by his superiors in Vichy to be so lax in applying their raid orders that they replaced him.

- There really was a lookout and alert system organized by the pastors and carried out by the Scouts, though many of the details in the novel are invented. It's also true that after the first raid, the pastors were regularly given warning when a raid was coming by an anonymous phone call to the parsonage.

- The story of the rescue of over one hundred Jewish children at the sorting camp of Vénissieux is real down to the last detail. The stolen telegram (it was the Abbé Glasberg who stole it), the all-night scramble in the dark barracks to convince parents to sign away custody of their children in the most wrenching circumstances, the disused convent used as a temporary hiding place, the warning and the flight to the back door, the fear that the cardinal might hand over the addresses when given assurances from Pétain. (He did not hand them over; he gave the operation every possible support.) Some of the children rescued in that operation were indeed hidden on the plateau.
- The rescue was carried out by the Amitié Chrétienne (a network of Catholic and Protestant aid groups) and the OSE (a Jewish aid organization). The OSE hid and supported thousands of Jewish children in France during and after the war, including smuggling about a thousand to Switzerland. The "dark-haired woman" behind the table in the convent is Madeleine Dreyfus, a Jewish social worker with the OSE who

placed hundreds of children in hiding on the plateau. The Cimade was a Protestant organization doing similar work.

- Though the real Pastor Losier did participate in the underground work I described, the leading role was taken by the dynamic Mireille Philip, wife of a Socialist leader who was in London with Charles de Gaulle at the time.
- The three-week police raid, with the police trying morning after morning to find someone, really happened. Sadly a few people were arrested in the end, some of them through identity checks on the roads as they fled the area; we don't know for certain how many. I know the names of three: Kalman Scherzer and Ida Besag, who likely both died in Auschwitz, and a man by the name of Steckler, who was later released.
- The story of the policeman falling into a farm cesspit the owners "forgot" to tell him about is also real.
- Jeannette and Maurice Berger and their friend Clément are inspired by Georgette and Jean-François Meylan and their brave and lively group of *passeur* friends on both sides of the

French-Swiss border, in the Jura mountains north of the Alps.

- The character of Antoine Duval is based on a real person: Léopold Praly, employed by the Vichy police to stay in the real Tanieux and gather all possible information on Jews and Resistance fighters. He was more of an inspector and less of an informer than he appears in the book — he actually made a few arrests himself.

- In the real Tanieux, as in the story, there was a quiet (or mostly quiet) tug-of-war between beliefs: the pastors and their adherents, who believed that Jesus taught nonviolence, and the Maquis and their supporters (some of them also church members) who felt it was the duty of the French people to resist the occupiers by force.

- The story of the pastors' arrest is real. The policeman did have tears in his eyes; the real Madame Alexandre had offered him supper when he came to arrest her husband.

- It's also true that in the camp they were sent to, the pastors were allowed to lead worship services, and that they held many friendly debates about the gospel with the Communists who were the majority of the political prisoners there.

- The two pastors really did refuse to sign a loyalty oath to Pétain even though they would have been released immediately if they had. Although they had accepted certain forms of lying, like providing Jews with false identity cards, they felt that taking a false oath to save their own skins was too much. They were released the next day with no explanation.
- There was no raid the day of their release. I invented that. But there was one raid — almost the only raid with no anonymous phone call beforehand — while they were gone, in which eight people were arrested by the French police. Unfortunately we do not know their names.
- It is true that the people of the plateau never attempted to convert the Jewish refugees, and that the pastor in the real Tanieux offered them the use of church facilities for prayers.
- The story of a convalescent German soldier "looking the other way" rather than betraying refugees he happened upon during a raid is not true in itself, but is based on the fact that a hotel

full of these men stood next to a boardinghouse full of Jewish children, and no one was ever denounced.

- The story of local people coming up to a deportation bus with gifts of food is real, but I've altered some facts. (It happened during the first raid, and there was only one person in the bus.)
- Julien's confrontation with Duval is fictional but is based on the fact that when asked why he did what he did, Praly said, "A man has to earn his living in one way or another."
- A small group of men from the Maquis (though not the local Maquis) really did assassinate Praly in front of his hotel in broad daylight. The pastor did hurry to the scene and urge Praly to repent before he died. Praly responded by closing his eyes.
- There was an international school in the real Tanieux like the one I described, meeting in a wide variety of facilities for lack of its own school building. Some classes did meet in a hotel — but not the same hotel Praly was shot in.
- The story of the raid on La Roche is real. The Gestapo (or possibly the German military police; there's still some

uncertainty) raided a boardinghouse housing young men of university age, both Jewish and non-Jewish. They surrounded the house just before dawn with machine guns as I described, and arrested eighteen young men and the director. It was the only time the Germans themselves raided the town. Of the nineteen, seven came back.[1]

- There really was a political arrest at that same house several weeks before the raid, and some of the men felt the house was targeted and started sleeping in the woods.
- It's true that a young refugee saved a convalescent German soldier from drowning in the local river — and that someone went to the Gestapo with this

1. I offer their names here, in their memory: Jean-Marie Schoen, André Guyonnaud, Jules Villasant-Dur, Félix Martin-Lopez, Sérafin Martin-Cayre, Pedro Moral-Lopez, and Antonio Perez survived. Georges Marx, Jacques Balter, Léonidas Goldberg, Herbert Wollstein, and Charles Stern died in the Auschwitz gas chambers. Daniel Trocmé, the house director, died in the gas chamber at Maidanek. Robert Kimmen, Frantz Weiss, Hermann Lowenstein, Camille Wouters, Alexandre De Haan, and Klaus Simon are unaccounted for.

story hoping to get the young person released. It was actually a young man from the real "La Roche," a Spanish refugee named Luis "Pepito" Gausachs. The pastor's wife asked two German officers to serve as witnesses and plead Gausachs's case while the raid was still in progress; the Gestapo released the young man. (He was not Jewish.[2])

- Although it is fiction, Elisa's escape from the Gestapo is inspired by the many, many stories of Jewish deportees, both men and women, who saved their lives by leaping from deportation trains.
- I based my story of the tip-off that the Germans had taken out a hit on the pastors on a story told in the real Pastor Alexandre's memoirs. The two pastors did go into hiding in 1943;

2. But a Jewish refugee did once save a German convalescent from drowning: Joseph Atlas, a sixteen-year-old from Poland, did it in August 1943. In an interview in 2002 he said he didn't realize till afterward that the man was German, but would still have done it if he'd known. When he saw the man's friends coming over, he fled immediately just like Elisa did.

though the reasons aren't clear, it does seem they felt it necessary for others' sake as well as their own. It was the assistant pastor himself, not his son (he had none) who became a *passeur* on the Swiss border.

- Pastor and Madame Cantal are based on Odette and Paul Chapal, who were involved with the Cimade and kept a safe house in Annecy which was a hub for several *filières,* clandestine networks smuggling Jews and other threatened people to Switzerland.
- The priest in Collonges in the last chapter is Abbé Marius Jolivet, a resister and rescuer; the details of the Collonges crossing are real, drawn from a written testimony by Pierre Piton, who worked as a *passeur* when he was a seventeen-year-old Scout. "The monks and their ladder" is a reference to another real group of rescuers, who under the leadership of Père Louis Favre passed roughly two thousand people into Switzerland over the back wall of a Catholic school built up against the border.

I should also say a word about the Maquis and the Resistance. Pierre's notion that the

Maquis would shoot at Vichy police is just that — Pierre's notion. The fact is the Resistance as a whole was not concerned with protecting Jews but with liberating France from the Germans. They derailed and sabotaged German supply trains, but not deportation trains. But there's good evidence that the armed resisters on the Vivarais-Lignon plateau, at least, saw the Jews as an integral part of the community they were sworn to protect; there was in fact a Jewish Maquis unit on the plateau, which helped to liberate the region in 1944 before Allied troops arrived.

As for Julien's confrontation in the woods with the Gestapo, no such thing ever happened. Resistance to the Nazis on the plateau was a quiet, humble thing, decidedly undramatic. Silence was these people's friend. But it's a writer's job to dramatize things. It's a writer's job to take characters and ideas and strike them together till they make sparks. I wanted to take the silent, humble spirit of the nonviolent resistance on the plateau and force it to speak its faith aloud. I knew I needed that to make my story work.

It wasn't till it spoke that I realized how desperately I had wanted to hear what it had to say.

The more I've read about the story of the plateau, and the more I've read about World War II, the more I have realized how utterly shocking it is that two such idealists as the pastors I've portrayed even survived the war. It was not a time for ideals. It was a demonic time, a time when the power to kill was worshipped as a god, when the Hitler Youth trained up young boys to the ideals of steel-hard pride and ruthlessness. A time when the powerless died by the millions, when the young learned the terrible lesson of the world: *kill or die.*

And yet these men who in following Christ refused all violence and power, refused not only to kill but even to lie to the Nazis to save their own lives — these men who *protested a Nazi roundup in writing* — not only survived but aided their people in saving thousands. It is almost unbelievable.

And it happened.

That is the story I wanted to tell. That is the story I needed to hear. The shocking story that hints that at the end of all things there is something more, that there is another Power beyond power, that the gun does not decide all.

Maybe these people were simply very, very lucky. Or maybe it's true. Maybe the meek shall inherit the earth.

ACKNOWLEDGMENTS

The person this book owes the most to never had the chance to read it. I don't know, any more than Elisa, whether the dead see us. But I want to thank Rich Foss. Thank you, Rich. For your friendship, for your listening, for not only using your precious energy to talk writing with me but actually wanting to. You found the heart of every single fragment I ever told you of my story; to see you seeing it kept me going. I wish I could remember every word you said. I miss you.

The other person this book owes the most to is of course my mother, Lydia Munn, who birthed not only me but also Julien and all his family. Thank you, Mom. For your patience, for the foundation you laid, for giving me the privilege of carrying it onward. Our partnership fed my roots, both in writing and in life. Thank you also to my dad, Jim Munn: you've been the best encourager either of us could wish for.

Thank you to all my editors at Kregel, present and former: Miranda Gardner, who started me on the journey and taught me that cutting is not violence but sculpture; Janyre Tromp, who believed in this series from the beginning; Dawn Anderson, who helped me see my words with different eyes; Joel Armstrong, who pushed till I came up with the last few vivid details, like late fruit on the tree as the frost comes; and Steve Barclift, who has been very kind.

Great thanks to Rachel Langer for answering so very many questions about Judaism, for your kindness and encouragement, and for taking the time to read over the manuscript at such a busy moment. I could not have written Elisa without you.

Warm thanks to J. J. Neulist and Małgorzata Madej: for all your encouragement which was like water in a dry place, for all our writing discussions, for knowing what it's like. For your excellent feedback and for being patient through so many versions of that scene where Marek almost falls out of the tree!

Deep thanks to Tim Otto for being the one I knew I could send the book to when it was far from perfect; for a phone conversation that brought me back to who I was, what I was doing and why; for another that gave me the space I needed for a new decision. You were there at exactly the right time.

Many thanks to Heather Clark for your listening ear as I flailed around trying to chart a true course through the treacherous waters of history. Thank you also to her husband, Greg, for that story about what it means to speak names. I'm glad I spoke the names I did.

All my thanks also to my husband, Paul: for seeing with me what I see in this one, for bearing with me long as I've paid what it was worth.

And to my son, Ian: thank you for being patient, thank you for being interested. Sorry for the spoilers, not to mention the bedtime stories about Nazis at four years old. Please don't be mad when you find out I didn't tell you everything. I love you.

ABOUT THE AUTHOR

Heather Munn was born in Northern Ireland and grew up in southern France, where her parents were missionaries like their parents before them. She has a BA in literature from Wheaton College and now lives in rural Illinois, with her husband, Paul, and their son. Her blog, *Gravity and Grace,* can be found at seedstoryteller .blogspot.com.